Pink Flamingo Soup

*I don't do autographs
Brian Philly*

Editor: Julie Bertoni

All rights reserved by:

The Daily Insurgent Press,

19 Hereford Gardens,

London,

HA5 5JR

Pink Flamingo Soup

Chapter 1

Proof, proof, proof – that's all some people live on. That's their bread and butter, their oxygen and two parts hydrogen. If you can survive on one plus one equals two, the Earth spinning around the sun and all that clear-cut codology, then fair enough: This story is probably not for you. I've been a librarian in Ballyfarnon, County Roscommon, for twenty-three years and I've seen all sorts come and go. Old men looking for a quiet corner to read the paper and mad young fellas searching for the meaning of life, they all take refuge in my dusty old library. Little Jessie fit into none of those camps. He was what some people would call an anomaly, the fecking PC gobshites. In truth he was a freak, a weirdo, a bloody nuisance, and I knew from the second I clapped eyes on him that trouble was on its way.

I was neck-deep in new books with shiny covers and ludicrous titles like *How to be Happy* and *Understanding your wife* when I got that creepy-crawly feeling that I was being watched. I popped my head over the tower of books on my desk and sure enough there was a baldy-headed child with goldfish eyes swimming behind a pair of milk-bottle glasses. I put me left eye on him and gave him the squint, but he didn't flinch, not in the slightest. A cheeky little fucker, I thought, and stood up, scratching my rickety wooden chair across the broken tile floor.

'What do you want there?' I barked at him and hocked up as much phlegm as my smoky lungs could muster. He smiled back at me—serene, calm and insolent. Right, I thought, this little fucker is getting a clip around the ear. I charged towards the countertop, swinging my bad leg, and was loading up my left hand to deliver a bit of smacht, when I saw the pile of books he was holding. I put the left eye on him again, watching for a grin, or a snigger— anything to give away a prank. Was this little fucker actually taking out books? In the twenty-three years I worked here no one under the age of eighteen had *ever* taken out a book. Of course the non-linear spontaneous stream of consciousness cataloguing method (implemented in this library by our resident visionary Dr. Benjamin Murphy) makes finding a book unassisted a near impossibility. The explicit nature of Dr. Murphy's method means children are never treated to the great man's help. I held my eye on him and noticed a strange sheen coming off his body.

'Well? What's your game young fella?'

'Hello John James, my name is Jessie and my mammy told me everything about you and how I could get any book I wanted from this library and how even if you don't have it you can call a man up in Dublin and he'll put it in a van and drive it all the way to Roscommon so that I can read it and it won't even use up all my pocket money cause I need that for buying nice paper for writing my stories that my mammy says are better than some of the books grownups have written,' he said, placing his selections on the counter.

As he crossed his arms I heard the faint sound of folding paper. Now if I walk through this village and meet a face with a new wrinkle I'm shocked, but this, well this took the biscuit.

'And who is your mammy young man?' I asked.

'My mammy is Mary and we've just come all the way from Japan where people eat fish without cooking it and don't speak English except for the boys and girls my mammy taught their ABCs.'

Well I should have guessed he was from that lot, bloody blow-ins, that Mary one was forever setting tongues wagging. Not a boyfriend in sight let alone a husband and she gets up the duff! Fecking hussy and here's the product. I pick up the books and prepare myself for another battle with the stupid fecking computer. Hang on a second, I thought, *A Naked Lunch*, *Fear and Loathing in Las Vegas*, *On the Road*, this is his mother's reading no doubt, ashamed to get the filth herself, sending her innocent child to do the dirty work for her.

'Here now Jessie. Who asked you to get these books?' I said leaning forwards on the counter, tapping the filthy, dirty trash.

'Nobody asked me to get them, John James,' he said, eyes still wide open.

Well, I thought, she has taught him how to tell bare-faced lies to adults too. A holy disgrace! A bloody damned outrage! Still he only learns what he's shown, poor fella, there's no substitution for parenting, he'll come to a bad end no doubt about it.

'Well Jessie, do me a favour will ya?' I said taking the poor lost soul into my confidence.

'Yes Mr. John James I will, I will.'

'You tell your mammy John James says everyone should do their own dirty work,' I said handing him down the long-haired weirdo propaganda I presumed (and hoped) would never return to the shelves of Ballyfarnon Library.

So you can see the boy was a freak, that is of course a subjective point of view. I'd never try to pass it off as the truth. Absolute knowledge has been proven to be a myth. Now I know some people swear green is never pink and mayonnaise never tastes like watermelon, but what can I say? There is always leaders and followers. Dr. Murphy is a prime example of a leader; he's the Daniel O'Donnell of librarian studies—a true genius and a shining light. After graduating from Trinity College with a gold medal, he pioneered the psychedelic cataloguing movement. His career was, however, cut short by a tragic accident involving the local fungi that grows wild in the fields around Ballyfarnon. He may be stuck in a wheelchair and borderline catatonic, but he can still pick out the location of *War and Peace* faster than any new-fangled modern jiggery pokery. So when three days later another gobshite, young and arrogant enough to think there are answers, approached the counter and said 'I can't find Dostoyevsky's *Crime and Punishment* under D,' I turned to the great man, spittle dried in the corner of his mouth, hair sprouting from his ear and said, 'Please Dr. Murphy would you be so kind as to tell us where *Crime and Punishment* is located.'

The great man's eyes, locked shut by inches of dried yellow pus, could be seen oscillating rapidly, mucus seeped from his nose and he began, '*Crime and Punishment*, garlic in my left sock, 1932, cheetahs on steroids waltzing to subterranean homesick blues, killer whales stuffed with mouldy underwear, nuns masturbating with sawn-off crosses under neon pyramids in Hampstead.— Aisle 5, Row 3.' I smiled at the baffled young pup and lead him to his chosen waste of time. As I handed him the book, I froze in shock. Across the dimly lit hall my good eye fixed on a baldy-headed boy, up on the desk, flattened under a pile of books. Now we've all seen *999*

Rescue. Fools have a talent for finding their end in the most ridiculous fashions and, to be honest, my poor heart feared the worst.

'Call an ambulance!' I shouted at the philandering philosopher and charged to Jessie's rescue. A tower of books stood, perfectly balanced on the back of the flattened child. I ripped him free and in a wild panic carried his incredibly narrow frame out the door. My bad leg was temporally resurrected by pure adrenaline, and I charged through Ballyfarnon, making for Dr. Crowley's surgery at the top of the hill. Well, I thought, he won't be coming to a bad end on my watch. I'll run him all the way to hospital if needs be. The lad's face was a horrible yellow-tea brown with ears folded flat on his cheeks. I began to lose heart when suddenly his big goldfish eyes popped open.

'YOU'RE ALIVE! Holy Mary immaculate sacred heart of the Jesus—thank FUCK for that!' I shouted in relief, accelerating with newfound hope.

'Where are we going John James?' said Jessie smiling with cheerful amusement.

'To the hospital child, you've been flattened by a tower of books,' I panted.

'I haven't been flattened John James! I was just taking a nap.'

I trundled to a stop, dull pain groaning in my bad leg, sweat pouring from my brow and an almighty urge to beat the living shite out of the boy bubbling in my stomach.

'You little brat ya! You nearly gave me a heart attack. Playing in the books! It will take Dr. Murphy months to fix all that. Wait till I box your ears for ya!' I said plonking him down but keeping a firm hold of his arm.

'I wasn't playing John James, I promise I wasn't! I was reading *The Magic Mountain*,' he said cowering and squirming in my grasp.

'Like hell you were—no one reads that book,' I said, giving him the first clip of many.

'I was John James, I was! How can you know I wasn't? Please believe me!' cried the child.

Well, I thought, the little fucker has found my weak spot. Am I now claiming absolute knowledge about his literacy? If he wants to waste the day pretending to read *The Magic Mountain* and then get a whipping so be it. I can retain my fidelity to philosophical scepticism and still issue just retribution.

'Were you now? Fair enough, you've till the end of the day. Then we'll have a little quiz.'

So I grabbed him by the ear and lead him down to the library, deposited him at the desk, located Thomas Mann's classic and threw it in his lap. I fixed him with my good eye, giving him one last chance at free admission, which he didn't take. If only Beckett had been right, I thought. If only hussies like Mary did indeed give birth astride a grave. If only the light gleamed but for an instant before all was darkness once more. I'd be free of the young pup; free to devote my undivided attention to the volumes of Blavatsky and Olcott, which had just arrived, in their original Russia, from Bombay. But alas if his mother wasn't going to take him in hand, someone had to. This is a temple of psychedelic cataloguing not a fecking playground.

I began reading the esoteric wisdom of *The Secret Doctrine*, but kept my good eye trained on the exit for any attempted escape. Closing time came round and I walked around the shelves to find the little fucker gone. Well, I thought, he's a coward on top of everything else, and I locked the front door. I searched the toilets. I looked under the stairs. I flung open the doors of each and every cupboard. Then as I searched the aisles themselves the light bulbs, hanging high in the rafters, began to flicker spasmodically. The periodicals were plunged into darkness. Maps of the geological survey vanished from sight. Text books and reference books and manuals of all sorts evanesced from the far wall. But as I turned into the fiction section, the filaments of the bulbs began to burn as if fuelled by very the souls of the damned. It was then that I noticed, sitting a loft a pile of books, a strange translucent volume.

No doubt the fucker's been playing in the stacks again, I thought. Long used to doing as he pleases and damn the consequences, I muttered. Well, he'll soon learn. He may have escaped this time, but there's no bog deep enough in all of Ireland to hide him from the wrath of John James. I grabbed the books off the desk, made my way back to the front of the library and handed the strange translucent volume to Dr. Murphy for re-insertion.

'No title on this one Dr. Murphy, what do you think?' I enquired of the great mind. He lifted the book to his nose and sniffed. A shudder passed through his being, and he began.
'Transylvanian marching band, pink flamingo soup, genital warts bleeding in the Indian dawn, Yoko yoyo marmalade sauce, the flesh became word! THE FLESH BECAME WORD!' he shouted, his eyes snapping open sending crusty yellow shrapnel flying in all directions. He leaped to his feet, vigorous and fecund, roaring, 'AND THE FLESH BECAME WORD!'

Well a lot of things began to make sense: the sound of folding paper when he crossed his arms, the familiar shine, yellow-tea brown face, slender width and preferred sleeping arrangements. I had never encountered Professor De Selby's theory of subatomic interchange in readers. I always believed the phenomenon to be confined to fanatical cyclists, but alas I was mistaken. The boy had, through prolonged exposure, turned himself into a book. I wouldn't have given a monkey's but for the effect it had on Dr. Murphy. He glided straight out of the library, grasping the book to his chest and began preaching the word according to Jessie.

This being a good Catholic town, his message of peace and love was met with stern resistance. Oh the holy mortifications I suffered watching the great man mocked and abused by the ignorant rabble. I was not, however, deterred. The apathy of Ballyfarnon's residents only served to cement my belief that human progress is achieved not by the carrot, but by the swift administration of the stick. I'm sure my case for more traditional theological methods, i.e. beating the living bejesus out of anyone who argued, would have gained favour if things had not come so rapidly to a head. Mary— mother of Jessie—decided, out of sheer petty jealousy, to undergo a transformation of her own: flagrant hussy to suffering saint in the blink of an eye. She circulated the village's seven public houses, howling ululations to the high heavens, whose filth I won't repeat, but suffice to say, Dr. Murphy was traduced. These baseless rumours would have petered out quickly, if it were not for the rampant gossip of old Fr. Quigley, relieved to find himself, for once, removed from the epicentre of paedophilic suspicions.

Now you don't need a PhD in human civilisation to know, two diametrically opposed worldviews cannot, will not, exist together for long. A battle was brewing and so it happened on the night Co. Roscommon lost their seventeenth consecutive all Connacht semi-final to arch rivals Co. Leitrim.

We turned off the old bog road and entered O'Donoghue's public house.

'Repent my children! The hour of salvation is at hand!' roared the great librarian, holding aloft the sacred volume illuminated by his gleaming scalp. The shebeening bastards, grown accustomed to this demand after three days of campaigning, simply continued to slobber pints of porter.

'See now, Dr. Murphy, if you'd just let me administer a couple of eye-openers with my cosh here we'd have their attention in no time at all,' I whispered.

'Patience, my child. The truth is only heard by those who choose to listen,' he replied softly. Well I'm not ashamed to admit it now—that display of ideological purity, in the face of such godlessness, brought a tear to my eye. This moment of awe was, however, cut short by an unmerciful scream. Out of the women's snug scurried our adversary in the kind of attire which would make the ladies of Leeson St. blush.

'You've taken my Jessie,' she screamed, springing forwards, with surprising agility, only to collide with Fighting Bill Tracy returning from the bar. Mary, mother of Jessie, having taken to the floor, remained there, howling like a banshee and displaying her arse to all and sundry. Needless to say, quite the crowd began to gather. Dr. Murphy, spotting his opportunity, stepped forwards. 'Yes my children. I have taken Jessie into my heart and now I beseech you – place down your pints of darkness and follow me into the light. THE FLESH BECAME WORD! Salvation is at hand!'

Fighting Bill Tracy, recovering from the crippling grief of losing four pints of Guinness, turned his hulking frame towards the great librarian.

'What the fecking hell are you jabbering about ya gobshite?' he boomed, his chest inflating with rage, setting off a series of excited jeers and whistles from the crowd.

'He has taken the poor helpless women's child,' snivelled the stoat-like face of old Fr. Quigley, bending down to restore Mary's modesty, much to the consternation of the gawkers. Dr. Murphy continued, not discerning the fact that *The Book of Jessie* had, somehow, joined that illustrious club of books that inspire murderous intent in the illiterate.

'Children of Ballyfarnon! Hear me now—'

'He's calling you a child Bill,' called a voice from the crowd, which after yet another humiliation at the hands of Co. Leitrim, were baying for blood.

'I'll show you children!' snarled Bill unleashing his famous right hook – a punch so exaggerated in swing, that it has never, in living memory, hit anyone. Dr. Murphy, being a gentleman of learning, was understandably stunned; I, however, reacted with the razor reflexes that years of Burmese boxing had instilled in me.

The unmerciful hiding received by Fighting Bill Tracy, gave the crowd pause for thought. In this brief reprieve, I seized Dr. Murphy, who due to fright had relapsed into his catatonia. Once again I found myself charging through the village, carrying an injured party, swinging my bad leg.

I locked the library door, deposited the great man in his chair and watched in horror as the mob, armed with hurleys and flaming torches, laid siege to the library.

'Come out, ya coward ya!' roared the inimitable voice of Fighting Bill Tracy. 'We'll have none of that foreign karate shite. Come out and fight like an Irishman, toe to toe, blow for blow!'

Finally discerning a purpose for the genre of celebrity biography, I began firing hardbacks at the approaching mob. This was, in retrospect, bleeding thick. Soon a bonfire of the vanities was licking the walls of the library. Not even I had envisaged this scenario when drawing up my one hundred and twenty page objection to the council's current *renovations* to the library, but needless to say the presence of paint thinner expedited proceedings. I did what any self-respecting librarian would do and rushed to save our prize collection of Medieval Poetry. Owing to the air's super-saturation with paint thinner, I was surprisingly euphoric as flames ripped through the fiction section. In a state of complete serenity I gathered volumes of Boccaccio, Hangland and Petrarch, but on placing my hands upon Chaucer, I was overwrought with joy. I opened *Canterbury Tales* and began reciting aloud, as if for the first time, that apogee of verse. In this state of reverie I floated, as if on angel's wings, from the burning library.

It was not until my lungs drew fresh air that the horror of my negligence became clear. I spun on my heels, just in time, to see the library implode, sending a fire-ball high into the night sky. Yes it's true – no point mincing my words now – I had, in his moment of need, abandoned the greatest mind of a generation. Struck dumb with grief I fell to my knees, and it wasn't long before the universe joined me in sorrow. A purple scar split the sky, the moon vanished, flowers bowed their heads and cows curtsied as the mob held back my attempts to rush back into the flames. It was at this moment, the lowest ebb of my existence, that the miracle took place. From the flames, bathed in a radiant light, holding aloft a slim translucent volume, walked Dr. Benjamin Murphy, who was immediately arrested by Guarda John Joe O'Reilly. My poor heart, unable to deal with the wild oscillations of faith, began to flutter, and in short I lost consciousness.

Well there you go now. That's how it all started. What's that you're muttering – proof? Paint thinners caused a mass hallucination? Ah, get the hell out of it will you! Of course I'm not claiming I saw a material object called Benjamin Murphy walking, untouched, from a burning inferno—*that* would be fecking ridiculous. I am, in the grand tradition of Berkeley's immaterialism, stating the following fact: The Lord Almighty Himself saw fit to stimulate that idea in our minds. Furthermore, if you were to accuse myself, or indeed any of the fine residents of Ballyfarnon of lies, or hallucinations for that matter, you would in fact be calling God Himself a liar and may you, for all Eternity, suffer the torments of Hell!

Chapter 2

Guarda John Joe O'Reilly was, for want of a more diminutive expression, the village idiot. A young fella so devoid of cop on that he spent three long years in fourth class. He does, however, possess the two essential characteristics of a Garda Siochana: nifty skill with a billy club and deep empathy with the machinations of the most idiotic members of society. Obviously these talents were no match for myself or the great Dr. Benjamin Murphy – intellectual titan, pioneering librarian and witness to God's latest manifestation on Earth— but every dog has its master. Inspector Finley Crawford Biggington, descendant of a long line of English landlords, was determined to continue the protestant tradition of persecuting the religious activities of Irishmen.

So we sat shivering, around a battered table, in Ballyfarnon Garda Station (a place most accurately summed up by the term bog-hole), our paradigm being subjected to, what the natural philosophers term, experimental scrutiny.

'So you last saw Jessie son of Mary, a ten-year-old child, sitting in your library reading a one-thousand five-hundred-page novel about, amongst other things, the diseased nature of genius,' said Biggington stroking a ginger moustache that completely hid his upper lip.

'That's correct Garda,' I said keeping my good eye fixed on the sneaky fucker.

'And at closing time you undertook an extensive search of the library for the expressed purpose of... let me see, now how did you phrase it? 'Administering a bit of smockt.''

'Correct again Garda. There is no substitute for good parenting.'

'Do not withhold discipline from a child. If you strike him with a rod he will not die,' said Dr. Murphy, adding erudite force to my comments.

Biggington leaning back in his chair smiled sarcastically to his fellow Garda. John Joe, unfamiliar with the act of condescension, misconstrued the smile for confusion.

'He means a bit of a clip round the ear does a young fella good, Serg.'

'I realise that, O'Reilly.'

'Sorry, Serg, I thought...'

'Shut up, O'Reilly.'

'Yes, Serg,' said John Joe grasping his club for comfort.

'So the child simply vanished, Dr. Murphy?' continued Biggington.

'The flesh became word and dwells among us,' answered the great man.

'He's talking about the book again, Serg!'

'Damn it, O'Reilly! I know what he's bloody well referring to!' roared Biggington his walrus face aflame. 'Do you actually expect us to believe the boy was magically transmuted into a book, Murphy? Do you take us for fools?'

At this juncture, seeing O'Reilly fidgeting with his club and his master rapidly losing patience with a reality his meagre intellect could not comprehend, I reluctantly took on the role of sophist. After begging permission to proceed from my intellectual senior, I began a treatise of Professor De Selby's theory of subatomic interchange.

Time and again it is proven, there is no force, in the entire universe, stronger than the inertia of the ignorant mind. In short my labours were rewarded with a fierce hiding. The handcuffs nullified my usual recourse to Burmese boxing and I was forced to rely upon the less effective art of Taekwondo, which failed me.

'The rod won't kill him, eh Murphy?' chuckled the sweating, bulbous face of Biggington as he watched O'Reilly work me over.

'All the day long they wrest my words,' answered Dr. Murphy, granting me a rare tobacco stained smile.

'I can see your determined to bowl a beamer, Murphy. So allow me to reveal what we have already caught in the field,' said Biggington producing a large folder. 'We know you were implicated in an intricate confidence scam involving a secret network of so-called clairvoyants while studying in Trinity College. We know you were temporarily suspended from said college owing to the discovery of several kilos of dried fungi – a case later dropped after the mysterious disappearance of all material evidence. We also know that in the seventies you were implicated in, and indeed subject to, monitoring by a special branch for smuggling firearms into the Republic from Libya for an organisation calling itself the I.R.B. Finally, and most relevant to this particular case, you were arrested in 1991 for indecent exposure in the vicinity of Mantua School for Boys, but owing to a sudden decline in health were unable to stand trial,' he said tapping the file with his sweaty digits.

'A false witness will not go unpunished, and he who breathes lies will not escape,' retorted Dr. Murphy to those scandalous slanders.

I was left, once again, in awe of the great man's restraint, my own temper, despite the beating I'd just received, baying for blood.

'Confess now and the judge will look kindly on your co-operation Murphy. Given your past mental problems I would recommend a guilty but insane verdict. Why make it harder on yourself?' said Biggington twisting the ends of his red moustache, pale green eyes gleaming from behind thickets of eyebrows.

'Behold, we count them happy which endure.'

'Have it your way Murphy. The detectives are on their way. They have the very finest apparatus in the sphere of forensic examination at their disposal. It's only a matter of time before we find the boy's body. I'm sure O'Reilly will love having you around for his little chats. Isn't that right O'Reilly?' laughed Biggington sadistically.

'Chats, Serg?'

'With your club, you bloody fool!' roared the frustrated sergeant.

'Chats with my billy club, Serg?' said O'Reilly, searching his club for an antenna or aerial of some kind.

'Here, have a chat with mine you simpleton!' snapped Biggington, brandishing his club with all the finesse of an old pro and delivering a pinpoint blow to O'Reilly's jugular, knocking the lad clean out.

Having waded into the arena of violence, Biggington decided it was easier to go o'er. I threw myself over Dr. Murphy and shielded his head from the blows raining down from above.

'If someone strikes you on the right cheek, turn to him the other also,' called Dr. Murphy from bellow.

I took the great man's advice, but the momentary relief of blows landing on unbroken bones quickly passed, as did my consciousness.

12

I woke slowly, a mucky fog obscuring my thoughts. The smell of damp earth and rotten air filled my nose, and I feared my worst nightmare had come true: They had buried me alive. I flailed around and feeling no wooden walls to my left or right was granted a momentary reprieve. I sat up slowly, my mind filled with Edgar Allen Poe-style horrors and listened carefully to my surroundings. The silence was absolute, not like a minute's silence before a GAA final, but a complete amputation of aural stimulation. Similarly the darkness was not simply impregnable, but seemed to deny the very existence of light. So they're reading from the CIA's manual on sensory deprivation, I scoffed. The torture caused by dismantling an individual's ego is less effective on a student of Zen Buddhism. Having studied under master Kim, in the foothills of the Seoraksan, South Korea, I was not only aware that the ego is an illusion, but that it is, in fact, the very source of all suffering. In short, their methods contained a logical fallacy which could inflict no pain on a masterful practitioner of meditation, but could, in actuality, lead him to enlightenment.

I decided to explore my surroundings, hoping to find a comfortable spot to sit full lotus. I quickly felt a wall before me and decided to ascertain the dimensions of this torture chamber. On and on I stumbled, each step increasing my incredulity. After a significant passage of time, I stopped my wanderings. I weighed two hypothesises: A – I am in a room of colossal dimensions; or B – I was in some naturally occurring subterranean amphitheatre, i.e. a cave. Perhaps they've left me here knowing I would seek egress and plummet to my doom, an accident easily explained as a novice error in potholing. I dropped down on all fours and felt my way ahead.

Perhaps it was a latent mental fog, symptomatic of mild concussions, or perhaps it was my taphephobia – whatever the case – it wasn't until my bad knee was stabbed, for a third time, by a protrusion of distinctly human origin, that the idiotic assumption, which hither to had lead my investigations, came into stark focus.

'Echo,' I shouted, testing my new hypothesis.

The absence of a response proved no surface was reflecting sound waves at any significant distance from my current location. The unending walk along this wall, the periodic stabbing of my knee and the absence of echo allowed me to conclude that the cell was, in fact, circular.

This information would have provided a sort of relief if I wasn't so well versed in the early Christian history of County Roscommon. I traced my steps to the spike in the floor, found a gully in the floor beside it and followed its angular trajectory across the cell. At this point I found another stake and a gully proceeding back across the room forming two sides of a triangle. I charged around the cell, swinging my bad leg, horror and delight battling like Achilles and Hector in my chest. It wasn't until I reached the sixth stake, completing the Star of David pattern made by the gullies, that I rested my aching leg. My scholarly instincts were, needless to say, enthralled at this discovery; my survival instincts on the other hand vibrated with the terror of the knell. There I was, interned in the fabled exorcism chambers of County Roscommon, death place of the last pagan priestesses of Ireland.

So the Church of Jessie has old Father Quigley worried, I smiled to myself. The true measure of a new paradigm is the rage it inspires in the old paradigm's faithful. Let the battle begin! As if hearing my proclamation, my jailers burst through a concealed door. Having been blinded by darkness I was now blinded by light, the only change being a sudden awareness of my nakedness. I took up a classic horse stance, maximising my ability to deliver debilitating open-hand strikes.

'I strongly recommend that you sit down and behave, John James. I'm growing tired of beating you,' came the voice of Biggington from behind the sheet of dazzling light.

Hearing my target, I charged. In five steps I was upon the threshold and began a Sok Glub Koo, Thai boxing's most devastating flying combo. I could almost hear the imitable crunch of nose and rib simultaneously breaking when I was swatted from the air by an icy column of water. Winded and dazed, I squirmed in a futile attempt to escape the attentions of the water cannon. Like a piece of fruit simultaneously beaten to mush and frozen, I lay helpless. The job of tying my limbs to the four stakes on the floor was not a difficult one.

'Would you look at your man,' said Father Quigley, his Jackeen accent revealing him. 'I've met every Bishop in Ireland, but this fella's purple hat takes the bleedin biscuit.'

'I apologise for the immodesty Fr. Quigley, but Dr. Cameron's research on...'

'Not at all Sergeant. You're grand. Sure I'm always happy to meet another Bishop,' said old Father Quigley, grasping my nether regions in his strangely effeminate hands and giving them a shake.

'You'll pay for *that*, ya shebeening bastard!' I roared, vulnerability doing nothing to temper my pugnacious nature.

'Well have ye ever heard the like of it, Biggo? Addressing a man of the cloth like that,' said Quigley.

'An irascible fellow but we'll soon make him malleable, Father,' replied Biggington, issuing me a switch kick in the bollix.

As the pain swelled up in torrents, I began the process of transcendental detachment by chanting the universal vibration: Ohm.

'Sweet mother divine bless us and save us, you've knocked the bleedin sense out of him!' shrieked Quigley. 'We'll have none of that violence, Biggo! Did Jesus ever kick his enemies in the balls?'

'Not as far as I'm aware, Father,' muttered Biggington.

'Well there you bleedin go. They threw rocks at 'im, spat at 'im, called 'im a Jew, and not once did he kick them in the balls. The Catholic Church is against all violence,' said Quigley proudly.

A look of profound bemusement crossed Biggington's face, the look of a child wading into water far beyond his accustomed depth.

'Well what about the Crusades?' ventured Biggington, as of yet only toe deep.

'What about them?' snapped Quigley.

'Well there was quite a bit of violence there, was there not?' – water rising above the knee.

'Of course there was. Those foreigners were barbarians and heretics for crying out loud!' shrieked Father Quigley.

'And the Spanish Inquisition?' – chest high and rising rapidly.

'Heretics!' screamed Quigley, growing delirious.

'Yes, yes of course...Hmmm what about the whole supporting Nazi Germany thing?' proceeded Biggington, up to his neck in it by now.

'For feck sake, Biggo – he was killing Commies, faggots, gypsies and Jews. Heretics, heretics, heretics, heretics.'

'Ah, I understand now, Father. My intellect is, I'm afraid, so under stimulated with that idiot O'Reilly. What you're saying is that if John James here continues with his heretic claims, I can kick him to my hearts content,' said Biggington, stroking his red moustache.

'Now we're singing from the same hymn sheet, Sergeant,' said Quigley, turning his attentions back to me. 'So Jimbo, what's it gonna be?'

Being deep in meditation I didn't give the bastards the satisfaction of a response. And so the kicking began, rose to a bloody crescendo and stopped as Biggington, frequenter of Macari's chipper, threatened to keel over from a heart attack. The coward instead enlisted the help of O'Reilly, who having spent most of his teenage years watching B-movies had more creative ideas. As the pliers attacked my nipples I seemed to watch from deep inside myself. My attitude should not be confused for stoicism – no good man is happy on the rack. Rather, each jolt of pain seemed to ask a question: Who are you? And in the brief moments of relief, I began to discern an answer. The words were still beyond me, but the voice of W.B. Yeats was unmistakable. I felt the illusionary fabric of the self being breeched, I was entering, or should I say re-entering, the superconsciousness.

How different events could have been, better or worse, I could not say, if the mystic spirit had fully entered me. Broken, beaten and starved in a subterranean torture chamber I was of course unable to observe, through normal sensory stimuli, the rise and fall of the sun or the waxing and waning of the Moon. How close had I been? Was I seconds or days or years away from a state of true enlightenment? We will never know, for soon the feckers found the weakness in my transcendental defences.

'John James we thought you might appreciate some company,' chortled Biggington.

I lifted my head, and through matted hair watched as he dragged Dr. Murphy into the cell and strapped him into the electric chair. I could see the great man's eyes sealed shut with layers of dark yellow sleep, and dried spittle formed a horrible ring around his lower lip, much like the make-up of a clown. This vesture, so humiliating to a man of his stature, undid all the composure I had so doggedly maintained over the previous days.

'Don't you lay a finger on him you bastards!' I screamed, struggling against my restraints. 'You're interfering with the very destiny of mankind!'

'Just sign this denunciation of the Church of Jessie, show us where the boy's body is, and we can all go home,' snivelled Quigley, hobbling into the cell, wearing a toothless smile.

'I'll kill you ya bastard! I'll *kill* you!' I said thrashing about me wildly.

'Be calm my son,' intoned Dr. Murphy suddenly. 'If Jessie brings you to it, he will bring you through it.'

In awe I looked at this child of the senses, built to soar on the wings of beauty, humbly accepting a destiny of pain. His bald head lolled from side to side shining like a beacon of hope on a dark sea.

'Ok, let the blaspheming bastard have it,' snorted Quigley.

The lights in the hall dimmed and Dr. Murphy was launched into a series of viscous spasms. Tears flowed from my eyes as his ear hair caught fire and mucus streamed from his proud nose.

There was a momentary silence filled with the smell of cooked flesh.

'Well, Benjo?' offered Quigley.

'Placenta milkshake, swollen vulva, shaven gibbons, bionic leopards gorging on quadriplegic orphans in a Kandahar brothel, the flesh became word, THE FLESH BECAME WORD!'

'Let him have it again,' squealed Quigley.

I closed my eyes and attempted to block out the sound of frying flesh by repeating the mantra Ohm, but Zen Buddhism could not help me for I could not, hearing Dr. Murphy's yelps of agony, believe its central tenant, i.e. I am the most important person in the universe.

'Had enough, Benjo?' said Quigley.

'The problem of social organization is how to set up an arrangement under which greed will do the least harm. Capitalism is that kind of a system,' vociferated the great man through chattering teeth.

Seeing the greatest mind of a generation reduced to such inane ramblings, I cracked.

'Enough! I'll sign the renunciation and bring you to the body,' I said, playing for time and hoping to improvise an escape.

It was a grand soft day when we emerged into the open air. A day I'd have spent drinking cups of tea and reading D.H. Lawrence before that little gobshite Jessie, blessed be his name, went and turned himself into a book. My hands and feet were shackled and after being bundled into the back of the car we drove back to Ballyfarnon.

'Where to now?' demanded Biggington as we stopped at the top of Dr. Crowley's hill.

'Jesus lads the hidings have me awful confused. I can't get my head around the directions at all,' I said studying my surroundings for any hope of escape.

'You're not codding us Jimbo. Now you either bring us to the spot or we'll head back and give your precious Benjo another jolt of juice,' said Quigley.

'I know the way. I only need a moment's thought,' I said, staring out the window.

Outside the post office, four state-sponsored layabouts, unemployed since 1973, queued for social welfare. Mrs. Maguire and Mrs. Falvey gossiped over the garden hedge, and way off in the back field I could see fighting Bill Tracy on his tractor.

'If we start at the library I can retrace my steps,' I said, seeing no succour here.

So down through the village we rolled, Garda Biggington sticking rigidly to the 20 kmph speed limit, allowing my good eye a decent gander at the town, but it wasn't till we passed Shannon's pub that I spotted the first weirdo. His jeans were rammed up his hole and he wore a vest a knacker wouldn't spit on. Down the street he strutted, in ludicrous pointy-toed boots, as if he owned the gaff.

'Gobshite,' we muttered in unison.

'One of McNoon's grandchildren over from England – I'd bet my life on it,' said Quigley.

'Fucking Brits,' said Biggington with that passionate hatred of ethnic minorities only found in fellow ethnic minorities.

We had barely recovered from the shock, when another and then another freak appeared. As we drove down the hill we found ourselves sinking into a mire of filth. The streets were thick with pierced lips, shaggy beards, leather jackets, tattooed necks, long-haired lads, skinhead girls and degenerates of every possible persuasion.

'Quick, Biggington! Get these off and let me administer a bit of smacht to these feckers,' I said, and the sergeant in his rage began undoing my cuffs.

'Not so fast, Biggo. We have bigger fish to fry,' said the sly old priest, robbing me of my chance to escape.

To our utter disgust the crowd of degenerates grew thicker as we approached the library, and outside Mrs. Bigginton's shop, which sold everything from bread to drill bits, from cider to holy water, we were forced to abandon the car.

'My god, they're looting the shop!' shouted Biggington and began cutting a path through the skinny bodies of these marijuana addicts with wild swings of his baton.

I contributed what I could with head butts and shoulder barges, but our rage was soon quieted when it became clear, on sighting the counter, that this mob of hoodlums were in fact making purchases. Is some natural disaster upon us? I wondered. Is the entire nation stockpiling essentials? Why come to Ballyfarnon to buy tinned meat?

We eventually arrived at the counter, where Mrs. Biggington, a woman who looks like she shrunk in the wash, worked at a furious but highly composed pace.

'What in the blazes is going on here?' boomed Biggington, his red moustache quivering with anger.

'Serving customers, dear,' sang Mrs. Biggington, her hawkish eyes, magnified by thick glasses, remaining firmly fixed on the cash register, which she played with the dexterity of a concert pianist.

'Yes I can see that woman, but what the bloody hell are they buying?' said Biggington, glaring with open hostility at the rabble.

'Souvenirs, dear.'

'Souvenirs! Souvenirs? Souvenirs of what?'

'Oh just the miracle, dear.'

'Miracle! Miracle? What miracle?

'Thought you would have heard, dear. A boy turned himself into a book,' she said wrapping I LOVE JESSIE t-shirts, translucent books and postcards of Ballyfarnon Library (pre-conflagration) in bubble wrap.

Old Father Quigley's lungs began rattling like a box of spanners and he steadied himself against what appeared to be a very lifelike rendering of Dr. Murphy in stone.

'But how did they find out?' asked Biggington.

'Something about tweeting and bogs and posting...A birdwatchers periodical I'd imagine.'

'The bishop is gonna have me guts for garters,' wheezed Quigley.

'How much money have you taken today?' said Biggington excitedly.

'Haven't counted, dear.'

'Damn it, woman! Give me an estimate!'

'Oh about nine, dear.'

'Nine hundred euros' cried Biggington joyously.

'Oh no, dear... I meant nine thousand,' chirped Mrs. Biggington, handing a fuzzy-headed freak his souvenirs.

Biggington began to dance a jig, his belly bouncing up and down on his knees. Around and around he spun, moustache curling up to meet his eyebrows as the long-suppressed dreams of restoring his family's fortunes flooded out in yelps of ecstasy.

The ruffians misconstruing this display of unbridled joy for religious celebration began imitating Biggington's surprisingly deft dance steps. Drums appeared as if from thin air, and of course these social leeches, having spent their time smoking wackeytobacky and indulging in the detestable reveries of music, could play better than any negro tribe. In short, all hell broke loose.

The music, if you could call it such a thing, may well have continued into the night if old father Quigley had not recovered, some ten minutes later, from his swoon.

'Heretics!' he screamed, bursting into the centre of the drum circle.

'Take it easy, man. We don't want any bad buzzes here, okay?' said a filthy rope-haired drummer in skin-tight cycling shorts.

'You're all going to hell,' shrieked Quigley, the birth-mark on his skull glowing bright red.

The rabble began shouting torrents of vituperations, and I stepped forwards to seize my opportunity.

'Quiet, please! A bit of whisht there now... Thank you. I'm Assistant Librarian in Ballyfarnon, colleague of the great Dr. Benjamin Murphy. I saw Jessie Son of Mary with my own good eye. I was there when he turned into a book, and I held that very book in my own two hands,' I said pausing to let the gasps of amazement settle down.

'Yes I was there. I witnessed the miracle and look what they are doing to me,' I said raising up my shackles, 'They've jailed me and tortured me and at this very moment they are holding Dr. Benjamin Murphy in their torture chambers. They're trying to kill the truth. They're trying to murder the miracle. But I'm here to bear witness. The flesh became word. THE FLESH BECAME WORD!'

The rabble, who moments before were dancing with Biggington now sought to murder him.

'Now, now. Please ladies and gentlemen, this is all a gross misunderstanding,' pleaded Biggington dodging miniature statues of Jessie and bound copies of Thomas Mann's *Magic Mountain*.

Fearing I would never free Dr. Murphy alone, I reluctantly saved Biggington from certain death.

'Please, brothers and sisters,' I said. 'At least allow the man to defend his actions.'

Biggington seeing the hold I had over the mob scrambled on all fours to my feet and began undoing my shackles.

'Forgive me. Oh please forgive me. I have betrayed Jessie. I was there myself that glorious night Dr. Murphy walked unscathed from an inferno; a fire no mortal being could survive. Out he walked from the flames holding aloft the sacred book. The flesh became word. THE FLESH BECAME WORD...Brothers and sisters I am a believer, but then, HE,' shouted Biggington pointing a rigid finger at Quigley, 'he dripped poison in my ear. He said if I arrested John James and Dr. Murphy he could get me the thirty county council votes I need to get the new Garda station. It was betrayal. Oh Jessie! I know it was betrayal, but how long must we wait for a toilet that flushes. How long...'

Biggington collapsed to the floor and flapped around like a heartbroken walrus. The mob, disgusted by the pathetic display, turned their fury on Quigley.

'The first one to touch me gets it,' barked Quigley, producing a pistol so ornate that the ruffians began laughing.

The joke was quickly extinguished as Quigley shot a woman fit for the first row of a rugby scrum straight between the eyes.

As everyone dived for cover, Quigley hobbled outside and escaped in Biggington's police car. Once again Dr. Murphy's life lay in my hands and I was determined, despite the concrete proof of Charles Berkeley's immaterialism garnered in the previous experiment, not to repeat my betrayal.

Now I know what you're thinking, surely I didn't associate with this mob of long-haired weirdos and social degenerates. No possible good can come from consorting with the lowest echelons of society, I hear you say. Granted, in most situations I'd be in absolute agreement with you, but even those with only a rudimentary knowledge of history will quickly recognise the role this bottom rung of humanity has played in every major revolution for the last two centuries. You don't have to look very far for an example either. Easter, 1916: On the steps of the general post office stood a disgruntled history teacher (a sophist of the worst genus) reading a proclamation so utterly devoid of poetic flare that when the Brits had finished blowing up half the town and marched Mr. Padraig Pearse through the streets of Dublin, locals turned out in droves to pelt him with rotten vegetables. Yet this flaccid event, once rewritten by the long-haired weirdos of the day, namely the balladeers, petty poets and pulp novelists, became the very foundation of the First Irish Republic. A republic that first bowed down to the Church, then to the Yanks and was now being left to rot by the Chinese. In short, a Second Republic was well overdue. There I stood, witness to a miracle, surrounded by the unemployed youth, and I thought to myself: Someone may as well make fecking use of them. With the brute force of the masses and the tactical prowess of the great Dr. Murphy I glimpsed a theocratic Ireland free to fulfil her artistic potential.

'To the jail!' I shouted, but my voice was drowned out by a strangely familiar howl.

I raised my fists and scanned the shop from left to right, but couldn't catch a glimpse of the inimitable source of those ululations: Mary Mother of Jessie. To my surprise, the pack of hooligans grew silent, produced slim translucent volumes from their pockets and began prostrating in the direction of the library. Not wishing to upset the spirit of communal buffoonery, so essential to the fermentation of revolution, I followed suit.

With these formalities dispensed with, the rabble sprung into action. Biggington, with all the fevered passion of the newly converted, began commandeering every available mode of transportation: buses, bicycles, tractors, roller skates and petrol lawn mowers. Soon a convoy of vehicles raced up the doctor's hill, past the police station and surrounded the parish church.

'Quigley. We have you surrounded,' I shouted through a megaphone. 'Give us Dr. Murphy, unharmed, and we'll leave it at a hiding. A fair couple of slaps round the head for you and that'll be that.'

'You're not gonna be laying a finger on me Jimbo,' snarled Quigley, emerging from the shadowy archway holding the ancient pistol to Dr. Murphy's head as it lolled from side to side in his wheelchair.

'There's nowhere to go Quigley. Take your hiding like a man and that'll be that,' I said, garnering shouts of approval from the mob.

Quigley scoffed and figures began appearing behind him. Fr. O'Neill, Fr. Morrisey, Fr. Sherran, Fr. Kelly and the twenty other members of County Roscommon's Holy Roman Catholic Church filed out in jet-black robes. Their faces were hidden under hoods and their hands clasped tight to golden staffs.

Well, I thought, we'll have a bit of fun after all. I was ready to leap into the thick of it when the tall red hat and floating gait of Bishop Ahern stopped me in my tracks. There was a collective gasp of amazement followed by total silence. Ballyfarnon locals, who had joined the procession out of curiosity, could be heard muttering Our Fathers and Hail Marys.

'My Children,' began Ahern mellifluously, 'what is all this fussing and fighting now? Have we completely lost the run of ourselves? Threatening a man of the cloth; a Shepard chosen by our Lord Himself to guide you to a world without end, and this is how you repay his love. If God Himself had told me I'd be witnessing this scene today I wouldn't have believed him. Not the good people of Ballyfarnon, I'd have said. They'd never turn to violence, I'd have said.'

Ahern tilted his head back wearing the look of a father having caught his child lying for the first time. This guilt led to a general lowering of weaponry and uncomfortable soul-searching in the mob.

'Says the man holding Dr. Murphy at the point of a gun,' I countered. 'As per usual it's one rule for us and another rule for this shower of shites.'

'Ah John James. There you are my child.'

'Don't you *my child me* you shebeening bastard. You're not fooling me with that man-of-cloth act. You forget I was in school with ya, Ahern. I saw ya dropping the hand on Julie Sweeney round the back of the bike sheds. I know who paid for her boat to England. I know why you did a runner to Rome. Why don't you tell all these people about that?'

Ahern did what every Catholic priest does when accused. He smiled meekly, imitated the vacant look of suffering favoured by Jesus Christ and acted as if his inability to answer was a moment of deep spiritual melancholy. Any other nation on earth would immediately ridicule such dramatics, but this was not any other nation, this was the nation were people go to pubs to drink depressant drugs and sing songs that make them cry. I looked around the crowd and the gobshites were deeply moved.

'He has no answer. Not a single word,' I roared, 'Don't fall for the cheap dramatics.'

'John James...John James my old friend,' sang Ahern's melancholy voice as he stroked his luxurious white beard. 'What is all this foul-mouthed raging? What is it that has turned a good man from the path of salvation?'

'Path of salvation my arse! We've seen the miracle of the Church of Jessie. The flesh became word. THE FLESH BECAME WORD!'

The rabble, ever-ready for a chorus, roared along with me for a few moments and settled down once more.

'And what is it that these words say?' asked Bishop Ahern with a raised silver eyebrow.

'Excuse me?'

'Well you say the flesh became word, so what exactly is it that these words say?'

'Well you see, eh the thing is that….well I couldn't exactly tell you as I've been eh how to say now...Well I've been detained and such.'

In all arguments there are two routes to victory: the vocal and the violent. When the first fails you there is no shame in the second, especially if you're correct and merely falling victim to a sneaky rhetorician. This argument, however, could not be settled in my preferred style owing to Dr. Murphy's vulnerability.

'He has no answer. No a single word,' said Ahern, turning my own attacks against me.

'Well I won't lie. I haven't read the Book of Jessie. Only one man has and he walked from an inferno unharmed. If you want to hear what the flesh become word has to say then let Dr. Murphy speak.'

All eyes shifted towards the prophet, pioneering librarian and all-round scholar who sat catatonic in his wheelchair drooling onto a blood-stained shirt.

'By all means,' chuckled Ahern. 'If Dr. Murphy can speak then let him do so.'

All ears strained to hear the great man speak, but were greeted only with the sound of rattling mucus.

'He needs a book,' I proffered by way of explanation.

'Oh by all means let him borrow mine,' answered Ahern, floating to Dr. Murphy's side and laying his black leather Bible onto the great man's lap.

Dr. Murphy began to vibrate. The rattling sound of mucus ceased and was replaced by a high-pitched whistle emanating from his flared nostrils. He jolted up into a rigid posture and bared his tobacco stained teeth.

'The Catholic Bible, grasshopper moon juice, unicycle nightmare, double-decker beaver burgers, April 1982, babies thrown from the Brooklyn Bridge, Ninja Weevils in a Hungarian trapeze, Isle 12 row 7.'

Needless to say, the entire crowd was stunned. The uneducated mind, when confronted with the non-linear random stream of consciousness cataloguing method, always is. Soon, wild theories and interpretations were circulating. Strange futures with totalitarian Weevil governments were being seriously discussed. Rival factions of reformists and traditionalists quickly sprung up, and all hell threatened to break loose.

'Maybe he's right, John James. Seems a lot of trouble is being stirred up with all this flesh became word business,' whispered Biggington, knowing any public disorder would fall within even his narrow definition of police responsibilities.

'You better hurry up if your gonna get your three in before the cock crows,' I growled.

'No need for bad blood now John James I'm only saying that...'

'And I'm sure they will be only too glad to listen. Pity about all that stock that'll rot away on the shelves. Can't imagine their will be too many buyers for marble statues of Dr. Murphy after you've had your say.'

Biggington's moustache began twitching frantically.

'But how could they turn their backs on the truth? The swine! The turncoat bastards! We cannot let it happen. We must act now,' he jabbered while attempting to run every which way at once.

'We need the Book of Jessie,' I said grasping him by the shoulders.

'The book of what?'

'The Book of Jessie you gobshite.'

Biggington's eyes glazed over and his moustache collapsed into an arch of desperation.

'The cause of everything that's happened you fool! The boy turned into a book. You took the book when you arrested us.'

'Uh you mean this,' said Biggington pulling the slim translucent volume from his inside pocket.

I snatched the book from his hands, swerved through the factions (now on the point of blows) and delivered the sacred word into Dr. Murphy's lap. Having spotted my lunge, Father Sherran and Father Kelly spear-tackled me into the muck. All hostilities quickly subsided, however, as the book produced the desired effects on the pioneering librarian.

Dr. Murphy rose majestically from his wheelchair with arms out stretched and palms facing the celestial orbs. He exhaled slowly from his nostrils, producing a limpid whistle that summoned all his bickering children back to his guiding hand. He opened his eyes slowly and with the next inhalation seemed to draw our very souls deep into the sanctuary of his bosom.

'Three things cannot long be hidden. The sun, the moon, and the truth,' he said at last.

'And the truth is what exactly?' sniggered Ahern with hubris.

'Listen and you will hear,' replied the great man, without as much as glancing at the bishop.

'And these people are meant to live by these wishy-washy proverbs are they?' jeered Ahern as Dr. Murphy studied each face in the crowd. 'Men need rules. Society requires a clear sense of right and wrong. What exactly is it that you believe in Murphy?'

26

The great man did not answer. Instead he seemed to drill into the very essence of his followers. In those moments I actually saw those divine flashes of inspiration, granted only to true genius, illuminate his pupils like forks of lightening.

'Look not a word of sense. Not a single...'

'Silence,' commanded Dr. Murphy with bone-rattling bass.

Ahern retreated a few steps to the safety of his rank and file. The ululations of Mary Mother of Jessie began once more at the library and the crowd fell to their knees to pray. With foreheads pressed against books and knees deep in Roscommon muck, we received the word according to Jessie.

'Listen now and you will hear the flesh become word. And say you not, when the days of judgement come, that you were not told.

'How can an idea be anything but an idea? How can a picture contradict your eye? Your eye is stimulated by God, but who stimulates the camera? I tell you that the devil is in that machine.

How can an idea be anything but an idea? How can a record contradict your ear? The breath of God kisses your ear, but who whispers his poison into the microphone? I tell you that the devil is in that machine.

'How can an idea be anything but an idea? How can money contradict labours done? Your hand is made strong by the will of God, but who deepens the pockets of banks? I tell you that the devil fills those vaults.

'How can an idea be anything but an idea? How can you create more energy than you are given? God charged your body with divine energy, but who charged the thick black oil hidden deep underground? I tell you that the devil is in that fuel.

'How can an idea be anything but an idea? How can your consciousness contradict your superconsciousness? The language of your superconsciousness is the lexicon of the gods. What goat-eyed scribe composed the banality of the consciousness? I tell you the devil is in those forms.

'How can an idea be anything but an idea? How can clothes enhance the flesh of your divine birth? God sculpted the contours of your body. Who attempts to mutilate his creation? I tell you the devil is in that cloth.'

These words, by now so ingrained in the fabric of humanity, were of course a revelation at the time. We were, each and every one of us, deeply moved by the resonance and poetry of the Commandments, but could never have imagined the width and breath of consequences they brought about. Even myself, the most ardent follower of Dr. Murphy, could not have foreseen the resulting coalition of unemployed historians, poets, musicians, magicians, economists, ecologists and pyjama-wearing single mothers that would change the course of Irish history forever.

One consequence, however, was abundantly clear as Quigley cocked the hammer on his antique pistol. The crowd surged forwards and were cut down in droves by the clergy's golden staffs.

'How can a dead man be anything but a dead man. Eh Benjo?' cackled Quigley, birth-mark glowing red.

The gunshot seemed to thicken time. I punched, kicked, butted and gouged, but the air was viscous. I couldn't reach him. I couldn't save him. The ancient pistol had emitted such a plume of smoke that Fr. Quigley and Dr. Murphy were completely obscured. Like boxers swinging underwater, neither the priests nor the mob could land a decisive blow. Back and forth we raged until the priests, far outnumbered, finally tired and we overcame them.

Unable to see Dr. Murphy, I followed the screams of agony until they too disappeared in the smoke. I scrambled forwards on all fours and my fingers felt warm blood staining the green grass. I followed this gruesome trail through the heavy smoke and finally touched a foot.

Blinded by smoke and tears I gathered the body up into my arms. I tried to run, but my bad leg had seized. I screamed for help and soon the others arrived. Together we lugged the body out of the smoke.

In fits of coughing and tears we gathered around our hero. I scoured my mind for the right words, but remembering the great man's Fifth Commandment spoke as he commanded.

'Self-erotic immolation, Shanghai swinging builders' bums,' I began and choked up with remorse.

I battled for composure and the wind conspired to help. A gust of air blew away the smoke. and I took a draft. I was ready to recommence my elegiac stream of superconsciousness when I saw the body (lying face down) was missing a hand. A mess of blood and tissue hung from the bone. It was only then I spotted the birth-mark and realised our mistake: We had lifted our mortal enemy from the battlefield.

As one half of the faithful began mutilating Quigley's body, I led the other half in a search of the church grounds. We scoured every bush and bramble, every pew and confessional, but could find neither sight nor sound of Dr. Murphy. The great man had vanished without a trace.

From Ballyfermot to Pluto: A portrait of a magician

Chapter 1

A loan moped wasped down the street as pubs emptied the dregs of Tuesday night drinkers onto Ballyfermot Road. Torn political posters calling jobless workers to hopeless protests flapped against the aluminium shutters of bakers, pharmacists, newsagents and bookies long finished opening up in the morning.

Hughey Harris ran a black wand along the iron railings of a dilapidated field. He imagined horses tossing shaggy manes and darting three steps away from the dull ring of the railings. As the moped vanished from the cold air Hughey heard the distant clip-clop of hooves on concrete. Memory stirred and Hughey held his step. Years of suffering had given him a sixth sense for the hazy boundaries between past and present. Tonight he would not welcome sorrow. Instead he gripped his wand and focused on the November frost descending on Dublin. He cursed the cold through chattering teeth. He pulled up his collar, blew hot whiskey breath on his fingers and charged for home, but all was a performance; an imitation of a sober man who could feel the cold; a desperate denial of those spooked horses of the past. Hughey turned onto Shelka Park Road and hunched further forwards as he passed rows of terraced houses. Not once did he remark the weed-ridden garden where Mr. O'Shaughnessy's roses once bloomed. Not a single thought was granted the boarded windows of Mrs. O'Toole's or the bone yard of cars outside Harry Hall's. Hughey didn't list his neighbours as he passed their doors. Why would he? Nothing had changed sure. On he walked, feigning cold, shivering off the pieces of past and present that did him no good.

Hughey reached his front door and took a deep draft of air. Two performances faced him still: the sober husband and the magician. He would tackle them in reverse order. Being a consummate professional he never carried keys, preferring to hone his lock-picking technique at every possible opportunity. With nothing more than a hairpin Hughey Harris, or Pluto Von Paradise, as he preferred to be called while doing such work, opened the door.

He stepped inside and, feeling revived by his performance, removed his trench coat with a matador's flair. Pluto stood tall. His barrel chest inflated, brandishing a wand in the favoured fighting stance of the fabled magicians of Budapest.

'Hughey is that you?' called Mrs. Harris from the kitchen.

'Yes love,' said Hughey, vanishing his wand with a wave of his hand.

He straightened his waistcoat, ran a hand through his slicked-back silver hair and stepped into a kitchen that smelled like the inside of a discarded teapot.

'There's a drop in the pot there,' said Mrs. Harris without taking an eye off her thousand-piece jigsaw.

Hughey looked down over her shoulder and shook his head. Every piece was pure white. He knew it would be. Mrs. Harris had long abandoned the superfluous niceties of constructing landscapes, portraits and still-lifes, but Hughey still hoped, in his heart of hearts, that the colours would one day return.

Hughey walked to the stove, poured a cup of tea, and sat down.

'Seems you have a new favourite trick,' said Mrs. Harris, slotting a blank piece into a blank puzzle.

'What's that now?' he answered.

'Making money disappear into O'Shea's pocket,' said Mrs. Harris, finally looking up from her jigsaw.

The moment their eyes met she softened. Despite his robust frame, heavy jowls and meticulous dress she always saw a vulnerable soul. Instinctively her hand dropped a jigsaw piece and reached across the family table to his cheek. There was a pause; a pause laden with love's full spectrum of joy and pain before Hughey pulled a handkerchief from his top pocket. He stuffed the handkerchief into his fist, tapped the fist three times and produced a bouquet of flowers.

'Can ya magic a vase for them as well?' laughed Mrs. Harris while accepting the offering.

'See, my favourite trick never changes,' said Hughey.

'What? The old bouquet trick.'

'No my love...making you laugh.'

Mrs. Harris stood up and walked towards a vase on the window sill.

'Looks like a frost is coming down,' she said shuffling the flowers with agitation.

Hughey grunted, loosened his tie and undid the first button on his shirt.

'Best set the alarm for seven,' she sighed.

'And why would you do that?'

'You know full well why,' she said retaking her seat and staring hard at the white pieces before her.

'Hasn't it started every morning this six month?' said Hughey leaning over his cup of tea.

'It has, and the summer before that it ran for seven months no problems, but the first day a frost came down it was dead as a dodo,' she says throwing down one blank piece and picking up another.

'And didn't I get it fixed for ya?'

'You did Hughey. That you did...only six weeks later.'

'Christ you'd swear I did you a disservice buying you a car.'

'Taking the bus was no bother to me Hughey Harris. One of the few things those shower of shites in Leinster House haven't taken from us.'

'Fine I'll sell it then. I'd only the best of intentions buying that for you, but a fat load of good it did me.'

'Yeah Hughey you're always full of good intentions,' said Mrs. Harris, standing up but deciding against such a cruel exit.

Mrs. Harris looked from the blank puzzle to the magician's flowers, out the frosted window and back to Hughey. His shoulders drooped off his frame. His eyes watched ripples spread across the tea as he tapped the surface with a finger.

'Come on up to bed. It's late,' she offered.

Hughey tapped the tea once more and suddenly jerked away from some impending thought.

'I'll be up in a minute, dear. Gonna finish my tea here. Need to get some heat in my bones after that frost,' said Hughey, finding another fictitious present to push away the past.

Mrs. Harris understood. She had fled, confronted, battled and accepted those self-same pains, and knew her husband's heart. She considered sitting back down. She imagined the conversation were confessions, acknowledgements and forgiveness were finally achieved.

'I'll set the alarm for seven,' she said turning away.

The two of them could never fill three seats. Maybe she thought Hughey should suffer for that, or maybe she thought it wasn't something for her to forgive.

Chapter 2

'No, Devorra, it is not something to grin and bear. It is completely and utterly unacceptable!' shouted Pluto Von Paradise down the phone line while sweeping back his cape in fury.

'I don't care about the recession, Devorra, I refuse to be treated like some small-time peddler of card tricks, some balloon-blowing clown – I have studied under the great magicians of Budapest! I have performed in the finest establishments in the world! And you are telling me I should accept the staff toilets as my dressing room!' said Pluto, brought to a stop by a lack of oxygen rather than words.

As the magician launched another volley of recriminations at his long-suffering agent, Joseph Blade slipped stealthily in the door. Perhaps, thought the young apprentice, he will ignore my tardiness if I polish the daggers, mirrors and Chinese water tank before my presence is sensed.

'…and after all these years this is how you treat me. Me! One of only two magicians to stick by you after the Oslo incident.'

Joseph worked the Hungarian throwing blades up to a brilliant shine. He checked his appearance in the steel, pulled his hair into a taut ponytail and moved on to the Chinese water tank.

'Since when? Ah he has finally abandoned you, eh? Well with the way you're treating me I think I might follow him...Oh...well I'm very sorry to hear that...Yes he was a dear friend to us all...Well at least he died doing what he loved, eh? Oh come on now, Devorra, the show must go on my dear...That's it! Chin up. Okay my dear, I really must run...Yes I'll see you at the funeral...Show's in ten...Okay goodbye.'

Pluto slowly lowered the phone from his ear, shook his head like a dazed boxer and drew a long breath.

Joseph, having completed all his chores, leaned against the wall with one hand in his pocket and the other cutting cards in a fifty-fifty split. He emitted, as always, a sexuality that could not be called feminine, but was certainly feline in nature.

'You're late,' said Pluto without turning.

'Oh...eh...well I was...' babbled Joseph, certain until now that his presence had gone undetected.

'I don't want your excuses Joseph. What I want—no, no...allow me to rephrase. What I *demand* is an apprentice dedicated to the art of magic who will watch attentively, study assiduously and, most of all, will be on time. If I've told you once I've told you a million times – In the art of magic, timing is everything.'

'I'm sorry but...'

'But nothing, you good-for-nothing swine!' roared Pluto spinning to face Joseph and brandishing one of the Hungarian daggers which moments ago Joseph had safely locked in its box.

'Wow, take it easy, Mr. Paradise. I can explain,' said Joseph Blade, eyeing a lunge behind the water tank, but fearing an even more terrible wrath would result.

'State Article 1 of the magicians' code,' snarled Pluto, cocking the dagger for flight.

'Oh Christ. Oh Jesus. How does it go now...'

'Damn you boy. I'll put this right between your eyes.'

'Article 1: Oppose the wilful exposure to the public of any principles of the art of magic, or the methods employed in any magic effect or illusion,' recited Joseph, thanks to the inspirational qualities of raw terror.

'And Article 4?'

'Expose false or misleading acts, literature, merchandise or statements pertaining to the magical arts.'

Pluto, despite receiving the correct answers, kept his dagger cocked and stared deep into his apprentice's eyes. In that long silence Joseph guessed the true source of Pluto's anger, and tension turned to melancholy. The master, sensing he had revealed himself, lowered the dagger and turned away.

'You saw the paper then?' said Joseph, staring down at his red leather shoes.

Pluto made no answer and leaned over the cracked sink to apply stage make-up.

'I was only trying to do what you told me. You know, make the magic my own,' said the ardent apprentice.

'That was not magic,' snapped Pluto.

'Well I respect your opinion but...'

'That is not an opinion. That is a fact. Doing a headstand on a unicycle for twenty-four hours on top of Molly Malone is an act of endurance. It is akin to running a marathon, climbing a mountain or some other artless pursuit. It is certainly not magic.'

'I only lasted seven.'

'What's that now?'

'I only lasted seven hours. A bunch of piss heads starting throwing chips and battered sausages at me, and I fell.'

'See? Even a drunkard has more taste in magic than you,' said Pluto, instantly regretting his words.

The apprentice had seen the hip flasks and bottles and cans. Joseph knew, on any night of the week, where his master could be found. They had never spoken of it, but if ever there was a chance to use that weakness, well here it was.

'Well at least I got my name in the paper, eh?' said Joseph, passing up his opportunity.

'Infamy is not the same as fame young man...Just imagine the plaudits you'd have received if you demonstrated your true talents,' said Pluto, reluctantly returning the kindness.

The magicians were saved from this uncomfortable bout of amiability by a creaking door. A woman's face, vulpine in nature, popped in the gap. Her head swivelled, as if unconnected to a body, and surveyed the scene.

'Everyone is waiting Mr. Harris,' said Ms. Sweeney in that flaccid tone all uncharismatic teachers use when impersonating authority.

'Good! Dim the lights and let the show begin,' said Pluto sweeping towards his audience.

'There will be no dimming of lights, Mr. Harris. There are health and safety regulations to be upheld, and as I mentioned earlier: no sharp objects, fire, smoke, violence, distressing images or disturbing stunts,' she said departing with a smile that sucks the life out of a room.

'A magic show *sans* magic,' laughed Joseph.

'And to think the minds of children are moulded by these dullards. Well today I solemnly swear to break each and every one of her little regulations,' said Pluto launching a dagger into the toilet door's No Smoking sign.

Salesians school hall bubbled with testosterone-fuelled chaos. If the din of PSPs, iPhones and mp3 players was impressive then the sheer diversity of foulmouthed abuse was breathtaking. Crisps, paper planes, pen tops and occasionally a plimsoll shoe could be seen sailing through the air. Some poor unfortunate had even lost his school jumper. It dangled high up in the rafters. Teachers scurried around the hall like firemen fighting infernos with watering cans.

A flash of light and a deafening bang jolted the carnival of hormones to a halt. Spotty jaws hung open, displaying massive balls of chewing gum as they stared into the thick smoke on stage. All necks, proudly sporting shaving cuts, craned forwards as the dark silhouette of Pluto Von Paradise began to appear.

Pluto allowed the tension to grow and then sprang forwards. He loomed over the audience, glaring at each member in turn.

'Boring...trap door in the stage that is,' called an insolent pup down the back who was quickly silenced by Ms. Sweeney who, although sharing the young man's distaste for events on stage, would not tolerate the insinuation that a health and safety violation, such as a trap door, could have existed under her very nose for so many years.

'Ladies and gentlemen, if you are of a weak disposition I advise you to leave now. For if you stay you will witness feats incredible, acts impossible and events unfathomable!' announced Pluto.

'But before I continue I wish to dispel a viscious and unsubstantiated rumour pertaining to my origins. Right here and now I wish to prove to you that I am neither angel nor demon. Indeed I am nothing more than man. And I will prove, once and for all that my heart beats as yours,' said Pluto sweeping back his cape to reveal a bare chest.

Pluto raised a hand high into the air and made a rigid claw. Tilting his head back, the magician lowered the claw to his chest. He began massaging his left pectoral. Ripples of laughter could be heard from the cynics in the back row, but they were quickly silenced as Pluto's fingers began disappearing into his own flesh. Blood streamed down the magicians chest and soon he stood in a pool of crimson.

As his hand completely disappeared from view Pluto Von Paradise fell to the floor with a scream of agony. Joseph Razor, trusted assistant, appeared from stage left and removed his master's cape. There now began a struggle of gargantuan proportions. Pluto twisted, pulled, grunted, bore his teeth and displayed the whites of his eyes. As the blood began dripping off the stage, flowing under the chairs of students, weary looks were exchanged. The liquid had the inimitable depth, viscous texture and metallic scent of blood.

Something was happening. The man was in real pain. The protective veil of passive voyeurism was coming undone.

'Call an ambulance,' shouted a member of the front row. And with that, Pluto collapsed face first into the stage.

'Get back,' ordered Joseph Blade turning Pluto over and beginning resuscitation.

The apprentice pumped furiously at his master's chest as the schoolboys were reduced to squealing schoolgirls. With teachers and students and janitors and secretaries charging in seemingly random directions Pluto began his death throes. His legs twitched violently and bile spewed from his mouth.

At the apogee of this chaos, a deep gong rattled the bones of all present and Pluto Von Paradise rose to his feet like the rewound hand of a clock.

'Silence,' ordered the magician, and the crowd complied.

All eyes fixed on the heart beating in Pluto's fist. Joseph Blade refitted the magician's cape and Pluto spun on his heels throwing the heart above the crowd. The boys in the back row began diving for cover.

'FLIGHT,' commanded the magician with his wand.

As the vital organ began its descent there was a collective gasp. The flesh was unravelling. Before their very eyes it bloomed into a flower of flight and swooped effortlessly over their heads. The eagle circled with menace, murderous claws ready for the plunge and mocked the screaming students with a shrill call.

Having in the last three minutes witnessed more health and safety violations than had occurred in the previous thirty years of her reign, Ms. Sweeney attempted to gain the stage. In a foaming sea of testosterone she waded forwards with razor-sharp elbows.

Having reached front of stage she demonstrated surprising agility in climbing up.

'Mr. Harris! This is completely unacceptable! I made it absolutely clear...' she shrieked with hair awry and face aflame.

Pluto Von Paradise, not wishing to lower himself to a response, issued an ear-splitting whistle. The eagle banked hard to its left and landed gently on the magician's outstretched arm.

'For my next trick I will need a volunteer,' announced Pluto.

'Mr. Harris this show is over. I have a right mind to report...'

'Ah Ms. Sweeney. Perfect. Mr. Blade, the restraints please.'

Before the headmistress could flee, the ever-adroit Joseph Blade clasped her in shackles. As the Hungarian throwing blades were produced, Ms. Sweeney's cries for help were drowned by roars of approval from students and staff alike. Soon the headmistress was spinning clockwise on a wooden board.

'Ladies and gentlemen, I must now insist on silence,' said Pluto.

'Mr. Harris, I had hoped not to make this a police matter but if...'

The brilliant ring of the metal blade striking the board above her head brought Ms. Sweeney's objections to a halt.

'Ms. Sweeney for your own safety I recommend complete silence,' said Pluto holding up a large chunk of Ms. Sweeney's hair for all to see.

The headmistress, having entered a fear-induced catatonia, was only too happy to oblige.

Pluto Von Paradise took up his fighting stance and proceeded, much to the consternation of Ms. Sweeney's embittered staff, to leave her flesh unmarked. Having thrown all eight blades, Pluto turned to receive the expected applause. It did not arrive.

'If I practised throwing poxy daggers all day I could do that. Any gobshite could,' shouted a member of the back row, garnering grunts of approval from all quarters.

Pluto grimaced and mumbled towards some invisible presence before regaining composure. The old performer, reading the minds of his audience, decided to further endanger their villain's life.

'She escaped the knife, but she will surely not escape the saw,' said Pluto.

Soon Joseph had Ms. Sweeney interned in a saw box. Her head hung limply from one end and her feet stuck out the other. Pluto spun the box around three hundred and sixty degrees thus demonstrating the impossibility of escape and produced a rusty saw.

'Boring...Boring...Booooooooooooooooooooring,' heckled a boy.

Pluto checked the descent of his saw and looked up into the eyes of his interlocutor.

'Is that another volunteer I hear?'

'Yeah whatever man. I saw all about dis on dat show...*Breaking The Magician's Code*. It's just like a false box or a mirror or whatever. Oldest trick in da book dat is.'

'So I suppose you could come up and perform it then ya gobshite,' retorted Joseph Blade.

'He could if he spent all his time doing dat crap couldn't he? It's just smoke and mirrors and trapdoors and all. It's not magic,' answered another student and the cynicism spread like a dose of weapons-grade smallpox.

Pluto tightened his grip on the saw. He recounted the steps of his next trick as if they hadn't become instinct. He rehearsed his lines as if he could possibly forget them. He summoned the nerves of a younger magician; a magician who wasn't hearing a multitude of teenage voices merging into one.

'Then what is magic?' asked Hughey meekly.

Seeing this authoritative male wither under their mockery, the schoolboys grew cocky. Torrents of abuse rained down on the stage followed by every available type of projectile.

One particularly oafish lad attempted to gain the stage. A skirmish looked certain until Joseph Blade pinned the oaf's tie to the stage with a dagger. This swift counterattack knocked the wind out of the schoolboys. Hoping to grasp this brief reprieve, Joseph Blade gently touched his master's arm.

'Mr. Paradise, we better leg it,' said Joseph, eyeing the riotous crowd and screaming headmistress with foreboding.

'Then what is magic son?' asked Hughey again.

'Eh, I really don't think this is the time, Mr. Paradise,' answered Joseph, suspecting another test.

'No, no... son, listen to me. Don't fall for that old lie. Don't buy into the cult of genius. You practise for months and years away from the watching eyes of the crowd. In secret places you hide your mistakes. Over and over again you reach for magic, but it slips through your clumsy fingers. You think it will never come, but then one day, the same as all the others, it does....Oh please son just listen to me,' pleaded Hughey, tears latent in his eyes.

'Mr. Paradise are you okay?' said Joseph, slowly realising his master was not staring at him, but rather through him.

'But you're wrong son. That's all magic is. The audience never sees the months and years of practise: We make the labours disappear! That's the secret to every trick. That's the only true magic.'

With his master engaged in a phantom debate on the nature of magic, a screaming headmistress interned in a saw box, a hall full of leery teenagers and the very real prospect of arrest, Joseph Blade took action.

In a burst of acceleration that rendered him a blur to the human eye, Joseph released Ms. Sweeney, unpinned the oaf, disappeared Pluto Von Paradise in a plume of smoke, and ferried their equipment from the stage.

Chapter 3

The rusty iron red of O'Shea's public house was chipped and peeling. Patches of navy showed here and there; a final testament to the former owners who sold up in '83. Two smokers hung by the door, cradling fags for feeble warmth. The base of O'Shea's door had been kicked clean of paint by drunken boots. Beyond that door, light halted and a silent gloom enveloped you; holding you silent and safe; letting you nod to the barman for a pint; letting you hand over the money without exchanging a word; letting you feel the drink flatten your emotions and letting you drift into the half-light.

Joseph Blade took the pints of Guinness off the bar and walked back across the muck-green carpet to where Hughey leaned over a small round table. As the drinks settled, they said nothing. The only other customers sat at the bar. The men chewed small blue pens, watched the horse racing and communicated by underlining important statistics in the form guide.

Another race began. The gates opened. Neither Hughey nor Joseph looked at the screen; instead they watched their pints, which defied the commentator's pace and remained unsettled as the final horse crossed the line.

The apprentice picked up his pint, but seeing his master was not following suit placed it back down.

'I haven't seen you do that trick in a long time,' said Joseph.

'Yeah it's been a while I suppose. It's hard to fit a lifetime's work into one show,' Hughey said with a smile and quickly snatched up his pint.

'The eagle's a great touch.'

'Well I was hardly going to turn it into a pigeon, now was I?' laughed Hughey.

'Still though. I've seen you do that – What? Fifty? Sixty times? And every time I get a buzz out of it. Fucking gets me here it does,' said the ardent apprentice shifting forwards and touching his chest.

Hughey replied by crumpling his forehead and burying his mouth in Guinness.

'Sorry bout the language,' mumbled Joseph before retreating to the Guinness himself.

The gate snapped open, starting another race. One horse remained in the stalls, tossing its head in defiance of the jockey demanding action with his whip. One of the gamblers swatted the bar with his form guide and stood up. Joseph watched the gambler, wondering if that was the end of ends. Is he all out of credit, debit, assets and options?

'So come here till I tell ya. Jennifer wants to go on a date,' said Joseph turning to his own financial needs.

'And who's Jennifer?'

'You know the Trinity head. Lives on my road. Green eyes, long legs, pierced belly button, tight bum, big...'

'I remember. I remember. Jesus spare me the details,' snapped Hughey.

'Right, yeah. Sorry. Well she saw my picture in the paper and finally agreed to a date. I was thinking of bringing her for a fancy dinner. You know? Impress her with a bit of sophistication...'

'McDonald's so, yeah?' said Hughey elbowing his apprentice.

'Ah feck off, will ye. I was thinking of an Italian or something.'

Hughey directed Joseph's attention to the gambler (who apparently hadn't reached the end of ends) returning to his seat.

'Gobshites,' said Hughey.

'Thing is you'd need a small fortune for that,' said Joseph.

'Damn right ya would. It's like my uncle Morris always said – You never meet a poor bookey,' answered Hughey.

'No I was talking about the restaurant.'

'What restaurant?'

'The Italian restaurant. You know for the date with Jennifer. I was just saying it would cost a fair bit of money,' said Joseph peeling the corner of his beer mat.

Hughey's forehead crumpled in confusion, relaxed in elucidation and crumpled once more.

There was of course a union rate for apprentice magicians. It was a nominal fee designed to meet the expenses incumbent on the student, i.e. polish, rabbit food, sharpening stones, balloons and bouquets of flowers. However, times were hard and Pluto Von Paradise had retained the services of Joseph Blade out of a paternal pride in his development when others would have lightened their load. If the master made money, the apprentice received his pay, but they had just fled a hysterical school mistress threatening to have them arrested. It was safe to assume payment would not be forthcoming.

'I see,' said Hughey at last.

'I hate to ask, Pluto—I mean, Mr. Paradise...but I don't know when I'll get another shot at this girl,' said Joseph tearing his beer mat in two.

Hughey knew the exact amount of money, down to the penny, sitting in his pocket. He also knew what each penny was destined to be spent on. He knew this because Mrs. Harris had told him. As Hughey listened to the cars thickening in the rush hour traffic, he was absolutely certain his wife's car was not among them. Frost had come and the car, a present he regretted every day, refused to start.

'Is that enough?' said Hughey handing over two crisp fifties.

'Jesus yeah. I mean I bloody well hope so. Thanks Mr. Paradise.'

'Well being a fiver under is the same as being one hundred under, so better safe than sorry, eh? Wouldn't want you ending the date washing dishes,' laughed Hughey.

As Joseph laid out his plan for conquest, Hughey laughed to himself. If he is fifty short for the repairs to Mrs. Harris' car he may as well be one hundred short. The money is gone. It has fled the mundane world of necessity into the magic of romance.

For a while Hughey smiled contentedly, but all Joseph's passionate talk began tugging heartstrings long fallen out of tune. She wouldn't even be angry, he thought to himself, she expects me to let her down. A wave of indignation swept through Hughey. How could a husband reach for ideals of love when weighed down by his wife's dull acceptance of his mediocrity? Hughey looked at the young man and envied him the irrational fights, jealous accusations and savage insults before him. Once Mrs. Harris had an ideal of Hughey in her mind; a beautiful ideal that when contradicted by his behaviour enraged her. Perhaps he could shock her once more. Could one trick change everything? Of course a magician would answer yes.

'...and you know once the ground work is done she'll probably come see my gig?'

'Your gig?' said Hughey.

'Uh yeah I meant to tell you. I'm doing a slot, nothing major now, just my own thing, just a chance to practise like...'

'In the International?' asked Hughey slowly.

Joseph Blade nodded.

'Christoph asked you?'

'Not directly, no. It's just a slot on the night. I'm not doing a gig for him. Just a little slot to practise in front of a crowd.'

Hughey washed down his words with Guinness. The young fella just wants a taste of the glory, Hughey told himself. God knows I'm hardly pulling in the crowds. And now they'll only pay for half-hour shows. How else is he going to hone his stage craft? Sure, weren't you chomping at the bit yourself at that age?

'You know if there were any other gigs I'd...'

'It's all right Joseph. I understand,' said Hughey pulling on his coat. 'We'll go over your act tomorrow and make sure you show them what's what, right?'

'Right.'

'Listen I'm gonna have to run. I have a few errands to run before the wife gets back.'

The master and apprentice shook hands with a professional courtesy that wounded Joseph. The apprentice wanted the gig, but he'd secretly hoped Pluto would forbid it. If the master had ranted and raged, how much easier it would be to justify a rebellion! Instead he was given permission; permission to put his interests before the feelings of his master.

"Yes you're right. I'm past it," are the words that Joseph read in Pluto's actions and he felt compelled by respect and loyalty to disagree in the strongest possible terms.

'See you tomorrow,' was all the apprentice managed.

Joseph stood, weighed down by words unsaid, watching Hughey walk into the cutting wind. Joseph considered cancelling the gig, but he knew that would be viewed as an act born of guilt. And there is nothing to feel guilty about, thought Joseph, I'm not even doing it for Christoph, just for the practise, and sure didn't Pluto even offer to help with the act. Would he do that if he thought I was betraying him? The apprentice brooded in the doorway until the sound of another horse race starting inside the pub and the prospect of seeing the true end of ends in that gambler's eyes set Joseph on his way.

Joseph walked past the shining glass and steel artifice of Ballyfermot community centre and remembered the T.D. delivering a speech full of dancing limbs, singing voices, eager minds and entrepreneurial drive at the opening ceremony. Joseph watched three grannies shuffling inside the youth centre for bingo. They, along with the babies who puked and crapped in the centre's crèche, made up the youth centre's entire patronage. All ages between grannies and babies had jumped ship. All able-bodied youth— bodies capable of saving the nation— had left. Well, you could work for ten years earning peanuts for the good of your nation, thought Joseph, or you could fuck off to Australia and have some fun. Patriotism was a little thin on the ground after we'd gone with the begging bowl to the EU and the British.

At the end of Boland Avenue, head starting to emerge from a beer buzz, Joseph scrolled through his phone book for someone to continue drinking with. The hundred from Hughey was off limits, but he'd enough money for six Dutchy and enough weed for a few spliffs. As the names of friends filed across the screen of his phone, Joseph recalled going-away parties: Good luck in New York; All the best in Sydney; Knock em Dead in Auckland. At twenty-four, Joseph's brother Mickey had been going to weddings every other weekend. They arrived like a deluge, and it seemed Mickey was never out of that Arnott's suit.

'Costing me a fucking arm and a leg, Joey. I've bought toasters for half of fucking Dublin by now,' complained Mickey on receiving yet another wedding invitation.

I suppose the weddings will arrive for my lot too, thought Joseph. I'll receive Facebook invites to ceremonies on tropical beaches, regretfully decline and snoop at the photos later. Better off anyways. I don't have the fucking money for presents and shite like that and aren't most of them bloody hypocrites anyway, taking solemn oaths before a priest when they haven't set foot in a church since their confirmation.

Joseph stopped outside the off-licence, which stood between an abandoned mobile phone shop and a battered ATM whose cracked screen permanently read, 'Temporarily out of service.'

Joseph opened the offo door and stood inside a perspex cage the size of a phone box. The shop had once allowed customers wild luxuries such as browsing foreign beers and tasting New World wines, but with the money gone, the robberies began. Joseph rang the buzzer. The owner emerged from the back of the shop and slid back a hatch in the perspex box.

'What do you want?' said the owner.

'Six Dutch please,' said Joseph handing money in through the hatch.

The cans were dropped into a metal box, which slid forwards allowing the customer receive the purchases.

'Here these are bleedin warm,' said Joseph picking up his beers.

'Yeah. And?' said the owner, his blood shot eyes glazing over and his unshaven jowls tightening with contempt.

'And nothing. They're bleedin warm. You can't drink warm Dutch— it's like drinking piss for Christ sake.'

'Do ye have a fridge?' enquired the owner.

'What? Of course I have a fridge,' said Joseph, thrown by this unexpected twist in the argument.

'Well go fucking chill them yourself. This is an off-licence not a fucking refrigeration service!' shouted the owner, slamming the hatch shut and strolling to the back of the shop.

'Come back here you robbing cunt! What kind of fucking off-license doesn't chill their beer?' shouted Joseph, lashing out at the perspex screen. 'This cage isn't preventing robberies— it's fucking causing them!'

The owner strolled back into view with a cordless phone, made a great show of stabbing nine three times and began reporting Joseph's attempted robbery to the police. For a split second Joseph considered waiting for the filth to arrive and laying forth his argument, but even the most cursory glance at his previous encounters with the law was enough to rubbish the idea that the Gardai Siochana could process rational discourse.

Back out on the pavement, Joseph stripped the cans of their plastic wrapper and hid them under his coat, preferring the armpits and small of his back as these recesses of the body offered best concealment. This achieved, Joseph made for home.

47

As he turned onto his road, Joseph spotted the twins sitting on the wall outside the house. His little brother and sister were not identical, but on viewing seemed to be two halves of either a Grecian hero or a Medieval villain. Nobody was ever sure what the merged halves would form. It all depended on which prevailed in the gene war – Dylan's sculpted cheeks or Shakira's pock-marked ones, the sister's button nose or the brother's crooked beak, the boy's greasy mop or the girl's curly locks. That is not even to mention the invisible battle between virtue and vice that would vie for control of the soul

Dylan's calloused thumbs moved in a blur across the buttons of his PSP as Shakira listened to her iPod and performed dance steps learned from that weekend's episode of *X-Factor*. Joseph, hoping to slip by unnoticed, reached into his pocket and produced one of the surplus pyrotechnics from Pluto's performance.

As the sound of a cheap cover version mixed with the screams of decapitated zombies, Joseph lit the firecracker and made a dash towards the front door.

The flash and bang drew the attention of the fourteen-year-old twins only momentarily, for, like a dog that always hears a bell before feeding time, the twins had long ago deduced the true meaning of this sound.

Joseph was quickly seized by his siblings in a classic pincer manoeuvre.

'All right, Joey, did you get us anything in the shop? Did yeh?' said Dylan eyes still glued to the computer screen.

'What's under you coat Joey?' giggled Shakira while under the guise of a loving hug she executed a thorough search of Joey's person.

'Get off me you,' said Joey untangling himself from his little sister.

'Well I'm glad to see you too! Look at your man Dylan – too big and too cool to give his little sister a hug now that he's a magician and all,' cried Shakira, sweeping back her strawberry curls.

'Mickey was never too cool for hugging was he, sis?' added Dylan.

'Never, bro,' confirmed Shakira.

'Always bought us little presents didn't he, sis?' continued Dylan, bringing the blood-curdling screams of zombies to a crescendo on his PSP.

'Always, Dylan.'

'Never brought booze under his ma's roof did he, sis?'

'Never, Dylan. Mickey knew Mammy'd hit the roof if she found any of us drinking in the gaff, and Mickey never wanted to upset mammy,' said Shikira with a nefarious grin.

'Of course he didn't. Sure you'd have to be a right cunt to be upsetting Mammy when she's working non-stop in the hospital and every day wondering if she'll still have a job in the morning,' said Dylan feigning deep melancholy as level-complete victory music came from his PSP.

Joseph considered grabbing the cheeky little fucker by the collar and giving him a good dig, but this course of action would only result in answering two sets of charges when his mother arrived home. The only other course was to plead with the twins; to convince them of his poverty; to beg they allow him this small pleasure, but Joseph knew only too well that these encounters were not about material possession. In fact the twins didn't even like beer, preferring alchopops or vodka. This was simply another episode in a lifelong battle of wits between him and his younger siblings, an episode he had to concede and hope to avenge at a later date.

Joseph opened his coat and took out two cans of beer.

'I hope you fucking choke on them,' he said tossing the cans into the rapacious mitts of his siblings.

'Here these are warm,' objected Dylan as Joseph put his key into the latch.

'Yeah. And?' said Joseph over his shoulder.

'And nothing. You can't drink warm Dutch – it's like drinking piss!' cried Shakira.

'That's exactly what I said,' answered Joseph, closing the hall door behind him.

The apprentice stood in the hallway listening for signs of his parents. He listened with a fearful hope – fearing being caught and hoping they'd actually be home early.

A television chattered in the living room, wind whistled though a gap under the warped back door, heat pipes coughed, taps dripped, wallpaper peeled, carpet frayed, tiles chipped, toilets moulded, stairs creaked and the entire house seemed to moan under the weight of growing entropy, but there was no sign of his parents. Joseph's dad would be working the double shift tonight in the train maintenance yard. He didn't work twelve- or sixteen-hour days for the overtime or the chance of a promotion. He took the shifts merely to avoid the machete of privatisation, which hacked away family men who preferred a little time at home to extra time at work. At the hospital Joseph's mam was taking similar precautions, acquiescing with all requests to work holidays and attempting to tend a nation of babies and invalids with half the resources required.

Joseph kept his coat on, fearing a raid by the twins and walked five steps down the hall to the living room. His granddad, as always, sat in the armchair beside the window with a Persian blanket across his lap. Mr. Blade's jaw, smashed decades before in a freak boating accident, was the first plastic replacement in the history of the Republic, and protruded at a morose angel. This scowl led all who met Mr. Blade to assume he was a laconic character; an assumption which only served to render his romantic tales of adventures on the seven seas all the more incredible to the listener.

'All right, Granddad?' said Joseph, sitting down on the sofa and crossing his legs.

Mr. Blade heard nothing of this greeting and stared at the footage of another round of union protests on the streets of Dublin and grumbled to himself.

'I said ALL RIGHT, GRANDAD?' repeated Joseph rising slightly to aim his words directly at his grandfather's ear drum.

Mr. Blade glanced sideways as if hearing a faint shout from the bottom of a cold country lane on a mucky winter's night.

'Ah how are you, son?' he said registering Joseph's presence, lifting his hands from under the Persian blanket and smiling as much as his immobile jawline would allow.

'Great, Granddad,' said Joseph giving Mr. Blade the obligatory hug and receiving the obligatory squeeze of the thigh in that sensitive flesh just above the knee.

'Jesus, Grandda,' said Joseph sitting back down and rubbing his leg, 'your eyes and ears might be on the blink but that bloody grip of yours is getting stronger.'

'Ah my hands are not what they once were, son. There was a time on the ships when I was pulling ropes and hoisting chains that you wouldn't have broken my grip with a sledgehammer,' said Mr. Blade in an accent disappearing from Dublin: working class but articulate, well spoken but unpretentious.

'Well I'm glad they're not what they once were then. Christ knows that grip is bad enough,' said Joseph, but Mr. Blade was no longer listening, having returned his attention to the television.

Incomprehensibly large numbers in bright red font told a nation what they already knew: A situation that could not get any worse was in fact doing exactly that. Mr. Blade grunted. The studio presenter returned and began conducting an interview with Gerry Adams about the possibility of entering into a coalition government with Labour.

'Do you know how they tame elephants, son?' said Mr. Blade.

'No idea, Granddad,' said Joseph smiling at another trademark tangent from his grandfather.

'Well I'll tell you. I learned all about it from a lad called Jong Cung Minh. Wiry little fella he was, but as strong as an ox and sharp as a tack. But I suppose I better tell you how I met him hadn't I?'

'If you say so, Granddad,' said Joseph settling in for a long story.

'Right you are. No how should I begin?...Well we put out from Le Harve. It was to be a long voyage with a crew more drunken and violent than any I'd bore witness to before...No, no too early. That scrape is another story entirely. Yes I have it now. Into the thick of things it is. Right here we go...

'I was working on a French merchant at the time which saw us doing lots of runs back and forth to the colonies. I can't remember what we were shipping on that run, but whatever it was was late getting to port. Horse and carts on mud roads have a habit of running into trouble you see, and Indo-China did not have what you'd call the firmest grip of law and order in those days.

'Anyway, by the time the cargo had arrived a bloody big typhoon had started, and in the resulting chop some damage was done to our hull. A layover of a couple weeks was on the cards so off we went on a session which ended up in a dark little opium den in the backstreets of Tourane, or Dan Nang as the locals called it.

'We lay on our sides on straw mats smoking bowls of opium and listening to a Dan Nguyet playing in the background when a little fella, talking fluent French, asked if could he join us for a bowl.

How he came to learn French, considering were he was from, I'll never know, but I do know that he was a happy man that day.

'Through the course of conversation, punctuated by bowls of opium, my shipmates and I learned his name was Jong Cung Minh and that he had that very day sold three elephants. This of course twigged our interest, and our line of questioning quickly established that Jong Cung Minh was a member of the famous elephant hunting tribe located on the shores of Lake Lok. At first, Jong Cung Minh refused to tell us the ancient methods employed by his elephant hunting tribe, but after we had bought him a number of bowls and assured him that we did not intend to take up his trade, being as we were career sailors, he agreed to reveal his secrets. I lay on my straw mat enjoying a vibrant somnolence as the dark brown face of Jong Cung Minh bounced around on the candlelight and told us the following:

'The hunters set out from their stilt houses at dusk. They move through the jungle silent as mice. They pick up signs of the elephants and begin tracking them. For days on end they watch the elephants and pick out the one that will bring the most money on sale. Having chosen their prey, the hunters scatter the herd using drums, horns, fire and dogs. All night they keep up this racket until the herd is forced to abandon their lost member. With their prey isolated they, set four huge posts into the ground and tie the elephant's legs to them.

Now they set camp. For days on end they leave the elephant tied to the posts without food or water. Naturally enough the elephant weakens and just when it is about to drop they begin to feed and water it. Now each time they feed Nelly they touch him, always watching for that big bloody trunk of his. Day by day they risk more and more contact with the elephant until he becomes accustomed to it. This achieved, the most senior hunter – in this case Jong Cung Minh – climbs up a tree and jumps down on the elephant's back. At first the elephant goes wild with fury, but just like he grew accustomed to touch, he grows accustomed to being ridden. Then after all this work, some three to four weeks in total, do you know what they do?'

'Bring it to the market?' said Joseph.

'No. They let it go,' said Mr. Blade, trying to smile, but owing to his jaw achieving only a sneer.

'They let it go?'

'Yes. They untie the elephant and let it walk back into the jungle to find its family.'

'After all that work, they just let it go?'

'Yes. They let it go and after three days, without fail, the elephant comes back to the village,' said Mr. Blade.

'It comes back by itself?' said Joseph.

'Yes, and do you know why?' said Mr. Blade, pushing himself forwards in his armchair.

'No idea,' replied Joseph, honestly.

'Addiction,' declared Mr. Blade with a grunt towards the television.

'Addiction?'

'Yes, addiction. The whole time poor old Nelly thinks he's just getting food and water from the hunters, but little does he realise that he's also being dosed with salt. When they let Nelly go back into the jungle he finds his family all right, but he doesn't find the salt that he suddenly craves. So back to the hunters he comes, tamed and broken by addiction.'

'I see,' said Joseph slowly watching more images of doom on the television screen.

'I hope you do, son, because after I heard that story I never went into an opium den again,' said Mr. Blade sitting back to look at the screen, which began relaying the sports news.

Joseph searched for some question or comment to offer his grandfather, but nothing arrived. No clarification was required. After watching highlights of Liverpool's sixth defeat in a row, Joseph rose and without a word made for his bedroom.

The floorboards moaned with every step and as Joseph approached the entrance to the twins' lair their scattered possessions grew into a dense swamp of roller blades, Frisbees, dolls' heads, water pistols, skipping ropes and objects that defied definition. He opened his own bedroom door, stepped inside and locked the steady creep of chaos out.

Joseph sat down on the edge of his taut bedspread and admired his freshly polished acoustic guitar sitting in its stand under the window, where the evening sun could play in the beautiful swirls of the wood's grain. He unbuttoned his coat, placed the cans of beer in two rows beside the alphabetically arranged CDs on his desk and hung his coat on the third hanger in the wardrobe – completing a series of coats, jackets and jumpers that descended from thickest to thinnest. Now he knelt down exactly two feet along the bed's length, put his hand under the bed and slid out a stainless steel box. He entered a combination into the hefty padlock (a number which he changed on the first Friday of every month as a precaution against the machinations of his siblings) and opened the box.

 The box contained five distinct compartments with five distinct purposes. The first contained a gunmetal Zippo lighter which was refilled with gas each fortnight and given a fresh flint quarterly. The second contained a selection of rolling papers ranging from Liquorice Superskins to regular Rizla cigarette papers. The third contained somewhere in the region of eighty pre-rolled cardboard roaches. The fourth contained a safety pin from a fire extinguisher, and the fifth contained the main ingredient: a bag of weed.

 Joseph opened a copy of Hot Press magazine and laid it flat on the desk. He placed the box on top of the open magazine and after careful consideration chose a packet of blue Rizla rolling papers. He removed three skins from the packet and placed the packet back in its compartment.

 Joseph licked precisely one inch of the glued portion of one skin and affixed another skin to it. He now licked the entire length of the third skin and fixed it to the back of the joined skins, thus reinforcing the structure. Having established a solid foundation, Joseph took a cigarette from his pocket and licked the length of its seam. He gently peeled away the seam and poured the tobacco onto the face of Mick Pyro, who was interviewed in that week's issue of Hot Press.

 Joseph now took the bag of weed and emptied the dregs onto the tobacco. For three minutes the apprentice mixed the two substances with his fingers, determined to avoid an uneven burn caused by surfeit marijuana (a slower-burning substance) on one side of the joint.

 Satisfied that this nuisance had been thwarted, Joseph placed his mixture within the skins along with one of the pre-made roaches. A look of intense concentration now took control of Joseph's features as fingers and thumbs worked with relentless exactitude, shaping and sculpting the joint.

Finally the joint was flipped. Joseph licked the glue and sealed his creation. His features did not relax, however, for there was still work to be done. The fire extinguisher pin was retrieved, and the head of the joint was poked firm before being twisted shut.

Joseph placed his joint on top of his Genaflex speaker and gently took the open magazine off the desk. The few shards of tobacco and weed that had been spilt during the process were dropped into the bin. The magazine was placed back into the rack, and then, sitting down at his desk, Joseph assessed his work.

It was beautiful. It tapered from a thick head to a neat roach. On all sides it was completely solid and symmetrical. The thought of smoking this creation did not enter into his mind for five smiling minutes and only then with a sense of blasphemy. All those hours spent rolling weedless joints had come to fruition. For over six mouths now he had replicated this exact joint every day of every week. And the lads aren't even here to see it, thought Joseph. He glanced at his computer. Maybe he could go online. Maybe someone would be awake in Australia and up for a chat. Then Joseph remembered how those chats inevitably went – Fucking paradise man, surfing this morning, 40C, BBQ tonight, road trip next weekend, did you see the pictures of my new moth? Bleedin gorgeous or what? How's Ireland?

The apprentice grabbed an ashtray and made for the bed. He lit the joint and, realising he'd failed to put on some music, reached to the bedside locker where he'd placed a remote control to counter this eventuality. Bon Iver played on the stereo. Joseph opened a beer and began a long, slow drift towards easy sleep.

The apprentice awoke to shouts from all quarters and, fearing a fire was about to envelop his room, decided to investigate.

'But Da I need the book for tomorrow or I'll be given detention, and if I get another detention I'll get a suspension, and if I get another suspension I'll have to have a meeting with Travers, and Travers said if he ever has to have another meeting with me I'll be kicked out of the school,' cried Shakira, standing in Welly boots at the threshold of the bathroom.

'If you get kicked out of school I'll bleedin brain ya!' roared Eoin Blade from inside the bathroom, which was steadily oozing water out onto the landing.

'Jesus Christ, Eoin, the ceiling's gonna come down if you don't get a move on!' shouted Geraldine Blade from below.

Joseph was long accustomed to the contrasting states of order between his private space and the public thoroughfares of his family, but this dose of chaos was stronger than even he expected. He sludged across the carpet to the bathroom in a state of disbelief.

'How's the head,' asked Shakira with malicious concern.

'Shut up, ya rat. What the fuck's going on here?'

'Joseph? Joseph, is that you?' called Eoin.

'Yeah, Da.'

'Finally someone with a bit of sense. Get your arse in here,' cried Eoin.

Joseph obeyed and was confronted with his father standing waist-deep in a bath full of water desperately plunging away at the plug hole as the tap steadily poured forth more of the offending liquid.

'Well don't bleedin stand there gawking!' roared Eoin, his shock of grey hair falling around his flushed face. 'Get that bucket and start bailing water into the sink.'

Joseph always felt the urge to rebel against the physical presence of his father – a former boxer and twice Joseph's size. The apprentice had inherited his mother's slight frame, and this urge to rebel, always smothered by fear, was merely a form of self-flagellation, for every man who knows he'll never best his father feels himself a failure.

Joseph picked up the bucket and did as he was told.

'Da, are you gonna give me the money for the book or what?' whined Shakira.

'I'll give you a box round the ears if you don't get the hell out of my sight,' shouted Eoin waving the plunger at Shakira, who fled down the stairs towards her shrieking mother.

'Could you not fix that bloody tap before the ceiling falls in?' said Geraldine, coming up the stairs.

'I can only do one thing at a time Ger,' said Eoin, pumping the plunger furiously.

'Well fix the tap first then,' said Geraldine, standing in silk pyjamas and slippers of a Chinese origin.

'The thing is, love, fixing the tap will take at least half an hour in which time the water will keep filling the bath and spilling out onto the floor,' panted Eoin before launching a fresh assault on the plug hole.

'If it's not one thing it's another in this bloody house,' said Geraldine.

'Could you not turn the water off at the mains Da?' asked Joseph pouring a pale of water into the sink and watching in terror as it refused to go down the plug hole.

'Oh that's a brilliant idea. That's exactly what I could do... if the bloody handle wasn't rusted shut!' said Eoin, taking out his frustrations on the plug hole.

'Uh, Da?'

'No oil won't help,' barked Eoin.

'No, Da it's not that.'

'What then?'

'Uh...the sink is uh...kind of uh...clogged too,' muttered Joseph.

A madrigal of screams broke out in the bathroom before Joseph was given instructions to accompany each pale of water down the toilet with a prayer to Saint Jude Thaddeus.

It was an hour before the clogs in the bath and sink were cleared and another hour before the tap itself was brought into an acceptable mode of operation. With the bathroom now saved from the onslaught of entropy, Eoin and Joseph were free to peruse the collateral damage to the rest of the house. Each fault was easily repaired in isolation, but each element was part of a system of delicate interdependence and soon the men found themselves driven to the brink of insanity by the complex permutations that arose.

'So we'll have to take up the carpet if we want the floorboards to dry,' said Eoin, sitting at the kitchen table and rubbing his lined forehead. 'We can't put the carpet outside because the knackers will rob it, but we can't put it in the attic because of the mice. So I suppose we'll have to get some mouse traps and get rid of the mice, but they're getting in somewhere so they'll be back quick enough. We could get a lend of your Aunty Ann's cat, but the cat will probably pull the carpet apart itself. I suppose I've no option but to search the attic again for the hole they're getting in through.

'Right well if I don't break my back crawling around in that attic, I'll need to get the heating on full blast to dry out the floor, but the boiler is on the blink. Now Colin across the road could have a look at it for us, but I'll have to throw him a few bob and with all the money it'll take for the repairs I'll have to work my night off to scrape it together. Fecking heating ain't gonna dry out that ceiling though, not with the draft coming in under that back door. Robbing bastards who sold me that. Bloody thing warped after one winter. I'll have to take it down and plane the whole thing flush. Christ I hate re-hanging doors. Then I'm gonna have to replace the bath taps. That requires a few bob. I'll have to save up over a few months and hope to God it doesn't break in the middle of the night again and set me right back to the start of these repairs...'

The thought of performing all these repairs for a second time stopped Eoin in his tracks. He lit a cigarette, smoked half of it in one drag and washed it down with a gulp of black coffee. As if on cue, Shakira appeared in the kitchen with Dylan in tow.

'Da, we need money for those books,' they began.

Eoin pushed his coffee across the kitchen table and looked Joseph in the face with a frankness that frightened the apprentice. Sons did not tell the truth to their fathers and they expected the same favours in return.

'Sometimes I think it's easier just to let this place fall down and start all over again,' said Eoin, finishing his cigarette with his second drag.

The twins began a fresh salvo of complaints, the wind whistled under the back door, water dripped from the ceiling, and Joseph felt his ribs squeezing his heart like a trapped bird.

Chapter 4

While leaning on his low garden gate, Hughey Harris spotted the approach of his old friend Marley Kempe and began whistling "Entrance of the Gladiators." Marley's giant red afro shone like a beacon, warning all those convinced of the seriousness of living that their antithesis was approaching.

Needless to say a seven-foot Irish-Jamaican clown caught the attention of the neighbourhood. Women's heads, wrapped in rollers, popped out of windows. Husbands tore their eyes away from TVs and peeped out the curtains. Children spilled out of gardens, jumped out of trees, hopped over fences and sprung out of manholes.

Marley, having taken a lifetime vow of clowning, was only too happy to entertain his audience. He spotted a tiny spider in his path and froze in terror. The children crept forwards cautiously to see the cause of his paralysis.

'You all right there, mister?' asked little Johnser Doyle.

Marley pointed towards the minuscule spider and twisted his face in terrified anguish.

The children began laughing.

'Jesus, it's only a little spider, mister,' said Johnser, bending down to pick up the offending creature.'Wouldn't hurt a fly, it wouldn't.'

The clown, being more versed in the dietary customs of spiders, was not inclined to agree. Seeing Marley's cowardice, the boy decided to give chase. The children howled with laughter as Marley tumbled over walls, leaped cars and tripped over curbs in his attempts to escape. The clown eventually found refuge high up a lamp post. The howls continued, but now began to take on the manic sound of youth suddenly discovering their power. Despite the children attempting to goad Marley into an early descent, the clown remained safely aloof and gazed down on them all with a melancholy innocence.

Eventually a deal was brokered between the shouting children and the silent clown. Marley threw down a balloon and through a process of mime communicated that the spider was to be interned there in. It took several attempts before the clown fully descended, as time and again he mistook assorted pieces of litter for members of the arachnid family.

Back down on his size-seventeen feet, Marley began performing balloon tricks. He twisted, moulded and sculpted with amazing dexterity, but each time burst his creation while tying the final knot. Soon he ran out of balloons and fell into a sulk. Spotting his opportunity, Johnser offered up his balloon. Marley made an effusive show of thanks, nearly shaking Johnser's hand off his arm. The clown made elaborate preparations, stretching his cheeks and fingers and launching into a sequence of lunges. At last he lifted the balloon to his mouth and inhaled the spider trapped within. The neighbourhood erupted in hysterics as Marley galloped off down Shelka Park Road towards the waiting Hughey Harris.

'As much as I love to see you perform, I was hoping to avail of your mechanical rather than your clowning skills today,' said Hughey, opening the garden gate.

Marley spotted some multi-limbed beast on the path before him and opted to dive over the hedge instead.

'Really Marley, the wife's gonna be home in a few hours. Did you even bring your tools?' said Hughey to the clown spread flat on his back.

In response, Marley began pulling wrenches, bugles, screwdrivers, ukuleles, pliers, water pistols and hammers from his baggy pants. Having disgorged his heavy load, Marley flipped up onto his feet.

'Bravo. Shall we get to it then, yeah?' said Hughey.

Marley pulled up his sleeves, surveyed his tools for the appropriate implement and made towards the car brandishing a stuffed giraffe.

Hughey opened the bonnet of the car, and Marley and his assistant giraffe began a highly animated, but absolutely silent, debate about the best course of action. After some minutes the conversation took a nasty turn and Marley stormed off in a huff. He sat down with crossed arms and refused to look in the giraffe's direction.

'Listen Marley, no one has more respect for the Stanislavsky method than I, but the wife's back soon. We really need to get this done,' pleaded Hughey.

Marley responded with waving arms and protestations indicating that it was not he, but in fact the unbearable arrogance of the giraffe that was holding up proceedings.

Having been through years of such antics, Hughey knew he had no choice but to play along. Pluto stepped out of the clown's sight and conjured a bouquet of flowers.

'Look, he says he's sorry. He asked me to give you these,' said Pluto handing over the bouquet.

The clown bit his bulbous red lips, broke into an enormous smile and proceeded to eat the flowers.

With the lovers' tiff resolved, work began in earnest. Marley placed his long-necked apprentice on a stool and began working frantically on the engine. Labours quickly halted, however, as the giraffe began complaining of an insufficient view of proceedings. After trying to ignore these protests, Marley finally relented. The clown hopped into the drivers seat, took off the hand brake and ran around the back of the car. With a massive effort Marley moved the car forwards inch by inch until the fastidious giraffe indicated his satisfaction.

'Right, I'll get the kettle on then,' said Hughey, happy that everything was now going to plan.

Marley now entered the engine stock bodily. As the car began rolling down the drive, his chopstick legs and canal-barge feet swayed happily in the air. The clown was seemingly so engrossed in his work that he neither heard the shouts of warning from the giraffe nor felt the motion of the car as it gathered pace down Shelka Park Road.

Hughey Harris returned with the tea to see his car on a crash-collision course with the heavy traffic on Ballyfermot Road.

'Why didn't you call me?' screamed Pluto at the giraffe and charged out of the garden.

With the car less than five metres from certain doom Pluto knew he would not reach them.

'You better pull this off, you maniac, or you're buying me a new car!' shouted Pluto.

And of course, the clown did pull if off. He hopped out of the engine, dusted off his overalls, closed the bonnet, jumped into the driver's seat and started the car with all the assurance of a man who speaks seven languages, plays seventeen instruments and retains the wisdom to know these intellectual adornments are nothing more than props in the comedy of life.

The clown rolled gently down the road and parked the car on Hughey's driveway. Despite Hughey's insistence, Marley refused all payment. The clown even demurred on a lift back home in the car he had resurrected. As Marley's 'fro wobbled out of view on a unicycle Hughey felt a tension in his chest. In the midst of grunting busses, speeding cars, wasping mopeds and the professional mania of the modern world, Marley's fall seemed inevitable. The eyes of commuters stared through glass panes with perverse detachment. No one smiled. They were all wrung out of laughs. It wasn't that they couldn't see the joke. Oh, they knew it was ridiculous for a seven-foot Irish-Jamaican clown to be craving through the traffic on a unicycle, just like they knew it was ridiculous to spend eight hours a day in an office chained to a machine, but they had heard the joke for so long now that they felt certain that if they laughed they were also going to have to cry and then... well then madness was only a hop, skip and a jump away.

Hughey felt the sweet tears and bitter laugh of madness welling up inside and quickly searched for some practical distraction. Picking his wife up from work was the undertaking he settled upon.

As Hughey pulled into the Supervalue car park he saw a huddle of women around the entrance. They marched in a circle waving placards and chanted in an incessant monotone. Hughey, not wishing to be spotted by his wife, stayed in the car, but rolled down the window to see what all the fuss was about.

'What do we want?' shouted Ms. Falvey (proud mother of seven half brothers).

'Equal rights,' replied the mob.

'When do we want it?'

'NOW.'

Hughey briefly considered their possible agenda: animal rights, environmental protection, anti-GM farming, vegetarianism, fair trade coffee, anti-globalisation....The endless stream of objections made Hughey feel nauseous. The magician rolled up the window and turned on the radio.

'...and the main headlines again. Roscommon Police have arrested two men in connection with the disappearance of Jessie of Ballyfarnon. Detective inspector Biggington of Ballyfarnon Guarda Station has appealed to any members of the public with information relating to the disappearance of ten-year-old Jessie Son of Mary to come forwards...'

Hughey stared into the radio's black liquid crystal display and felt his mind reversing the radio waves. He felt himself sucked into the receiver, flung across the sky to a radio mast and down a wire to the newscaster's microphone. Hughey tried to stop it there, but he couldn't. Back he went towards the source of this story. Hughey put himself in the father's position. He wanted to run through the streets questioning every stranger. He wanted to beat every suspect into a pulp. Hughey heard the police tell him to let the professionals do their work. He heard them insist that the best thing he could do was support his wife. He heard them tell him to be composed. He heard them tell him to do the things he knew he couldn't.

The radio began blasting out the top twenty and Hughey switched it off with a grimace. The silence thickened around him. Sweat ran off his forehead and he noticed his knuckles had turned white from gripping the steering wheel. Hughey rolled down the window and stuck his head out into the open air.

'High-heeled slappers! No! No! No! Jammies and slippers! Yes! Yes! Yes!' shouted the protesters, stomping round and round.

The lifeless drone of their chant momentarily masked the meaning of the words from Hughey.

The magician watched with bemusement as they circled in cosy nightgowns, snug pyjamas and oversized fury slippers. Hughey looked to their placards for an answer and read slogans such as:
Mum not Model
        Down with fashion fascists
        Super Mams against Slapper Value
        Tarts giving BJs, NO – Mams in PJs, YES

Mrs. Harris emerged from her besieged supermarket and was instantly swamped by the mob.

'Think you're too good for us, do ya? Think your da bees knees don't ya?' shouted Ms. Falvey while jostling Mrs. Harris and blocking her path.

'Look all we're asking is that you wear some clothes like everyone bloody else,' snapped Mrs. Harris, shoving her captors aside.

'Not everyone else has seven children do they? Some of us are busy rearing kids you know? We don't have time for tarting ourselves up like fucking sluts,' replied Ms. Falvey, pushing Mrs. Harris back into the throng of protesters.

Having until now watched with mild amusement, Pluto Von Paradise sprung into action.

'Get your grubby fingers off my wife,' roared Pluto striding forwards, brandishing a wand.

Ms. Falvey spun on her furry-slippered heels and with fists on hips sneered at the magician.

'Ah look it's her majesty's knight in shining armour. And just how are you gonna make us let her go?' said Ms. Falvey.

Pluto reached into his pocket and the crowd, expecting a knife or baton, made ready their placards for a charge. The appearance of a deck of cards threw everyone, including Mrs. Harris, into total confusion.

'For Christ sake, Hughey, this is no time for tricks! Call the bloody police!' said Mrs. Harris.

'Pick a card,' said Pluto, ignoring his wife and fanning the cards for Ms. Falvey to pick from.

'Fuck off, you cunt,' spat Ms. Falvey, swatting the deck of cards onto the pavement.

'The Joker,' said Pluto with a grin.

'Ya what?' said Ms. Falvey.

'The card you picked... it's a Joker.'

'I never picked a bleedin card, you gobshite.'

'Ah but you did, young lady. Perhaps you should look in the pocket of your delightful bedroom attire.'

Ms. Falvey stuffed a paw into her dressing gown and pulled out a beautifully hand-painted Joker.

'Oh you're bleedin rapid, you are. I suppose you're gonna get your bunny rabbit to batter us now, are ya,' said Falvey. 'Bleedin thick. I'm gonna fucking kill...'

'SOLAS,' shouted Pluto with a wave of his wand.

The Joker in Ms. Falvey's hand exploded with a blinding phosphorous flash. As the mob stumbled around in their slippers, Pluto led his wife from the field of battle.

The car started first time and Hughey looked to his wife for praise but received none.

'Jesus, you think you've seen everything in life and something like that happens, what?' laughed Hughey.

Mrs. Harris watched the mob gathering their senses and picking up their placards.

'I mean, what in the bleedin name of Jesus do they think they're at?' continued Hughey reversing the car away at speed and swinging around towards home.

Hughey put the car through its paces, overtaking BMWs and cutting off shiny Mercedes.

'Not too bad eh? Running like clockwork she is. I had Marley come over and fix it. Now before you start...'

But much to Hughey's surprise, Mrs. Harris did not start.

'...I know how you feel about him and I agree with you up to a point, but really there was no other choice at such short notice.

'Anyway he wouldn't take a penny from me. Cycled off home on his unicycle without asking for as much as a lift home. You should have seen the looks on the neighbours'...'

'What's wrong with people?' said Ms. Harris.

'What's that, love?'

'Is it too much to ask for people to get dressed in the morning before coming to a public place?' she said turning towards Hughey and demanding an answer.

'They're just lazy good-for-nothings, love. Don't be fretting yourself,' said Hughey, still enjoying his jaunt in the car.

'But that's just it. They're not lazy. Not in the slightest. They're been marching and chanting and writing letters and calling radio stations and harassing staff all over Dublin for two months now. We are the forty-fifth supermarket they've picketed. In Rialto they swarmed an IKEA and chained themselves to the beds. It took twenty guards and the fire brigade to get rid of them.'

Hughey Harris erupted in laughter and began slapping the steering wheel.

'Why are you laughing?'

'Why am I laughing?' said Hughey between volleys of laughter. 'These people are running around in pyjamas shouting – Tarts giving Bjs, NO... Mams in PJs, YES – and you're asking me why I'm laughing!'

Mrs. Harris shrugged and turned away from Hughey's hysterics.

'Yes, I suppose it is funny,' she said, her ashen face devoid of a smile. 'But doesn't it worry you?'

'Ah come on now, love. There's nothing to be fretting about. As soon as a good plot line starts on the soaps they'll disappear.'

'No, Hughey. There's something not right,' replied Ms. Harris.

'Ah get out of it, will ya.'

'Well why would mothers go marching around supermarkets in their pyjamas? Why would young girls get all dressed up to get so drunk they can't walk? Why would people stab each other over a bag of chips? They're all trying to say something Hughey. It just comes out all wrong.'

'Their all bleedin mad is what they are. Equal rights for pyjama wearers! Have you ever in your life heard the like of it,' laughed Hughey, but he laughed alone.

By the time they arrived home, silence had settled between them. Mrs. Harris sat at the kitchen table drinking tea and wondered what malaise had gripped Ireland. Everywhere she turned her thoughts, she saw energy being splattered in chaotic patterns. It was only a matter of time before someone picked up a brush. It was only a matter of time before someone used that energy to create. What would they make?

The image of her son flashed through her mind. She saw him at twenty, still clean, with a Mohican haircut, playing a low-strung bass guitar and splattering his energy across a crowd of angry young men.

She shuddered because she knew the other half of that question: What would they destroy?

Chapter 5

The upstairs of the International Bar was packed to capacity with forty applauding people. Despite the enforcement of a smoking ban since 2005 the room still smelled of cigarette smoke. It was as if smokers, seeing the fascist turn politics was taking, had hidden their favourite aroma (Ann Frank-style) in this rundown backroom.

Joseph Blade bowed up on the stage and slipped behind the dark red curtain. Mr. and Mrs. Harris were first upon their feet and soon the whole crowd was standing in ovation. Hughey pumped his hands together with ardent force. The sound he made was not simply for now. No the applause needed to travel through time as well as space. He had watched the hands of his apprentice move like his own. He had heard the proclamations, warnings and jokes infused with his influence. And so Pluto applauded more than tonight's performance. He applauded the realisation of years of interwoven labours: teaching-studying, speaking-listening, acting-mimicking, disciplining-reforming. He applauded Joseph's ability to make those labours disappear: the essence of all true magic.

Hughey smiled at Mrs. Harris who, seeing her husband welling up with pride, couldn't help but think of a graduation ceremony. Although she had hardened herself against the lure of fictions, nobody is immune to metaphor. Mrs. Harris allowed imagined present and impossible future to mingle and was soon matching Hughey tear for tear. Through watery eyes she stared at the beautiful young woman up front who had listened to Joseph's every word as if trying to memorized an incantation.

'Another woman loves him,' she thought, and with proud resignation added, 'but I'll always be his mother.'

Indeed the young woman, Jennifer Patrice, was falling for our Joseph. Her lips tingled with a remembered kiss and the memory of a romantic meal still glowed in her heart when she arrived at the International Bar. The sight of her suitor commanding attention on stage made her hungrier still for his heart.

As the up-lighting on the dark red walls faded and a lone spotlight trained on a crack in the stage-curtain Jennifer quickly fixed her hair and then retook her seat like the rest of the crowd.

Joseph Blade strode back on stage and took a low solemn bow.

'Thank you ladies and gentlemen. Thank you...' said Joseph waiting for the applause to die down.

'Now for my final trick I will need the assistance of four strong men. Four strong hard-working men.'

Four men with the build of rugby forwards goaded each other into action.

'Ah, the very kind of men I need,' proclaimed Joseph. 'A round of applause for these strapping young gentlemen.'

The four men lumbered up onto the stage, each one a variation of the following: tree-trunk neck, bushy eyebrows, floppy hair, expensive shirt and tailored trousers. The largest of the four, Mr. Fallon, smiled at the crowd and gave a wave.

'Thank you, gentlemen. Now if you could form a straight line from the front to the back of the stage,' said Joseph, and his volunteers complied.

'Yes I can see you are all very athletic hulks of men who could make a young magician very happy,' said Joseph garnering some cheap laughs, 'Would you mind telling me your max bench in kilograms please.'

'75kg...70kg...72kg...73kg,' lied each man in turn.

'Excellent,' said Joseph clapping his hands together, which summoned some apparatus from stage left.

A long rectangular frame approximately eight feet high and six feet long was wheeled onstage by none other than Christoph McFee. Mrs. Harris instinctively reached for Hughey's hand but found his arms stiffly crossed. She patted his leg, a consolation he rebuked with a jerk of his knee.

'Now gentlemen, if you'll please stand inside this frame. Thank you.'

The four men now stood in a perfect line so that only the first was visible to the crowd.

The willowy Christoph McFee had no problem slotting a panel above the rugby players' heads. Only the walls of the rectangular frame remained open.

'Gentlemen if you could lift the panel above your heads please,' said Joseph and the men pushed the panel up with the palms of their hands.

'Now brace yourself to hold a weight, gentlemen,' said Joseph hitting a button on the edge of the frame which shot up perspex walls to the left and right of the rugby players.

Only the front face of the rectangle remained open, where the audience soon witnessed Mr. Fallon straining under a terrible weight.

'Just a little more gentlemen,' said Joseph turning a dial on the frame.

A collective grunt came from the four trapped men. Mr. Fallon's legs began shaking and sweat poured from his brow.

'It's too heavy. Turn it off it's too heavy,' shouted Fallon, 'I'm gonna have to jump out the front.'

'We can't hold it by ourselves you fucker,' screamed the men trapped behind him in the box.

'It's too heavy,' moaned Fallon, his knees knocking at a furious pace.

'If you drop it we're all dead,' shouted his comrades.

With that Joseph Blade strode forwards, relieved the helpless Mr. Fallon of his wallet and produced what appeared to be a mobile credit card machine.

'Pin please,' said Joseph swiping Mr. Fallon's card through his machine.

'What the fuck?' said Fallon partially blinded by sweat.

'You gentlemen told me you could hold a collective weight of 640Kg. You are currently holding under 600kg and have ruined my trick. I am charging you five hundred euros.'

'You're what?!'

'I'm charging you five hundred euros for spoiling my trick.'

'Fuck off!' screamed Fallon.

'Give him the pin Fallon. For God's sake give him the fucking pin,' moaned Fallon's comrades.

'Why should I pay?'

'Cause we're all gonna be crushed to death if you don't, you prick! Now just give him the poxy pin!'

The audience gasped as Fallon clearly considered jumping rather than paying, but it's a rare genre of human that makes decisions off pure principle and damns the consequences: Fallon was neither sadistic saint nor holy psychopath.

'2008,' he said at last.

Joseph typed in the pin, charged the fee, stuffed the receipt in Fallon's pocket, released the weight with the press of a button and vanished in a plume of smoke.

The rugby players stumbled forwards on jelly legs. Not a single member of the audience applauded or spoke or dared to move. Events had been so extraordinarily strange that they floundered around in their minds for a possible explanation. Had they just witnessed a robbery? Were they about to be robbed? Who would help these poor men? Would these poor men expect help from them? As the questions became more and more frightening the people did what people always do: They stopped asking questions, hoping the situation would go away.

Even Fallon, despite finding himself five hundred euro lighter, was slow to act. He and his comrades stared dumbly at the stage curtain sure that Joseph Blade would re-emerge and explain all. As the minutes passed and it became obvious that the young magician had no intention of reappearing, Fallon and his comrades grew in anger.

Soon the police were mentioned. Some braver elements of the audience agreed to act as witnesses, but Fallon and company would not be so easily sated in their thirst for justice. Spotting Christoph McFee in the wings they sprung forwards. Fallon lifted McFee two inches off the floor by the scruff of the neck.

'Where's the fucker who stole my money?' demanded Fallon.

'I've no idea what you're talking about,' laughed McFee, displaying a mouth of blindingly white teeth.

Fallon twisted his fist and the purple silk collar of McFee's shirt began cutting off the circulation to his brain.

'You've got seconds before I rearrange your face,' said Fallon drawing back a fist of gnarled knuckles.

'But no one stole from you, dear sir,' croaked McFee.

'I've a receipt for five hundred blips in my pocket that says otherwise.'

'Perhaps you should look again, my friend.'

Fallon eyed his prey with suspicion before lowering him. He did not, however, remove his grip. Fallon fished in his pocket and produced the receipt.

With lightening speed Joseph Blade appeared from behind the curtain and snatched the receipt from Mr. Fallon. As the rugby players closed in upon the young magician he quickly tore the receipt to shreds and stuffed it in his mouth. Joseph swallowed the paper and instantly went into convulsions. Not wishing to be vomited upon, the rugby players hesitated. Blade brought his retching to a horrible climax and then stood stock-still. He lifted a hand to his mouth and began pulling a slip of paper from his lips.

'Your money sir,' said Joseph handing Fallon a pristine five-hundred euro note.

Fallon checked the watermark and smiled. The audience, offered the opportunity for relief, snatched it with two clapping hands.

'If only every crunch ended so well for the hard-working man,' said Joseph with a wry smile.

The young magician bowed and, before exiting stage left, blew a kiss to Jennifer Patrice. She was first upon her feet for this ovation. Her heart palpitated with the discordant rhythm of applauding hands. Everyone cheered and whistled; everyone except Hughey Harris, who sat with arms crossed and jaw set.

The longer the cheers persisted the lower Hughey's head sank until finally he glared at the stage from under his eyebrows, chin touching chest.

Long after the applause had subsided and the crowd had begun to disperse, Hughey remained rigid in his seat. Some members of his row, impatient to be on the road home, attempted to rouse Hughey from his meditations, but quickly abandoned their attempts when Pluto Von Paradise laid his crazed eyes upon them.

'Come on, Hughey we'll get a bag of chips on the way home,' said Mrs. Harris.

Hughey stood up.

'That's right, love. We'd better be hitting the road before—'

Hughey pivoted left, marched to the end of the row, executed another abrupt turn and charged through the stage curtain.

Mrs. Harris did not give chase. She knew the only thing that angered Hughey more than being in the presence of Christoph McFee was Mrs. Harris being in the presence of Christoph McFee. She sat down and gripped the handle of the handbag resting in her lap.

Hughey opened the fire-escape door and began descending the stairs. This was not a search. Having led a renaissance in Irish

Illusion from this very venue, Hughey knew every creak in every stage board. His hard leather shoes slapped off the iron stairs and the dull ring would have announced his presence to Joseph Blade if the young magician hadn't been so engrossed in retelling tonight's victory with Jennifer Patrice and McFee.

'...and the look on the audience's faces was priceless. They didn't know what the fuck had happened,' laughed McFee doing an excellent impression of a startled rabbit.

'You had them all going Joey,' cooed Jennifer. 'You nearly had me going too! God if I didn't know what a big softy you are I really would have believed you were gonna just—'

'Oh of course he wasn't going to rob the simpletons! Even if they did deserve it. No, no, the point is you made them believe you were doing exactly that. Brilliant,' said McFee.

'Well I'm glad you liked it. I wasn't sure it would work...it's brand new. I call it The Credit Crunch,' said Joseph, lighting a cigarette and leaning against the bare brick wall of the cellar room.

'Topical. Current. Brilliant. Oh this could be big, Joey. You're onto something here, my boy,' said McFee, his huge set of pearly teeth glinting under a bare light bulb osculating back and forth on a frayed wire.

'You're going to be famous, baby,' said Jennifer, jumping up off an old leather trunk and wrapping her arms around Joseph's neck.

'Yes, my boy, you're—'

'He's not your boy, McFee,' boomed Pluto, announcing his presence from the thick shadows beyond the doorway.

McFee and Joseph fixed each other with worried stares. Joseph broke the look first, throwing his cigarette onto the damp floor and stamping it out.

McFee, his back to the door, took a moment to arrange some emotional furniture, then, bearing his massive smile, turned towards Pluto.

'Merely a turn of phrase, Master Paradise. No offence intended as I'm sure you know...Oh how things come around Pluto – in the venue where you built a legend, your student, this very night, writes the first chapter of his own,' said McFee, garnishing his speech with elegant gestures and nostalgic tones to which the shadows made no response.

Joseph was immobile against the brick wall that separated him from his master. McFee attempted to fill the tense silence between master and student with fawning platitudes, but Pluto and Joseph heard none of it. All they heard were unspeakable words, and all they felt was a growing distance.

'This was the proudest night of my life right up to when it became one of the most shameful,' said Pluto from the shadows.

McFee, in the middle of another nostalgic anecdote, swallowed his words. Having failed to stave off this battle between master and student, he decided to steer clear of the blows. He turned to his trunk and pretended to be arranging props within.

'Who's that and what's his problem?' whispered Jennifer.

'Shut the fuck up, will you?' snarled Blade.

Jennifer, in a state of confusion, chalked this profane outburst up to hubris and decided to take a stand.

'So you think you're the bees' knees now, do ya? Well I've got news for you buster – nobody speaks to me like that,' she said storming out the door, past the hidden Pluto Von Paradise and up the iron stairs.

Joseph and Pluto listened to her high heels ring fainter and fainter on the iron steps until another silent stalemate ensued.

'So you call that last stunt magic, do you?' said Pluto.

'It was a trick wasn't it?' replied Joseph.

'Conning someone is a magic trick? Three shell-and-ball hawkers are magicians now, are they?'

'There was a little more to the boy's trick than that,' mumbled McFee from the corner.

'McFee, if you speak to me again I swear I'll kill you,' said Pluto with the unnerving calm of a fatalistic man.

'Well there was more to it, wasn't there?!' shouted Joseph, rousing himself from his slouch and addressing the shadows head-on.

'The audience could see exactly how it was done! The mark knew exactly what happened to him. You trapped a man in a box and robbed him. Where was the magic?'

'It was a metaphor. It was a reflection of what these people swallow everyday. They saw what happened and they still applauded,' said Joseph jabbing a finger at the hidden Pluto Von Paradise.

'So, you're a politician, not a magician.'

'I conjured a five hundred note for him didn't I?'

'Oh yes, I forgot about that. What a way to finish a night of the most technically accomplished material I had seen in years. What a finale – load, ditch and simulate. A ten-year-old could do it.'

'Christ, I'm just trying to do something different! I'm trying to make the magic my own just like you always tell me, but the minute I try, the second I stray from your way, I'm betraying magic. This is my own, don't you understand? This is my own.'

'Oh it's your own all right. It's not something I'll be associated with.'

'Don't be then, you fucking hypocrite,' shouted Joseph slamming the door on the shadows.

Mrs. Harris had seen Jennifer Patrice hurry past her in tears and she had heard the shouts from backstage punctuated with a slammed door. As the stage curtain was breached by the frame of Hughey Harris, she stood up and tried to wring a smile from the handle of her handbag. Even here in the impossible future she was forced to play peace keeper. When will I learn? she scolded herself. A momentary weakness is punished the same as an eternal one.

Mrs. Harris picked up Hughey's coat from his chair and draped it across her arm, but the magician did not halt at their row. Crazed eyes led his feet at a pace they struggled to maintain. He went straight down the narrow stairwell lined with photos of his glory days and out into a Dublin cold that wrapped itself around his bones.

Mrs. Harris stared at the exit and then turned towards the stage. They need one another, she thought, the old protect art from the savagery of youth and the youth protect art from the nostalgia of the old. Mrs. Harris wanted her lost son and fleeing husband to understand; she wanted them to be happy. A decade before she would've rushed back stage and taken on Joseph's load. She would've chased down Hughey and taken on his load too. She would've brought the lightened men together and let them float into forgiveness. But now her legs were unsteady, her back ached and if she carried even a gram more pain she'd buckle.

Hughey had crossed Dame St. and was turning into Temple Bar by the time Mrs. Harris caught up with him. He heard the clip-clopping of her shoes but did not slow. He heard the wheezing of her breath over his shoulder but did not turn. In silence they walked under the stacked concrete slabs of Central Bank. They moved down the gentle cobblestone slope of Crown Alley and tourist pubs with names like Molley Malone's and The Irish Rover stood mute. Even the Roma gypsies, forever stationed at the ATMs of Temple Bar square, had abandoned their posts.

Hughey turned onto Dury St., entered the multi-storey car park and (ignoring a waiting elevator) took the stairs to the third floor. The magician waited at the passenger door of Mrs. Harris's car and inhaled the scent of spilt oil, worn break pads and exhaust fumes. Mrs. Harris, having elected to take the elevator, was not far behind. She walked to the driver's side and while jiggling the keys in the lock somehow found a smile that said so much; too much; far more than Hughey wanted to hear.

Mrs. Harris sat into the car and unlocked the passenger door. Hughey, sure tonight's cosmic alignment meant only further exasperations, remained standing outside.

Mrs. Harris turned the key in the ignition. The car sputtered, coughed, groaned and finally ceased any pretence of cooperation.

'Give us your bleedin money,' came a strangely saccharin voice behind Hughey.

The magician turned and involuntarily issued forth a sound that was half chuckle, half convulsion. Our mugger, Barry O'Neil, unaccustomed to such a reaction responded by raising his weapon, a dramatically blood-splattered syringe, towards Hughey.

'Do you want to get bleedin stabbed or what? Give us your money now,' said Barry, doing his best impression of an inner-city knacker.

'I'm afraid you are out of luck. I haven't a penny on me,' said Hughey looking straight into the junk-hungry eyes of Barry O'Neil.

'Well what the fuck is that then?' shouted Barry, tapping a bulge in Hughey's pocket.

'Your mind's playing tricks on you, young man. My pockets are empty,' said Pluto, displaying a pocket which Barry O'Neil would swear contained neither wallet nor mobile phone nor silver cigarette lighter.

'Well what the fuck are you doing out on the town with no money?' said Barry in exasperation.

'Well what are you doing out on the town with no money?' retorted the magician.

'Trying to get some fucking money that's what.'

'Well you better keep looking hadn't you?' said Pluto gently pushing the syringe away from his throat.

'Fuck sake. Trust me to rob a broke nutcase like you!' shouted O'Neil shaking with junk hunger.

'That habit is going to kill you, you know.'

'And what habit is that?' said O'Neil a black nihilism hijacking his mellifluous voice.

Pluto quickly reached out and pulled a cigarette from behind O'Neil's ear.

'Smoking,' answered Pluto, popping the fag between Barry's lips, producing a silver lighter from his empty pocket and lighting the cigarette.

Oblivious to events outside, Mrs. Harris turned the key in the ignition and to her surprise the car started without objection.

Hughey and Barry looked into each other's eyes. While trying to decide if he was being mocked, O'Neil found himself being drawn into Pluto. The magnetic poles of empathy held the men together— because whether you fail after or before success, the feeling is about the same; the latter harks after an idealised future and the former after an idealised past.

'Thanks,' said Barry shedding his circumstances to relapse into the person he once was: barbershop alto tenor, Dublin Minor footballer and loving fiancé.

'Look after yourself,' said Pluto, a handshake masking his left hand dropping a silver lighter into Barry's pocket.

Hughey sat into the car and Mrs. Harris began their descent through the concrete maze of pillars and walls. Hughey's eyes followed the white painted arrows directing them down ramps and around hard corners. He had given away an item that he had guarded for twenty years on a whim. He had given it away to a stranger who had tried to rob him. He had given it away, and he didn't care. Hughey imagined Barry nestling down in a doorway, muttering bitter recriminations instead of prayers, and finding the solid silver lighter. He'll pull it out slowly. He'll stumble to his feet and move towards a street light. He'll hold this piece of divine succour aloft and turn it in the orange light. The bulb will blink, a wind will shimmer through the trees, the city will hold its tongue, and Barry will see the engraved words: Joy is of the will which labours.

And will he overcome? And will he triumph? Or will he pawn it off for a pittance and stick the money in his arm? Hughey knew the odds, but desperate men dream the wildest dreams.

Chapter 6

The staff finished their ritualistic post-work pints and left Christoph and Joseph alone in the narrow downstairs bar of the International. Joseph, incapable of slouching even in a state of depression, sat erect on a barstool cutting cards with one hand and swirling whiskey around a glass with the other.

Christoph had spent the day answering phone calls, chasing down distributors, booking acts, interviewing staff, balancing books, staging performances and cashing tills, but as the day came to an end his energies showed no signs of waning. As Joseph drank, Christoph polished glasses, tables and drinks taps while cursing his staff's cheap imitations of assiduous care.

Joseph threw back a chest-burning gulp of whiskey, but before he could set down the empty glass Christoph snatched up a bottle of Jameson, unscrewed the cap and refilled it.

'Tired?' asked Christoph, placing the bottle back on the shelf and spotting a smudge on the mirror behind.

'Not really, but Christ you must be, ' said Joseph, watching McFee remove every bottle from the shelf and begin polishing the mirror.

'Me?' scoffed McFee. 'Never. Meditation, my boy. That's the trick.'

'Meditation?'

'Two hours of meditation reduces the sleep required by the average adult male to four hours. I meditate for three hours each and every day and am far beyond the capabilities of the average adult male as I think you'll agree.'

'You think right,' said Joseph raising his glass to Christoph's Bollywood smile.

'Yes it's a commonly held belief that the R.E.M. cycle of sleep, in which the conscious is concomitant to the subconscious, holds the key to physical and cerebral regeneration,' said McFee expounding on his theme while stretching simian limps incredible distances to banish the faintest smudge.

'Nothing like a good night's sleep, eh?'

'Well that's where you're wrong, my boy. You've fallen for one of modern science's many myths. The truth is there is nothing like a good morning's meditation... Did you know Buddha lived for forty-nine days without sleep or sustenance while in a meditative state?'

'No, never heard bout that. American magician?'

'Indian, actually. But the point is that when we retune the string of our being to the universal vibration, anything is possible. The magic is in our hands,' said Christoph.

'I think I've had my fill of magic for the minute,' muttered Joseph.

'Nonsense! You just need to empty the glass if you want to refill it,' declared McFee placing the last bottle back in front of a spotless mirror.

'Well that I do understand,' said Joseph, affirming McFee's aphorism with a heroic gulp of whiskey.

McFee shook his head, laughed and pulled up a stool beside Joseph.

'Pluto taught you more than card tricks, eh?' said Christoph pouring himself and Joseph another drink.

'And what does that mean?' snarled Joseph, whiskey bubbling in his blood.

'Ha ha, easy now my boy. No offence intended. Merely commenting that if you were so inclined, a fine career in boozing lays before you.'

'Well as Pluto says, repetition is the mother of all skill,' replied Joseph.

'I was hoping you'd say that. I have just the place for us to get some practice in, unless of course you're tired,' said Christoph emitting a low meditative hum.

'No, I'm up for it.'

'Excellent,' said Christoph, reaching into his blazer pocket. 'First a little something to sharpen our senses.'

Bus Eirean was bright and silent. The last buses bound for Leitrim, Galway and Cork had departed. No passengers graced the hard plastic seats in the waiting room. The coffee shop and newsagents stared each other down from opposite sides of the hall. Two employees stood behind their respective tills, waiting for the last buses to arrive from Donegal and Sligo. The only thing that punctured the monotony of the graveyard shift was some lunatic ordering a double espresso at 3 a.m. or a habitual masturbator purchasing a copy of *Horny Housewives.*

Across the road from the bus station stood the modern grey artifice of Store St. Garda Station. The police cars were all double- and triple-parked, making a speedy response to some incident impossible. Depending on your point of view, this parking arrangement indicated quiet streets and therefore a job well done, or criminal insouciance. In addition to the police station and bus station, Store St. possessed a number of hostels falling into two distinct categories. The first housed tourists operating on a strict budget, and the second housed the frequenters of Store St.'s methadone clinic. Life was very convenient on Store St. A tourist could arrive at the bus station, have a meal in Issac Butts, find a hostel next door, be mugged in the alley and report to the Garda station across the road. The junkies could arrive by train (the suburban terminus being a mere two minute walk), collect methadone at the clinic, rob a tourist, buy the real drugs and make a daring escape to Roscommon on the bus. It was all very convenient, and it was to this one-stop shop of depravity that Christoph McFee and Joseph Blade hastened.

'...and this from a magician,' shouted McFee in disgust as they passed a sign advertising 'The Paddy Waggon' – seemingly a tour of Ireland's cultural epicentres, i.e. the pubs.

'I don't see what being a magician has to do with it. The fucking ball was two foot over the line. The lads on the bleedin space station could see it was a goal.'

'Ah but it wasn't a goal was it?' cried McFee as if springing a beautifully disguised checkmate.

'What the hell are you shiting on about? It was two bleeding foot over the line!' rejoined Joseph with a cry of his own.

'But the referee didn't think it was two feet over the line, did he?'

'Cause he's blind as a fucking bat.'

'Irrelevant. The referee did not think it was two feet over the line, and therefore it was not. The scoreline, league table and history books shall forever testify to the fact that the goal was NOT scored.'

'Not scored! You're off your rocker— it was a mile in! It doesn't matter what the referee or the FA or the bleedin history books say. This isn't the Stone Age, Christoph. We have video evidence. Everyone in the world knows that ball crossed the line. For years to come, people will talk about that decision as the biggest fuck up in football,' said Joseph, following McFee down an alley of rotten brick perfumed with urine.

'And that is exactly my point,' laughed McFee.

'What is exactly your point?' shouted Joseph halting his stride and refusing to move until certain clarifications were given.

'My point is this,' said McFee turning to face Joseph, clearing his throat and arranging his elegant features to lend maximum effect to his discourse. 'As you said, my boy, people will talk of this game for years and decades and indeed centuries to come. Supporters will bare grudges with religious conviction. Players will be vilified. Alternative histories where the goal was awarded will be dreamt up. Debates will rage as to whether or not the mythical goal would have changed the final outcome. In short the artistic faculty of man will be engaged to the fullest. What fun, eh? What craic?'

'Bleedin tragedy is what it is.'

'Yes, it is a tragedy. You're absolutely right. It is another entry in that most noble cannon of stories which hold our souls rapt. Now just imagine if the goal had been awarded. What would be the outcome? A fair scoreline; the players shake hands; the managers exchange compliments; the commentators struggle to fill thirty minutes of airtime talking about an even contest; supporters leave the ground content, but are they enthralled? Are they incensed? Are they alive? Not a bit of it! And in the morning the world awakens and nobody mentions the game. Nobody bears a grudge. Nobody creates villains or heroes. Nobody dreams up alternative histories. Nobody argues about truth and myth and justice and beauty. That is what you condone with your avocation of goal-line technology. You condone the theft of drama from the theatre of football.'

'You know what, Christoph?'

'What, my boy?'

'You talk the biggest amount of shite I've ever heard.'

'But what entertaining shite, eh?' laughed Christoph, stopping in front of a spiked metal fence that bared entry to a derelict building site.

Joseph looked over the field of deep muck peppered with concrete mixers, dumpers, shovels, generators, picks, bricks, flax and assorted debris that defied naming.

'And why in the name of Jesus are we going in there?' said Joseph as Christoph swung a loose railing aside and squeezed through the skinniest of cracks.

'I could tell you, my boy, but I'm afraid you'll only accuse me of talking shite as you so eloquently put it,' answered Christoph, weaving a nimble path through one of the Celtic tiger's many bone yards.

Joseph heard a shout from the end of the alley, a siren, a grunting bus arriving from Donegal and two junkies discussing last night's disallowed goal. Before McFee disappeared from sight, Joseph took off after him.

Four blocks of apartments gazed down on Joseph as he dodged bog-brown puddles, tetanus-tipped nails and mud infused with frozen swirls of oil like fossils of extinct species. The apartment blocks stood fifteen to twenty storeys high, all starved with black, hollow eyes; beaten and naked and broken. These buildings, yearning for the glamorous lives of bankers, accountants, traders, engineers, software designers and their happy families, gazed down on the smashed windows, rotten doors and cracked plaster littered around their feet. They gazed down upon the bile with empty stomachs and wished that they too could simply lie down and cease this half-existence.

'This way,' called McFee as he walked across a thin plank cast across a pit twelve feet deep.

'Are you fucking mad?' said Joseph.

'You walk in a straight line every day, my boy. Surely you can recreate the feat here,' replied Christoph, arriving safely on the opposite side.

Joseph took stock of his surroundings. To the east the path was tantalisingly dangerous with cranes holding pills of brick overhead, concrete arches threatening collapse and vast swamps rigged with electrical wire. To the west a gentle path wound its way through the debris and offered fine vistas of the bone yard. To the south lay the exit. The northern path, in contrast to the others, offered neither thrill nor view nor simple escape. It was a long monotonous route and the apartment block at its end was neither the most ruinous nor the most pristine on offer.

The art of misdirection is making your movements appear natural, thought Blade— someone had gone to great lengths to make this way naturally repulsive. The magician cursed his professional curiosity, took a deep breath and set off across the plank.

The rest of the way was exhausting. They'd scramble up mounds only to follow an elaborate series of planks back the way they came. Paths wound around swamps in concentric circles. The tiniest progress would be followed by fifty meters of neck-high insulation, which absorbed every step and sapped their strength for the sprint up a fifty-degree incline that immediately followed. Finally, after forty-five minutes of leg-burning, heart-straining and lung-heaving labour, they entered the lobby of the apartment block.

Their footsteps sounded like an agony to the bare concrete walls; an echo of dead hope; the false memory of unrealised dreams. Newly married couples never hurried towards waiting beds. Children never charged on tireless legs towards school. Nobody ever paused on the stairwell, passport in hand, fleeing a final fight, their mind spinning in the vertigo ease with which we can alter our entire lives.

McFee stopped at the elevator and pressed a button, which, much to Joseph's surprise, lit up.

'Listen, Christoph, I don't know why I've followed you on this wild goose chase, but I do know that I'm not getting into an elevator in a building that's falling the fuck down.'

'It's in perfect working order, my boy. Mr. O'Donnell who lives on the twelfth floor was chief engineer for Hitachi's elevator division. He keeps this mechanism in a pristine state of operation.'

'Mr. O'Donnell who lives where?'

'On the twelfth floor,' said Christoph as the elevator arrived with a pleasant chime and opened smoothly for its passengers.

McFee stepped inside and began combing his hair in the elevator mirror. Joseph stood in the aborted hallway dazzled by this sudden dose of precise functionality. With the ghosts of Sunday shoppers, hungry children and cantankerous grandparents jostling him forwards, Joseph stepped aboard.

'Twenty-fifth floor, my boy,' said McFee pulling a platinum dragon from his blazer pocket, clicking its tail and snorting cocaine from its nostrils.

Joseph turned towards the elevator panel to see a mosaic of hand-painted tile, bronze engravings, blown glass and carved wooden buttons. The last button, number twenty-five, was a gold Celtic brooch affair complete with green gemstones. Joseph, unable to pick a question from the throng demanding answers, simply pressed the button and remained silent as they ascended.

'My boy! My boy! Prepare yourself for the weird and the wonderful. Keep your ears, eyes and most importantly your mind open. Do as I do and we'll have a wonderful time. A resplendent time. A splendiferous time,' said McFee, offering Joseph the cocaine.

Blade accepted the offer like a child drinking spoons of tonic before the onset of winter.

The elevator stopped and the doors opened to reveal a cavernous room with goings on quite beyond Joseph's immediate comprehension. Regrouping, he decided to deal with what was immediately in front of him: in dancing candlelight, eight individuals, each of wildly contrasting appearance. As they dismounted bike machines that were wired to the elevator, Joseph wondered if he'd ever seen such an assortment of angular hairstyles, long beards, archaic hats, neon scarves, piercings, tattoos and pointed shoes. The answer was of course that he hadn't.

'I told you he wasn't alone,' said Victor Hall rubbing his firm thighs. 'We'd never have been four seconds off pace if he was alone.'

A bout of relieved chatter broke out amongst the cyclists, who, Joseph noticed, all possessed thighs worthy of classic Grecian sculptures.

'Sorry to have scared you,' laughed McFee, 'My friend Joseph Blade here just performed one of the best magic shows I've seen in the International since the great Pluto Von Paradise, so I insisted he come out and celebrate.'

All eyes turned to Joseph, who gaped at ceilings painted with enormous murals, abstract sculptures lurking in alcoves, perspex floors under-lit with shifting colours and musicians pumping out deranged music to a throng of wild-eyed dancers.

'High praise indeed...Welcome, Joseph. We're happy you choose our humble abode for your celebrations,' said Victor Hall.

Joseph shook Victor's hand as if debating his existence. The magician inspected the Arian chin, blonde comb-over, high-necked shirt, suspenders and ankle-length trousers while holding Victor's hand far longer than decorum dictated.

'Well I'll show him around then, Victor,' said McFee, ushering Joseph away.

'We'll be in the hub,' answered Victor. 'See you later, Joseph.'

'Bye,' mumbled Joseph, following McFee like a drugged psychiatric patient.

Christoph was greeted with smiles and nods from all quarters as they approached the source of the pumping music. A meticulously bald man with a swooping nose towered over a microphone and with a single fluttering hand and Dylan-esque sunglasses spat syncopated rhymes and juxtaposed images. Above his rasping bass floated an ethereal harmony delivered by a woman who appeared to have recently escaped a Grimm's fairy tale. On a raised platform behind the vocalists a man sat half-lotus, his plated beard and knee-length grey hair hiding his face as he played the sitar. To the left of the stage three bodhrán players, all dressed in grey woollen jumpers and sporting masses of brown curls, beat out a spine-quivering rhythm while yelping and whistling intermittently. To the right a man clad in the uniform of a suburban bouncer – black shoes, black trousers, black shirt and short black hair – sat with a serene smile and closed eyes as he played a hot-pink accordion.

In the crowd, limbs strived to translate music's functions of time into dance's functions of space. Two shirtless men performed Capoeira with telepathic synchronization - legs swung at lightning speed over ducking heads and under hopping feet. Around their dance orbited a woman in tap shoes, her Irish dancing apparel offset by neon laddered stockings and natty dreadlocks. Another group to the right made for equally dramatic viewing. Their movements, however, were not locked into the time signatures followed by the musicians. Instead, they hunted for a gesture or a movement to articulate the emotions behind the music. Their dance was a rebellion against time and a worshipping of space.

The song switched to double-time and all attempts at melody were abandoned in favour of primal noise. Never had an accordion struck such fear into the heart of man. Never had a sitar threatened to unlock the very gates of Hell. The two vocalists, in a fit of passion, fell to the floor and tore at each other's clothes (and resulting bare flesh) with tooth and nail. The crowd began pounding their chests and circling in a classic mosh pit. Soon bodies were colliding and bouncing around the circumference of the pit. The slender frame of Joseph Blade was helpless in this sea of iron thighs, and all that saved him from serious injury was his lightning reflexes. En route from one sweaty chest to another, Joseph suddenly felt himself airborne. He bobbed on a manic sea of hands like a little rubber duck. This aleatory music was, however, following some mysterious rules as the musicians clairvoyantly pulled the plug on the chaos with a synchronised jolt that sent Joseph spinning downwards in a whirlpool of feedback.

The crowd applauded the musicians who bowed and motioned towards the back of the hall. The crowd now turned and applauded a group of twenty or so cyclists with wobbly legs stepping off bike machines.

'What the fuck?' said Joseph, stumbling to McFee's side.

'This time of year you have to supplement the solar panels with a little bit of pedal power,' said McFee, receiving a flaming glass of bright green liquid from a passing waitress.

'What the fuck?' repeated Joseph.

'Absinthe, my boy! Absinthe with a sprinkling of mescaline and a pinch of MDMA. Fine mental lubricants. A fillip for the night's exertions,' giggled McFee, blowing out the flames, dropping a spoon of chemicals into the drink and mixing it thoroughly.

'What does it do? What will happen to me?' said Joseph taking the pro-offered glass.

'But that is entirely the wrong question, my boy. It is not what happens to you or indeed what is done to you. That is the first step on the road to victim-hood. Oh no, it is all about how you react. The murder of a man could be the damnation of your soul or its glorious liberation, depending on your internal judgement of the external act...'

Joseph watched McFee digress into a maze of profound gibberish. Every syllable of his speech was marked by a gesture of intense pleasure. His eyes rolled. His chest swelled. His fingers fluttered. Whether 'What will happen to me?' was the correct question or not was irrelevant to Joseph. He could see what was happening to McFee and, quite frankly, it looked like fun. It had been a night of extremes for Joseph –full-blooded rebellion followed by blind acquiescence: Why stop now? Joseph knocked back the concoction.

'McFee, are you going to pedal your piece for once?' came a shout from behind.

Joseph and Christoph turned to see Lance Roche, great-great-grandson of the legendary Steven Roche, pointing at them with his metal whistle.

'More than happy to, Lance. More than happy,' said McFee placing down his glass, unbuttoning his jacket and beginning a series of elaborate stretches.

'Today, if you don't mind,' shouted Lance with a nefarious grin.

'Best to get this over and done with now, my boy,' said McFee, leading Joseph towards the bikes. 'When our little tipple takes effect, we may find ourselves incapable.'

The eighteen other cyclists began jeering as McFee adjusted the height of his saddle with extreme fastidiousness. Joseph, a newcomer to manual electricity generation, had not grown as greedy for maximum efficiency and sat on the saddle with bowed legs.

'Are you right or what?' boomed the gargantuan Roche, raising his whistle to his lips.

'Clear your mind and obey nothing but the speedo. It is god,' said McFee fixing an intense stare on the LCD screen before him.

Joseph watched the other cyclists enter into similar states of concentration and stifled a laugh. Roche blew the whistle and the pedalling began.

The band, now receiving sufficient electricity, began tuning their instruments.

'This one's called 'Shuttle Sprints To the Moon',' announced the bald lyricist, summoning yelps of terror from the cyclists and screams of delight from the dancers.

'Roche, you bloody sadist! You know I'm no use in the mountains. I'm a time-trial specialist, damn it! A time-trial specialist!' screamed Christoph.

'We'll get a piece of pedalling out you for once, McFee,' cackled Roche, clicking a remote control that clasped restraints around the feet of the riders, making escape impossible.

Joseph pedalled on with a casual smile, events being so strange in general that one specific oddity was impossible to concentrate on. A blonde dressed in nothing but an elaborate tattoo walked past; inch-long nipples pointing towards the sky; hips swaying with heavy lust. Joseph's speedo dropped below the required rate and a jolt of electricity shot through his legs.

'Jesus Christ!' yelped Joseph.

'Keep your eyes on the speedo,' cried McFee. 'We haven't even begun the climb and you're falling behind.'

And with that, the band erupted into a frantic rhythm and the bikes went up ten gears. The cyclists rose from their saddles and began pumping the pedals furiously. Joseph's legs screamed lactic objections. His lungs ignored his pleas for more oxygen. Even his bones joined the rebellion – knees threatening to explode under the intense pressure.

Joseph's thumping heart rate rushed the chemicals ingested minutes before quickly to his brain, and he felt himself cycling into a delirium. As the musicians finished the first of their shuttle sprints, Joseph's mind began to warp. He sat back down and felt a cushioned leather saddle beneath him. He heard springs squeak under his weight. He looked down and saw an old black metal bike with curved handlebars and a dainty bell. He saw the dancers move to either side of the room. A road opened up between them, and he began cycling up it. The air was cold. The cold air of early mornings in the mountains before the sun has risen over the peaks. The road was potholed and littered with broken branches and pebbles. Trees arched over Joseph and filled his nose with the smell of yesterday's rain. Now the road twisted and began to climb. Joseph looked down for the gearshift, but his grandfather's bike never had gears. He stood up and began rocking from side to side with each push. The sinuous path grew steeper and steeper, but he pushed on, telling himself the next turn was the end. And each time he was rewarded with yet a steeper climb. And each and every time he thought of stopping, but peddled on from habit and as disappointment faded he thought of how far he'd come. He thought of the miles of pain behind him and wondered what they stood for. If only he knew how far. If only he knew how much would be asked of him. Was reaching the finish even possible? Joseph looked at the spectators on the side of the road. They danced and cheered and clapped him on.

'How far? Is it much farther?' he shouted to them, but all they did was dance and sing and cheer louder.

Then all of a sudden the peaks and valleys drew away their veils, and Joseph saw the true summit. Bare rock loomed hundreds of miles above. Joseph's eyes tumbled down from the summit, each twist and turn of the path filling him with dread. Then he spotted a lone rider far above him and far below the summit. He could not discern a solitary attribute of that lone rider – not size, not colour, not gender – but each rotation of Joseph's pedals led him from suspicion to absolute certainty: the lone rider was Pluto Von Paradise.

'He's still fucking pedalling,' groaned Joseph Blade. 'After all this time he still hasn't reached the end.'

The scale of what would be asked and the distance yet to be travelled stretched Joseph's will upon the rack. He could no longer convince himself that the next turn was the end. He could no longer drown the pain by saying, 'One more time.'

Joseph fell onto the dance floor, lay and gazed dumbly at the applauding dancers and musicians.

'That's the longest version of that song I've ever heard. A five-minute accordion solo nonetheless. Bastards. Fucking bastards,' shouted McFee towards the musicians and collapsed at Joseph's side.

'A fine piece of pedalling,' said Lance Roche, bending down to give Joseph's thighs an appreciative squeeze.

'Hughey's still cycling,' muttered Joseph.

'Who?' said Roche turning to ensure no unsupervised pedalling was occurring on his watch.

'He can't make it. We have to tell him. It can't be done,' said Joseph, turning pleading eyes to Christoph.

'Hmmm. I can see you need a rest, my boy. Understandable. Perfectly understandable,' said McFee, pulling Joseph to his feet as he muttered on.

'I've never seen a novice complete 'Shuttle Sprints To the Moon' before. With the right coach, you could go far,' said Roche, squeezing Joseph's thighs once more.

'Yes very good, Roche, but have to get going,' said McFee, ushering Joseph away.

'Consider my offer, Joseph. It's not every day I offer to train a champion,' called Roche.

'Well, if he wants another near-death experience he knows where to find you,' jeered McFee, leading Joseph through the dancers and out of the hall.

They stopped before a large disc-shaped door, which rotated on its horizontal axis to reveal a blindingly white amphitheatre.

Spectators, each and every one engaged in heated debate, sat on white cushioned benches that circled a large pit in the centre. On the right of the pit was a huge blue leather armchair and accompanying bookshelf with blue leather-bound books. On the left, the same furnishings were replicated in red. Seated to the right, dressed in a suit, was Turloch McNeil, and to the right, dressed in pyjamas, was Molly Lawler.

McFee lead Joseph, who struggled to regain both breath and sanity, to an empty seat and procured a couple of beers.

'Are you all right, my boy?' enquired Christoph.

'Uhhh I'm not sure.'

'Well there's nothing a pint can't fix, eh?' said McFee, crossing his legs and bouncing with excitement as Victor Hall appeared in the pit.

'Ladies and gentlemen, welcome to the hub. It's time for tonight's main event,' announced Victor. 'In the blue corner, weighing in with a degree in International Business, an MA in Market Modelling and a Ph.D. in E-commerce, it's the real deal, McNeil.'

The crowd cheered, odds were shouted from certain quarters, and money began changing hands.

'And in the red corner, straight from the school of hard knocks, weighing in with six children, one divorce, two repossessed homes and more hard graft then you can shake a stick at, it's the street brawler, Molly Lawler.'

The referee summoned the two debaters from their armchairs, and they shaped up eyeball to eyeball.

'I want a good clean debate. McNeil, watch the polysyllables. Lawler, watch the cursing. Let's keep it clean. Let's keep it comprehensible. When the bell rings, come out debating. Let's get it on,' said Victor Hall.

The two debaters touched flashcards, retreated to their armchairs for some last-minute cramming and came out for the bell.

'What are they debating?' said Joseph, finally grasping what he was witnessing.

'Everything,' replied McFee, momentarily breaking away from furious declarations of odds and exchanges of hard currency.

'How can they be debating everything?'

'Post-Darwinism my boy. The ideas with the strongest memes survive,' answered McFee, turning back to his labours. '5 to 2 on the nose for red. Takers? Takers, please... Ten euros? Come back when you're ready to make a man's bet...'

Joseph began forming another question, but turned to the pit instead: Tonight's answers seemed only to lead to exponentially more questions.

Above the pit hung multiple microphones and video cameras. The wires from all this apparatus streamed towards a large metal dish at the top of the amphitheatre.

'...granted, but the old didactic view of left and right is no longer relevant,' said Turloch O'Neil. 'Both pure nationalisation in communism and pure privatisation in capitalism have failed us. Only New Government can save us now.'

'And what in the bleedin' name of Jesus is NEW government when it's at home,' laughed Ms. Lawler.

'New Government is the creation of distributed responsibility enforced by a centralised government. Under New Government, each citizen will be a bank. Each citizen will be a police officer. Each citizen will be a creator of electricity, cleaner of water and helper of the elderly. The greedy will no longer be able to horde currency. The lazy will no longer be offered handouts. Money will never again be made without work that's of value to mankind.

'We will all be shareholders in our future. We will all suffer from our failures, and we will all prosper from our victories. This is New Government, and this is true freedom,' proclaimed Victor, setting off a bout of furious betting in the amphitheatre.

'You can shuv your New Government up your bleedin' hole,' retorted Ms. Lawler. 'You only have to look around this madhouse to see that the yawdaas from Foxrock and Killiney like you and your mates here didn't fare too badly in the aul credit crunch. Members of the Pyjama Wearers' Liberation Army from Ballyfermot to Belfast haven't two pennies to rub together and yous lot are throwing money away on sculptures made out of shopping trolleys and toilet roll! The rich blagards who crippled this country are now turning round and telling me to be me own banker and policemen and all – why? Cause they gave all the tax to the fucking...'

'Language, Lawler,' said Victor Hall.

'Ah go and shite,' she said, brandishing a slipper. 'They gave all our money to the banks and now they can't pay the real policemen, so they're trying to lump it all onto our shoulders. You call that freedom? Sounds like fucking slavery to me.'

'The rich did not cause this crisis, Ms. Lawler,' said McNeil.

'Didn't they? Well how come us ejiots at the bottom are cobbling together pennies for a loaf of bread while they're sitting pretty?' wailed Ms. Lawler.

'Well I can explain it to you if you like,' smirked McNeil, straightening his tie.

'Can you, yeah? Go on then. I can't bleedin wait to hear this.'

'Well, the crisis began with a sub-prime credit bubble bursting in America. This bubble was created by NINJAs,' began McNeil.

'Ninjas?'

'Yes. NINJA mortgages – no income, no job, no assets. NINJAs were sold all around America. The idea was that when people ran into problems with their repayments, rising house prices would allow them to re-mortgage. This was all well and good while interest rates were low, but in June 2004 the American Central Bank raised interest rates. Home prices began to fall and NINJA lenders began defaulting on their loans.

'How did American NINJAs result in a global crisis? you may well ask. Well that is explained by CDOs.'

'UFOs?'

'No, CDOs – Collateral Debt Obligations. Ninjas were bundled into CDOs and sold to hedge funds around the world. When these CDOs full of ninjas crashed, they ruined the hedges and it caused a massive black hole in the banks' finances. The result: the credit crunch,' said McNeil finishing with a standard 'and there we have it' gesture.

'So you're telling me that ninjas bundled into UFOs crashed into a load of hedges which caused a massive black hole and that's why members of the PWLA from Clondalkin to Belfast are suffering?'

'CDOs, Ms. Lawler, not UFOs,' replied McNeil.

'CDOs! UFOs! What's the difference? Still sounds like a load of waffle to me. And where I'm from people waffle for only two reasons: Either they're full of shite or they're lying through their teeth.'

'Excuse me, Ms. Lawler, but I doubt you'll find a more informed person on the causes of our current economic...'

'Lies it is, then.'

'Oh for heavens sake, are you completely incapable of reasoned...'

A siren erupted from overhead, calling an end to round one. The two debaters were separated by Victor Hall and sent back to their respective armchairs.

A colossal screen lowered from the ceiling displaying a plethora of pie charts, percentages, t-tests and standard deviation calculations. Victor Hall provided a running commentary while pointing to various figures with a red laser pen.

'And we can see, Mr. O'Neil is faring well in the blogsphere. The Times and Independent message boards are abuzz with favourable comment. If you look at the quotation quotient, you'll see he's being referenced quite frequently.

'Oh and look at this – Wikipedia have created an entry for 'The NINJA Incident.' We're creating history here, ladies and gentlemen.

'Yes, and as you'd expect the public is latching onto the Ninja/UFO element. And wait for it, wait for it, yes there it is – a video of Ninjas crashing UFOs into a hedge outside NIB has been posted on YouTube.

'Now the number to watch here is the Facebook link index, and look at it go. Thousands are reposting the link. My Lord, it's been Tweeted by Senator Nicky Byrne; Nobel Laureate Cecilia Ahern has given it a thumb's up; it's going, it's going... It's gone viral!' shouted Victor Hall in excitement.

Joseph sat transfixed by the sight of his own fingers as a maelstrom of cursing and cheering erupted around him. Christoph McFee, having taken large wagers for very favourable odds on Blue, was forced to fork out bundles of cash.

'Gobshite. Bloody Gobshite!' screamed McFee towards McNeil. 'Play to the gallery not the balcony.'

The siren sounded for a second time, and the debaters emerged from their armchairs, flicking through flashcards.

'Would it not be more productive if instead of blaming hard-working, successful people for your woes, you put on some clothes and got yourself a job?' swung McNeil, dispensing with reason and delivering the quotable sound bite.

'Get a job?! I have a job. I'm a mother. My job is raising the children of this nation. My job is not rewarded with big bonuses and flashy cars and tropical holidays to the Costa del Sol, but someone's gotta save our young fellas from the drugs and crime and depression caused by greedy bankers and...'

'And you'll battle drugs, crime and depression dressed in your pyjamas, will you?' grinned McNeil, imagining the resulting YouTube video.

'Do I have time for dolling meself up when five hundred young fellas and young ones a week are saying enough is enough and jumping off this sinking ship?! We'll be a nation of babies and old men while our youth is off making foreign countries rich. How many Americas and Australias are we gonna build before we fix our own country? How many? So yeah I will do it in me pyjamas cause I don't feel like putting a fecking pretty face on it for you.'

'Pyjama man!' shouted McNeil, running around the pit doing a commendable impression of a superhero.

A door burst open at the back of the amphitheatre. Insistent hysterical screams punctured the crowd's laughter.

'IT'S HAPPENING!' screamed the voice.

The cackling of odds, trading of money, cheering and cursing dissipated and a hum of excitement rushed into the vacuum.

A young man carrying a stack of newspapers reaching to his chin skipped down the stairs of the amphitheatre and plonked his load at Victor Hall's feet.

Victor grabbed a newspaper, scrutinized the front page, flicked to page two and after speed-reading the contents lowered the paper to reveal a face fixed in determination.

'It's happening,' he confirmed in earnest. 'We leave at dawn. Prepare your bicycles.'

As Victor exited the pit followed by the other executive members of the Store St. commune, the crowd spilled into the pit and soon newspapers were circulating the entire amphitheatre.

'It's happening my boy. It's finally happening!' cried McFee.

'What's happening?' replied Joseph, his eyes rising from his palms with a hunted expression.

'He's back,' said Christoph, tossing a newspaper into Joseph's lap.

Joseph gazed down at an old man with prodigious tufts of hair sprouting from his olfactory organ and yellow puss seeping from his tear ducts.

"Bonfire Prof!" declared the red top headline.

Chapter 7

At the bottom of the garden, past the apple tree, rhubarb patch and blackberry brambles, nestled deep in assorted shrubs and dwarfed by the cold perimeter wall of Cherry Orchard industrial estate, stood Hughey Harris' garden shed. Mrs. Harris stood, wrapped in heavy layers of clothes, glancing nervously left and right at the hissing brambles, hiding place of rats from the dormant factories.

'Hughey love. I've left some supper in the oven for you,' she called through the bolted door. 'You just need to heat it up.'

Beyond the door, by the light of a lone storm lamp, Hughey stood at a solid oak cabaret table performing finger dexterity drills. He spanned his fingers and lowered single digits and alternating pairs with a speed that only comes when thought is cut from the equation.

'You should really eat something, love,' continued Mrs. Harris as the wind picked up, drowning her voice in the hissing brambles and making her shiver.

Now Hughey rolled two old Irish pennies, on either hand, across his knuckles in opposite directions.

'Well I'm off to bed. Don't stay out to long love. You'll catch your death of cold,' said Mrs. Harris, straining to hear the slightest sign of acknowledgement from Hughey.

Hughey, surrounded by card guillotines, turnover boxes, magnetic casino chips, pirates' knives, bi-fold picture frames, ring escapes, pendulums, witches' stakes, Dr. Hopzinger's hands and the general apparatus of his life's work, gave no such sign.

Mrs. Harris turned away from the shed that smelled of weeping sap and chemical preservatives. The rhubarb patch was bare, having been heavily pruned in July. Mrs. Harris thought of the bags full of red stalks she'd harvested. She remembered the days and nights she'd spent making jams and crumbles. Hughey used to love the smell of fresh jam in the kitchen, but so had their son. Sean would come home from school and work through half a pot with nothing but a spoon. So now Hughey hid in the pub until Mrs. Harris finished stirring vats of jam and had given all the fruits of her labours away. Her neighbours had grandchildren, beautiful, strong, sugar-hungry grandchildren, living in American and Canada,

Australia and New Zealand. Each neighbour received the jars of jam with smiles, but each smile was heavy. They all longed for things grown in the soil to feed the feet upon it. The neighbours longed to watch grandchildren grow in the self-same kitchen where their parents had been raised.

Mrs. Harris stepped inside the back door and into the kitchen. She gently closed the door behind her, but left it unlocked. She caught her reflection in the glass and stood transfixed by the faded figure. She could feel the mucky night surrounding the garden shed and imagined Hughey had stepped outside. She tried to see past her colour-drained form to the bottom of the garden, but there are no windows when all is dark outside, only dull mirrors. Could I say something more? she thought. Could I not offer more than dinner waiting in the oven? She could, but that meant walking back down that dark path, past the bare patch and into a tangle of brambles; it meant standing in the light of a lone storm lamp surrounded by memory's sleight of hand. She could give more: She could suffer the way Hughey choose to suffer, but would it help?

Having finished his finger dexterity exercises Hughey picked up his cards and began a biography of magic. He performed everything from Pinetti to Copperfield, Hofzinser to Charles Bertram, Robert-Houdini to Blaine. His hands moved without volition and into this empty space the subconscious flooded. Each sleight of hand remembered its place in time, and Pluto was transported back to remake his mistakes.

Normally when Pluto arrived to test new material in the International Bar, the crowd was abuzz, but not that night. And even McFee's praise and obsequious gestures seemed like mere habit. There was a summit to which Pluto plotted his course, but for the first time the magician felt a loss of momentum. Surely this was not as far as he would rise. Surely this was merely a beginning. Hughey drove home in a red Opel Cadet, assuring himself that renewed labours would wield renewed progress, but for reasons he couldn't place, his mind replayed scraps he'd fought from boyhood to manhood. He remembered the cheering pack at the top of the school steps. He remembered the feeling of inescapable conflict. He remembered punches thrown and punches received, but his own bruises weighed heavier on the memory, and so Hughey skipped over his victories and dwelt on his defeats. With adrenaline pumping and pride moaning, Hughey arrived on Ballyfermot Road. He slowed as he passed the new church and gazed into the fenced green surrounded by sleeping terraced houses. His headlights threw the long shadows of railings across the grass and the horses, unshod and untamed, bolted. They tossed their heads in fury and their nostrils shot hot breath into the cold air. They charged to the far side of the green and finding the grass here still infested with sinister shadows sprinted to another corner. As Hughey turned onto Shelka Park Road, the horses settled down. He saw them standing inside the metal fence, surrounded by row after row of concrete terraces and felt keenly their need to run; a need to escape far beyond these restraints.

Hughey opened the front door to see Mrs. Harris standing in the hallway with her arms crossed, lips pursed and eyes narrowed.

'You better talk to your son,' she said.

Hughey knew this face as the precursor to bitter tears.

'What's he done now?' said Hughey setting down his bag of magician's tricks.

'He says he's leaving college and...'

Articulation pushed Mrs. Harris from anger to sorrow, like her very words were a betrayal of her hopes.

'Come on now. Come on,' said Hughey, putting his arms around her but being pushed away.

'Well, can you at least tell me why he's quitting?' said Hughey, angered by the rejection.

'That band of course. What else? What else but that fecking band? ... I wish to God you'd never bought him that bloody guitar, Hughey,' she said, turning away from her accused husband and retreating to the kitchen.

Hughey unwound his scarf and dropped it over the banisters. He unbuttoned his coat and climbed the stairs towards the sound of music roaring from Sean's room.

Hughey knocked on the door twice. There was scrambled motion in the bedroom – the wardrobe slammed, something fell off the bedside locker and the music dropped ten decibels.

'It's your Da,' called Hughey, there was no acknowledgement, 'Christoph gave me a copy of the poster for your gig.'

The door swung open and Sean, attempting to muffle his excitement, sat down on the bed. Red curls hung down over his green-brown eyes. His delicate pale lips hung open, loaded with the arguments he'd been planning, reciting and perfecting for months. Hughey spotted the trap and opted for misdirection.

He popped his cap onto Sean's head and pulled it down over his eyes. The son of a magician knows a plant when he sees one, but Sean smiled nevertheless as Hughey displayed his empty palms and sleeves.

'Oh get on with it Da,' laughed Sean.

'Oh no. Oh shit! I've lost your poster' said Pluto executing an elaborate search of his person.

Sean rolled his eyes and laughed despite himself.

'I know this is going to sound crazy, absolutely nuts like, but maybe it's under this hat on my head,' said Sean.

'Ah yes very good, son. Very good indeed,' said Pluto snatching the cap from Sean's head and staring down into it with a frown.

'Hmm, seems to be torn,' said Pluto pulling strips of paper from the cap.

'Oh no,' cried Sean in mock terror, hands on both cheeks.

'I'm sorry, son. I thought the poster would be safe up there.'

'Can nothing be done?' said Sean on cue.

'No, nothing. Nothing except maybe, but, no, no, you wouldn't have one of those,' said Pluto.

'What is it? What do you need?'

'Well, if only we had a wand I could melt the pieces back together, but you don't have a wand do you?'

'Damn it, I left mine at the drycleaners this morning,' mocked Sean.

'Are you sure you don't have a spare?'

'Sorry. No go.'

'But you haven't even checked. You might have left one in a coat pocket for instance. Maybe you should look in that leather jacket over there,' smirked Pluto.

'Oh come on you haven't even been over that side of the room... Yesterday? But I was wearing that all day! When did you— Oh Christ it's 24/7 with you Da, it really is,' said Sean, smiling with pride at the elaborate preparations made for his entertainment.

Sean walked across his room and searched his leather jacket.

'Oh would you look at that. There was one in the inside pocket after all,' said Sean tossing the wand to Pluto.

'Excellent!' boomed Pluto, taking up the classical fighting stance favoured by the fabled magicians of Budapest and pointing his wand at the cap containing shreds of paper.

After a few minutes of intense concentration that produced beads of sweat on Pluto's brow, the magician lowered his wand. Pluto reached his hand into the cap and began slowly pulling a poster of impossible length from the shallow cap.

Sean applauded with the deeply felt admiration of a connoisseur: the trick had been expertly planned and beautifully executed.

As Hughey unfurled the poster he saw in the face of his son the self-same excitement he'd felt on seeing his name at the top of a bill for the first time.

'Ah that's gift, that is,' said Sean, and Hughey felt his son's surge of invisibility, the doped air filling him with strength, the world waiting to receive his greatness and the certainty that he could talk his way into anything and, if needs be, fight his way out.

'The first of many headliners, son,' said Hughey, letting the poster roll itself closed, tossing it to Sean and sitting beside him on the bed. Now, they waited for the real discussion.

'Your Ma is very upset, son,' said Hughey at last.

'I know,' said Sean, lowering his head with unwanted shame.

'Do you not think you should hedge your bets and have the degree to fall back on? You've seen the struggles I've gone through and well, at the end of the day son, nothing's for certain in the entertainment business.'

'I know that, Da, and yeah I've seen everything you've had to put up with and the commitment it took to get where you are now. You gave it everything. You gave it absolutely everything, and if you were where I am now you wouldn't be spending half your time studying crap you don't give a shit about— you'd be chasing your dreams, wouldn't you?'

Hughey knew the answer and, no matter what advice the father felt impelled to give about back-up plans and the value of education, the son knew approval was implicit. Sean only had to look at Hughey's life for the answer.

At the back of the garden, standing at the cabaret table Pluto performed another set of misdirections and simulations with a cold grin. The storm lamp cast his shadow high up onto the roof where it hung ominous and still except for fluttering fingers that moved with the panic of a trapped bird. Hughey knew the tricks of faith, he mirrored them with expert precision, but was still powerless to escape them. On the night Sean arrived home, he had stood in the exact same position, taking earlier steps upon his long journey in magic; a journey of assiduous effort that never ended, but rather slowed, despite his will, to a desperate crawl.

The brambles were thinner in their youth and shot up year after year towards unobstructed views of the sun above Cherry Orchard Industrial Estate wall. Autumn fruit was thin on the stretched limbs of the brambles, and the apple tree, as yet unmarked by pruning saw or axe, was also busy reaching for the heavens rather than dropping its seed down to the earth. Hughey stepped from the shed as the sun disappeared behind the wall. He wore a tired smile that only came when all energy and effort had been expended. Now rest was justified because rest was all he was capable of. He took a deep draft of melancholy autumn air, a sweetness only captured in the turning days between seasons. He heard a shoe polish tin hit the paving stones and the girls next door laugh as they played hop scotch. A swing screeched on a rusty chain bearing giddy legs up into the fading light. School uniforms, bedsheets, white shirts, blue overalls, babies' bibs and lacy underwear hung from clotheslines and rippled in the insufflations of winter, but the cold had yet to shake the smells of baking bread and fat sausages and melted butter from the breeze. Past the rhubarb patch and under the apple tree walked Hughey. He opened the back door and bleach burnt all other aromas from his nose. He looked at the chairs standing in perfect symmetry under the kitchen table, cups hanging in order of colour and size over the sink, and began wiping his feet vigorously. He then checked if he had dirtied the mat and finally decided it was best to simply remove his shoes. A relentless scrapping could be heard above, and Hughey followed it. The floors of his home seemed to receive his dirty steps with contempt. The newspaper rack in the hall, normally bulging with unread opinions, had been culled. Only two titles remained: both Mrs. Harris'. Up the stairs he went, following the harsh rhythmic scraping to the bathroom. The door was ajar and, gently pushing it open, Hughey saw Mrs. Harris down on all fours attacking the grouting between the bathroom tiles with a cold violence. She knew there was no dirt there. This two-week campaign of cleaning had banished all grit and grime from her house in the first day, but on she scraped. The wire wool opened tiny cuts on her delicate fingers, which the bleach gladly burned, turning her fingers a purged red.

Hughey was about to speak. He was about to intervene. He was about to beg for an end to hostilities when the doorbell rang. Mrs. Harris ceased her scrubbing and listened. Hughey felt himself holding his breath and then the doorbell erupted in Sean's favoured volley of rings. Mrs. Harris threw down the wire wool, rose to her feet and wiped her hands in her apron. Hughey stepped back out of sight as his wife exited the bathroom and began descending the stairs.

'Do you not want to welcome your son home?' she called over her shoulder to Hughey, who had presumed himself unnoticed.

The hall door swung open as Hughey began his descent.

'Sean!' shouted Mrs. Harris, genuine pleasure battling genuine concern in her voice.

'All right, Mam,' said Sean throwing his arms around his mother and lowering his head to her shoulder so that his face was obscured by his mop of red hair.

'Ah, the warrior returns,' shouted Hughey, making the foot of the stairs and instantly regretted his choice of cliché as Sean released his mother and looked up.

A warrior had returned (for a short visit) and the battle was written all over his hollowed cheeks. The question of course was – who was winning?

'God it's good to see you, love. Great to see you. You must be awful tired what with the travelling. Doesn't he look tired, Hughey?' said Mrs. Harris.

'Well thanks a bunch, Mam,' laughed Sean, 'and here was I trying to look my best for the homecoming.'

'Ah don't get me wrong now, son. You look good. You look handsome as ever. Just a little tired is all,' said Mrs. Harris, taking

Sean's guitar case, rucksack and sleeping bag from his hands and putting them under the stairs.

'Welcome home son,' said Hughey, trading a proud handshake with this new man, 'Why don't you come into the kitchen and tell us all about it.'

'Hang on a second there, the pair of yous. Let me get a good look at my son first,' she said rushing back from the stairs and gently elbowing Hughey aside.

She took Sean by the shoulders, then the cheeks, and looked hard into either eye.

'You haven't been eating properly, son,' she said after deliberation. 'Well, I'll put that right quick enough. We'll have your energy up in no time at all with some good wholesome food.'

'Ah Mam, stop fussing will ya. I'm grand,' said Sean, breaking free of Mrs. Harris' inspections.

'I'll fuss all I want. My son is home. My only son is home and I'll fuss all I bloody well want,' she said forcing a laugh and shooing Sean into the kitchen.

As Mrs. Harris traded her campaign of cleaning for a new campaign of cooking, Hughey took in this new man before him. The boyish ease and well-fed airs had been starved off Sean's bones. They were now replaced by a swagger and a look of ruthless determination.

'So the gigs are going well over in London then?' said Hughey across the kitchen table that he and Mrs. Harris had avoided since Sean's departure.

'Brilliant, Da. Really and truly brilliant,' answered Sean with slow nods of his head and a grin that belied contradiction.

'Good crowds then, yeah?' said Hughey, mining for more detail.

'Great crowds and growing with every gig. You'll have to come over and see for yourself, Da. The raw energy is hard to describe. It's like...it's like we step up on that stage and just let go. It's like we let go of the nine to five, the grind, all our inhibitions and then even time seems to slip away. It's like we're travelling towards something else, and the crowd sees us going and they trust us enough and believe in us enough to follow. Then it's like...it's like we're this hungry monster up on stage feeding off the crowd's energy— except for every ounce they give us, we give them four and then they give us eight and off we go, up and up and up,' says Sean, eyes shining with the memory of glimpsed treasures.

Bacon hit the frying pan behind them and masked the silence of Hughey's thoughts. Not when he has just walked in the door you old codger, thought Hughey, there will be time enough for that. The lectures on the cult of genius, the myth of given gifts and the fallacy of instantaneous perfection could wait.

'So how is the song writing going?' he said instead.

'Very well, Da! Actually bloody brilliantly to be dead honest,' said Sean sensing his father's change in mood. 'We're rehearsing every day. Everyone is working on their instruments every spare minute and the songs are just pouring out of us. They are literally just coming out of nowhere. Night and day, they magically appear.'

'They're not coming out of nowhere, son. They're coming out of the hard work you're doing,' said Hughey, unable to hold back.

'Well that's a kind of chicken-and-the-egg thing isn't it, Da?' laughed Sean as Mrs. Harris slid a plate laden with scrambled eggs, black pudding, bacon, buttered toast and hash browns in front of him.

'Right, get this into you for starters while I get a proper meal on the go,' said Mrs. Harris. 'Hughey, we've no milk or bread left. Could you run around to the shop please?'

Hughey sat battling with his thoughts, oblivious to Mrs. Harris' orders.

'Ah Jesus, Mam, I've enough food here to feed an army. Don't be sending Da out for supplies,' laughed Sean through a mouth full of toast.

'And what's your beloved Da gonna eat for breakfast if he doesn't go around for supplies?' said Mrs. Harris, ruffling Sean's hair and casting a look of warning at the brooding eyes of her husband.

'Supplies?' said Hughey from behind leagues disconnected thought.

'Yes bread and milk and some biscuits if you can manage it,' said Mrs. Harris, returning to her cooking campaign.

'Right... Well the warrior needs feeding,' said Hughey, slapping his palms down on the table and telling himself there was plenty of time to dislodge the ideas loaded in Sean's mind.

Alone in the shed, Pluto performed the plant, loading his sleeve with the required card and felt a wave of nausea.

He remembered the call from London, some time after Christmas, on a crackled line. A party with whiskey-laden shouts and lusty laughs bubbled in the background.

'We have a showcase in Berlin. They want to sign us. We basically just have to turn up, play and sign a deal,' said Sean with irresistible excitement.

Did Hughey have the money to give? No. Did he find the money and give it? Yes. Mrs. Harris would scream to high heavens if she found out, but she wouldn't find out until the result was revealed. Contracts and advances and ticket sales were not the attributes of worth to which Hughey subscribed, but they were the attributes, which could soften Mrs. Harris' conviction that her husband had silently encouraged their son to throw his life away. This flourish could transform her protests to applause.

At the oak cabaret table, Pluto looked up at a framed picture of Sean on the shelf and performed the final flourish of his card trick. There was no accompanying memory: life had provided no such magic.

Dawn stumbled forwards, heavy clouds muffling the starting shot of day. Mrs. Harris, hearing the birds finally convince themselves that day had arrived, glanced at her alarm clock. She had slept, but all the while listening for the back door, and so she slept with waking in mind and was not rested.

A knock on the front door jolted Mrs. Harris from her pillow. She quickly threw on a dressing gown and slippers, allowing herself to imagine Hughey laden down with bread, sausages, bacon, eggs, black pudding, orange juice, tea, milk and even flowers. Hurrying down the stairs, she was sure she could see the silhouette of shopping bags through the glass of the door.

Mrs. Harris swung the door open and was greeted by the sight of Marley Kempe in oversized pants balancing on a unicycle.

'What do you want?' snapped Mrs. Harris.

Marley fell from his unicycle and summoned the most melancholy frown since the great Jean Gaspard Deburau.

'Typical,' snorted Mrs. Harris and began closing the door.

Marley performed a backwards roll into the driveway, honked twice on his red nose and pointed towards Mrs. Harris' fully functioning automobile.

'Yes, well, thank you for that...but one good dead doesn't undo a thousand bad,' said Mrs. Harris, crossing her arms.

Marley hunched forwards, languidly picked up his unicycle and began dragging his seven-foot frame away from the door with silent sobs.

'Oh for Christ's sake, come back,' called Mrs. Harris.

Marley hopped on his unicycle and pedalled into the house.

'He's in the shed. Been in there all night. He has had a fight with young Joseph,' explained Mrs. Harris while leading Marley to the back door.

Marley pulled a bouquet of flowers from his pants.

'Don't think they will do the trick, Marley,' said Mrs. Harris.

Marley tossed the flowers over his shoulder and produced a bottle of Jameson.

'Don't you bloody dare!' said Mrs. Harris, confiscating the offending article.

At that, Marley shot down the garden path on his unicycle, fearing a thorough search of his breeches would result in further expensive losses.

Two heavy bangs on the shed door had no effect upon Hughey Harris' personal re-enactment of card trick history, neither did the five-, six- or seven-shot volleys. Marley Kempe, accustomed to the frustrations arising from a lifetime vow of silent clowning, paused and considered alternative methods of announcing his arrival.

Two honks upon his nose was the method settled upon.

Distracted in the middle of a difficult flourish, Hughey let the cards spill upon the cabaret table. All night he'd transmuted these dead forms into the realm of magic, but with one slip, they returned to the inanimate. The magician drew his fingers down his face, hoping for anger, for rage or for disappointment, but nothing came.

Marley heard the bolt slide back on the shed door and, abandoning all pretence of composure, burst in the door.

Hughey was thrown back upon his cabaret table and Marley landed upon him.

'What the hell has gotten into you?!' shouted Hughey, struggling from under the clown's panting chest.

Marley regained his footing and shoved a newspaper in Hughey's face.

Having spent the night performing card tricks in near darkness Hughey's eyes were in no state for reading.

'Wait till I get my glasses,' said the dishevelled magician, searching through endless piles of bric-a-brac while Kempe's size-seventeen foot tapped impatiently behind him.

'Ah, here we are,' said Hughey turning to read the paper. 'Right let's see what all this about. Riots in Co. Roscommon after seventeenth consecutive all Connacht semi-final loss...this is what the fuss is all about? Do you have family down their or something?'

Kempe snatched the paper from Pluto and jabbed his finger towards a smaller accompanying article.

The magician froze in shock as Marley Kempe launched into a tirade of highly animated, but absolutely silent expressions. Pluto closed the paper, and his entire being seemed to stiffen.

'Murphy,' said Hughey at last, drawing the word from a place of cold hatred.

Pink Flamingo Soup

Chapter 3

There are three types of people I never trust: men who don't drink, men who drink American "whiskey," and Jackeens. I've said it before and I stand by it still – nothing good, or even halfway descent, has ever come out of Dublin. What about Wilde? I hear you say. What about Beckett and Joyce? you cry. To which I answer: West Brit fairy, protestant Francophile, and pretentious peddler of smut! The only admirable attribute of this so-called capital is that it's aptly named: Dublin – Dubh Linn – Black Water! Even the Vikings new a shithole when they saw one.

 So you can imagine my feeling when a letter arrived with a postmark from that degenerate metropolis. I poured myself another mug of tea and fixed my good eye on the envelope. It had that putrid grey hue of recycling. Only a Jackeen would send you a letter that could possibly have wiped the arse of an Englishman in a previous incarnation. This factor, when coupled with that obnoxious stamp, which sported a bright, modern bridge, supposedly representing modernity, progress and all that cock and bull they go in for in the pale, created a fierce urge to throw the letter in the fire. It was only a strange prognostication as to the letter's topic that stopped me burning it.

 I set my tin mug down on the table, which had received the dead bodies of both my parents, and wondered if my mentor would now be laid out to wake here too. This thought, a thought too terrible to comprehend, held back my hands. Well is this not what you've wanted, I reasoned. Open the letter and you'll know if all is lost.

 Oh dear reader, how I wished to abandon my beliefs in philosophical scepticism that night! How I wished to convince myself that opening the letter was not part of the murder, but had Schrodinger not slaughtered cats on sight? Had Heisenberg not proved that observation alters the previously unobserved? Had Dr. Murphy not began each and every commandment with the truism: How can an idea be anything but an idea? Under this terrible weight of responsibility, I wavered, and in truth it was hours before I mustered the courage to open the letter, which read:

Dear Mr. John James,

Please forgive the tardiness of our little communiqué old boy. Rest assured that the days have not been spent in idleness, and our intention was not to keep you in a state of apprehension. Alas, the struggle ahead requires materials, stratagems and personnel which we have been busy acquiring, but you'll see all this for yourself soon enough.

    To the point: Dr. Benjamin requests your presence. For reasons that will be obvious to a man of your intelligence, we cannot disclose our position. Dr. Benjamin insists this will suffice: *Great Expectations*, *Notes from the Underground*, *The Magic Flute*, *Finnegan's Wake*.

    I hope you have the means to elucidate this encryption and that the meaning remains as hidden from unwanted eyes as it is from ours.

The flesh became word.
Executive Council of the IRB.

    Well, I hardly need to say the effect this glorious news had upon me; like a leper touched by Christ; like Packie Bonner after saving a peno; I was awakened from my stupor by an excelsior of the gods. After dancing around the kitchen table, swinging my bad leg, knocking over my tea and scaring poor Edwin Mirr (my Scottish terrier) half to death, I settled down to re-read the letter.

    The words, like all true poetry, were better on re-reading. Not only had my mentor, the greatest mind of a generation, requested my presence, but he'd hinged my ability to realise his wishes on my proficiency in the non-linear stream of consciousness cataloguing method.

    I began steadying my breath. My nose hairs ceased their erratic fluttering, and my eyes stared straight ahead. I emptied my mind of immediate stimulations, un-hearing the sound of rain on the tin roof, un-smelling the tar-black tea simmering in the pot, and un-seeing Edwin Mirr licking his own vomit from the floor. Having entered the bubble of my consciousness, I allowed it to expand slowly. I heard the old oak tree moan in the wind and threaten the destruction of my cottage— I heard it, but passed no judgement. I smelt the months of rancid bacon fat sitting in the frying pan. I smelt, it but passed no judgement. I saw Edwin Mirr cock his leg and urinate on a collector's edition of *A Drunk Man Looks at the Thistle*. I saw it but passed no judgement. Every inhalation drew the web of the world into my lungs, and every exhalation sent my soul out vibrating across the silk.

'*Great Expectations*,' I said, beginning my mantra '*Great Expectations, Great...*'

I chanted on and on until the words became sounds and the sounds lost meaning, and there, in the realm without language, the stream of superconsciousness began.

'*Great Expectations*, dead virgins buried in their wedding shrouds, Julio Iglesias lapping at Mary's menarche, three hundred and sixty-five yards short of a marathon, splutter Pip yo-yo, row, row, row your boat, rip out her fucking spleen, merrily, merrily, merrily, merrily, life is but a dream, Aisle 6, Row 24.'

On I streamed, finding each title in turn and thus revealing an encoded telephone number. After recovering from my exertions and giving Edwin Mirr a good kicking for his disrespectful choice of urinal, I set out for the village, more specifically for the telephone in O'Donoghue's public house.

Up Tinkers' Hill, past Fighting Bill Tracy's farm, round Pike Lake and onto the old bog road I went, arriving at the lop-sided entrance of O'Donoghue's Pub sometime after midday. I stepped inside the pub, and the raucous crowd, consisting of Ballyfarnon's three most dedicated alcoholics, attempted to lift their heads from the bar, but failed. Joe, Jimmy and Jessie were their names, but owing to uniform baldness, wild beards, blotchy complexions and incomprehensible slurring, no one could discern who was who. It was even rumoured that the three men actively propagated this confusion owing to the benefits of polygamy, an allegation their wives stridently denied, each woman proffering a certain idiosyncrasy of their husband's reproductive organs, its resistance to manual stimulation being high amongst the list of candidates, as proof of identity. No one, understandably enough, volunteered to investigate the validity of this evidence, and hence the rumour lived on.

'Lads,' I said to the polygamists and hurried towards O'Donoghue's phone, which, before the invasion of wireless mobile telecommunications devices, served as the point of contact for fire brigade, Garda Siochana, ambulance, exorcist and (in one of Ballyfarnon's greatest scandals) a late-night sex line operated by old Maurine McCooth.

I dialled the number and waited and waited until the dead tone led me to doubt my proficiency in psychedelic cataloguing. These doubts were cut short by an incoming call.

'O'Donoghue's public house. John James speaking,' I announced, hoping my rendition of standard procedure would lead to the least ear wigging.

'Ah John James, my old boy. Very glad to hear from you. We were worried our encoded message would prove impenetrable,' said a Dublin accent of the worst possible genus – the type that says croissant with a French intonation.

'Hello. HELLO? Are you there?'

'I'm here all right,' I said, masking my contempt for the sake of Dr. Murphy, who had clearly been accosted by yet another group of degenerates.

'Very good, old boy. Listen I'll have to be brief. Time is pressing. Be at Connelly Station, Platform 9, tomorrow at midnight. Don't worry about finding us. We'll find you. Got it?'

'I've got it all right,' …and you're going to get it off me soon enough.

'12 sharp, old boy, and make sure you're not followed,' said the Jackeen voice before being replaced by the infinitely more pleasurable sound of a dead tone.

Only weeks before, I was the proud servant of psychedelic cataloguing. I passed my days on the winged verse of Boccaccio, Hangland, Petrarch and Chaucer. Quiet contemplations of these apogees of form were rarely intruded upon, and then only by some young gobshite looking for Jack London or Nietzsche or some other such rubbish. I would ask the great Dr. Murphy for assistance and watch a brilliant mind go to work. Now I was without library, separated from my mentor and about to embark on a trip into the greatest cesspit known to human civilisation. That little fucker Jessie, blessed be his name, had a lot to answer for. I decided to take a drink for my nerves.

I sat in the corner nursing my whiskey, mind spinning with unanswerable questions, when the door of O'Donoghue's opened. Now, Ballyfarnon had seven pubs, and those seven pubs catered to seven distinct genres of patron. Shannon's catered to the god-fearing mass-attending social drinkers. O'Toole's was adjacent to the bookies and so housed men hooked on the dogs and horses. Pearse's dealt with the GAA crowd. The Greystone masqueraded as a hotel and so was venue of choice for christenings, communions, confirmations, weddings and funerals – not necessarily in that order. Nobody ever went to the Crown and Arms, which was owned by an absentee landlord by the name of Nigel Cadbury Buckworth, and so all shady business involving brown envelopes, extra-marital affairs and pornographic material took place there. Clancy's Pub was a shag heap and kept afloat by selling alcohol to under-age drinkers, which everyone was happy to tolerate as it kept the little fuckers out of the decent pubs. Finally, there was O'Donoghue's, which was frequented by only serious drinkers who didn't want distractions such as music, television, soft drinks or women in their pub. So you can imagine that the appearance of a seven-foot clown of African decent went somewhat against our clear system of segregation. Not only did he fail to meet the requirements for O'Donoghue's, but he defied our system of categorisation all together.

I engaged in a good minute of open-mouthed gawking before I realised the enormous clown was accompanied by a man of Hungarian-like origins wearing a long black macintosh and black leather gloves.

'How are yous now?' said the publican, little Matt O'Donoghue, beady eyes swelling under bifocal glasses. 'You're very welcome. Sure we're only too glad to have fellas like yourselves here. There'll be no hassle for ye at all. Not an ounce of hassle. Not in my pub. Sure didn't we have a Chinese fella from Vietnam working in the post office in Carrick for years. Lovely fella he was. At least that's what I was told. Never met him. Didn't go in for drinking you see, and well isn't that his right! … strange as it might be. I for one welcome a bit of diversity. A change is as good as a rest and all that. Not a racist bone in me body. I can promise you that.'

The giant African clown greeted this gushing welcome with a silent grin, which, owing to his enormous frame, had an ominous air.

Little Matt O'Donoghue, whose welcomes normally went no further than 'What are you having?', began to panic.

'Well what will you be having, big man? This one's on the house. It's not every day we get such fine, upstanding people in O'Donoghue's.'

'He has taken a clown's vow of silence,' said the Hungarian, attempting to calm little Matt O'Donoghue's terror.

The publican either failed to hear this explanation or, owing to its utter strangeness, decided to ignore it. Whatever the case O'Donoghue began shaking with fear.

'A pint of the black stuff for you then? I mean the Guinness. Not that there is anything wrong with the black stuff. Sure don't we *only* love the black stuff here, and black people too, or should I say Africans, or African-Americans, rather. Well what does it matter, eh? As long as the heart's in the right place and you can bet your life *mine* is,' said little Matt O'Donoghue, passionately thumping his chest.

The clown shrugged and looked to his Hungarian associate for help.

'Well I hate to break this to you young man, but we're both from Dublin. I'm Hughey Harris and this is Marley Kempe. As I was trying to tell you he has taken a clown's vow of silence and so never talks. He will, however, drink a pint of the black stuff, and so will I.'

My interest up until that point had been one of mild amusement, but on learning they were Jackeens I felt a rush of adrenaline. First the letter and now these two. Why were they here, and what were they looking for?

'Right you are?' said little Matt O'Donoghue, darting towards the taps and starting to pour the pints.

On hearing stout hit the glass the eyes of Joe, Jimmy and Jessie fluttered open, for into seemingly impenetrable depths of catatonia they could descend, but still retain the uncanny ability to miraculously surface as soon as a round was being got.

'And one for meself,' they slurred in unison, each suspecting the other of pulling a fast one.

'It's not your round I'm getting now, lads,' giggled little Matt O'Donoghue nervously.

'Well who the fuck is it for then?' said an incredulous member of the polygamist trio.

'Easy now, lads. Wait your turn like everyone else. All are equal under this roof as they are equal under God's good sky or Allah's good sky or whatever deity one assigns ownership of the sky ta. We'll have no discrimination here, but I hardly need to tell you lads that having stated my passionately held beliefs in equality to ye many times. And well if only ever race was as...'

At first Joe, Jimmy and Jessie attempted to follow this stuttering egalitarian nonsense, but even they, possibly the drunkest men in all of Roscommon, soon realised this high-philandering codology could not possibly be intended for their ears. And so, they began casting their bleary eyes around the bar for an explanation for little Matt O'Donoghue's queer turn. I can see now, with the benefit of hindsight, how wildly I underestimated their drunkenness: They were not merely the drunkest men in Roscommon, but without doubt the drunkest men in all of Connacht, for it took them a good five minutes to spot the seven-foot African-Jackeen clown sitting on the opposite side of the bar.

'Jesus H. Christ, would you look at the fucking head on your man!' said one of the trio, falling from his stool in a kind of parody of reflexes – arms flailing left when they should have went right, legs shooting forwards when they should have gone backwards.

'Oh, the lads love a joke! Mad for the craic, they are. Big part of Irish culture you know, but of course you do know being IRISH yourself, being more Irish than the lot of us put together,' blabbered little Matt O'Donogue.

'Well fuck me sideways! Your man's as black as the ace of spades!' said another of the trio.

At this point, little Matt O'Donoghue dispensed with Guinness pouring etiquette and topped off the pints quickly.

'Here you are. Two of the best for two of the best,' he said handing over the pints to his guests and beginning a speech that drew on everything from Martin Luther King to Nelson Mandela, from Rosa Parks to W.E.B Du Bois.

'Well I'm sure the Americans will be glad to hear of your love for their Declaration of Independence. Thanks for the pints,' said Hughey Harris as he swept back his black macintosh before taking a seat at the bar and drinking his pint.

Joe, Jimmy and Jessie, already stunned by the appearance of a seven-foot negro clown in their pub, were simply flabbergasted by the miraculous appearance of three quadruple whiskeys under their noses. Not wishing to draw attention to this apparent blunder on behalf of the publican, the trio necked the devil's water and duly slipped back into catatonia.

'So we've heard some weird things have been happening around here?' said Hughey Harris in a hushed tone that I strained to hear.

'Well I'm not going to lie to ye lads. It's not every day we get such ethnic diversity here in O'Donoghue's, but I for one welcome it. Much like in the United States I believe the cross-pollination of...'

'I was referring to events at the library,' said Mr. Harris, reaching into his jacket pocket and producing a newspaper clipping, which even at that distance I could recognise owing to my assiduous cataloguing of all Dr. Murphy's media appearances.

'Oh right yeah, you're talking about the boy who turned into a book are yeh?' said little Matt O'Donoghue with a heavy sigh.

'The boy who did what now?' laughed Harris.

Little Matt O'Donoghue cast a quick glance in my direction and, fearing a revival of the chaos that had ravaged his pub in the previous weeks, attempted to shush his guests.

'Well I can see how from an external point of view these things may appear strange and perhaps even humorous, but as people of ethnic diversity I'm sure you can respect the culture differences that arise between races. I hope that you keep, as I do, an open mind and look not on these cultural differences as a source of fear but as the wellspring for advancement of all human kind. For is it not in variations of form, garnered through the mix of genes, cultures and worldviews that we evolve towards our true potential as children of God? As Darwin himself pointed out...' lectured little Matt O'Donoghue with chest thrust forth.

I had hoped to slip out of the bar at some opportune moment, but the guests, quickly realising this speech was for the benefit of a third party, began looking around the bar for its cause. In short, I was spotted and could not beat a hasty exit without raising further suspicion.

Harris interrupted Matt O'Donoghue's speech, which was expounding on the dangers of homogeneity, and there was quick whispered exchange. After a brief delay, Harris and Kempe rose and approached my table.

Hughey Harris stood smiling at the threshold of my table with the enormous clown looming in the background. They wanted an invite and I was happy to allow them wait till the cows came home. I stared out the pub window, which owing to the building's uneven descent into the bog, was at an odd angle to the horizon.

'Can we join you?' said Harris at last, pulling out two stools from my table.

'Oh I'm sure you can, but may you?' I answered, watching a murder of crows rise from the bog and make for a lone tree reaching its bare arms towards the grey sky.

'Spoken like a true librarian. Very good. Very good. I like a man who takes pride in his work. May we sit then?' said Harris, taking his seat.

'You may of course. I'm away soon enough anyway so you'll have the table all to yourselves,' I said, visualising a swift headbutt for Harris' nose and a stool across the shins for the clown.

'Off somewhere in particular?' inquired Harris, rolling a penny across his knuckles.

'I don't see that that's any of your business,' I snapped, eyeing the door but knowing my bad leg, seized since last week's exertions, would not facilitate a daring escape.

'No, you're absolutely right, Mr...'

'John James.'

'You're absolutely right, Mr. John James. It's none of my business. My business is one thing and one thing only: magic. Would you like to see some magic?'

So it's a pair of cheap critics we have, I thought. For what is clowning but a critique of life lived in earnest? Clowns are but leeches on those attempting to hear the words of God. They mock our endeavours, our presumptions, our dreams, our false victories and our real failures. How easy it is to mock and parody, but what alternative does the clown offer us? Nothing but buffoonery. And what is a magician? Nothing but a peddler of copies and imitations. He dedicates his entire life to executing fraudulent miracles and in doing so attempts to drag all that's divine into the realm of human deceit. So a pair of cheap critics it is – one who calls all life a joke and the other who calls all life a lie.

'Well do you want to see some magic or not?' repeated Harris, displaying empty sleeves.

'You can show me nothing but lies,' I said, finishing my whiskey and slamming the glass down on the table, creating a plume of cigarette ash.

The clown attempted to mimic my gesture, but the glass slipped from his hand and sailed through the air towards Joe, Jimmy and Jessie.

Much like the sound of pints being poured - the sound of smashing glass never failed to awaken the trio from the deepest of slumbers. This sound, however, did not summon a slurred "And one for meself." Instead, it summoned clenched fists and bared teeth. Thus Joe, Jimmy and Jessie began stumbling around the bar throwing wild punches at imaginary attackers.

'Well perhaps it is lies, John James. Perhaps it is. Let's see,' said Harris waving his hands back and forth over my glass, blocking it from view and then revealing a book in its place.

'Is it only this fake that you're selling, Harris, or do you have some counterfeit Rolex watches under that big black coat of yours?'

'Oh I can see you don't like my work. What a pity. And here was I under the impression that this particular trick was very popular in Ballyfarnon these days,' said Harris, tossing the book to Kempe who began making all kinds of holy gesticulations towards the volume.

'People can always tell a miracle from the lies you peddle, Harris,' I answered.

'Can they now? Well find me one miracle that I can't replicate with an illusion and I'll hang up my top hat and cape for good,' said Harris.

'Oh I'm sure you're more than capable of mimicking and criticising all and sundry, but come here till I tell yeh: Everyone knows your work is cheap tricks, whereas they believe absolutely in the work of God.'

'They know my work is an illusion because I tell them the truth. They believe other tricks are works of God because those performing them lie,' said Harris, banging his fists down on the table, which attracted the stumbling gaits of the polygamist trio who were still searching for the hand that threw the glass.

'You have no *choice* but to tell them your work is a trick, Harris. They'd know it anyway. The beauty of Chaucer, Yeats and Boccaccio is absolute because the spirit of God moves through them.

The human soul feels the breath of his maker in this beauty and quivers in ecstasy. This is a breath you've never tasted and the hunger has made you bitter,' I said as Joe, Jimmy or perhaps Jessie, swung a viscious left into the side of Harris' face.

Soon the clown was conducting a slapstick brawl of Charlie Chaplin-like proportions. I was tempted to watch the fight to its conclusion, but instead made good my escape onto the old bog road and resolved to head to Dublin without delay.

Chapter 4

It was a cloudless night in Dublin, but the filth of the capital infected even the heavens above, turning them a jaundiced yellow and smearing away the stars. I stood on Platform 9 of Connelly Station as the red electronic sign read 00:00. The platform was a long concrete affair dotted with hard black metal seats that were designed to be as uncomfortable as possible, presumably to banish from the minds of commuters, from the very start, any idea that public transport could be a pleasurable experience. To distract myself from the cold that hunted my flesh and the foreboding that stalked my soul, I walked from a small wooden signal hut at the top of the platform down to the other end. Walking from bottom to top, I viewed trains pulling into a long maintenance yard where machines could be heard lengthening the lives of other machines and shorting the lives of the men who were forced to work the hours of timeless tools. Walking from top to bottom, I viewed tracks beginning their journey across the nation, a sight that could have endowed a poet with romantic feelings if it wasn't for the fact that the Republic of Ireland only possessed two major railway lines.

  I was entertaining myself with the mental construction of a satirical novella in the style of Jack London involving an Irish hobo riding trains in agonizing monotony back and forth from Galway to Dublin and Dublin to Cork when my good eye detected movement to my left. I swung about, expecting a brakeman to fling me to the tracks shouting, 'Hit the grit!' but was greeted with nothing but bare concrete. I heard the swish of a cape behind me and spun around to see another train slowly approaching the platform. I backed slowly up the platform, readying myself to jump on the first blind when one hand wrapped around my mouth and another wrenched my arm up into an excruciating lock. My years of Brazilian jujitsu told me this was the work of a trained martial artist and that my only chance of escape was to relax, remain alert and to tire my opponent with passivity.

  My deadweight was dragged backwards up the length of the platform and into the small signal hut, which smelt of oil and engine grease. Here I became aware of a third party, who bound me hand and foot with a rapidity and precision that belied belief. My legs were now swept from under me and if it wasn't for the cushioning blow of the wall, I would surely have split my skull on the stone floor. Observing that I was completely winded and incapable of anything more than gasping, my captors gagged me without haste. As they stuffed a rag into my mouth, my eyes adjusted to the gloom and by the jaundiced hue of the Dublin night I first guessed their identities.

Black boots, black trousers, black coats, black balaclavas and black gloves can only hide so much, and a seven-foot clown with beehive hair and size-seventeen feet is conspicuous no matter what disguise is employed.

So the pugnacious polygamists met their match, I thought to myself and wondered if medical science would finally succeed where Ballyfarnon had failed and unravel the mystery of Joe, Jimmy and Jessie's identities. A major obstacle remained, however: Delirium tremons could very well drive the trio out of the hospital and back to the pub before a thorough investigation of their private parts could be undertaken.

I lay on my back and as the moments passed I gathered my thoughts. How had this pair of critics followed me? Had I blundered in my execution of anti-surveillance measures? Why were they looking for Dr. Murphy? And who was it that we now awaited?

I watched Harris and Kempe crouch on either side of the hut door as the blank windows of the train filed past. The procession halted with a screech, and my captors tensed for battle. Feet could be heard falling upon the platform and whispering voices approached. Harris and Kempe made hand signals communicating the fact that six men were approaching and to attack on Harris' mark. Three shadows crept past the door and as the second group of three passed, Harris gave the signal.

Kempe leaped first and began executing noogies, foot stamps, eye pokes and other slapstick manoeuvres. Harris followed with more orthodox moves. Shouts, grunts, curses and moans filled the air, but owing to the homogeneous black attire and balaclavas of the fighters, it was impossible to say who was hitting whom. This was not a problem unique to yours truly, for it soon became apparent that the fighters were also finding it difficult to ascertain their target and thus spent as much time apologising as they did attacking. Harris took full advantage of this camouflage and mimicked the voices and objections of his opponents when struck. At first this confusion led to a lull in fighting, but as paranoia took hold, the fight descended into a free-for-all, with Kempe contributing trips, wedgies and kicks to the arse.

As the battle raged outside, I pushed myself along the wall to the signal levers. I placed my hands over a rusted lever and began furiously sawing at the rope.

'Do you need a hand there?' said an invisible voice in the dark before me.

I ceased my labours, bent my knees and positioned myself to deliver the only blow I was capable of within these restraints: a dropkick. I gazed into the darkness hoping to spot his advance, but although the man could be no further than ten feet away, I could see no sign of him.

'Didn't we tell you we'd find you?' said a young man materialising from the shadows à la Bram Stoker, an impression heightened by the appearance of a dagger in a hand that moments before had seemed empty.

As this undead youth stepped into range, I threw my entire weight behind a dropkick. The youth spun adroitly away and with a nifty piece of footwork was quickly standing above me with his dagger raised. With no hope of escape, I took a deep breath and prepared to meet my maker.

'Credo in Deum Patrem omnipotentem, Creatorem caeli et terrae...' I began, when suddenly I felt my restraints cut free.

'Let's go. Dr. Murphy is waiting,' said the youth, dragging me out of the hut and allowing me no time to savour survival.

Our appearance on the battleground had the effect of freezing fists, kicks, head butts and eye gouges in mid-execution.

'Joseph!' said Harris, pulling up his balaclava and restoring much-needed clarity to the chaotic conflict.

Kempe mimed shock and horror while pointing at Harris' back and proceeded to pull a dagger of Eastern-European–looking origins from that very spot.

'They told me you'd joined the IRB, but I didn't believe it' said Harris, receiving the dagger from the clown and making a few threatening slashes at the air.

'The country's falling down Pluto. There's no point in working to fix what'll only fall down anyway. The flesh has become word. The time for change has come,' answered Joseph, stepping forwards with his knife raised.

'And how quickly they've taught their little parrot to squawk their lies,' said Harris.

Kempe pulled a stuffed parrot from his pants, began coercing it to speak and on hearing something highly offensive trampled the bird underfoot.

'Truth becomes fiction when the fiction's true; real becomes not-real where the unreal's real,' said Joseph garnering blood splattered grunts of approval from his associates and revealing the teachings of Dr. Murphy in his thinking.

'And there's no need to ask who's been teaching this little birdie to talk,' said Harris with bitter contempt before staring hard into Joseph's eyes.

'Did I teach you nothing?' pleaded the magician.

'You taught me everything I know,' answered Joseph softly.

'Then state Article 4 of the magician's code,' demanded Harris, taking up some strange frightening stance that, despite my vast martial arts experience, defied categorisation.

'None of that matters anymore,' said Joseph, mirroring Harris' stance.

'So you've forgotten then have you? Well let me refresh your birdbrain,' said Harris, swishing his dagger through the air. 'Article 4 states: Expose false or misleading acts, literature, merchandise or statements pertaining to the magical arts.'

'Well didn't they mislead us and ruin our country with the fucking Celtic tiger? Didn't they write bill after bastarding bill to save the banks and rob ordinary people? Didn't they state that the bailout was our only chance of survival? What good does exposing their illusion do if you don't have a fresh illusion to replace it with?' said Joseph, jabbing home each point with a thrust of his dagger.

'I'm not talking about politics, I'm talking about the art of magic,' screamed Harris in exasperation.

'What's the difference?'

'Everything,' cried Harris, attacking Joseph with the passion of a martyr.

All eight men watching the knife fight did so without as much as a blink, for it seemed certain that the fatal blow was milliseconds away. The agility, technique and speed of their blade work were breathtaking, but steel seemed incapable of striking flesh. As the seconds turned to minutes it became clear to all and sundry that Harris was somehow communicating his intended attacks before execution. It was the only explanation for Joseph's clairvoyant defensive parries and blocks that drew the battle into the realms of the interminable.

By the time Harris and Joseph were halted by exhaustion, the spectators had long lost interest. Kempe was juggling balls and my balaclava-shod associates were chatting casually amongst themselves about the coming revolution.

Harris panted for breath with both hands on his knees. At first I thought he was having some form of respiratory attack, but soon realised that he had begun sobbing.

'I can't lose another one. I can't. I can't lose another one. Not again...' said Harris with a desperation painful to witness.

'I'm sorry, Hughey. I'm sorry,' said Joseph, turning his face away from the sight of his crumbling master.

'Oh Lord. Oh Christ! I can't do it again. Don't ask me to do it again. I can't lose another one,' said Harris, ignoring Joseph's apologies and instead addressing something very distant; something past; something the magician clearly believed was not going to listen.

'I'm sorry, Hughey, but I can't climb and climb forever by myself. I'm not like you. I'm not as strong as you. I can't ignore everything that's happening to my friends and family. I can't climb above it. ...So what else can I do? I have to try and change it,' said Joseph, turning his back on Harris and letting his knife fall to the concrete.

'He understands nothing. Christ, he understands nothing,' cried Harris, starting to fall and being caught by Kempe.

If only I'd known what a pain in the arse those pair of critics would be for the Church of Jessie, I would've picked up the dagger and struck them down in their moment of weakness. Indeed the notion crossed my mind, purely out of contempt for their philosophical viewpoints, but being as I was in unfamiliar company, I decided to keep a low profile.

As the clown led the lachrymose magician into the jaundiced glow of the Dublin night, Joseph began struggling with tears of his own. His associates removed their balaclavas and tried to comfort

Joseph with aphorisms bearing all the hallmarks of the great Dr. Murphy. Now the words may have come as comfort to me, but the faces delivering them did not. If they were not pierced with some barbaric tribal ornamentation, then they sported ridiculous tufts of facial hair or, worse still, were vandalised with Indian ink.

'Dr. Murphy is waiting,' said Joseph, regaining composure as the train sounded its horn behind us.

In pairs we took to the couplings between the carriages, Joseph and I standing between the restaurant car and first-class carriage. The wheels groaned over the bare metal tracks, crushing stray gravel and litter tossed from the platform. I watched as a half-eaten sandwich was mangled by the train and felt my stomach lurch in fear. As Joseph began nonchalantly rolling a cigarette I wrapped myself bodily around a ladder.

What a big girl's blouse – you might say and I'm not ashamed to admit that I was indeed terrified, for deep wounds, when inflicted on the young, leave scars that do not fade, but only grow darker and more pronounced with age. My bad leg began to throb hard and fast, remembering the circumstances that reduced me from the greatest leap in Co. Roscommon Hurling to the worst hobble in all of Munster.

We had finished our Inter-cert, last port of call for fourteen-year-olds destined for the farm or apprenticeships in the trades. I of course had no intention of following my peers into this drudgery and was already planning a beautifully protracted convalescence in the nation's centres of learning. Nonetheless I agreed to join Billy Ahern and Julie Sweeney for a couple of flagons of cider down by the train tracks. It was a lovely June night; with the cider loosening our tongues and the soft syllables of the river filling our ears, Ahern, Julie and I talked of our great futures: ecclesiastical, clerical and academic, respectively. As the night wore on, the fire began dying down and I went to get some more wood.

With a belly full of cider Ahern was as horny as a billy goat, an attribute which explains why, in his current role as Bishop of Roscommon, he abstains completely. And so it was I returned to the sound of slopping saliva, fumbling fingers and frustrated groans.

'For Christ sake give a rest will you,' I barked, throwing more wood on the fire.

'Oh sorry John James,' said Julie, straightening her clothes and pushing the insistent Ahern off her.

'Come on,' groaned Ahern, thrusting his pelvis against Julie's leg.

'Stop it. Have some consideration for John James,' said Julie, still young enough to feel ashamed of her lascivious nature.

'Ahh he's just jealous, aren't you Jimbo?' laughed Ahern.

'Let him be,' said Julie.

'Oh come on, I can see his stiffy from here,' giggled Ahern before being silenced by a swift smack from Julie.

I poked at the fire while picturing a naked Mother Theresa defecating in a Calcutta drop-toilet in a desperate attempt to rid myself of the aforementioned erection.

'Come on, I have to tell you something anyway,' said Julie taking Ahern by the hand and leading him up the steep riverbank, out of the trees and onto the railway line.

I don't know how long I was alone, but it was long enough to finish my flagon of cider and for the fire to become a mound of embers.

I heard a train approaching from a mile down the track, not by the grunt of the engine or the blowing horn, but by the strange whispering vibrations that ghost up the tracks far in advance. Now the engine emerged from under Cope Bridge and filled the valley with the rhythm of its wheels. The leaves shook in time. The river shimmered. The embers pulsed and my legs (both of which were good) bounced. Everything prepared itself for a Doppler crescendo, but then a lone instrument rebelled with a disparate key and rhythm; something soft; something terrified.

The train was a mere three hundred meters away when I realised I was hearing cries for help. I rose to my feet and found the earth unable to bear my weight. In addition to the ground's apparent putrification, the trees pitched and rolled as if attacked by a ferocious hurricane. I made it three or four steps before the horizon jumped up and struck me in the face.

'Jimbo,' shouted Ahern, galloping down the river bank and vaulting clean over me, 'Julie's foot is trapped under the fucking tracks. She's stuck. She's stuck in front of the fucking train.'

Hitherto the strongest language I'd heard in Ahern's mouth was 'damn'. This mild expletive was caused by the tragic demise of his prize violin (a family heirloom of some four generations) in a bicycle accident. The future Bishop atoned for this slip of tongue with a rosary bead session lasting a marathon seventy-two hours, which only ended after the personal intervention of the parish priest, who advised Ahern that ostentatious praying was also a sin.

So you can imagine that his utterance of the F-word banished any suspicions of a prank from my mind. Unable to stand, I scrambled up the riverbank in a simian fashion, and on seeing Julie Sweeney was instantly sobered. She had crossed the line from wild hysteria to paralytic terror. There were no screams or tears, just a blank expression and a methodical tugging on her trapped foot. The train blasted its horn as tonnes of metal defied the screeching breaks with sheer momentum. Ahern and I punched, kicked and pulled at Julie's leg. I watched in horror as Julie's shadow, cast long by the headlights of the train, shortened and shortened as if sprinting towards an ineluctable destiny. As the gravel shook beneath me I gripped Julie's ankle with both hands, took a deep breath of diesel smoke and wrenched the bone from its socket. The headlights were blinding me, but I could feel her foot, now capable of unnatural movements, coming out from under the track. I stood up to pull her free when Ahern rugby tackled me from the side and sent me sailing towards the river. In mid air I felt my trailing leg struck with bone-crunching force and I was launched into a flat spin before tumbling down the riverbank.

It seemed to me then that there was a moment of pure silence. The river stopped babbling its sibilant vowels, the wind held its peace, the trees bowed solemnly and as I looked up at the heavens even the stars ceased their incandescent dance.

And then it all came flooding back: Ahern's curses, running feet, screaming sirens, panicked instructions and, in my leg, the first pangs of a nauseating pain which was to last the rest of my days.

Would it do any good to describe to you the mess one hundred tonnes of metal makes of a nine-stone girl? Is there any beauty to be found there? No dear reader - rape, murder and gore may be the fashion of the day, but I will take the quixotic stance of damning it all to where it belongs, i.e., hell.

Suffice to say the memory, after the passage of more than three decades, was horrific enough to make me grip the ladder on the restaurant car with all my might. As we exited the station and approached a large intersection, the train sped up to a slow jog.

'Okay, Mr. John James, you can unravel yourself now,' said Joseph, leaning with crossed legs against the passenger car and casually smoking.

'I've already been present at the death of one person under a train....Now I don't mind it being two as long as it's your body dismembered and not my own,' I replied, wrapping my good leg around the ladder for extra support.

'Not very bleedin grateful, are you?' said Blade, flicking the end of his cigarette up towards the moon, which hung in the Dublin night like a myopic cataract.

'Grateful? Grateful for you dragging me onto one hundred tonnes of murderous metal? You're even thicker than you look,' I snarled.

'I was talking about rescuing you from Pluto and Kempe, but if you feel like that then fucking stay here for all I care. In thirty seconds we're jumping off this train. If you want to see Dr. Murphy again you'll jump too. Otherwise, see ya later,' said Joseph, sticking his head out from between the carriages as the sounds of a train approaching in the opposite direction reached my ears.

'Why in the name of Jessie is it necessary to jump off a train to see Dr. Murphy?' I said.

'Counter-surveillance,' replied Joseph, bending his knees and readying himself for a leap.

'But there's nobody fecking following us,' I pleaded, Julie McSweeney's mutilated cadaver terrorising my mind.

'Maybe there is. Maybe there isn't. There defo won't be after this though,' said Joseph as the headlights of the approaching train appeared on the opposite track, 'We won't be risking another mission to find you John James. So stay here or jump in 5, 4, 3...'

There have been many well-documented cases in medical science (a branch of natural philosophy I will only lower myself to mention this once) of adrenaline glands entering a state of hyperproduction, thus causing the myth of human volition to be exposed. Even the most cursory glance at these cases will show grandmothers lifting cars off grandchildren, crippled men carrying whole families out of fires, and Irish soccer players scoring goals on the half-volley from thirty yards after a barren spell of seven years.

Can these people will actions they are incapable of conceiving? Can an idea be anything but an idea? Of course not. And thus the illusion of human will is exposed and the hand of God revealed.

It was this state of adrenaline-induced superconsciousness that I entered and I found to my surprise that I had followed the youth into the air.

My feet hit the grit between the tracks and I instinctively entered a forward role, which brought me to a stand some six inches beyond the bloodthirsty roar of the train behind me.

I remained perfectly still, hoping to receive further instructions, hoping I had finally transcended the illusion of free will, but God in his divine wisdom returned me to the tribulations of human madness.

'Let's go!' shouted Joseph, grabbing me by the shirtsleeve and leading me up an embankment to a thicket of trees.

We piled onto four high-powered motorbikes and shot off on a sinuous path that more than once seemed to return to its beginnings before careering down a new set of alleys, backroads and housing estates.

After some forty minutes, we arrived at an abandoned building site in the centre of Dublin city. The bikes were brought in through a gap in the iron fence and hidden under piles of rubble. Now we set off on foot. Through swamps of muck, across elaborate systems of planks and over towering mounds of broken brick we went, before arriving at the entrance to one of the dilapidated buildings. We ascended to the twenty-fifth floor in a surprisingly well-maintained elevator, and as the doors of the mechanism opened I got my first glimpse of the now legendary Store St. Commune.

My good eye twitched in delight as sculptures gave way to frescos, which bled into light installations, which in turn complemented exquisite paintings. My soul, sullied by a day of Dublin drudgery, delighted in this phantasmagoria.

'Yeah I was a little stunned the first time I saw it too, but the boss is waiting for us so you'll have to have a nosey later,' said Joseph, leading me towards a round door at the far end of the room.

Beyond that rotating door, I was dazzled by pure white light and the sound of thousands of murmuring voices. I squinted through my good eye and discerned that I was in some form of amphitheatre. One by one the multitude came into focus and I was confronted with everything from bearded women to men wearing make up. The only attribute constant across this collection of freaks was abnormally developed quadriceps – something that struck me as deeply sinister at the time.

'Let us rejoice! My son has returned,' came the imitable voice of Dr. Benjamin Murphy from the centre of the amphitheatre.

All eyes watched as I descended the stairs to my mentor's side.

'Jessie be with you,' I said, voice cracking with emotion at the sight of him unharmed.

'And Jessie be with you,' replied the great man, halting my attempts to prostate myself at his feet. 'Be seated, my son. The hour of judgement is upon us.'

Choking back tears of gratitude I took my place at the right-hand side of Dr. Murphy and, in this state of bliss, barely noticed the jealous sneers of certain members of the IRB Executive Council.

'Right....So like I was saying before Jimmy Bob here arrived – I reckon we dig up the stuff we didn't hand over under The Good Friday Agreement and blow the fuck out of them as they come out of Leinster House,' shouted a woman wearing what appeared to be a dressing gown, while banging her fists down on the table.

'They are not following Jessie who resort to violence,' replied Dr. Murphy, much to the disappointment of the amphitheatre.

'So we'll just persuade them to give up bleedin power over a cup of tea and a few bickies, will we? You forget that the PWLA has been out there struggling on the frontlines. We've faced the water cannons and the dogs and the batons in our pyjamas and let me tell yeh something – a load of bleeding waffle ain't gonna change fuck all,' cried Ms. Lawler, swishing her dressing gown belt through the air.

'Don't be jealous of violent people or decide to act as they do. Be mindful of the commandments at all times,' said Dr. Murphy softly.

'Ah go and shite. I couldn't give a rat's arse about the bleedin commandments. Well except for the one about clothes mutilating God's creation and all. We like that one. In fact we'd die for that one, but you can stuff the rest of them where the sun don't shine,' said Ms. Lawler, turning to receive nods of approval from the army of pyjama wearers behind her.

'Remember, child, that the commandment you love so dearly begins thus: How can an idea be anything but an idea?' replied Dr. Murphy.

'And what in the name of Christ – I mean Jessie, blessed be his name – is that supposed to mean?' said Ms. Lawler, pulling at her wild hair with both fists.

'If I may, old boy,' said Christoph McFee, rising from his seat in the executive council. 'I might be able to put this is terms more readily understood by Mrs. Lawyer.'

'Go into the world and preach the word of Jessie onto every creature,' said Dr. Murphy, granting McFee the requested permission.

'Very good, old boy. ...Well as the great Dr. Murphy has said – How can an idea be anything but an idea? And what, you may ask, does this mean? Well, allow me to demonstrate,' said McFee, removing his top hat, sweeping back his cape and producing a white rabbit.

'I think we can all agree that there is a rabbit in my hand. Now as I lower the rabbit we can agree that there is a rabbit in the hat. I tap the hat three times with my stick and, lo and behold, the rabbit has disappeared,' said McFee, displaying the empty hat and even receiving some mild applause from the backbenches.

'And what the fuck do rabbits have to do with anything?' shouted Ms. Lawler, waving a slipper over her head.

'Absolutely nothing, old girl, but imagine if instead of a rabbit I made your livelihood, pension and life savings disappear. I'm sure you'd be very interested in where exactly they'd disappeared to, and more importantly what I suggested you did to get them back,' grinned McFee, waving his hands around like some sort of Italian fairy.

'If someone doesn't start talking sense around here, myself and the whole of the PWLA are leaving,' threatened Ms. Lawler.

'What Christoph is telling you is that you don't need to make the rabbit disappear. You just have to make everyone *believe* the rabbit has disappeared,' interjected Blade.

'Precisely, my boy. Revolutions of blood and guts are so last century. We live in an information age where the truth is whatever truth garners the highest viewing figures. We don't need to launch a

130

ruthless coup, we just need everyone to *believe* we have,' said McFee, clapping his hands together.

'So you're saying we can just fucking pretend our way into power?' laughed Lawler.

'Exactly.'

'That's it. We're leaving,' said Lawler, summoning her army to their feet.

'But don't take it from me. Dr. Powers here can tell you it's all been done before,' said McFee, motioning towards a man whose beard flowed seamlessly into colossal eyebrows before merging with a wild mop of chestnut hair, giving his face the appearance of a small child hiding behind a bush.

'Yes, thank you, Christoph. I can, yes, of course, with absolute certainty, positively confirm the validity and accuracy and – hmmmm how should I put it now? ...Ahhh yes, the rectitude of what Christoph was saying. Ms. Lawler, I assure you, I guarantee you and indeed I stake my reputation as president of the Unemployed Historian's Alliance on the fact that the self-same tactics of illusion have been employed in Hitler's Germany, Stalin's Russia, Pinochet's Chile, Thatcher's Britain, Bush's America, Videla's Argentina....The list is endless, bottomless, topless–"

'Don't get fresh with me, sonny Jim,' said Lawler, advancing threateningly.

'No, not topless, excuse me, and certainly not bottomless, I beg your pardon. The list is fully clad, dressed very respectfully, in a shirt and trousers, possibly even a tie,' babbled the retreating Dr. Powers.

'Ya what!' shouted Lawler, cracking her dressing gown belt above Dr. Powers' head.

'That is to say if it wished to be so attired. The list could very well be, and given the demands placed on its time you'd imagine this very much to be the case, dressed in pyjamas and a dressing gown. In fact, and I think I speak for all involved when I say this: we would very much prefer them to be more casually dressed.'

'You're damn right we would,' shouted Lawler, before turning to her supporters and beginning to chant, 'Mams in PJs, YES! Slappers giving BJs, NO!'

Dr. Powers had no idea what the PWLA were chanting about, but he knew a roused rabble when he saw one and stepped bravely forwards.

'Yes the list, dressed head to toe in bedroom attire, stretching backwards through all of history, has little time for skirts and lipstick and high heels. She is no tart. No, no, indeed she is the very herald of truth. Of course, in all probability, you've yet to hear of this; you've been cunningly distracted from the truth of the role, of the influence, of the part that illusion has played in the shaping of mankind's destiny. This ignorance, or oversight, or intellectual travesty is no doubt a consequence of the great historian unemployment epidemic— a sad, sickening, and utterly disgusting, time— but soon that will be over, finished, dispensed with, when we smash the cameras and crack the iPhones and shut down the blogs and snap the microphones! The day, the hour, the time is upon us when historians, scholars of the past, painters of time, will again be called upon to mine the truth, the absolute truth, the absolute historical truth from the dark pit of facts,' said Dr. Powers, rising to a howling crescendo.

'We'll burn the eye of the devil!' screamed another member of the UHA.

'We'll petrol-bomb the banks, ' answered one of the delegates from the Distributed Economists Committee.

'And smash the coal stations!'

'Rip up the magazines!'

'Tear up the chick lit!'

'Destroy the CDs!'

'Make them pedal their piece!'

'Distribute all banking!... Ban banality!... Enforce poetry!... Banish demand!... Worship beauty!... One country under Jessie!!'

The crowd were on their feet now, hissing and spitting venom across the amphitheatre. Fists pumped through the air. Pupils widened. Feet stamped on the floor. Adrenaline filled our nostrils, and every man, woman and child got that mad whore of a look in their eye, spotted on any young fella, outside any chipper, on any Saturday night, in any town in Ireland: the look of bloody fucking violence.

'And all in our pyjamas,' screamed Ms. Lawler, dropping all reservations and hurtling forwards on the ineluctable wave of revolutionary fervour, imaginary or otherwise, sweeping through the amphitheatre.

Dr. Murphy sat unperturbed in this maelstrom of unemployed historians, reader-less poets, fanatical cyclists, pirated musicians, distributed economists and avid pyjama wearers. The great man smiled upon his excitable children with a fine set of tobacco-stained teeth. I on the other hand felt absolutely certain that this harebrained scheme would land us all in a pauper's grave.

Was it too late to return home and see out the long winter nights, surrounded by volumes of Dante and Milton and Chaucer, with the dog curled up by the fire and the kettle whistling on the stove? Was the time past when I would sit in Ballyfarnon Library, ensconced in the very womb of genius, fingering manuscripts, proudly apprenticed to the leading light in librarianship? Could we not return to those golden days once more? With tears of nostalgia filling my eyes, I leaned forward and whispered into the great man's ear.

'You know there are three rooms in my house, Dr. Murphy, and I only really use the kitchen....Sure, you know yourself 'tis warmer sleeping by the auger. We could easily fit our prize collection of medieval poetry in the front room and purchase some choice fiction for the bedroom. It wouldn't be a library worthy of the pioneering non-linear stream of consciousness method, but it could tide us over till the council gets us a new building,' I said, knowing full well how long it took Biggington to get a toilet from the county council.

Dr. Murphy turned his pale green eyes upon me and gazed down to my very soul.

'Know well what leads you forward and what holds you back, and choose the path that leads to wisdom,' said the great man, delicately touching my cheek with the back of his hand.

That look of infinite compassion from my mentor, pioneer of psychedelic cataloguing, prophet of the Church of Jessie, greatest mind of a generation, filled me brimful of shame, for in it my cowardice trembled naked. Dr. Murphy knew I doubted what he believed absolutely, but he also knew these doubts were born of love. He forgave me my weakness because it was the weakness of a child who would let an entire nation rot to save his father.

There and then I swore to Jessie, blessed be his name, to cast away all doubts and give body, mind and spirit to the struggle ahead.

Through the long, cruel winter months, I strived. I sat on every committee, chaired several sub-committees, established a dozen quangos and acted as dialogue facilitator between our most disparate factions, i.e., the PWLA and the Distributed Economists Delegation. I became an expert in the mad, bleedin, off-de-rocker inflections of Dublin's inner-city idiolects as well as an effective interpreter of the wilfully obfuscating argot of the Distributed Economists Delegation. Issues of translation overcome, as completely as my whirlwind apprenticeship would allow, there remained but one major issue: For reasons that never became clear to me, the existence (or non-existence) of intergalactic ninjas became a major stumbling block in negotiations. Months of negotiations eventually lead to both sides agreeing that one of the first acts of the Second Irish Republic would be to enforce a blanket ban on Ninjutsu (a martial art I never held in any esteem owing to its sneaky nature) and implement tight controls on intergalactic travel.

In addition to resolving in-house tensions and forming a cohesive manifesto around the commandments of Jessie, I partook in front-line preparations for our coup d'etat. For the first time since my ill-fated summer as a fisherman off the Aran Islands, I took to the sea and ran the greatest consignment of fireworks seen on these shores since the opening of the 2003 Special Olympics. I also liaised between the Executive Council of the IRB and Sergeant Biggington. With the capital gained through souvenir sales in Ballyfarnon, Biggington managed to persuade his contacts in the Garda Siochana to recruit certain individuals (Jessie sympathisers each and every one) into the riot squad and had the most sympathetic unit scheduled for duty on the day of our rebellion.

Through all these labours I got to know something of the mettle of my comrades. Despite their freakish appearances and contemptible modes of speech, I began to have begrudging respect for their inventiveness. It was the poets, each and every one reduced to penning filth for the popular press, who came up with the notion of staging our coup on the Friday before Christmas. They assured us that all other journalists would be either on holiday, busy shopping or out to a liquid lunch when the story broke. This would allow the poets to report the story in the most sensational market-panic-inducing terms possible. The distributed economists, all beleaguered stock market traders, in turn plotted to pull vast swathes of capital out of Irish banks the moment the news struck, leading to a stampede of funds and the eventual insolvency of the First Irish Republic. It was the musicians, however, who came up with the masterstroke. Having long suffered the humiliation of composing songs for talentless gobshites who appeared (and promptly disappeared) on television talent contests, they decided to turn the tool of their torture into the key of our salvation. A song of such heart-wrenching Celtic melancholy was composed that, for weeks, meetings and workshops descended into teary-eyed declarations of eternal brotherhood every time the musicians began rehearsing in the neighbouring rooms. The song would make its début on the finale of the television talent contest, but in the meantime the Executive Council was forced to intern the musicians in a soundproof room to make any progress in our preparations.

After months of meticulous planning, we were beautifully poised to spring our trap.

It snowed all night on the eve of our coup and when we awoke in the morning, not one man having slept from nerves, we found ourselves surrounded by four feet of snow.

There was a scramble for ice picks and snowshoes. In lieu of huskies, the PWLA attempted to hook up a team of Chihuahuas to a breadboard. The Unemployed Historian's Alliance began quoting Scott and Sackelton's advice to would-be polar explorers. The cyclists stood beside their steeds like recently orphaned children of the Muscovite aristocracy, stripped of their silver spoons, raking impotent forks through bowls of grey gruel.

Even McFee and Hall expressed severe doubts about the ability of the riot squad to arrive in time for battle. It was all threatening to come undone. But a quick call to Sergeant Biggington assuaged our doubts. The truncheon-wielding Jessie sympathisers, foreseeing the logistical problems caused by bad weather, had set out two hours ahead of schedule. This apparent clairvoyance of the riot squad would be masked by all clocks in the barracks being set two hours fast. When the request for a riot squad came over the radio, the self-same clocks would be set two hours back. In the resulting confusion, Biggington would personally convince the hungover administrative staff that the riot squad had not been gone two hours, but had in fact just departed. This, he assured us, could be easily achieved using a combination of screaming, whispering, bribing and bullying.

We were back on! Boots were laced. Knives were sharpened. Sights were zeroed. Pyjamas were straightened. Dressing gowns were tied. Wooden spoons were unsheathed. Derivatives were checked. Bond prices were calculated. Sales were readied. Then the poets, as is their romantic nature, began waxing lyrical about pathetic fallacy, heavenly omens, and one of their number, perhaps suffering from the latent effects of Stockholm syndrome, remarked how well the photos would look in the newspapers and history books. Naturally enough the Unemployed Historian's Alliance reacted with fury and threatened to pull the plug on the whole shoot and shebang. They hadn't come this far only to have the historical narrative once again wrenched from their grasp by photographers or cameramen or any other impudent peddlers of so-called realism. It would be they, the Unemployed Historian's Alliance, who would create a unified tale of cause and effect out of the aleatory acts of humanity. It would be them or it would be nobody! Dr. Powers was by now squaring up to one of the more Byronesque poets and all hell was threatening to break loose.

Only a characteristic flash of genius on the part of Dr. Murphy avoided the abortion of the Second Irish Republic. He nodded to the musicians and they began to gently play their heart-wrenching ballad. All contretemps dissolved in free-flowing tears as men sang at the top of their voices and held each other in passionate embraces.

And so, off we set from Store St. Commune in five squads singing one anthem. The Distributed Economist Delegation led Alpha Squad towards the Central Bank. The UHA led Bravo Squad towards RTE Headquarters in Donnybrook. Those musicians not required for tonight's performance led Charlie Company to the server racks of Google Ireland. The PWLA, despite storms of protest from all other factions, led Delta Squad to Arnott's. Finally, Dr. Murphy and I led Echo Squad to the steps of the General Post Office.

From Ballyfermot to Pluto: A portrait of a magician

Chapter 8

The kettle howled on the gas stove as Mrs. Harris sat at the kitchen table, elbows holding her up against the gravity of numbers written in bold red upon the bills. The pitch of the kettle rose and rose until it was nothing more than a stuttering screech. Mrs. Harris shook herself out of her meditations, acknowledged the kettle with a twitch of her chin, discerned its meaning and stood up to make her third pot of tea in as many hours.

She opened the lid of the shiny metal pot, glimpsed the insides turned black and dropped in two tea bags. She poured in the boiling water, which although drawn from the same reservoir as her childhood, tasted more and more chemical with every passing day. She slipped a subdued yellow tea cosy over the pot and stood the tea to brew on the kitchen table. The cosy was conspicuous for its lack of flowers, chicks, stripped patterns or playful polka dots, and betrayed, to those who cared to notice, a ruthless pursuit of the sober.

Mrs. Harris began shuffling through the bills once more, but each figure that hit her eye forced her to flee to the next until she worked herself into a tizzy and dropped the entire pile onto the table.

Hughey wasn't the only one capable of pulling tricks from his sleeve. Having let the bills fall, Mrs. Harris left them there and produced an old handkerchief. She pressed the first present Sean had ever bought her against her cheek. Her breathing steadied, inhaling a fragrance she had long stopped wearing, but still purchased every year to scent her handkerchief with. Not with photos or music or wine did she attempt this journey into the past. She only trusted the sense of smell. For that ancient sense had not evolved the trickeries and machinations of the others. It did not warp and distort memory with current needs and wants. She inhaled deep and felt herself transported back to a time before tragedy. Knowing happiness had been real, not merely an illusion born out of ignorance of the future, she felt strengthened. She slipped the handkerchief back up her sleeve and made a silent resolution to face what was before her. She took up the calculator, punched in fifteen intimidating figures, made one meagre subtraction, and faced the deficit in block digits.

Mrs. Harris heard the keys in the front door. She placed the calculator down without erasing the deficit and poured herself a cup of tea.

In the hall, Hughey removed his long back mackintosh, black top hat and black leather gloves. His moustache was powdered with snow, which had fallen all through the night, and gave him the appearance of a child having just gulped his daily dose of milk. Hughey turned to the hall mirror and winced at the sight of his receding raven hair, his worry-creased brow and his eyes sunken in age-bruised sockets, but it was the moustache that made him shudder: today a milk moustache; tomorrow a nappy for incontinent bowels.

Hughey wiped away the snow on the back of his sleeve and walked into the kitchen.

'There's tea on the pot,' said Mrs. Harris.

Hughey, freezing cold from a night of chasing shadows around Dublin, ignored his wife's offer in favour of a cold glass of water.

'Thirsty, are you?' accused Mrs. Harris.

Hughey replied by dropping the glass onto the metal drying board.

'Well, I suppose a night of pissing your money up against the wall would make anyone thirsty,' continued Mrs. Harris while shuffling the bills into an orderly pile.

'Not that you'll care, but I've actually been out gathering information. Very important information. Something is afoot. Something big. ...Did you know that over sixty-five percent of schools in Ireland have reported their history teachers missing?' said Hughey, striding forwards to face his wife.

'No, I didn't.'

'Well, they have – and that's not all. That bunch of pyjama wearers have suddenly vanished, McFee hasn't been at the International Bar for months, Joseph's family haven't heard sight nor sound of him for six weeks, and there are even rumours that Murphy has infiltrated the Garda Siochana with his lunatic followers,' said Hughey, working himself into a state of breathlessness.

'Did you see about any more work?' answered Mrs. Harris.

'Did you hear anything I just said? Don't you care at all? They're plotting something!' shouted Hughey.

'No, I don't care, Hughey. I really don't care about a grudge you hold against some mad old magician from Roscommon,' said Mrs. Harris, calmly.

'Some mad old magician! Oh he's just any old loon now, is he? The man who–'

'Killed my son?' snapped Mrs. Harris, nails clawing the table. 'Is that what you're going to say, Hughey? Is it? Are you gonna try and peddle me that old lie again, are you? Tell me this and tell me no more – if that bloody fool had sold Sean a car would you be blaming him for a crash?'

Hughey's red eyes sank deeper into the shade of purpled flesh, and with the vacant air of a sleepwalker he sat down opposite Mrs. Harris.

Mrs. Harris stared down at her husband who no longer fought these battles, having suffered such resounding defeats in the past, and her anger gave way to pity. Hughey poured himself a cup of tea and stared down into it. Mrs. Harris retook her seat, poured a drop of milk into Hughey's tea and added two spoons of sugar.

'Thanks,' muttered the magician, picking up a spoon and clinking it off the side of his cup with a methodical swirl.

The sun crawled over the roofs of the terraced houses and hit the snow-covered gardens. The brilliance of sparkling white drew Mrs. Harris' eye and she looked out the kitchen window down to the apple tree. Every branch and bow was traced in white as if the heavens, staring down with the eye of a painter, had sought to transmute the crumbling beauty of the old tree.

'What's the damage, then?' said Hughey, tapping the pile of bills.

Mrs. Harris delayed her answer, instead letting her eye rove around the winter scene, drinking in the beauty of a bridal garden waiting for summer. She wanted to lie about the black digits on the calculator. She wanted to get bundled up in hat and scarf and boots and bring her husband out into the garden. They could take pictures under the tree. They could look for the robin who visited every year with his chest thrust forth. They could build a... At this thought, a childishness too far, she stopped.

'See for yourself,' said Mrs. Harris, sliding the calculator across the table.

'I think you've got one too many zeros on their love,' laughed Hughey nervously.

'Check it for yourself,' said Mrs. Harris walking to the coat rack on the back door.

As Hughey began muttering curses and punching numbers into a machine that made no efforts to soften the blows, Mrs. Harris wrapped herself up warm.

The snow crunched lazily underfoot as Mrs. Harris walked on the hidden path to the tree traced by the heavens. The sky, a perfect clean blue, seemed higher than usual, as if the air had expanded its domain. Mrs. Harris stood under the main bow of the tree and began to form another memory, another source of succour. Through her nose she inhaled the slowed smells of wood and earth – no longer giddy and striving in this cold, but rather still and satisfied. Mrs. Harris closed her eyes and smiled knowing she had attained another place where happiness could not be denied her.

The back door burst open. Hughey's feet kicked at the snow as he charged past Mrs. Harris. He unlocked the garden shed and slammed the door behind him. There was ten minutes of rifling and clanging before Hughey emerged carrying a sack full of magical apparatus.

'What are you doing?' asked Mrs. Harris, moving out from under the tree.

'Paying the bills,' replied Hughey, eyes fixed dead-ahead in a cold rage.

Ireland is a country whose infrastructure relies on a very narrow band of normality and completely ceases to function outside of these parameters. Roads begin to melt in thirty degree heat, towns are flooded after two days of constant rain, famines are predicted by farmers after a drought of two weeks and a few inches of snow shuts international airports. Hughey knew all this when setting out on his journey to Talbot Street, but if he gave reason a chance to catch up with his blind rage, he would never do what he was about to do. So Hughey braved two hours of cancelled trains, buses, taxis and treacherous bipedal motion to reach Messrs. Phelan Pawn Shop.

The pavements had not been gritted or shovelled and Hughey slowly trudged past people executing spectacular falls on every corner.

The majority of shops still had their shutters down, employees presumably stranded in the suburbs, but Phelan's was, of course, open. Hughey pushed open the door with its welcoming metal grill and stood in the stale warmth. The magician felt his legs began to itch, meltwater having crawled up his trousers. While sporadically scratching, Hughey surveyed the glass cabinets that lined the walls of the pawn brokers. They were full of silver earrings, diamond rings, gold watches and other valuables that the rightful owners, by whatever disasters of faith, had failed to reclaim.

'Is that the great Pluto Von Paradise, or do my eyes deceive me?' cried Phelan with rapacious delight.

Hughey said nothing. He pulled his sack to the counter and kept his face lowered to avoid Phelan's stoat-like eyes dancing behind the metal grill and perspex screen.

'No hello for an old friend then, Master Paradise? Not going recount the tale of woe?' said Phelan, his jagged nose burning an excited red as he rapped his fingertips together.

'I'm sure it's the same one that you hear every day, Phelan,' said Hughey, rummaging in his sack and trying to decide what indispensable item to dispense with.

'The recession, eh? Terrible thing it is. An absolute disaster for this country, but an accident waiting to happen, you'll admit, and just like when any accident occurs people turn to the emergency services for help. If your house is on fire, you call the fire brigade. If you're having a heart attack, you call an ambulance. And in our case if – '

'– you want to be rapped, you call Messrs. Phelan,' interrupted Hughey.

'Not in the slightest, Master Paradise. You'll find everything thing here absolutely consensual,' said Phelan, issuing his stoaty giggle. 'In fact, brokerage has a lot in common with our shared passion, namely magic. We take static wealth, convert it into cash and transform tragedy into opportunity.'

'Nothing you've ever done, past or present, has anything to do with magic,' said Hughey, head emerging momentarily from his sack.

'Well I'd never claim to have reached the heady heights of the great Pluto Von Paradise, but having served my apprenticeship in the streets and clubs I'd say my opinion is relatively well informed,' said Phelan, crossing his arms and licking his lips.

'Three cups and poker tricks do not a magician make,' said Hughey, rising from the sack with his prized Hungarian throwing knives.

'Well, those lowly arts seem to have landed me in a slightly better financial situation than others I don't care to mention,' said Phelan, tapping his fingers together and enjoying himself immensely.

Hughey closed his eyes, red ringed with exhaustion, inhaled deeply through his nose, and slowly lowered himself into the classical fighting stance of the great Erik Weisz. Could that fabled magician of Budapest have escaped these circumstances? Would he too have been subjected to such humiliations? In today's world would even the great Houdini, in the face of mounting bills and shrinking options, be forced to grovel to such a scurrilous swine as Phelan? Even admitting such a possibility made Pluto's very spine hum with rage. Deep in his fighting stance with daggers in hand Pluto visualised the precise shot, which would pierce Phelan's stomach, rupture his spine and turn that self-satisfied grin into the last voluntary movement his body would ever make.

'This glass is actually bulletproof, Master Paradise, so unless you're planning on pawning those magnificent pieces of workmanship I recommend that you put them back into your sack,' said Phelan with an arched eyebrow.

For a few moments, Hughey felt certain that the gods could not ignore the sheer volume of his rage and that his blades, if thrown, would be granted passage through the bulletproof glass to restore balance and justice to the universe.

'Well whenever you're ready, Master Paradise,' said Phelan, turning nonchalantly to his television, inserting series three of *Dynasty* into the DVD player and sitting down on his stool.

Hughey's body vibrated with swallowed curses and, like a young boy pulled from a fight before he'd evened the score, his eyes welled up. He sank forwards, plodded to the counter and threw down the blades.

Hearing the ring of precious metal, Phelan spun around in elation.

'Are you sure you're ready to part with these, Master Paradise?' said Phelan, his fingers creeping incredulously forwards.

'Take them,' snapped Pluto, pushing the blades into Phelan's grasp.

Phelan popped a magnifying glass into his eye, switched on a lamp and began groping the blades while stifling yelps of excitement.

'Exquisite pieces. Absolutely exquisite pieces, Master Paradise. I can't believe you'd part with them,' said Phelan, switching off the lamp and stealing a glance at Hughey's cadaverous pallor. 'Nothing to be ashamed of, of course. If you break your arm, you call the ambulance. If your cat is stuck up a tree, you call the fire brigade. And if you need to temporally liquidate assets, you call Messrs. Phelan.'

'How much?'

'Two hundred a piece,' said Phelan, folding his arms.

'You bastard, they're worth a *hundred* times that! They were handcrafted in the foothills of Stara Planina from Spanish steel. They're encrusted with the finest stones known to the Ottoman Empire! They are the most sought-after throwing knives in all the magical arts!' shouted Pluto, hooking his fingers into the metal grill and fogging the perspex screen with his breath.

'Well, if you can find a magician willing to pay you that type of price, I recommend that you sell to *him*,' said Phelan, sliding the daggers back to Hughey's side of the counter.

'You were a magician once...surely you appreciate what these are worth,' said Hughey, stepping back from the blades, knowing he couldn't part with them twice.

'No, I was a ball-and-cup trickster and a poker cheat. That does not a magician make,' said Phelan without pity.

'I need at least five hundred each. Two hundred isn't going to fix my problems,' pleaded Hughey.

'Two fifty is the best I can do, but if you let me see what else you have in that sack of yours, we'll see if we can make up the difference,' said Phelan, his eyes widening with anticipation.

Hughey had chosen to pawn the daggers and thus cure himself of rotting debt with one savage amputation. Now that his most prized possessions had fetched so little, the thought of accepting even more insulting prices for his other loves made him nauseous. The magician rummaged in the bag wondering if he wanted to be slapped, kicked or spat upon first.

'Come, Master Paradise, there's no shame in asking for help when...'

A thundering explosion bent the air and bowed the windows of every shop on Talbot Street. Street lamps, metal shutters and shop grills hummed with the savage release of energy. After the echoes had died away down the alleys of Dublin, a tense silence followed.

Hughey, momentarily deafened by the explosion, palmed the side of his head in an attempt to rid his ears of some viscous fluid. After trading shouts which neither Phelan nor Hughey heard, the magician walked to the door of the pawn shop. Hughey saw his bemused expression repeated on the faces of every pedestrian and shopkeeper on Talbot St.

'What the hell was...'

Another explosion hurtled down from O'Connell St., and Hughey caught glimpses of fire over the building tops. The pedestrians, observing the phenomenon was not some one-off accident but something far more sinister, began to run. This reaction turned out to be far more threatening to their immediate health than the distant explosions. Old women began performing unwilling, but admirably executed, backflips, and their bodies added further obstacles to the icy path. Soon mounds of tangled limbs were dotted all along Talbot St.

Hughey did not panic. He walked to the counter. He took up his blades. He put on his black top hat and he strode out onto the street. Hughey walked through a maze of spilt groceries, moaning bodies, crying children, four-wheel drifting buses and suicidal cyclists. His step did not waver. His eyes stayed fixed on the metal spire marking his destination: O'Connell St.

The magician's nose drew the smell of gunpowder in for analysis and discerned the source of the explosions to be fireworks of North African origin. As the magician pulled level with the cast iron statue of James Joyce leaning casually on a walking stick, he took cover. At the south end of O'Connell St., Hughey could see a riot squad, six men deep and over fifty men wide. They were not advancing, some of their number wisely judging truncheons and tear gas to be no match for explosives. To the north, in front of the General Post Office, was a chest-high barricade constructed of shopping trolleys, wheelie bins and crates looted from the surrounding businesses. Between the opposing forces there burned a number of buildings. Even from a distance Hughey's eye could detect telltale signs of illusion. The scatter pattern of rubble on the street revealed to the trained eye that the explosion had proceeded from inside out, rather than outside in, and was therefore the result of a detonated package rather than an artillery round. Well, there are plenty of bomb makers left in Ireland, thought Hughey, fighting the urge to jump to conclusions.

Leaning against Joyce, Hughey took a deep draft of air through his nose. The magician searched the smoky odour for further clues, and with eyes raised up to the heavens, he banished all doubts concerning the protagonists of this rebellion. On top of the GPO, flying full mast in the icy wind, was a dark green flag. A golden book, brilliant in the pure winter light, fanned out in the flag's centre like an eagle soaring towards the sun.

'The flesh became word,' snorted Hughey.

A good twenty minutes passed without explosions, shots or violence of any kind. This lull in proceedings quickly ended with the mysterious arrival of several cameramen, photographers and journalists who seemed to be on very close terms with the riot police. The media men were escorted to vantage points along the road, and only when the journalists had set up their equipment did the riot police begin their advance.

The gentle sound of crackling timber was smothered as the riot police began to crunch through the virgin snow with heavy, methodical steps. All else was silent. The IRB, coiled up behind the barricades, did not make a sound.

As Hughey watched the disciplined step of a well-trained riot squad, he shuddered. How did McFee and Joseph think they could stand up to these lads? thought Hughey. They've been blinded by Murphy's waffle and now they're going to have their heads cracked open before spending the rest of their lives in jail.

As the riot squad moved within twenty metres of the barricade, a shrill whistle sliced through the air. Hughey saw the balaclava-clad faces of the IRB rise with guns raised. Jesus Christ, thought Hughey, Murphy kept a stash.

'Take aim, my boys,' called a voice, which Hughey instantly recognised as McFee's.

The riot squad, long accustomed to bashing protesters armed with nothing more than bad language, froze in the face of superior firepower. Their surprise was so complete that the majority did not even attempt to gain cover.

'FIRE!' ordered McFee, and a volley of shots rang out.

Riot police up and down the line dropped into the snow with screams of agony. Hughey watched men cradling their own bowels, hands picking up severed limbs, eyes blinking in faces devoid of jawlines and a level of bloody carnage not seen in Ireland since the riots following Roscommon's seventeenth consecutive all-Connacht semi-final loss to Leitrim.

The riot squad aborted all attempts at advance and frantically tried to pull their injured comrades to safety. Soon the snow was a red slush and the riot police, already impeded by their cumbersome armour, slipped and slid all over the street.

'Take aim!' ordered McFee, allowing no time for retreat. 'FIRE!'

The number of standing officers was now halved, with men executing elaborate swan dives, exquisite pirouettes and commendable re-enactments of scenes from Vietnam war movies.

The horror was spectacular; every drop of blood was vivid in the snow; every scream was distinct in the icy air, and Hughey began to wonder if perhaps this was really it. Had they dug up the guns? Had they prepared the bombs? Had they abandoned the old ways of the Illusionist Republican Brotherhood and decided to lay down their lives?

For laying down their lives is what they were about to do. Shooting police officers armed with sticks was one thing, but engaging in a full-scale fire fight with the Irish army was quite another.

A respect for foolish self-sacrifice (an instinct ingrained in the Irish psyche) was beginning to complicate Hughey's hatred for the IRB when a riot officer emerged from a shop alcove near by. Without warning, the officer's chest exploded, spraying blood, bone and stringy fragments of lung across the snow. The officer did not scream. He did not drop. He did not even wince. Instead he stood rooted to the spot fingering his gaping wound, cursing irritably as if he'd stubbed a toe. Hughey waited for adrenaline to abandon its pretences and for the scream to begin. Instead the officer shrugged, tucked the gore back into his chest and strode forwards.

After a few strides the officer realised he was being watched. His eyes darted from side to side hoping to find some means of egress, but finding none he decided a belated performance was better than none at all. The officer dropped on two knees, screamed to the heavens and collapsed face first into the snow.

Hughey emerged from cover, strode into the line of fire and rolled the fallen officer onto his back with a good kick. Blood began oozing from the officer's mouth as he screamed for help. Hughey reached down, took a dollop of blood on his finger and licked it clean. Over a lifetime of performances Hughey had spilt gallons of blood and shed innumerable pounds of flesh. None of it had been real, but all of it contained an imitable taste: the chemical taste of fraud.

Hughey now drove his hand deep into the officer's chest and found exactly what he expected – rubbery prosthetics and a series of pipes feeding fake blood to the wound.

'Help! Help! He's trying to rip out my heart!' screamed the officer to some comrades sheltering behind a parked car.

'What did Murphy pay you for this?' demanded Hughey, holding a threatening fist above the officer's face.

'He's one of them. He's trying to finish me off. Help me! I...'

The pleas were cut short by three sharp blows, one to each eye and a finale on the nose. The officer, until now assuming this encounter to be nothing more than some brilliant improvisation on the part of a talented actor, was stunned to silence.

'Whatever Murphy has told you is lies. The plan will never work. People will see through the illusion,' said Hughey into the officer's ear.

'How can an idea be anything but an idea?' replied the officer, smiling as if emerging from a dream.

'Another one of Murphy's parrots, eh? Well, I'll stop your squawking,' said Hughey, readying his fist, but stopping as the officer's comrades made a charge forwards to recover his body.

Now suspecting the entire riot squad of being in the pay of Murphy, Hughey took up his classical fighting stance and prepared for battle. The IRB, however, saw fit to intervene.

'Take aim!' shouted McFee. 'FIRE!'

The riot officers dove for cover and then watched in disbelief as Hughey not only remained fully upright, but actually began to approach the barricades.

'Shoot me, you fools! Come on and shoot me!' shouted Hughey, spreading his arms wide and mocking the IRB with a carefree dance.

A fierce debate could be heard raging behind the barricades and in the moments it took for a resolution to be reached, Hughey's quixotic antics had garnered the attention of the few remaining (and thus genuine) riot police.

'Uhhh we don't believe in shooting civilians, old boy,' said McFee hidden behind the barricade.

'You don't believe in shooting anyone, McFee. That's why you're firing blanks and those actors over there are rolling around in pools of fake blood,' shouted Hughey, setting off an energetic reprisal of moans and screams from the injured actors.

'We do not trust in our bows; our swords do not bring us glory, but Jessie gives us victory over our enemies. He puts our adversaries to shame. In Jessie we make our boast all day long and we will praise his name forever,' said Dr. Murphy, rising from behind the barricades, standing on top of a wheelie bin and holding aloft a strange translucent volume.

'Well let's see if he puts me to shame,' said Hughey, sprinting towards the source of his pain with daggers raised.

The magician took flight and time began to unravel. As Hughey's knife rushed towards its ultimate goal all the pain of the past flooded into the present. All the lost future streamed back to the tip of his blade. The entire weight of all that had been, and could have been, and should have been, condensed to a point and waited to explode again into some better arrangement of reality.

Murphy made no attempt to dodge Hughey's lunge, but remained statuesque on top of the wheelie bin. As the magician's knife descended towards flesh, the translucent volume above Murphy's head burst open and flapped wildly in a ferocious breeze descending from Parnell Square. Hughey's eyes swam in wind-cut tears, but even through the watery haze he detected some movement before him. Something had changed below his knife, but his target was too alluring to abort now. This knife could cut through time and slaughter pain. The years of assiduous study and dedicated practise would result in magic.

Hughey felt the steel drive through flesh, past the collarbone and down into the lung. They fell, tangled together into the snow. The magician felt Murphy deflate and exhaled in unison. The body began shaking beneath him and to his surprise Hughey began to shake too. His wind-summoned tears dropped gently into the bloodstained snow and his vision came back into focus.

The magician waited for the IRB to charge him down, but they did not. He waited for screams of sorrow, but they did not come. The revolutionaries just stared at Hughey with a vacant inertia as he gripped his dagger, still deep in flesh, with both hands. Could they not imagine a single act without their leader? Had he remade the world so completely?

Hughey looked down and saw the reason for the strained silence: he saw Joseph. In disbelief, Hughey lurched away and scrambled backwards. He looked up at the wheelie bin and found Murphy still standing statuesque with the translucent volume flapping in the breeze above his head.

'No. No,' muttered Hughey with a manic laugh. 'No, it's not real. I didn't stab the boy. I'd never hurt the lad. He's pretending. He's turning his own learning on his teacher. It's another trick...'

Hughey scrambled to his feet and began stumbling around the battlefield as if assailed by accusers on all sides. He remonstrated with light posts, chided dust bins and swore blind to anything in his path that nothing was as it seemed.

The riot police, having watched Hughey cut down Joseph without retaliation, reasoned that the rebels were out of ammunition. The officers gathered into a pack of twenty and charged the barricades.

The IRB, armed with nothing but imitation rifles and pistols, were quickly overwhelmed and the revolution would have come to an end there and then if reinforcements had not arrived in the shape of the Pyjama Wearers' Liberation Army. Armed with rolling pins, sweeping brushes and wooden spoons pillaged from Arnott's department store, these night-attired warriors rounded the corner of Mary St. with a stirring battle cry. The sheer enormity of the sight gave the riot police pause, and this was all the opportunity the PWLA needed. Over the officers they swarmed, aiming wooden spoons to the delicate spots only mothers know how to hit. With reddened arses, stinging thighs and swollen ankles, the riot police beat a hasty retreat to O'Connell Bridge.

Pink Flamingo Soup

Chapter 5

And here's what mercy gets you in the end: nothing but a pain in the arse. Harris had crumbled that night on platform nine, but did I rid the world of him? No, I didn't, and now the entire jig was up.

Oh we'd scared the living bejesus out of the markets all right. The poets had flooded the news with Armageddon-heralding headlines written in various pentameters. The musicians having taken the entire staff of Google Ireland hostage redirected all internet traffic to revolution-related stories. The distributed bankers dumped massive swaths of Irish stocks on the market and pulled mountains of capital out of the banks, causing general hysteria across global trading floors. All was going exactly to plan. Everything except for the fact that Harris had exposed our lack of ballistic weaponry. Admittedly, this fact was known only by the few officers who'd escaped the wooden spoons of the PWLA, but that would be enough. The officers would inform the army, and the protracted surrender negotiations, which our plan relied upon, would be cut short. Lads in tanks don't negotiate with ladies armed with wooden spoons.

Hidden behind the barricade, my bed leg throbbing in the melting snow, I gazed at Dr. Murphy, greatest mind of a generation, sitting full lotus in a shopping trolley while chanting incantations to Jessie. The desolate shame of a man who does half a job welled up in my chest. For what else is mercy but half a job? The Italians (as effeminate a race as they are) knew what they were about when they slaughtered the sons after murdering the father.

While shivering in the snow, listening to the frightened whimpers of young Joseph, the incantations of Dr. Murphy took on the aspect of ululations. The bursts of icy wind racing down from Parnell Square completed the mood of desolation. Our morale was shot— the most dangerous wound for any soldier.

'We're on the front page of The New York Times!' shouted McFee, attempting to rally the troops with news he garnered with the use of some strange mobile telecommunications device.

'The Tehran Daily is calling our revolution the single most important act in the spread of theocracy for thirty-five years...'

The plaudits came thick and fast, and each was greeted with a cheer louder than the last. Someone began singing our anthem, and after a stirring rendition— of all thirty-two verses— some measure of confidence was restored.

Tanks rolled onto O'Connell Bridge. Large cannons followed, and when snipers were spotted on surrounding rooftops, we were forced to take shelter inside the general post office. There was a deathly silence amongst us, and as time passed we became aware of something deeply disturbing: the soldiers appeared to be singing the entire score of *Joseph and the Amazing Technicolor Dreamcoat* while making preparations to blow us to kingdom come. In retrospect, this could have meant only one thing, but in that tense hour, frozen half to death, my senses were not what they should have been.

'Surrender peacefully and there will be no need for further loss of life,' came a voice over a megaphone, which I instantly recognised as none other than the legendary Captain Fintan O'Reilly.

'We no longer recognise the validity of the First Irish Republic, and as a result its institutions hold no authority over us. If YOU surrender peacefully we'll guarantee your safety as well as prominent positions in the army of the Second Irish Republic,' answered McFee, hanging out a smashed window in the cavernous lobby of the GPO.

'And a wise move that would be. If any lessons are to be drawn from the campaigns in Iraq and Afghanistan, it is that the dissolution of already existing civilian police forces and armed defence forces in favour of completely new institutions manned by unseasoned staff is a process fraught with difficulty and gross inefficiency often resulting in institutions less effective than their predecessors, further hindered by the fact that the previous members of those institutions are hell-bent on fighting the members of the new ones. I commend you on your practical approach,' said Captain Fintan O'Reilly, having lost none of his passion for military history.

'Uhhhhh...thank you, old boy,' said McFee, his learning clearly not a match for this titan of academia.

Now, I don't pander that term around lightly. A titan is exactly what he was. While I served as librarian in the Irish Army's Congo campaign, Captain O'Reilly was my only active cardholder. He withdrew, on average, five tomes of military history every week.

152

Many a long night, over manys a bottle of stout (which the captain alone knew how to acquire), I was treated to treatises of every campaign from Genghis Khan in China to Rommel in North Africa.

'There does, however, remain at least one obstacle to your transition of powers,' said Captain O'Reilly, thoughtfully.

'And what's that, old boy?'

'Well, you see, you haven't overthrown the existing powers. Now, as an apolitical entity duty bound to protect the democratically elected institutions enacted under the constitution, I cannot allow you to seize power by force. If, of course, you had already seized power, rewritten or perhaps suspended the constitution, I could listen to your case, but you've neglected to do any such thing.'

'I see...' said McFee, turning to shrug at the enquiring looks of the IRB.

'Your only other course of action, as I see it, would be to persuade me that the constitution of the first Irish Republic no longer represents the will of the people of Ireland, thus invalidating all its institutions and laws. Even if that were possible, and I see no evidence of it on the streets of Dublin at present, their would still remain the small matter of demonstrating yourselves to be the true voice of the Irish people,' said the captain, now pacing back and forth on top of a tank, dressed in full parade uniform.

'Uhhhh... I see,' muttered McFee, before I sprang forwards and seized the megaphone from the spluttering gobshite.

'What are you doing?' barked McFee.

'Stopping us from getting blown to kingdom come,' I answered, elbowing him away from the window and garnering a nod of approval from Dr. Murphy.

'Well it's quite clear by your paucity of words that you do not possess the means to fulfill the criteria I have laid out. Therefore, I'm left with no choice but to demand an unconditional surrender. You have one hour to meet my demand,' said the captain.

'We're going to need more time discuss our terms,' I ventured.

'Who is this?' demanded the captain.

'Corporal John James, sir,' I replied in clipped military tones.

'THE Corporal John James? 151st Ranger Unit?'

'The very one, sir.'

'Ah, very good. Great to see you back on the battlefield, Corporal,' said the captain, pulling out field glasses to get visual confirmation of my identity.

'Thank you, sir,' I said, offering a salute from the smashed window.

'I told you you'd tire of civilian life, Corporal. Once a military man, always a military man,' he said, beginning to pace once more around the top of the tank.

'Yes, sir.'

'Well as I'm sure you understand, I'm very keen to give these tanks a whirl, Corporal. Damn United Nations terms of engagement mean my boys here never get a shot away in anger these days,' said the captain, emotion creeping into his austere tones.

'I understand, sir,' I said, playing for time before choosing my course.

'One hour it is then, Corporal.'

'We will need longer sir,' I said apologetically.

'Longer? For what?'

'Well, firstly representatives must be elected from each member group of our umbrella organisation and then the terms of surrender will have to be thrashed out by those mandated negotiators,' I said, angling for the captains main weakness – electoral procedure.

'What terms, Corporal? I'm demanding unconditional surrender. Is that not clear to you?' barked the captain, suspecting insubordination.

'I understand completely, Captain. Your terms seem more than fair to *me* given the circumstances. That said, our organisation is composed of several subgroups, each with its own cultural, political and economic agenda. Our group here in the GPO could of course offer our own unconditional surrender, but we couldn't unilaterally accept for the other groups owing to our democratic ideals. The danger is that if you force us to be hasty, our organisation could splinter and you may well find yourself fighting several small factions and eventually embroiled in endless small-scale negotiations of complicated interrelation,' I said, silencing the howls of disapproval behind me with a sly wink.

'Always better to negotiate with a single entity in control of its people.'

'Exactly, sir.'

'Very good, Corporal. I see my lectures in the Congo did not go to waste. ...Well three hours it is then,' offered the captain.

I glanced down at my watch and saw that it would be four hours until our secret weapon would be unleashed.

'We'll need at least five, sir,' I said apologetically.

'Out of the question, Corporal,' said Captain O'Reilly, stamping his leather boot down on the metal tank.

'If it was a straight count I'd gladly meet your demands, Captain, but the smaller groups, as they are absolutely right in doing, will only agree to a system of proportional representation. Therefore, a further two hours will be needed to recast ballots after the first vote,' I said.

'Uhmmm. I see. Well, as you know I've always been against the first-past-the-post system, Corporal. Have we not seen the polarising effects it has had on American and British life? Very good. Proportional representation is the only correct course, but tell me, do you have in place an electoral commission to ensure the fairness and validity of the vote?' enquired the captain.

'We do not,' I conceded.

'Well good god, man, what are you playing at? Create one at once! Its members must be drawn from the most upstanding members of society. They must be immune to partisanship or financial sway. An electoral commission is essential to any election,' shouted the captain in exasperation.

'I'm afraid five hours won't be enough time for such an undertaking sir,' I sighed.

'Then take six, man. For the love of god, don't cut corners. Do it right the first time and you'll only need do it once.'

'Very good, sir,' I said, tossing the megaphone into McFee's lap and walking away from the window victorious.

The victory was, however, short lived.

We were in the midst of deciding constituency boundaries, the Unemployed Historians Alliance holding up proceedings with wild accusations of gerrymandering, when Captain O'Reilly interrupted proceedings.

'Corporal John James, get your fucking arse out here,' screamed the captain down the megaphone.

All debate ceased as I approached the smashed window.

'Here, sir. What's the problem, sir?'

'I've just had some disturbing news, Corporal. Some very bloody disturbing news,' said the captain, standing beside a riot officer.

'And what's that sir?' I said, feigning ignorance.

'That you don't have any ammunition in those rifles, Corporal, that's what! Are you attempting to make a mockery of the Irish Army, Corporal? Are you trying to make a joke out of the defenders of the nation?'

'No, sir. Of course not, sir.'

'Then why are you, an unarmed rebel force, trying to extract a seven-hour surrender negotiation, complete with electoral commission and proportional representation, out of the Irish Army?' shouted Captain O'Reilly, leaning so far forwards on the balls of his feet that it seemed certain he would fall from the tank.

'With all due respect, sir, the electoral commission was your suggestion,' I said.

'Shut up, Corporal, this situation is already bad enough. The press are going to have a field day with this. You've dragged the Irish Army into the worst public relations disaster since the great deafness epidemic of the 1990's. Negotiating for seven hours with unarmed rebels! Think of the headlines...'

'We are armed sir,' I interrupted.

'Then why were you fighting this good officer here with nothing but wooden spoons, Corporal?'

'We don't believe in using excessive force on the civilian population, sir.'

'LIES! Bloody lies, Corporal! Excessive force is the only kind of force that works on civilian populations. They must be shocked and stunned before they realise their sheer numbers can overcome your weapons. If I taught you anything, I thought you that. You're trying to make a joke of me, Corporal,' said the captain.

'My own personal opinions are not necessarily the democratic will of...'

'You have ten minutes before I send a shell down your lying neck,' said the captain, opening the tank's hatch and disappearing from view.

Inside the GPO all hell broke loose. The PWLA proposed one last glorious charge to our martyrs' deaths. The Irish Illusionist

Brotherhood, adept at feats of contortion and balance, suggested crawling through attic spaces and traversing rooftops. The most bizarre proposal, however, came from the members of the Stage Actors Guild who suggested adorning An Post uniforms, beginning to sort mail and claiming complete ignorance of any revolutionary activity within our workplace. The analysis of each proposal's advantages and disadvantages was cut short by the deep thud of a tank barrel and the whistle of a shell arching towards us. We all cringed, like children waiting for the pin to burst the balloon, before the right-hand corner of the GPO disintegrated.

My recollections of the events that followed, as you can understand, are dim and scattered. I remember dust, grey dust; so much fecking grey dust that when I awoke from my stupor I thought my legs had been blown away. After digging my lower body from the rubble with cracked fingernails, I gripped a broken plank and pulled myself up. There must have been an unmerciful racket—screams, gunfire, running feet, falling bricks etcetera—but all I heard was the high-pitched ring of defeat.

I attempted to walk, but my bad leg, sick and tired of abuse, had given up the ghost. I was forced to hop through the rubble, falling on several occasions and, on achieving a difficult egress, was greeted with the muzzle of a gun.

We were captured. Every one of us was chained hand and foot and then chained together in a long line. Not a word was said between us, owing to the temporary deafness caused by the explosion, and I think, if you asked any of those great men now, they'd admit they were thankful for an excuse to remain silent.

In the time it took to organise us into an orderly formation, young Joseph collapsed. The soldiers, on finding his wound, unchained the lad and hurried him away on a stretcher. Clearly, Captain O'Reilly's fortnightly lectures on the intricacies of the Geneva Conventions had continued in my absence.

With Dr. Murphy at the front, our chain gang began its march from the battlefield. Being aurally impaired, we made no attempt to coordinate our steps with a military song, and this circumstance, when combined with the inappropriate footwear of the PWLA, meant we soon found ourselves tangled on the snowy ground. Needless to say, the lack of discipline demonstrated by our shoddy marching did nothing to ingratiate us to Captain O'Reilly.

On discovering blanks in our rifles, fireworks in our knapsacks and prosthetic wounds on the injured police officers, Captain O'Reilly's anger was driven to genocide-inducing levels. In a fit of rage he even cursed the Geneva Conventions, summoning gasps of shock from his rank and file, before ordering us marched to Pearse St. Garda station.

And so we marched across O'Connell Bridge, flanked on all sides by soldiers, synchronising our steps to the rhythm of the doomed. All along the quays of the Liffey, cars could be seen bumper to bumper, most abandoned by their owners. The drivers, as it turned out, had not gone far. The moment we stepped onto D'Olier Street, men in suits of cheap modern cut and women in skirts well above the knee began pouring out of cafés, restaurants, bars, bookies, hairdressers and beauticians.

'You gobshites made me two hours late for my aqua aerobics,' screamed one woman launching a tortilla wrap at Dr. Murphy's face.

'I missed my round of golf with Andrew Healy because of you fecking ejiots,' rejoined a man, tossing a cappuccino or frappuccino or grande macchiato over my head.

'I'll have to pay the babysitter overtime...'

'I had that spin class already paid for...'

'If I miss the finale of *X-Factor*, I'll bloody brain the lot of yas...'

The objections of the hard-working Irish public, forced into cafés and hairdressers by the glorious uprising of the Church of Jessie, came thick and fast. Smoked salmon bagels, sushi lunch boxes and green tea lattes rained down upon our heads. The soldiers, initially happy to expose us to abuse, were forced to intervene (owing to their religious devotion to the Geneva Conventions) when bottles and cans replaced the softer projectiles. Batons were raised, warning shots were fired, and the murderous mob was dispersed.

We proceeded to Pearse St. Garda station where we were stripped of belts, shoe laces and all personal objects, including the Book of Jessie, causing the great Dr. Murphy to lapse into a state of catatonia.

We were bundled into a long, narrow cell furnished with a single plastic bench. Dr. Murphy sat crumpled against the wall, bathed in a pale winter light pouring in from a lone barred window through which the chimney stacks of Trinity College could be glimpsed. The great man, who normally emitted a grace and profundity of immeasurable depth, seemed hollowed out and haggard by the events of the day. His hair, which usually reached towards the sky in viral tufts, was limp and lifeless. His skin, so ethereal and angelic when preaching the Word of Jessie, was ashen and shrivelled.

'The night is always darkest before the coming of the dawn, my boys,' said McFee.

We have all heard this ridiculous aphorism before, and normally I would simply point out, as anyone with a elementary grasp of physics would, that night is darkest at the midpoint of that cycle owing to your position on Earth being at the maximum distance from the sun, but reason abandoned me and that other human instinct, the instinct to destroy something for the sheer bloody pleasure of it, took over.

I landed five joy-filled blows on McFee's mug before being restrained by a half dozen members of the IRB executive council. Still I wouldn't rest. I'd seen a boy turn into a book, suffered public ridicule, lost my library, overcome religious suppression and plotted a revolution. I'd suffered kicks, punches, head butts, hosings and been blown to holy hell by a tank round. All that I took ... but McFee's waffle was the limit. All the evenings I'd lost, evenings that would have been spent on the winged verse of Chaucer, coursed through my veins, and I swore blind that I'd kill every single one of the bastards if they didn't set me loose on McFee.

The soldiers, obviously watching the proceedings on closed-circuit television, were forced to enter, and I was incapacitated by some form of electric shock to the jugular.

In a paralysed state on the floor, I observed that the soldiers had not entered alone. In the door there stood two personages. Captain Finton O'Reilly and another man, slightly taller than the captain's five feet, six inches but at least twice his width. The man's jowls throbbed a repulsive red like some kind of tropical frog. This anatomical likeness was heightened by the man's breathing habits – he flared his whistling nose on every inhalation and pursed his bulbous lips into a type of O on every exhalation.

'Well, which one of the lads here is Murphy?' said the man in an accent robbed of its natural country lilt by the leather cosh of the Jesuits.

'The man you refer to is seated on the far right of the bench adjacent to the window, sir,' answered Captain O'Reilly, betraying the identity of his interlocutor.

For there were only two men in all of Ireland that Captain O'Reilly would consider himself subordinate to, and seeing as Ireland had still not outgrown the reprehensible habit of electing women presidents this could be none other than the Taoiseach.

'Doesn't look much for it now does he, Captain?' scoffed Taoiseach Heffernan.

'Well I've seen more likely boys for sure, sir, but I've never witnessed the blind bloody cheek of this lad; if you'll excuse me speaking so freely, sir,' said the captain.

'Not at all, Captain. A blind bloody cheek is exactly what it is. What do you mean copying our revolution, Murphy?' shouted the Taoiseach.

Dr. Murphy's head fell down onto his chest and a long stream of drool began pouring onto his tattered shirt.

'How can an idea be anything but an idea? How can...' mumbled McFee from a bloody mouth.

'Well, it's our bloody idea!' interrupted the Taoiseach. 'We're the Republican Party. We're the fecking rebels and everyone knows you can't rebel against the rebels. That's just bloody ridiculous!'

'Some rebels! Some fucking martyrs to the cause. All you did is steal our jobs and houses and pride and dignity. What's the difference between you Republicans and the English landlords?' said McFee, tears of frustration mixing with the blood on his face.

'How dare you accuse my party, the party that won this country's freedom, of being English. Eighty percent of our TDs are fluent as Gaeilge. Ninety percent of our members are active figures in the Gaelic Games Association. There's more Irish blood in my little toe then in the lot of you put together,' roared the Taoiseach, sending spittle flying across the entire audience.

'Well, I'd prefer if you were fluent in Korean, avid supporters of tiddlywinks and didn't destroy our nation with greed and corruption,' said McFee, drawing howls of approval from all members of the IRB, except for myself who hadn't recovered the use of my larynx.

'Hang the bastards!' shouted the Taoiseach, jowls shuddering with rage.

'Excuse me, sir?' said Captain O'Reilly in shock.

'I said string the insolent fuckers up by their necks. Are you soldiers still hard of hearing, O'Reilly?' said the Taoiseach, turning his pulsing red jowls on the Captain.

'No problems with my hearing, sir, or with any man in my brigade. Our extensive musical education program keeps the aural organ well exercised. Sing any air sir and my men will transcribe the music note for note. They can even compose suitable harmonies on the fly. The dark days of deafness are far behind the Irish Army sir,' said the Captain, visibly deflated by this chiding.

'Then what's your problem, soldier? Put a rope around these fuckers' necks and let's see them swing.'

'Very good sir. No doubt they deserve it sir, but there are the Geneva Conventions.'

'Is this Geneva?' roared the Taoiseach.

'Absolutely not, sir. This is the first and the ONLY Irish Republic, sir. ...Unfortunately, the constitution of our republic specifically bars the death penalty,' said Captain O'Reilly with a resigned sigh.

Taoiseach Heffernan's jowls throbbed with anger. It seemed that at any moment he'd envelop the captain with a tirade of vitriol, but like all sneaky politicians Heffernan gained control of the internal and focused instead on his external goals.

'I'm disappointed, Captain. Deeply disappointed. To think I once considered you a potential member of the Seanad, but you're clearly a man who sees problems not solutions,' said Heffernan, shaking his head mournfully.

'Well I'm flattered that...I didn't want to seem...that is to say...perhaps there are other options here. It's wasn't my intention to sound fatalistic. There are perhaps other means that could be employed,' said the captain, reduced to the flattered stutterings of a schoolgirl being seduced by the headmaster.

'Such as?' said Heffernan, narrowing his amphibious eyes.

'Well, if you could demonstrate that the constitution no longer represents the will of the Irish people then you could suspend it, sir. You would then of course have to demonstrate yourself to be the true voice of the people and...'

'Demonstrate! We are the democratically elected representatives of the people! Our mandate is unquestionable. Our powers are guaranteed by the Irish Constitution,' barked Heffernan.

'Very good, sir,' said the captain, meekly.

'Glad that's understood. So in the powers vested in me by the Irish Constitution, I hereby suspend the constitution and order these men hanged,' said Heffernan, puffing out his chest.

'Excellent, sir. I will consult the Table of Drops at once.'

From Ballyfermot to Pluto: A portrait of a magician

Chapter 9

As Hughey Harris stumbled up Ballyfermot Road, his passionate debates with inanimate objects went unnoticed by the general public. It was true to say Ballyfermot was no stranger to drunks and junkies babbling incoherently on its streets, but that was not the cause for Hughey's invisible passage. There was an air of the unhinged about town. Cars, in no apparent rush, casually ran red lights. Shops were either open, but
devoid of staff, or had their shutters drawn with sounds of frivolity emanating from inside. A dozen men stood in the centre of Ballyfermot roundabout, smoking cigarettes, drinking from hip flasks and punctuating their discourse with passionate bursts of profanity. Even the animals were in on the act— a dog standing aloft a motorbike surveyed the traffic as if preparing to take off on some urgent errand.

The Church of Jessie's uprising had sparked a thousand micro rebellions in the hearts of Ballyfermot's populace. For no reason they could explain, it suddenly seemed acceptable to disregard work and traffic lights and the social conventions regarding public discourse.

Hughey bade a bus stop a hearty valediction and on setting off again (on a pigeon-like course for home) was passed by a horse. The animal galloped at full whack, snorting its contempt for its surroundings and tossed its mane in a mocking salute. Hughey teetered on the edge of a lucid thought, but quickly banished it by remonstrating with a post box.

Mrs. Harris sat at the hall table begging the phone to ring, but praying that it wouldn't. Two phone calls of that sort was enough for one lifetime, let alone for one day.

Maybe he went to the pub with Marley, thought Mrs. Harris. He's drunk as a fool in the corner of some pub without the foggiest idea of what's happening to the country.

'How dare you! I'd never lay a finger on the lad. I taught him everything he knows. You've ten seconds to withdraw that allegation before I kill ya stone dead!' came a shout from beyond the hall door.

Mrs. Harris jumped to her feet, flung open the door and saw Hughey pointing a knife at the garden gate. She wanted to sprint down the narrow path. She wanted to slap Hughey's face for making her worry. She wanted to cry from relief and bury her head in his chest, but Mrs. Harris had seen that look on her husband's face before. It was the look of madness.

'What are you doing, love?' said Mrs. Harris softly, approaching with slow steps.

'9, 8, 7...' continued Hughey.

Mrs. Harris noted the torn coat and the snow-soaked trousers, but on spotting the blood-splattered shirt she stopped in her tracks.

'What have you done?' gasped Mrs. Harris.

'I've done nothing,' screamed Hughey, turning his crazed eyes on his wife.

There was no love in Hughey's stare. There was not even a hint of recognition.

'Give me the knife, love,' said Mrs. Harris, smothering her terror and demanding the knife with an open palm.

Hughey raised the knife higher and bore his teeth.

'Hughey, give me that knife this instant and get your arse into the house. You've had me worried sick all day. Is it not enough that we're stone bloody broke? You disappear without a word and then turn up and start this carry on,' said Mrs. Harris, feigning exasperation.

Hughey jumped up in the air and landed cross-legged on the pavement. The magician moaned and began rhythmically hitting his forehead with the butt of his dagger.

'He'd only give me five-fifty, the robbing bastard. I couldn't sell them for that. They're worth one hundred times that amount. I told him. I said they're worth one hundred times that amount...but if I'd sold them then I wouldn't have...no but that was an illusion, you see. Another one of Murphy's tricks. I nearly had him, love,' said Hughey, looking up at his wife now like a terrified child. 'I nearly undid it all. I nearly made it all ok.'

Mrs. Harris opened the garden gate, knelt down before Hughey and slowly unwrapped his fingers, digit by digit, from the knife.

She rose, walked slowly back up the garden path and into the house. Once inside Mrs. Harris abandoned all pretence of calm and sprinted up the stairs into the bathroom. She pulled the cistern lid off the toilet and hid the dagger within. Now she began to shake and stifled yelps began to escape her chest.

'No, no...' she said with increasing conviction, gripping the sides of the sink with both hands and staring hard into the mirror.

She couldn't join him. She didn't have the luxury of letting go because that would be the end. For the sake of them both, she denied herself the gentle ease of disintegration, but she'd also refuse Hughey the comfort of lies.

I'll be damned if I'm doing this a third time, thought Mrs. Harris, doubting she even had the strength to pull Hughey out of madness for a second time. He has to accept it all now. He has to hit the absolute bottom and fight his way back up under the full weight of the truth.

Mrs. Harris descended the stairs, inhaling deep with every step and emptying her lungs before stepping again. She fixed her mind on one thing and one thing only – the wounding words, which could kill her husband, but still needed to be said.

Hughey had not moved from his cross-legged position on the pavement. A minibus reversed up the street at over thirty miles an hour, blasting deep drum and bass, but Hughey rocked back and forth, oblivious.

'All in Murphy's pay, you see. Actors each and everyone,' continued the magician, performing card tricks with a compulsive frigidity.

Mrs. Harris knelt down and took Hughey's face between her hands. She kissed him on both eyes and smiled a heavy goodbye. She didn't know how long he'd be gone, but that he'd depart she was absolutely sure.

'Hughey, love...We've done this before haven't we?' she said beginning to cry, 'Well we're here again and I'm going to try and drag you out of it, but I'll have to be cruel. I'll have to be harsh. I'll have to be real enough for the both of us.'

'...it's easily done you see. A trick as old as the hills. I could probably teach you to do it in an evening sure...'

'Joseph is dead,' said Mrs. Harris, forcing Hughey to look her in the face by yanking the hair on the back of his head.

'His Mam called from the hospital. He's dead.... Do you hear me? Joseph is dead. He's dead. He's dead. He's dead...'

Mrs. Harris repeated the fact without mercy, each time jerking back Hughey's head and each time growing louder. Hughey diminished with every iteration and soon hung flaccid before her. Only then did Mrs. Harris rest.

She rose to her feet, took Hughey's hand and led him into the living room like a sleepwalking child.

And in that sleep Hughey remained, staring blankly at the television screen as the afternoon sunset of a Dublin winter began. With the bright sunshine of a cloudless day giving way to the bitter cold of a clear night, everyone made for the shelter of four walls. They did not, however, fall into their normal arrangements. A type of nervousness, which nobody really acknowledged, drove people to pay unexpected visits to neighbours or relations, which were in turn received with a strange relief. Men who only drank as occasion demanded suddenly turned up in pubs and were greeted like regulars. The events of the day, events that only happened in places like Egypt or Tunisia or Libya, had forced people out in search of normality. They wanted confirmation that nothing had really changed. Their cause was of course self-defeating. For how could Mrs. Tracy feel normal when Mrs. Cleary, whom Mrs. Tracy hadn't seen in eighteen months, was nattering superciliously and nibbling biscuits Mrs. Tracy feared had gone off months ago? How could Mr. Murray laugh off the day's events as nonsense when he was drinking in a pub he never frequented surrounded by men he normally avoided? No, the search for normality was having the exact opposite effect. Strange rumours, casually invented in sitting rooms, were transported to pubs via husbands tired of gossiping wives and resurfaced all the way across town thanks to sons and daughters giddy for change. By the time Taoiseach Heffernan appeared on the evening news, the minds of the entire nation were buzzing with conspiracy.

As the leader of nation began his address, layers of make-up doing nothing to hide his scarlet jowls, the eyes of every citizen turned to their television screens.

'People of Ireland,' began Heffernan, voice crackling behind layers of mucus he was forced to clear from his throat before continuing, 'Uh, hm! Right. Well as by now you are all aware at approximately nine o'clock this morning a group of terrorists seized control of several buildings around Dublin city. An Gardai Siochana responded to what they believed to be a civilian protest and were fired upon. In the ensuing fighting, many of these brave men were shot and killed. Our thoughts, first and foremost, are with the families of these brave defenders of the nation through whose efforts these terrorists were captured and defeated.

I know you must all be asking yourself, as I am – Why? Why would fellow Irish men and women attack the nation which the blood of many a patriot won for us all those years ago? Is this the thanks that O'Leary and Pearse and DeVelera deserve for winning our freedom? Is mother Eire...'

As the old clichés and rallying calls began, people turned down the volume or changed the channel altogether. They'd only granted Heffernan their ears to confirm what they already knew – the men in charge had even less idea what was going on than they did.

The rumours got more fevered now. ATMs, which had been bled dry by jittery account holders, stopped dispensing cash and led to reports of bank collapses. Copycat insurrections were being reported in Arklow, Mote and Ballyfarnon. The armed forces had apparently split into two warring camps, and the high-security prison in Clondalkin had spilt all kinds of crazed lunatics onto the streets of Dublin.

There was shouting, jostling, panicked phone calls, looting and record sales of flights on Ryanair.com, but all this settled down when an event far more important than the disintegration of society began, i.e., the finale of *X-Factor*.

Mrs. Harris set down her tea as the show began. She glanced at Hughey, slumped, head on chin, in the armchair, and turned up the volume. The presenter, a woman tailor-made to complement the arm of any professional footballer, made the usual hyperbolic introductions before Raymondo and Jesinta bounced onto the screen.

Raymondo sported platform Dock Martins, tight brown pants, suspenders, a shirt buttoned tight to his neck and a six-inch blonde quiff. Jesinta appeared to have half a haircut – left eye completely hidden by red hair and right ear surrounded by nothing but stubble. Her green dress was similarly cut, going from mini-skirt on the right to ankle-length dress on the left.

Mrs. Harris waited for the high-octane beats and frantic dance moves to begin, but instead a gentle rhythm, devoid of electronic force, emerged from a shadowy figure seated on a stool at the rear of the stage. Still the audience awaited the pyrotechnic takeoff, suspecting this to be a cunning ruse that would inevitably give way to synthesizers, distorted bass and auto-tuned vocals. Instead the drum began changing tone and pitch and those wild enough to draw such conclusions attributed the sound to a bodhrán. The camera cut to the judges, who exchanged looks of derision and mockery. Now it swung around to the crowd who, attributing this freakish sound to some technical fault, began booing.

The appearance of fiddle and flute players (stage left and right respectively) transformed the boos into gasps of amazement. This was no error. The high-octane, hammer-n-thongs, tits-and-cock pop act were attempting a ballad. And not just a Boyzone, Westlife, bums on stools, arms spread wide-type ballad, but a full-on i-dilli-o traditional ballad complete with fiddles and all.

The entire country grinned and sat back to enjoy the car crash. For although seeing one of our number succeed is something we enjoy, seeing the confident fail, thus revealing themselves to be no better then the rest of us, is something we enjoy a little more.

Jesinta's right leg glistened under the gently throbbing lights and the long dress covering the left leg added an additional element of the voyeur. Her proud neckline was also on display – the shaved right-hand side of her head negating the possibility of hair obscuring the view. Raymondo stood square with a thumb hooked under his suspenders and a cheeky grin on his face. They stared into each other's eyes and began the ballad, swapping vocals on alternate lines.

'She was the queen of the Steven's Green Mall,' began Raymondo with a wink.
'*He had a job in the department store*,' replied Jesinta.
'She strode through the crowd so proud and so tall,
When it comes down to shoes a girl always needs more.
I put serving her always just down the chance—
Credit card bills nearly scuppered my plans.
I slipped on her shoe she asked me to dance
So Beny became Kathy Ni Houlihan's man.

We arrive like stars in Lillie's Bordello.
He asked for Guinness but I ordered champagne.
Her dance drew the eyes of every fellow,

From a quick little kiss I couldn't refrain.
On Grafton St. I gave her my coat.
I knew I should but I didn't go home.
A busker sang a song we knew note for note,
I said I couldn't, but he still brought me home.

That night it seemed to last forever,
A night we seemed to steal from time.
And then we fell asleep together,
I heard the morning bells begin to chime,
Dreams filled with boats and holidays,
I washed and dressed before he woke,
The world upon a silver tray,
Night talk of love now seemed a joke.
I awoke to find upon her pillow...
Nothing but strands of hair turned grey.'

Now Raymondo strode forwards to the centre of stage. Jesinta turned to display her opposite profile. The short skirt became a long ankle length dress. The punky shaved hair gave way to a cascade of shoulder length red curls. The proud neckline was hidden from view and the young pop star, hunching slightly forwards, seemed to age thirty years in one turn.

With tears falling down his cheek and eyes passionately closed, Raymondo brought the song to a crescendo.

'I searched for her each and every day,
But found nothing but strands of hair turned grey.
Now up forty thousand feet flying to the USA,
I've nothing but strands of her hair turned grey.
While dark in a cell Benjamin Murphy
Still kisses the strands of her hair turned grey,
Yes the prophet of the Church of Jessie
Still worships the strands of her hair turned grey.'

'Free Benjamin Murphy! Long live the Second Irish Republic,' shouted Raymondo as the song ended.

There was silence. The audience did not clap or boo or cheer or whistle. In sitting rooms across the country people stared at screens with intense concentration. In pubs pints were set down and all necks craned towards the television. They had come out looking for assurance that the world had not changed. They wanted to see Father Sheeran codging pints left, right and centre. They wanted to hear neighbours moaning about water rates. They wanted to hear the Taoiseach babble inarticulately about things he'd no clue of. They wanted to look around the world, recognise the old problems and accept them, but only if they were the same problems; only if they fit like an old shoe. Brainless pop stars suddenly turning into politically conscious balladeers did not fit like an old shoe. In fact it did not fit at all, and there was a blister coming; a blister that was gonna have to pop.

Pink Flamingo Soup

Chapter 6

I've seen some things in my time that would turn the legs of Our Lady's statue to jelly. The mess that train made of Julie Sweeney isn't even the start of it. In the midst of a tempest, I saw Pio Tearnan decapitated by a snapped mast – eyes blinking as he bobbed off towards the jagged rocks of Inishmore. Worse still, I once saw Kieran Divilly round four players, sell the keeper a dummy, score a screamer of a goal and then collapse with a hurly dissecting his skull. Worse again, in the Congo I saw a young negro rolling cigarettes with pages torn from rare editions of Boccaccio and Chaucer. I've seen all these things, but nothing gave me a cold chill like stepping onto the weighing scales in Pearse St. Garda Station.

'Ninety-seven kilos!' shouted the police officer, confirming my suspicion that stress had reduced my robust frame to nothing more than skin and bones.

'One hundred and sixty-five centimetres,' answered Captain O'Reilly, personally overseeing preparations for our hangings.

We were each weighed in turn and then treated to the sight of our ropes being measured and cut. The swines even slipped the nooses over our heads to insure no anatomical oddity would delay our demise. There would be no John Babbacombe Lee miracles here. The gallows had been constructed with fastidious attention to detail, thus ruling out any hope of trapdoor malfunctions, and Captain O'Reilly's meticulous adherence to the Table of Drops ruled out any hope of a half-hanging.

In that mucky yard, the size of a decent county GAA pitch, surrounded on all sides by high stone walls, staring at the lengths of rope that would snap our necks, I actually found myself thankful that modern advances in hanging would avoid decapitation and allow us decent burials.

'Any last requests, lads?' said Captain O'Reilly, holding a hangman's hood.

My comrades made the usual requests – smokes, whiskey, phone calls or (in the case of those really getting into the role of the martyr) notes to be delivered to lovers. As Dr. Murphy groaned, eyeballs rolling in the back of his head, I requested one final prayer with the sacred book of Jessie.

'Out of the question, Corporal. The Taoiseach has given direct orders regarding that translucent volume,' said Captain O'Reilly.

'This is still the First Irish Republic, isn't it?' I said.

'You're damn right it is, Corporal. The first and might I add ONLY Irish Republic,' snorted the captain.

'Well then, my right to religious freedom and conscience is guaranteed under the constitution,' I argued.

'The constitution has been suspended by the Taoiseach, and I'm under direct orders not to give you the book, Corporal,' said the captain, dusting his hands.

'Under what authority can Heffernan order the leader of the armed forces to do anything if the powers vested in him by the constitution have been suspended?' I said.

'It's a fine point well made, Corporal, but you are still not getting the book,' said the captain with a childish petulance.

'You're willing to break the constitution for a fecking promotion?' I mocked.

'How dare you!' screamed the captain. 'How bloody dare you!...If you had studied the constitution more carefully, corporal, you'd realise the state reserves the right to suppress the right to religious expression if it threatens public safety.'

'Public safety, my hole. Tell me this, Captain: Does the Senators' pension plan come with a replacement soul?' I said, before receiving a viscous backhand to the face.

This violation of the Geneva Conventions drew gasps of amazement from the soldiers. The very man who forced them to endure fortnightly lectures and bi-quarterly workshops on the proper implementation of the Geneva Conventions was now openly striking a prisoner. Captain O'Reilly, seeing his men exchange glances and mutter admonishments, bent forwards to deliver his words to my ear alone.

'I was going to hang you first, Corporal, for old times' sake, but I can see you need a lesson in respect. I'm going to let you watch each and every one of these blaggards swing by his neck before you join them,' whispered the captain with serpentine venom.

172

'String them up!' ordered Captain O'Reilly, striding towards the gallows.

The captain waited at the trapdoor lever, full military parade dress rendering the hangman's hood redundant.

The Unemployed Historian's Alliance, eager to join the figures they'd spent their entire lives studying, volunteered to be hung first. The constant stream of abuse the PWLA dished out to the soldiers saw them elevated into second place. Next came the Distributed Bankers Committee, the Stage Actors Guild, the poets, the musicians and finally the IRB Executive Council.

Dr. Powers, as president of the UHA, was first to step upon the trap door. With pride he declined the priest's offer of a last confession and declared himself to be a son of Jessie. Behind his conjoined hair, eyebrows and beard, Dr. Powers' eyes hardened in determination.

'For crimes of treason against the state you've been sentenced to hang until dead. May God have mercy on your soul,' said Captain O'Reilly, placing a hand on the lever.

'FREEDOM!' screamed Dr. Powers before the trapdoor opened and he plummeted down towards the mucky remains of yesterday's snow.

His neck snapped loud and clear in the winter air and sent a shudder through us all. This moment of mourning was, however, robbed of its appropriate sobriety as our brains began to process the farcical nature of Dr. Powers' final words. Dr. Gerard Trimble Powers, PhD, scholar of early Irish history, founder of the Unemployed Historians Alliance, sworn enemy of photography, films, blogs and social networking, had chosen to quote a Hollywood film riddled with historical inaccuracies at his moment of departure. His fellow historians and academic rivals, like children at Sunday mass, stifled fits of giggles. It was all the poor gobshites could do to stop laughing, and they took the noose around their necks with a look of relief.

'FREEDOM!' screamed each and every one, setting off a bought of hysterics, before the trap door opened and freed them from the cruel torture of stifled laughter.

If Dr. Powers' death had been perversely comic, then Ms. Lawler's was simply perverse.

She strode onto the gallows dressed in slippers, pyjamas and dressing gown. The noose was barely visible in the mess of curls sprouting from her head.

'I'll go out the way I came in,' said Ms. Lawler as Captain O'Reilly read the sentence.

Despite having her hands bound behind her back and a noose around her neck she still managed, by some feets worthy of Harry Houdini, to shed her clothes as the trapdoor opened.

Down she shot, sending her pendulous breasts up to slap her in the face. Having gained freedom, the colossal mammary glands would not be halted – up and down they bounced, striking the knees and then the face in a perpetual motion. Above the muck of the yard, Ms. Lawler's sagging flesh swung. Veins bulged in her hefty thighs and a quaint mole the shape of County Donegal throbbed on her stomach. I was on the verge of erotic thoughts, but was saved when Ms. Lawler's bowels emptied down the inside of her legs.

Needless to say, the other members of the PWLA followed suit, and when the soldiers began to wretch Captain O'Reilly was forced to intervene. The PWLA's ankles, wrists and waists were wrapped tight in masking tape, thus rendering the doffing of nightwear an impossibility.

Things proceeded at pace now, each snapping neck sending a shudder through our ever-diminishing ranks.

As the first musician stepped onto the gallows, he began to sing. The aching melancholy of the anthem began to stir our souls. The song now had an irresistible poignancy, given the end our beautiful ideals had met, and I'm not ashamed to admit it... there wasn't a dry eye amongst us.

'For treason, you're hanging. God bless,' said Captain O'Reilly, hurrying to choke the dirge of the doomed.

Down went Tadgh Cooke, but his voice was not lost from our choir. As he swung over the slush and muck, surrounded by stone walls, feet twitching in his death throes, his voice still sung the lines of our anthem. It came from far above in the night air; gentle and distant, but distinct and clear. We raised our voices to the heavens, and in reply the departing spirit of Mr. Cooke raised his.

The soldiers began to exchange nervous looks; omens being harder to dismiss when your job consists of the binary states – kill or be killed. Even Captain O'Reilly was given momentary pause before thoughts of his senators' pension plan drove him on.

'Get them up here!' shouted O'Reilly.

The captain dispensed with formalities now, pulling the lever as soon as the noose was fastened around the jugular.

G. Hansard followed D. Rice followed C. Davey followed D. Dempsey, but still our chorus could not be diminished. Instead, our anthem seemed to be approaching from all directions. Every soul set free drew a legion of angels to their aid. The song was so loud now that Captain O'Reilly was reduced to hand signals.

It became obvious in the second verse that the soldiers were being deeply affected by this musical phenomenon. It was not that they ceased to follow orders, but their actions lost the gusto of men who believed in their work. What could Captain O'Reilly expect after embarking on the largest musical education program ever attempted in modern military history? His reasoning had been sound at the time: well-exercised aural organs reduce the probability of hearing impairments, thus banishing the scourge of deafness from the Irish Army forever. How could the captain have foreseen these men of Aries being moved to mutiny by the sheer beauty of a rebel ballad sung from the heavens.

'I searched for her each and every day,
But found nothing but strands of her hair turned grey...'

The anthem began its climax as Dr. Murphy was lifted from his wheelchair onto the gallows. At the sight of the noose tightening around the great man's neck, our song took on the aspect of a plea. If Jessie could add legions of angels to our choir, could he not then lift his prophet from harm? Could he not snap the rope? Could he not smite our executioners down with terrible vengeance? Oh the childish accusations I levelled at divine providence. What philosophical naivety. What foolish doubts.

'Dark in a cell Benjamin Murphy
Still kisses the strands of her hair turned grey...'

Hearing our leader's name on the lips of heaven stopped Captain O'Reilly's men in their tracks. The captain, unable to be heard over the glorious chorus, made threats with clenched fists and bulging eyes that his diminutive stature rendered ridiculous. The soldier charged with placing Dr. Murphy on the trapdoor turned his back on the captain, added a beautiful harmony to the chorus and began removing the noose. The captain drew his side arm and began climbing onto the gallows to deliver a bit of smacht.

As the captain gained the platform, an almighty racket began at the yard gate. Rapid blows of various degrees of strength were raining down upon the wooden structure, which began to bow and bend in the maelstrom of abuse.

With Captain O'Reilly's gun at his temple, the solider was a tad more willing to discharge his duties. The situation was quickly complicated, however, by the remaining soldiers (now singing in baritone, tenor and soprano) training their rifles on the captain. In a burst of inspiration, the captain saw a simple solution and placed the muzzle of the gun in Dr. Murphy's face.

'In a godless land the Church of Jessie
Still worships the strands of her hair turned grey...'

There was an unmerciful bang, and all heads, in all directions, ducked. The yard gate burst open and a flood of bodies spilled into the square. Old men on walking sticks, young girls in mini-skirts, businesswomen in power suits and spotty young fellas in Celtic jerseys quickly surrounded the gallows. Not even the residents of this degenerate metropolis could deny the sound of angels singing above. They had been spurred into action by the voice of God Himself. From small cottages nestled in the foothills of the Wicklow Mountains, from proud country estates lining the shores of Blessington Lake, from the rows of houses running along the rocky beaches of Bray and Greystones, from the narrow terraced streets of Booterstown and Sandymount and Irishtown, from the high rises of Ballymun and Clambassile Street, from the apartment blocks of Smithfields and Dundrum and Kilmanham, from each and every nook and cranny in this dirty old town they came. With Jessie in their hearts and destiny within their grasp they sang songs of deliverance. The future was theirs and they would not be denied.

'In a darkened cell Benjamin Murphy
Still kisses the strands of her hair turned grey!
In a godless land the Church of Jessie
Still worships the strands of her hair turned grey...'

On and on they sang, a look of complete serenity on each of their faces. The kind of look never seen amongst the hesitant. The kind of look never spotted amongst the unbelievers. The kind of look that is only seen when the avant-garde is aware that behind them on the streets, and beyond them in parks, and further out in the estates, and further still on the back roads and thoroughfares, there is a body of opinion raising its voice in such swelling number, that to be at the front is not to be some daring trailblazer, but rather the herald of an ineluctable wave.

They had gone out into the old pubs and the old churches in the old neighbourhoods of the old republic. They had gone out to find solace in the same old talk in the same old fashion. But they had found everything made a new. They had found themselves free. And now they were coming. They were all endlessly coming, and their will would not be denied.

Up on the gallows Captain O'Reilly kept his pistol against Dr. Murphy's head. The pension plan, chauffeur-driven car, expense account and tri-annual trips to Brussels were only a squeeze of the trigger away. I screamed for the soldiers to shoot, but they began adding heartbreaking harmonies to the chorus instead and the song was transmuted to the realms of the eternal and absolute. For true beauty is not subjective. Admittedly, some would swear they honestly believe the work of talentless fools like Ginsberg or McGough to be superior to that of Chaucer or Yeats, but the explanation for that is simple: those people are godless heretics. Their ears have been clogged with filth and they no longer hear the word of God. Beauty is nothing more than communication between souls at the level of the superconciousness. It is the breath of God Himself, and if someone cannot appreciate a true work of beauty it is because they are godless.

Luckily, O'Reilly had not sunken to that level. He may have been a lair, a thief and a murderer, but he was still a man of God. The beauty of the music, a manifestation of the Holy Spirit moving through us all, brought him back from the brink of damnation. He lowered his weapon, ordered that we be unchained and approached me with a smile on his face.

'Close call there, Corporal' shouted Captain O'Reilly, struggling to be heard over the intensity of Dublin City's choir of believers. 'I wasn't in touch with public opinion, you see. I didn't have access to all the facts. All's well that ends well though, eh Corporal? The constitution has been suspended, and the public clearly believe you are representative of their will,' he said, surveying his surroundings and blinking in amazement as our supporters, who, now unable to squeeze into the courtyard itself, began to form a human ladder and climb up onto the walls in order to secure a clearer view of their prophet and saviour: Dr. Benjamin Murphy. 'I stated my conditions at the outset. They have been met. ...I'm willing to hold up my end of the bargain if you're willing to hold up yours?' said Captain O'Reilly, awaiting a handshake to seal the deal and save his neck from the gallows.

I won't deny it, the image of his body swinging from a rope was very appealing. He had quashed some of our brightest lights: scholars, scribes, poets and minstrels, who, had they had lived, would've enriched the lives of every citizen of the Second Irish Republic. The snap of his neck would have been sweeter to the ear than Petrarch, but if we've learned anything from the troubles up North it's that the beast called revenge has an insatiable appetite. We could not allow a vicious spiral of attacks and reprisals to destabilize our young nation. Indeed, if we were to survive the threats from beyond our borders we would need to be absolutely united within their confines.

'Captain O'Reilly, head of the armed forces of the Second Irish Republic,' I said, shaking O'Reilly's hand, 'now we'll be needing the Book of Jessie, Captain.'

The book was fetched, and I climbed onto the gallows where Dr. Benjamin Murphy waited in his wheelchair. I knelt on one knee before the pioneering librarian, prophet of Jessie, leader of the world's first immaterialistic revolution, and laid the translucent volume in his lap. The great man began shaking. A murmur went through the crowd, his lips tore away a seal of dried spittle, and mucus poured from his olfactory organ. Not a breath was taken from Pearse St. to the Phoenix Park, though beyond them in the mountains and high up in the heavens the chorus of angels continued to sing, and as their voices soared, Dr. Murphy's eyes snapped open and sent a shower of yellow pus across the expectant crowd.

The great man arose slowly and surveyed the waiting crowd with a benevolent smile. His breath steadied. The limpid whistle of his nose silenced the entire audience, and every inhalation seemed to pull the souls of his followers into the sanctuary of his bosom. With arms outstretched and palms facing towards a legion of angels still singing from the heavens, Dr. Murphy began a speech which would echo through the souls of Irishmen forever more.

'My children, today we are victorious,' said the great man, summoning a roar of approval from those lucky hundreds within the courtyard walls. But the truth, the sheer glory of the words rolling forth from this man so potent with prophecy, could not be contained by bricks and mortar assembled by human hands. No, these words could transcend every obstacle and be delivered to all of those with Jessie in their hearts. Over the wall and down the alleyways and across the fields and above the mountains the young, the old, the rich, the poor, the believers and the unbelievers all heard the words of Jessie and could not but confirm their truth. They raised their voices in affirmation, and the very soil of Eire awoke to the dawning of a new age.

Dr. Murphy awaited silence and his will and the will of Jessie were communicated throughout the country and silence descended upon the flock.

'Yes my children, tonight Jessie's will was done, but this victory is merely a beginning. We have won nothing but the chance to plot our course. We have gained nothing but the opportunity to question our direction. ...So let us not shy away from these hard questions,' he added in sober tones.

'I ask you, how can an idea be anything but an idea? What is our nation but a collective thought? Therefore, let our nation be thoughts of beauty. We will ban banality. We will assemble armies of authors. We will export poets. We will float music on the stock exchange. We will paint masterpieces upon the concrete streets. We will perform plays at the United Nations. We will create sculptures in the rubbish heaps and wines in the sewers.

'And how will we do these things, you ask? And I answer, how can an idea be anything but an idea? You are the people. You are the dreamers. You are the nation, you are the tools and you are the way. How can a nation be anything but its people? At the dawning of the Second Republic, one nation under Jessie, I tell you all that you're finally free. You are free to dream and make this nation a thing worthy of dreams. So dream, dream, dream, dream...' said Dr. Murphy, rising in intensity, gazing towards Jessie above and leading his followers as they began to chant along with their leader.

How to describe that moment? The moment all worries and fears were abated. The moment all hopes and dreams were fulfilled.

All the superlatives in the all the languages of all the world could not do it justice. The pains of the past had gained us a perfect future—is that not heaven?

Peter Smash – The Truth

Chapter 1

I swore I'd never do it again. I swore I'd never sit down and read, let alone write, a load of bleedin waffle. If you'd grown up in the dark days of the Second Irish Republic, you'd understand. If you'd attended Jessholic School you'd snap every pen and burn every book that crossed your path. What am I at, then? Why am I dictating this shite to my ghostwriter Jonathan sitting over there in the corner with his girly little laptop? Why am I about to spend day after day telling that poncey blondey-headed dipshit my life story and watching him type down my words like a fucking robot. ...That's right, Jonathan, you're a cunt. Put that down in black and white seeing as you write so good [sic].

    Anyway, why am I doing it? Were the years of composing odes to Ashen Hurls and receiving beatings from Jimbo James not enough? Well they were, but me agent tells me you lot are willing to pay top dollar for my story of adversity skinned, impossible odds nutmegged and all that Hollywood horseshit. Well fine. Give the people what they want, I say. It's simple supply and demand. If you want to waste your bleedin time reading about how I made it to the top instead of busting your balls to get there yourself, then that's fine by me. It's one less moron for me to beat back into place. Just don't expect any trip-hop Joycean, new-wave Beckettonian or post-isotonic Yeatsian crap here. Yeah, Ireland may have won the Nobel Prize for literature seven years in a row, but try getting your toilet plumbed or your door hung or your carpet laid during those years. It's all very well for some professor in France or Italy or New Abyssinia to praise the results of the Second Republic's education system – they weren't neck-deep in refuse because the bin men were too busy composing poems using words cut randomly from magazines, newspapers and breakfast cereal boxes. So again, if you've picked up this book expecting an Irish sports star to write his autobiography in the style of Modern Irish Literature, I'll be forced to insist, once again, that you fuck right off.

    This story will start at the start and end at the end. Everything in between will be cold hard truth. I'll list everything that happened and describe exactly how it happened. And if that poncey little dipshit in the corner doesn't type what I say, exactly how I say it, then I'll brain him.

You hear me, Jonathan?

Good.

So again, if you've picked up this book expecting symbolism, methadones [sic], philosophical moralising or Berkelian consumerism [sic], then fuck off. Grand, that's all settled then— the start it is...

I was born on Christmas Eve in the year zero. The Second Republic was exactly one day old and already the whole shoot and shebang was going to shite. The airports were jammed with stock market traders, businessmen, photographers, music producers, movie directors, doctors and nurses. The last two being fairly important when you're trying to get born. For forty-eight hours, I tried to force me head out, each hour halving the number of doctors in the hospital. Long story short, me Da was forced to reach for the callipers himself. I was a slippery fucker even then and it took all me Da's strength (which isn't a lot, mind) to reef me out. For my entire career there have been rumours about the two scars on my temples. I've heard everything from brain transplants to electric shock treatment. ...Well here's the truth: the scars are from me Da pulling me out me Ma's gash with a pair of pliers.

Me Da said I left me Ma's privates looking like the entrance to Dante's Inferno. Dante's what? Well, don't worry about it. If you're lucky enough to have never learned volumes of medieval poetry by heart, then count your blessings. The point is I left me Ma's privates looking like the entrance to hell – something me Da (James W.R. Smash) loves to repeat when trying to prove I'm the spawn of Satan.

So me Ma died. I suppose you expect a list of attributes now. You expect me to say she was a lighter in the wind; a dandelion in a field of weeds; a tender-hearted angel with a singing voice that brought tears to parties in the park when we laid out a picnic and me aunts and uncles had a skin full of Chardonnay and me and me cousins were high on sugary drinks and warm summer air...but I won't. This book is called The Truth and the truth is I know only one thing about me mother for sure: she was a woman. She could have been Mother Theresa or she could have been an old cunt. Odds are that she was just that—who else would marry me Da but an old cunt? Whatever the case may be, it makes no difference to me. Her presence in my life consisted of a grey headstone in a rainy graveyard, which is about as much presence as a chair, except a chair is of more use.

Right, that brings us to the years before school. Again I have no proper memories of that time except for bits of crap all jumbled up in me head. Well, you paid good money for this shit so I suppose I'd better get Jonathan to write it down with his beautiful manicured girl's fingers...and if he grins at me again I'll put me [sic] size elevens up his Swissroll. That's right, blondey, keep your fucking eyes on the screen.

Anyway... I remember my big blue teddy bear, the smell of my pillow, the fluff under the bed and plumes of smoke unfurling from me Da's lips. I remember my cot and the bars that kept me captive at night. Yeah, even then I hated sleeping. How do I know I hated sleeping? I know because I did as little of it as possible. How do I know I did as little of it as possible? I know because it's one of the many pieces of evidence me Da presents when trying to prove I'm the spawn of Satan. He of course slept half the bleedin day away, woke up and then smoked himself into another sleep while playing the poxy Sitar. I must have known even then that he was a waster because everything he done I done the opposite. I never lay there in the dark all helpless and vulnerable. Nah, I kept one eye and both ears open and only then for a couple of hours. Then I'd start screaming to be let out of my cot.

Me Da claims he tried for six months to lull me to sleep. He claims he played his entire catalogue of Indian lullabies and only stopped when I started throwing the contents of my nappy at the sitar. He's lying through his teeth, of course. He probably had the industrial earmuffs on from the first yelp. But as I would do again and again, I turned adversity into opportunity. The bars of my cot were my first obstacle, and they wrecked me head for a long time.

I'll list my attempted solutions in order:
1) On discovering that my legs and arms fitted between the bars I tried squeezing myself in various positions (ass first, shoulder first, folded in half) out the bars. No matter what brilliant feats of stretching and bending I achieved it all came to nothing because of the size of me head. Yeah I'd had a

huge head on me back then—the first of many indications that I was gonna be a big strong fucker when I was older. That was little consolation to me at the time though and I spent manys a night suspended in midair – legs, arms and torso outside the cot – head stuck between the cot bars.

2) Me Da, cheapskate waster that he was, had bought me the cheapest bedding money could buy, and one night, probably driven mad with frustration by the size of me head, I began chewing my bedding. After a few hours of this I sat up to have another whack at squeezing meself out the bars and discovered I'd chewed a small hole in me bedding. This gave birth to me second tactic: tunnelling. Night after night I worked on that hole, hiding the bits of bedding in my pillowcase or occasionally swallowing a piece when hunger got the better of me. I never tired of the work. In fact, I enjoyed it. When you're teething the need to chew is uncontrollable. Even at that age I was quick to accept the way things were and make them work to my advantage. Me spatial relations weren't the best at fourteen months, but after a few weeks I was sure I must be on the verge of a breakthrough. Soon I'd be free of these bars. Soon I'd be free to run (or at least toddle). I remember breaking through the bedding like it was yesterday. I remember that first taste of victory and the devastation when it was snatched away. I'd made it through the bedding all right, but who was to know that there were solid wooden planks underneath? It was a hard lesson, but one I never forgot. If something is worth doing, it's hard to do.

3) I'd failed to go through the bars. I'd failed to go under the bars. So I now tried to go over the bars. Now I know what you're thinking – a fourteen-month-old baby couldn't possibly generate enough power in his quadriceps to clear a bar set at one-and-a-half times his own body height. Well of course he couldn't, but try telling a fourteen-month-old boy that. Night after night I leapt, gaining a millimetre here and a tenth of a centimetre there. In the afternoon, when me waster Da eventually got out of the leaba, I continued doing squats, burpees and lair walks – an early hint of the kind of discipline I'd bring to me training in later life. After weeks of

184

leaping, I was now able to smash me head into the railing at the top of the cot bars.

You better take that smirk off your face fairly sharpish, Jonathan, before I come over there and put some manners on ye. Dats [sic] righ [sic] bury dat [sic] stupid blondey head under your girly little laptop.
You reckon a fourteen-month-old child is incapable of generating that kind of power in his gluts? Well, if you'd been force-fed O'Nolan, O'Brien and na gCopaleen in Jessholic School then you'd know all about the jumping Irishman. Africans can run, Welsh can sing, Canadians can slide strange circular stones across the ice and Irishmen can jump. FACT
3) [continued].... So as I was saying, owing to a scientifically provable genetic advantage, I was jumping to such a height that my big head was slapping into the railing on the top of the cot bars. I was sure I'd be leaping clear over the thing in a week. It seemed a simple enough equation. X amount of training got Y amount of height therefore 2X amount of training would get me 2Y amount of height. Despite increasing my daily routine of squats, burpees and lair walks I was shocked to find progress actually slowing. Jesus, the hard lessons I learned in that cot! While other kids were gooing and gaaing and laughing at moons and stars hanging from strings, I was learning about the law of diminishing returns. I was learning that the work needed to go from third to first is far bigger than the work needed to go from last to third. So yeah there I was eking out a millimetre here and a tenth of a centimetre there and starting to lose all hope when lady luck shone down on me.
It had been a long night of jumping and I'd gotten no closer. Me forehead was throbbing from slapping it off the railing so I decided to give it a little rest by leaping backwards. I gave a little run from the back of the cot, jumped, turned in midair and slammed the back of me head into the railing. I crashed back into the cot, but realised my cot was now rocking from side to side. At fifteen months I'd no idea of leverage. I hadn't the foggiest notion of forces being more powerful when exerted at greater distances from the fulcrum. That said even a fifteen-month-old lad can suffer from boredom. My forward leap had brought me nothing but a sore head. At least this new backward technique was adding a little rocking and rolling into

the mix. I gave the second leap some serious gusto, hoping to enjoy a good bit of rocking when I landed. The back of me head slapped into the railing. I waited to fall back into the cot, but soon realised the cot was falling too. We both crashed down onto the bedroom floor, and I was free. Free to roam around me bedroom till me Da appeared in the afternoon.

    I suppose you expect a list of feelings now. You want me to talk about the joy of victory. Rewards following hard work. Contentment. You'd love me to describe happy nights playing with my building blocks and big blue teddy bear. Well that's exactly why you're a loser. You're only interested in the rewards. You're only interested in what comes after. Winners, people like me, don't care about after. We care about achieving what we set out to achieve and the moment it's achieved we're thinking about achieving something better. Why? I'll tell you why – cause what you achieved in the past proves only one thing, i.e., what you could do in the past. It proves nothing about what you can do now. And if you're a winner proving what you can do now is all that matters.

    So yeah I got out of the cot and started immediately sizing up the door. It was a problem far more complicated then the cot. A problem I didn't get a proper crack at for a long time cause the Da tried everything his little stoner brain could think of to keep me locked up in the cot: meshing, hinged flaps, restraints and a half dozen other methods. It was a battle of wills and I wanted to be out of that cot far more than me waster Da wanted to think of new ways to keep me in it. I won't bore you with the details, but needless to say I overcame everything he put in my way.

    Around the time of my second birthday he finally gave up. My cousins had been over. We'd been thrown together in the sitting room to play, but within five minutes I'd given me six-year-old cousin a black eye for touching me dumper truck and was strapped into me high chair. I remember bobbing me head left and right to dodge spoons of cake and finally slamming my fists into my plate. Could me aunties leave it at that? No, of course they couldn't. Me Da may have been a good for nothing waste of space. He may have worn industrial earmuffs when I cried. He may have nailed a wooden door onto the top of me cot, but he never covered my face in spit. He never squeezed me cheeks. He never lifted me out of my chair and tried to smoother me against his chest. He never tried to rock me asleep where I'd be all unconscious with me eyes all closed and vulnerable and all. He was a good-for-nothing waster, but at least he never tried any of that craic.

So when me aunties started in with all that messing, I went bananas. I caught hold of one by the hair, another by the ear, and from this position aimed kicks at the other attackers. My months of leg training didn't let me down. I landed devastating blows to the eyes, lips and noses of me relations.

The party finished early. Me Da, me aunties and me uncles were crying and looking at me all sorry and all. Looking at me like they pitied me or something. Looking at me like I was the one who got battered.

'Poor Peter. Poor little baby Peter. If only his mother was here. His mother is all he needs to set him straight,' they were saying like there was something wrong with me.

I almost fell for it too. I almost fell for that classic loser tactic of making the winners feel guilty. I almost began to believe that winning had been wrong. Here I was all alone with everyone else pitying me. I was a loner. But why was I a loner? I was a loner because there can be only one winner. Even at age two, I knew it was better to be a loner than a loser.

So yeah the Da knew he was fecked. I'd battered me cousins, aunties, uncles and him all at the same time. He'd gone all in and been beaten. At least the waster knew when to quit. After a few days he abandoned the restraints and hinged doors and I was free to backwards leap onto the bedroom floor every night.

Now I could tackle the door. It was a solid wooden door, so squeezing was out of the question. Leaping was gonna get me nothing but a headache. So tunnelling seemed me only option. I scouted around the room and found that the floor in the far left-hand corner of the room screamed when I jumped on it. Every time I smashed me feet down onto it there was a little cry. The harder I kicked the louder the cry. I was hurting it. I was breaking it.

My days of leg training began again. Now I focused on generating downward instead of upward power. This needed a total overhaul of my training techniques. Instead of burpees, squats and lair walks, I undertook a gruelling regime of explosive kicks. I kicked chairs. I kicked tables. I kicked walls. I kicked my dinner. I kicked the TV. I kicked me Da and his sitar and his cup of coffee and his bag of chips. I kicked me aunties and uncles and cousins. I kicked everything, be it alive or dead, that came into kicking range.

So yeah night after night I rained a barrage of kicks down on the floor in the far left hand corner of me room. And every morning the Da arrived earlier and earlier to stop me. It got to the point that the fucker was getting up before midday. He stopped smoking joints. He even started going for a jog in the evening. The fucker was changing his entire lifestyle to try and keep me in me room at night.

Well if I was gonna have less time to kick the floor I'd have to come up with more powerful kicks. On me big blue teddy bear I slowly perfected a move; a move that generated such momentum; a move that generated such power; a move that could be thrown with such supernatural speed that it made me the sports star I am today. That's right... I invented the world-famous Peter Smash spinning-720 shin-cracker axe-kick at age 2 years, two months.

As it turned out, practising on a soft teddy bear and slamming your heal into solid wooden floorboards are two different things. Yet again I learned a valuable lesson. If you've missed something in training, competition will find it out and make you pay. I jumped, spun 720 degrees and slammed me foot down on the floor. The boards screamed like never before, but so did I. As a weird warm feeling spread across me foot I bit my lip and rested me head off the wall. The pained started throbbing, but I wouldn't cry. I wouldn't call for help. I wouldn't give that waster Da of mine the pleasure of seeing me foot all banjaxed.

As I caught me breath and calmed me heart I began to hear something on the other side of the wall. The other side of the wall where me waster Da slept with industrial earmuffs. It started low. For the first few minutes I thought it was just in me head. But over the course of ten minutes the noise built up to a faint but clear moan. Then suddenly it became a scream. Someone was being hurt. Me Da was hurting someone in his room. I started kicking at the floor like mad with me unbanjaxed foot. The screaming and moaning got so loud that I couldn't even hear the floor crying when I slammed me heel into it. Me waster Da had finally lost it. He was strangling someone in his room. I was next. Then with a heavy grunt the noise stopped.

I put me ear against the wall. The bed creaked. He was coming for me. I grabbed me plastic sword and crouched beside the bedroom door where I could spring a surprise attack.

Right, you little blondey-headed puff, put up your fists!
I don't care if you can't type with your hands up.
Yeah I know what I said.
Well there you go Jonathan you've managed to smirk yourself into a no-win situation haven't ya [sic]?
No more chances. So what will it be? Gonna give me a fight or what?
Suit yoursesfghjkop;'\456+\\\
Learned your lesson?
Good. Where was I?

Ah yeah. So you reckon it's obvious what was going to do, yeah? Well, I'm telling you the FACTS. I'm laying down the gospel truth here. And the truth is that even if I had known about the birds and the bees at age two years and two months I'd never have believed any women would go in for me Da. The man talked shite, looked like shite and smelt like shite. So yeah, even if I knew what riding was I never would have believed any women would give me Da a go.

So anyway, I woke up in me cot the next morning all panicked and sweating. How long had I been lying there all unconscious and vulnerable and all? Had I crawled back into the cot meself? And if so, how did I get it back up on its legs? No, me Da must've done it. Me shite-talking waster Da had picked me up and put me in the cot without as much as a kick in the bollix. The thought made me so angry, I got sick on me shoes.

After I'd finished emptying me guts I started screaming. I wasn't screaming for help. I was screaming out of pure rage. Rage at me cot. Rage at the door. Rage at the crying floorboards that I couldn't break. Rage at me broken foot. Rage at me Da picking me up and putting me back in my cot. ...But mostly rage at meself for having slept through two training sessions.

Me waster Da had picked me up and I'd done nothing. He could've brained me there and then, but he didn't. He knew what would hurt me most. He left me sleeping there all vulnerable and all, wasting the whole day away. I'd missed me early and late morning training sessions. I still had me afternoon and evening sessions, but if you know anything about physical conditioning then you'd know missing a session means two sessions are required just to get back to the level you were at before. That meant me whole day would be spent training for a level of power that still wouldn't be enough to break through the floorboards.

So yeah I screamed just to get rid of the frustration, but who comes running in? None other then the Da. As if that wasn't shock enough the shite-talking waster had done something to his hair. It was all facing in one direction like grass under a stone where all the creepy-crawlies live. He'd gotten rid of the dressing gown too. He was wearing a shirt and trousers and a tie. But there was something else. Something I couldn't put me finger on.

And then I saw it. An insect. On his lip. Long and brown. Getting ready to crawl up his nose. It had already eaten half his hairy face off. That's what the screaming and moaning had been. That's what lying around all unawares gets you. Killer creepy-crawlies are free to munch off half your face in the middle of the night.

As me Da came towards the cot I bolted, jumped, twisted in midair, slammed the back of me head off the railing and brought the whole shoot and sheebang down on his foot. One broken foot each evened the odds. As the Da hopped around the room cursing, I made for the far left corner of me room.

'For fuck sake, Peter, don't make a show a me, will ya?' muttered the Da, giving chase.

Before he could grab me I unleashed an unmerciful spinning-720 shin-cracker axe-kick on the floor.

Now, the adrenaline of competition, that now-or-never feeling, does give you that extra 0.0001 percent, but the FACT is it's 0.0001percent of what you've already got in the locker. If you're a hair's breath away in training then you'll do it on the day. I hadn't been a hair's breath away. The extra .0001percent wasn't enough.

The Da caught hold a me. I tried to kick meself free, but the Da had me against his chest. I couldn't get a good swing. Me teeth hadn't fully developed so biting didn't do the job. I punched and pushed and pulled but couldn't break free. Me training had all been leg work. I'd neglected me upper body. There I was aged two years, two months, convinced I was about to be eaten by a creepy crawly, all because I'd skipped push-ups, chin-ups and bicep curls. I'd learned a valuable lesson, but I'd learned it too late – you're only as strong as your weakest muscle.

Soon me undeveloped pectorals, biceps and lattisimus dorsis were exhausted and I hung limp against me Da's chest. When we got to the kitchen me eyes started going all cloudy. Me breathing went all choppy and I felt water running down me cheeks. What all this craic meant was beyond me, but I knew it couldn't be good. The creepy-crawlies must be near. I was gonna be eaten.

But I wasn't eaten. I was strapped into me high chair. The watery crap was still all over me eyes, but I could hear me waster Da waffling away to someone else. Someone female. Had me aunties been possessed by creepy-crawlies too? Were me cousins in the sitting room with centipedes crawling out of their eyes? Was me cousin Robert pushing my dumper truck around the sitting room with a caterpillar hanging from his nose? The thought of that gobshite touching my dumper truck made me so fucking angry that I shook the watery crap out of me eyes and started pulling at my restraints.

It was then that I saw her. She was sitting on a stool. Her legs were crossed. One shoe hung off her painted toes. One arm was crossed under her stomach pushing up her chest. Her wrist was cocked near her mouth, cradling a cigarette. Her lips were dark red. Her hair was long and blonde, but it was her eyes – blue and jade – that stopped me in me tracks. She was the most beautiful thing I'd ever seen.

'Well who's an angry little man this morning?' she said, smiling at me.

'Peter, this is Helen. Helen, this is my son Peter,' said me waster Da, walking towards me high chair.

I was so stunned, so completely flabbergasted, that me Da was able to come within kicking distance, plant saliva on my face and stand with his arm around me. In a state of shock I looked up and realised the killer creepy-crawly under me Da's nose was actually a strip of hair. Up until then I'd thought me Da's hairy face was just another one of his physical disabilities. When I realised he had actually chosen to look like a bleedin monkey, I went physco. The Da was forced to retreat to Helen's side as I kicked and punched in all directions.

'Oh, a very angry little man altogether,' said Helen smiling at me Da. 'Well I'm not much of a morning person either, Peter. In fact I'm barely human till I've had three cups of coffee and a pack of cigarettes. When you're old enough I'll introduce you to these little cures for the morning blues.'

Helen and me waster Da started planting saliva on each other's faces and smiling and laughing and all.

A few minutes ago I was sure I'd be eaten by creepy-crawlies. I was positive me lack of upper body training would be the death of me, but this craic, this gorgeous woman sitting in me kitchen necking with me waster Da... this was far more terrifying.

With me gob wide open I gawked from me Da to Helen to me Da and back to Helen.

'Hello gorgeous. H e l l o Peter. Say Helllllooo,' said Helen waving towards me.

'He doesn't talk yet,' said me Da, taking Helen's hand and stealing away her attention.

'But how old is he?' she asked with concern.

'Twenty-six months,' answered the Da.

'Hmmmmm.'

'Yeah, we're all very worried,' lied me waster Da. 'My sister in laws know a speech therapist up in Beaumont who's going to help us out.'

'Poor little fella,' said Helen turning her jade-blue eyes on me.

'Yeah, we've tried everything, but I think it's time for professional help,' sighed me Da.

Me waster Da was lying of course. He hadn't tried everything to make me speak. He'd tried everything HIS little stoner brain could think of. His first method was to pick one of me favourite toys, me dumper truck for example, and to point at it for hours repeating – truck, truck, truck, truck. Then he'd put the dumper truck somewhere I could see but couldn't reach. He'd just stand there waiting for me to ask for me truck. But I knew what the fucker was up to. I knew if I gave in even once I'd eventually be forced into talking twenty-four bleedin seven. I only had to look at the carry on of me cousins. Not only were they asking for food and water and toys and all, but the poor bastards were actually forced to look at books full of letters and numbers and all kinds of useless crap.

So yeah me Da stood there waiting for me to talk and I stood there waiting for him to need another joint. Needless to say I always won, and the second he pissed off to roll up I'd figure out some way to get me dumper truck back.

In fairness the Da's second tactic for making me talk was pretty clever for a stoner. He'd obviously seen me training four times a day. Sure you'd only to look at me bulging quadriceps to see the amount of protein I needed. Me diet at the time consisted of three food groups – eggs, dairy and as much red meat as I could get hold of. So what did the Da start putting in front of me? Porridge, pasta, vegetables, fruits, seeds, and all kinds of useless shite. Every afternoon I'd be strapped into my high chair and given a bowl of bleedin porridge while me Da tucked into sausages, rashers and eggs. The fucker knew exactly what I wanted, but he wouldn't give it to me until I asked.

Dinner was the same craic. I'd be given mushed up potatoes with cauliflower, broccoli, carrots and peas while the Da cut into a steak. The fucker would catch me staring from my high chair, muscles wasting away on me legs, and point at his slab of beef saying – steak, steak, steak, steak.

I don't know how long that went on for, but I do know that I kept training. Me muscles weren't growing, but I was losing weight. The increase in my power to weight ratio meant I kept making progress in me jumping. This led to me tactic of fasting, a tactic that eventually led to me passing out in one of me gruelling early morning training sessions.

The Da may have been a shite-talking waster, but even he knew that a two-year-old child dying from starvation was bad news. The Second Republic believed teachers who said they couldn't come to work cause they'd tapped into the poetic superconsciousness and needed to stay home to write their opus. They entertained you swearing green was pink or that mayonnaise sometimes tasted like watermelon, but not even those pack of lunatics would believe a two-year old starved himself to death trying to get a better power-to-weight ratio in his jumping technique. The aul fella would've been pedalling his piece in Dun Laoghaire Power Prison for the rest of his days.

So yeah, I eventually got the grub I wanted and never had to speak a word. They wouldn't be wasting my time with waffling and reading and all. I'd train and eat and that'd be it.

But when Helen, with those big gorgeous eyes, started talking to me something funny happened. It was like her words...in me heart...Jessie, how do I explain it? It was like her voice was... no, that's not it. Fuck how do I describe it now?

What's that, Blondie?
No, I won't slap ya, you fucking pussy.
I promise. Come on, say it again.
Well fuck me sideways, Jonathan! You've actually decided to be of some fucking use, have ya? Butterflies in my heart— that's bleedin great, that is.

Right where was I? Ah yeah, Helen started talking to me.
'Well don't you worry little man. There's no need to be rushing. You take your time and speak when you're good and ready,' said Helen and it was like heavenly music spilled from her lips and the butterflies in my heart began to dance.
'Thank you, Helen,' I replied with a smile.
Me Da spat his coffee across the kitchen table and started staring me down. I suppose Helen thought me Da was staring out of surprise. She thought it was a look of loving wonder. I know it was a look of hate. The hate losers have for winners.

He now knew what he'd only suspected before – that I was refusing to talk because HE wanted me to talk.
'Well that's one worry off the list, then,' laughed Helen, kissing me Da's shaven face.

The Da broke eye contact first. He couldn't even beat me at that. He looked up at Helen and that watery crap that had blinded me earlier started rolling down his cheeks.
'Thank you,' he said to Helen, pretending to be all grateful and all.

Helen and the Da started putting saliva on each other's faces again and hugging and laughing and all. It was a horrible sight. I thought they were never gonna give it up.

'Well would you look at us forgetting the real star of the show! Doesn't Peter deserve a kiss for his hard work?' said Helen, breaking free of me Da.

She began walking towards me high chair. It was a walk I'd never seen before. Me aunties all fecked one foot in front of the other. They all just plodded along in their slippers, flabby bodies hunched forwards under their pyjamas. Helen was playing a different game altogether. Each step was an event. She choose the exact spot for the ball of her foot to hit then shot her leg down to hit it. That wasn't the end of that step though. Jessie no. The move carried on up through her waist and chest into her opposite shoulder. And up and down those shoulders jutted until she reached me high chair.

'Uh, I wouldn't get too close unless you want a broken nose,' warned me waster Da.

'Excuse me?' said Helen, her skinny eyebrows doing a weird kind of dance on her face.

'Oh not from me of course,' laughed the Da. 'Lord no. I'd never – in my whole life I've never— but of course you know that. Yes. Well it's just that Peter doesn't like people touching him. The sisters-in-law have the bruises and broken bones to prove it. You'd be surprised by the power in those little legs.'

Me waster Da was right, of course. I didn't go in for all that hugging and kissing malarkey. And if there was one thing I hated it was people putting saliva on my face. Me aunties had learned that the hard way. Helen would've got the boot too if the Da hadn't stopped her just outside kicking range.

'Oh he wouldn't kick his good friend Helen. Would you, Peter?' said Helen smiling at me.

'He would and he will. Don't say you weren't warned,' said the Da.

And I would've. I would have given her a good hard front kick in the nose and followed if up with a round house to the ear. Me toes probably would've got all tangled up in her dangly earrings. While the Da tried to free her I probably would've aimed a couple of shots to the mouth. I dunno, maybe I would've went for the eyes instead. You never really know what you're gonna do in the thick of battle, but whatever I did it would've been bloody.

Anyway, FACT is I didn't kick her. Not because I wanted to be hugged or kissed or anything. No, that wasn't the reason. I didn't kick her because me waster Da was so cock sure I would. I'd already shown him I didn't talk because I didn't want to talk to HIM. Now I wanted the Da to see that I didn't hate ALL people touching me, I just hated shithead wasters like him and me aunties doing it.

As Helen put saliva on me face I fought the urge to stitch her a loaf.

'See? He's just a little dote,' said Helen undoing my straps and lifting me out of me high chair.

All me instincts and years of training told me to kick with all my might, but I controlled meself. As Helen held me against her chest I could hear the waster Da starting to cry. Helen held me tighter. It was dark in there. It smelled nice too. Helen was all warm and soft and lovely. I could hear her heart ticking away and the deep echoes of her words as she spoke to me waster Da. She didn't put me down when she spoke. Me waster Da was all upset and all, but Helen didn't put me down. I was the one getting the hugs and kisses. Not him. I was getting them and I didn't even like them. The thought made me smile and then, there in somebody's arms, while being touched and kissed and all, something *mental* happened, something absolutely fucking mental: I fell asleep.

I'm grand.

I said I'm fucking grand! A fly went into me eye.

Oh you didn't see a fly, Blondie, did you not?

Well that's hardly fucking surprising seeing as it's in me poxy eye.

No, I don't need a fucking doctor. We'll stop for lunch now, right?

I don't care what fucking time it is. If I say it's lunchtime then it's fucking lunchtime, alright?

Good. Now, piss off.

Chapter 2

You're late.

Yeah, I know I didn't say a time. Were you eating a ten-course meal or what?

And it takes ya half an hour to eat a poxy sambo?

Do you think this is the fucking civil service or something? I'm not paying you to swan around drinking cappuccinos!

That's right, I'm paying you to write what I say exactly how I say it.

Save it, Blondie. If it happens again, you'll be out on your ear.

Right so we've covered the first three and a half years or so of me life. As you've probably gathered yourself those years were spent between the four walls of me Da's gaff. Now don't get me wrong I'd been to the park and the swimming pool and all, but I'd spent most of the time knocking around the bedroom, kitchen and living room. So when journalists ask me what it was like growing up at the start of the Second Irish Republic I say – it was normal. I mean yeah me aunties all wore pyjamas twenty-four seven, me uncles performed plays in the front garden and me Da pissed around on the sitar all day, but I didn't know any different, did I? Yes, everyone was mad into cycling. No, I never saw a camera. Yes, I saw people sleeping under piles of books on the street. No, I never laid eyes on a TV. But that was all I knew. I'm sure if you asked those young fellas who grew up with wolves they'd tell ya the same thing. Everything seemed perfectly normal.

It wasn't till I started school that the lunatics in charge began to have an effect on me. Well that's what you're paying for, isn't it? You want to here about them fecking me up. Oh, poor Peter Smash is like this because at age four that happened. Oh, poor Peter Smash is like that because at age ten they made him do this. A load of bollix if you ask me. I'm me cause I'm me, but it's your fucking money.

I'd been hearing about this big boy school for months. The Da seemed really excited about the whole thing. Just three weeks now Peter…. Just two weeks now Peter – he'd say. When the Da brought me to the playground he pissed and moaned all the way there and back. So why was he so happy about bringing me to this big boy school? I knew something was up.

Apart from the Da being all excited there were other little hints of what was coming. I'll list them in order:

1) All me normal clothes – jumpers, jeans, runners and t-shirts disappeared. I woke up one morning and found me wardrobe empty except for three brown sacks and three pairs of brown open-toe sandals. As it turned out, the sacks were the perfect gear for kicking. They were airy and non-restrictive. There was none of that chafing malarkey that the jeans went on with. The sandals had their pluses too. While still providing protection for the soles of me feet the sandals were lightweight in design. This meant I could execute me kicks a couple of milliseconds faster. So yeah, me clothes had disappeared without warning or explanation, but all in all I was fairly happy with me new wardrobe.

2) Me waster Da, a couple of weeks before the start of big boy school, started putting these bleedin massive milk bottle glasses over me eyes. Needless to say I was having none of it. I fucked them into me dinner, out the window, under the couch and down the toilet. The Da was determined to make me wear them though, so off went his little stoner brain inventing ways to fix the glasses onto me face.

String was the first port of call, but no matter how many Boy-Scout or sailor techniques the Da found on the internet, I found a way to undo them.

The Da's second tactic was a chain and padlock. That had me stumped for a few days till I realised I didn't need to pick the lock or snap the chain. All I needed to do was snap the arms off the glasses. Easily done.

When his first two tactics failed the Da took to tying me hands behind me back. At that time me physical training worked every muscle in the human body. I was doing everything from lifting me toy box with me neck to opening jam jars with me toes. But having me arms tied behind me back was my first introduction to the importance of flexibility.

I'd seen Helen doing all kinds of stupid stretching and bending every morning. I'd laughed as she touched the back of her head with her toes. Waste of bleedin time— I thought— you'll never generate explosive power in your muscles with that carry on. With me bulging biceps and rippling pecs nullified with nothing more than a piece of rope, I learned another valuable lesson: power is nothing without the flexibility to unleash it.

So every morning I copied Helen's yoga routine. Progress was slow. Partly because I'd neglected me stretching for so long and partly because me hands were tied behind me back. Downward-facing duck and the like were pretty hard on the face, but after a few weeks I was getting close to freedom. Very close. And on the day me aunties and cousins came to visit I was a hair's breath away.

As usual, me cousin Robert was fucking around with my toys in the sitting room. I saw him edging towards me dumper truck and felt adrenaline flood through me system. I hopped up onto me feet and started controlling my breathing. As Robert started pushing me dumper truck across the floor I said a deep ohm and reached me hands down to my heels. It felt like me shoulders were gonna pop. It felt like me wrists were gonna crack. It felt like me collarbone was gonna snap in two. Me cousin Robert crashed me dumper truck into the couch, and I was so fucking angry it took me a couple of seconds to realise I'd stepped my feet between my arms. I picked up a building block and launched it at Robert's head.

Now Robert may have been a snivelling snot-nosed thief, but the fucker knew how to throw a building block. When it came to close-quarters combat, my kicks destroyed him, but in a long range battle Robert held his own. Anyway, long story short, me building block missed and Robert picked up an orange triangle to retaliate. He took aim for his favourite spot, a spot he hit every time: the eyes. A brilliant tactic, really, cause once your opponent is blinded you can bombard him at your leisure.

The triangle came straight for me eyes. Even with my razor sharp reflexes I knew I was fucked. But what did the triangle hit? Not me eyes. No it hit the poxy glasses. I didn't even get a scratch. You should've seen the look on Robert's face. Not only did I lash him out of it with building blocks, but when I ran out of ammo I went over and gave him the kicking of his life too.

So yeah it turned out the glasses had their advantages too, and from that day on you couldn't get me to take them off.

3) One night I went up to bed and the yoke I was meant to put me head on - you know? The soft white yoke... well that yoke was gone. Instead there was a pile of books. Blue and red and green

ones that smelt like tea, and one weird-looking see-through one. Pretty strange, I thought. But as you know, I never slept. I didn't care if they put a pile of broken glass where the soft white yoke used to be...made no difference to me.

So yeah there were hints. Hints of things to come, but at age four everything seemed strange. Birds and muck and fluff and flies and gravity – it was all a bleedin' mystery. So yeah, the big day arrived and I kind of just rolled with it.

Me waster Da got me dressed in me sack and sandals. Me, Helen and the Da ate breakfast in silence for once. That was nice. Helen and the Da even laid off the hugging and kissing. That was nice too.

'Right. Time to go, Peter. We don't want you to be late on your first day in big boy school,' said me waster Da, leading me out of the kitchen.

'Wait,' said Helen, stepping between meself and the Da.

'Helen...Helen I know how you feel. I feel the same way, believe me. But he has to go. It has to happen,' said the Da over Helen's shoulder.

'Yes, James. I've heard all about what *has* to happen. But I have to say my goodbyes if that's all right with you,' said Helen, keeping her back to the Da.

'Of course,' muttered the Da, shuffling out into the hall.

'Now Peter, listen to me, love,' said Helen crouching down to talk face to face, 'You be a good boy in big boy school. No hitting or kicking your classmates unless they hit you first, okay?'

'Okay,' I lied.

'There's a good boy,' smiled Helen, her jade-blue eyes going all watery. 'I'm going to give you something, Peter, but you have to promise not to show it to anyone. You have to promise to keep it hidden under your clothes till you're in bed and everyone else is asleep. You can't show it to anyone. Not even your Da. Okay?'

'Okay,' I said, slightly insulted that she thought I'd show me Da anything.

'Promise me. Promise me you'll keep it out of sight till you're alone in bed and everyone else is asleep,' she said all serious and all.

'I promise,' I said.

Helen grabbed my hand and stuffed a plastic kind of paper into it. I tied to see what it was but she stopped me.

'What did you just promise me?' snapped Helen.

'Oh yeah, sorry,' I said, putting the piece of paper inside me sack.

'Goodbye, love,' said Helen putting saliva on me face as watery crap starting rolling down her cheeks.

'Laters,' I said walking out to the front garden.

I hopped onto the back of the Da's bike, and off we went. Helen waved till we turned out of the estate into the morning traffic.

It was handlebar to handlebar. There was tricycles, quads, tandems, e-bikes, recliners and I even saw a massive seven-foot clown carving his way through it all on a unicycle. As we cycled over the narrow bridge into Leixlip Village, I saw hundreds of businessmen canoeing down the Rye River. Outside the little cottages in Leixlip Village the aul ones and aul fellas had set up drinks stalls. But these were no village fete or country fair yokes. Nah, these were bleedin high tech. Cyclists blasting over the bridge could beep their Distributed Banking Identification Card off a scanner and the stall owners, having received payment, would pull a lever and through a complicated system of pulleys, an isotonic sports drink would be lowered into the path of the cyclist. The fuckers could rehydrate without dropping a single RPM.

We made our way through the village and turned left to the foot of the Captain's Hill. I looked up the steep climb and thought, whoever named this wasn't fucking joking. Years later I would leap-frog up this hill, lair walk back down and crab crawl all the way back up again. But at age four I wondered how anyone made it up this mountain alive. The fucker just got steeper and steeper.

The Da went at it like a bat out of hell, hoping momentum would carry us up. It didn't. About halfway the Da's legs started to go.

'Get out of your saddle and give it some gusto, man!' roared a cyclist from behind.

'Get over the pedals and push down through your toes!' shouted another.

These weren't friendly shouts of encouragement. They weren't helpful pointers or tips. Nah, these were desperate fucking demands. If me and the Da started rolling backwards, there was gonna be one hell of a smash up at the bottom of the hill. There'd be bones snapped in spokes, eyes gouged by break levers, necks throttled with chains and stomachs disembowelled by gear clogs.

'He's not gonna make it,' screamed an old woman on a fixed gear to our left.

With that, two huge fuckers appeared on either side of us. They rode bright blue titanium alloy bikes. They wore blue wrap-around shades. At first, I thought their bodies were blue too. I could see the definition and curve of every rippling muscle on their torsos. Maybe their blue skin colour was the result of some amazing protein supplement I hadn't heard of. Then I spotted Guarda Jessie written across their backs and realised they were wearing some sort of Lycra uniform.

As they pulled level with the Da, they shot out an arm each and linked fingers behind me Da's back. Lights started flashing on their helmets. Sirens began roaring from their saddles, and we shot up the hill.

Having made it to the top of the hill, the guards pulled us over onto the grass.

'Identification,' said Guard A as Guard B started giving me Da's crappy bike the once-over.

'Rusted chain. Worn brake pads. Balding back tyre. Missing dust caps,' reported Guard B.

'You don't seem to have made the proper physical or technical preparations for your cycle today, Mr ...uhh, Smash,' said Guard A, handing the identification card to Guard B.

'I'm very sorry, Guard. I've been a little under the weather recently. I thought I was over it, but obviously the virus took more out of me than I thought,' said the Da, setting off on a bout of coughing.

The cough was real enough, but that stoner never had any fucking virus.

'And the dilapidated state of your bicycle?' said Guard A, crossing his arms and flexing his massive biceps.

'Well to be honest with you, Guard, I'm more of a walking man. Now don't get me wrong, I pedal my piece like everyone else, but if I'm going somewhere local I'd rather walk. Bad knees, you see. Anyway, today is the young fella's first day in school. We were running a little late, so I thought I'd better take the bike. I didn't realise what a state it was in till we got going. I probably should've turned back, but I didn't want the young fella to be late on his first day in school.'

'A walker, eh?' said Guard A, flexing his biceps again.

'17.5 kW,' shouted Guard B from a computer screen on the back of his bike.

'Pedal your piece, do ya?' barked Guard A.

'I generate what I need,' muttered the Da.

'All you need for twelve months is 17.5 kW of electricity?' scoffed Guard A.

'No, Guard. Of course not, Guard. Like I said, I've bad knees. The Mrs. does most of the pedalling for us,' said the Da.

'So you send this poor young fella's mother out to pedal while you sit around doing nothing?' said Guard A, sizing me up on the back of the bike.

'Helen isn't...my partner isn't...I'm a widower, Guard. And I don't sit around doing nothing. I'm actually working towards a doctorate in Indian folk music.'

'Indian folk music! Pah! May as well be doing nothing. It's wasters like you...'

'What instrument?' interrupted Guard B, trotting over from the computer.

'Uhhhh...sitar, mostly,' answered the Da.

'Do you mind?' said Guard A, trying to regain control of the conversation.

'Gift. I'm playing the tabla meself. Who're you inta?' continued Guard B, stepping between his partner and me Da.

'Ravi Shankar, Pandrit Nikhil Banerjee and the Khans of course...especially Ustad,' said the Da.

'Ustad's the shit, man. Pushes boundaries. Music is a living, breathing thing at the end of the day— a universal language. You don't hear us speaking like fucking Shakespeare, do ya? So why should music stay the same?'

'You're preaching to the converted my friend,' said the Da.

'Cool, cool. So do ye get to jam much?' said Guard B, taking off his blue shades.

'Everyday, man.'

'Oh, you lucky bastard. I just can't find the players. I mean tabla is beautiful unaccompanied, but you can get so much more of a groove going when there's other musicians to buzz off, you know?'

'I know...,' said the Da hoping and praying this wasn't going where he knew it was going.

'Your address is 24 Ryevale Lawns, right?' said Guard B.

The Da grunted.

'Well how about I pop over for a jam tomorrow at say...two?' said Guard B.

'Well...'

'If you're too busy don't worry about it, Mr. Smash,' said Guard B, popping back on his shades.

'No, no, two is fine, man. Two is perfect. I'll have the kettle on and the sitar tuned,' said the Da, doing a weird girly laugh.

'Great stuff. Great stuff altogether. I was gonna send the PWLA round to check you out, but you're clearly a good skin. There won't be any need for that,' laughed Guard B, giving the Da a slap on the back.

The Da didn't laugh. The Da didn't even fucking breath.

'Finished?' said Guard A, having watched the proceedings with hands on hips.

'Oh sorry, partner,' said Guard B, turning to whisper in Guard A's ear.

'You must be fucking joking,' said Guard A between his teeth.

There was another bout of whispering, which moved from argumentative to strangely intimate, before Guard B slapped Guard A on the ass and walked back to his bike.

'Right, well, let's see now...', said Guard A all flushed and hot under his Lycra, '...seeing as it's your young fella's first day in school, we're gonna let you off with a warning, but I'm telling you here and now if I catch you pedalling like that again it'll be off to Dún Laoghaire with ya. Understood?'

'Understood, Guard,' said the Da with a half bow.

'Well off with ya now before the young fella's late for school,' ordered Guard A.

'Thanks, Guard,' said the Da, pedalling off.

'See you tomorrow,' called Guard B.

'Can't wait,' replied the Da, shuddering from shoulder to shoulder.

We pulled up at this big boys' school. They hadn't been joking when they named this place either. Bleedin thing was massive. A slimy, snotty wall topped with rusty metal spikes surrounded the grounds. With me years of jumping experience I could appreciate the genius of the design. You could try backwards jumping over that lad, but you were only getting one shot. There'd be no practising. You either got over or you got dead.

Behind the wall were trees. Huge black trees that growled and spat every time the wind blew. Under the trees you could see fuck all, just shadows creeping around waiting for some gobshite to go wandering where he wasn't wanted.

After the trees there was lots of dark green grass and then the school. Now I'd never seen a building that size before, three-bedroom gaffs were the biggest I'd laid eyes on, but even I could tell something was up with this place. It took me a while to place it, but then I realised it was made of three separate parts. The far left was all pointy and sharp and all. It had pointy windows with spiky coloured glass. It had a pointy green roof with a big metal spike pointing up to the sky. It had pointy doors and pointy corners and pointy statues in pointy alcoves. But everything wasn't just pointy, no it was ancient too. Now I'd seen old buildings in ghost estates and all, but you knew they'd fall down in the next stiff breeze. This place was a different story. It looked so old; so ancient; that you got the feeling it had already taken everything the world had to throw at it. Now don't get me wrong, it looked like it was going to fall down all right, but it was so ancient you knew it wouldn't. You knew if it had any bloody intention of falling down it would've done it a long bleedin' time ago.

To the right of big pointy ancient yoke was a long rectangular modern yoke. The long rectangular modern yoke was grey like the ancient yoke, but it wasn't pointy or nothing. The windows were all the same size. The four doors were all brown and they were all equally spaced along the wall. The black plastic gutters came down to black plastic grills over square shores that were spaced equally between the brown doors. Like I said, it wasn't pointy or ancient or nothing. It was all modern and measured and precise.

Looking at the ancient yoke beside the rectangular yoke was like looking at two long-distance runners. The aul fella dressed in a twenty-year-old pair of Asics Gel, short shorts and grey vest. The young fella dressed in Nike Air, special hamstring-supporting leggings and sweat-wicking t-shirt. The young fella looked hot to trot, but one glance at the aul fella with his scraggy beard and wild hair told you all you needed to know. The aul fella had the miles of a hundred marathons in those legs. The young fella might run a marathon in under four hours, but what was he gonna do when the aul fella arrived an hour later and just kept running....and running....and running?

To the far right were six massive cardboard boxes. They were kinda just plopped there. There was no order to it. One was parallel to the rectangular yoke, the next was at forty-five degrees and another was at right angles. They were the newest part of the building, but were defo gonna be the first to keel over.

So yeah, you get the idea. The place was weird.

The Da hopped off the bike and pushed a button on the big iron gate.

'Place your ID on the scanner,' crackled a voice over the intercom.

The Da did as he was told.

'Ok. I'm all scanned,' said the Da.

'Just a moment, Mr. Smash,' crackled the voice.

We could hear the cameras on top of the gate zooming in and out and scanning left to right before a loud buzz went off and the gate started to open.

The Da hopped back on the bike and set off towards the school. The driveway was all gravel, and as any cyclist knows you're losing something in the region of 12.5 percent of your power on that type of surface. What with this morning's climb and this crappy surface, the Da was bollixed. We'd only gone a hundred meters when he got off and started pushing.

Needless to say I was less than happy about wandering through the poxy forest. The trees growled at us. The leaves blocked out the sun, and every time the wind blew the trees spat down the back of me neck. As if that craic wasn't bad enough there was stuff walking around in the shadows. As we got deeper into the woods the fuckers started making noises too. Shouting and singing and grunting and all. I eventually spotted one of them strolling through the trees, arms spread akimbo, throwing his head left and right talking to the branches and leaves and acorns.

'When it suddenly ceases, I find myself
Pursuing no longer a rhythm of the duramen,
But bouncing on the diploe in a clearing between earth and air,
Or headlong in a dewy dallops or a moon-spairged fernshaw
Or caught in a dark dumosity, or even
In open country again, watching an aching spargosis of stars.'

We made eye contact, and all three of us froze. We froze cause we were scared shitless, but the madman went a kind of purple-maroon colour, so I guess he must have been embarrassed or something.

'Welcome, welcome,' said the mad bastard, shaking off his embarrassment.

Seeing this thing coming at us, the Da hopped back on the bike and gave it everything he had left. As we shot over the gravel more and more crazy fuckers appeared from the shadows. One was warbling her voice around. The next was dancing like his hair was on fire. People were swinging swords, banging drums, swishing ribbons and performing acrobatics.

I'd been in this big boy school for all of two minutes, but I'd seen enough. I was fucked if I was gonna be hanging around with a bunch of loolahs. I'd be doing a legger fairy sharpish.

Anyway we made it out of the woods. The loopers had obviously put the wind up the Da too cause he didn't stop pedalling till we were right up to the school door. That done, the Da collapsed face-first into the gravel.

'You're late, Mr. Smash,' said a fella with the body of an eight-year-old, but the face of a eighty-year-old, standing in the pointy doorway.

'Hill...gravel...me legs...can't....stand,' panted me waster Da, still laid out on the deck.

'Well, Principal John James is about to begin the assembly if you'd kindly follow me to your seats,' said the dwarf, sweeping back his gown, pulling out an iron key and carefully unlocking the door.

'O...K...,' said the Da, struggling to his feet and lifting me off the back of the bike.

'This way please,' said the dwarf, disappearing into the building and around a pointy corner.

We shot after him, but as we rounded the corner we saw the tails of his black gown disappearing around the next corner. The Da broke into a jog, then a run and eventually an all out sprint, but no matter how fast we went, the fucker was always disappearing around the next pointy corner.

Even with all my training, I was feeling the burn. The Da must've been on death's door.

We tore around the last corner and found the dwarf tapping his pocket watch. The little shit hadn't even broken a sweat.

'So you finally decided to grace us with your presence, have you? Well it's not a moment too soon,' said the dwarf, snapping his pocket watch closed before opening another big pointy door and bringing us into a hall full of mammies and daddies and young ones and young fellas like meself.

Cause we were so late there were hardly any seats left. Why no one had taken the two seats right up the front in the middle of the row was beyond me. In me four years of experience I'd always found it better to be in the thick of the action. Like in the cinema for example – you didn't want to be down the back were people made grunting noises and put saliva on each other's faces. You didn't want to be in the middle either cause there was always some lanky fucker with curly hair blocking your view. Nah, up the front is your only man.

I sat in me seat and sized up the other kids. Bunch of snot-nosed wimps by the looks of things. They all had chicken legs and underdeveloped torsos. Half of them were crying and the other half were clinging onto their mammies' and daddies' arms like gobshites. Not much competition, I sighed with regret.

Why regret? Well! If you were a winner, if you were a real champion, then you'd know. You'd know that a great competitor is worth a thousand training sessions. You see his face when you're sprinting your final hundred meters. You hear his voice when you're doing your final set of lifts on the bench press. You taste his sweat when your arms are screaming they can't do it but you're forcing them to pull you up. When you're sick, and thinking of skipping training, you picture him picturing you and you go to the gym even though it nearly kills ya. And in the end, when you beat him, you don't destroy his ego. No, you've lived with him for too long for that. Nah what you do is you steal it. You steal his ego and you add it to your own.

So yeah I was fairly disappointed with the quality of opposition so I turned me attentions to the stage.

You've never *seen* such a bunch of weirdos. They were seated in a long row. Some sat bolt upright, some slouched, some crossed their legs, some crossed their arms, some had huge mops of hair, some were totally bald, some were unbelievably old, some were unbelievably young, some were male, some were female, some were in between, but they all had the same look in their eye. A look of sheer bleedin' madness.

Now if you came round my gaff you may have seen the Da playing sitar behind a wall of cannabis smoke, you might have seen Helen doing yoga completely naked at dawn, you may have seen the uncles doing interpretive dance on the garden shed and you might have heard me aunties yodelling out the attic window, but if you looked into their eyes you'd see a forced kind of enthusiasm. They all looked like a young fella at a teenage disco giving it socks to impress some piece of skirt. He looks like he's having the time of his life, but then you catch him looking around to see who's watching. You realise he's thinking about what other people are thinking. In other words he can't be having the time of his life cause he's worrying about whether you think he looks like he's having the time of his life or not.

The heads up on stage were a different kettle of fish. They weren't worrying about what you thought. In fact they didn't give a flying fuck what you thought cause they were one hundred percent sure what they were doing was the bollix. Now this absolute belief has got nothing to do with the absolute belief of a sportsman. A fighter may believe he is the greatest fighter of all time, but at the end of the day he has to go and prove it in competition. If he loses, he can no longer claim to be the greatest. Even if he wins the first couple of matches, nothing's proved. He as to win and win and win again right up till he retires. Point is a sportsman is constantly tested. He can't just talk the talk. He has to walk the walk. But talking and writing and waffling on is all artists do. The fuckers will even call competition irrelevant. They can claim to be the Mohamed Ali of freeform poetry without any fear of one day finding themselves knocked out cold on the canvas. A sportsman may believe he's great, but at the end of the day he tests that idea against reality. An artist believes he's great, declares all tests to be irrelevant and ignores any bits of reality that don't agree with his beliefs. In short, artists are plain old nuts, but manage to convince everyone else they're something else; they convince everyone else they're artists. And that's why these heads on stage, these artistic types, gave me the shivers.

The chitting and chatting in the hall suddenly stopped. Everyone stood up. The Da reefed me up by the scruff of me neck. Then I saw this aul fella walking up the hall, swinging his left leg in front of him. He had a face like an old oak that had gone ten rounds with a chain saw. He scowled around him with his left eye, heads bowing wherever he looked. He climbed the stairs onto the stage and stood before the podium.

'Suigh sios' said the aul fella.

Everyone sat down and the Da pulled me back onto me chair by the scruff of me neck.

The aul fella gripped the sides of the podium with two thick-knuckled hands and looked around the crowd. He kept his right eye closed like he was taking aim, like he was about to throw a building block. Well let him, I thought, ain't nothing getting through these glasses. I looked around at the other kids, wondering who was about to get a building block in the eye when I realised they were all wearing glasses too. Not only that, but the fuckers had brown sacks and brown sandals as well. Maybe we have some kickers after all, I thought, resolving to keep me wits about me.

'Some four years ago, at the birth of one Nation under Jessie, the holy prophet Dr. Benjamin Murphy, stood aloft the gallows that had threatened to abort our hopes and dreams, and asked the people of Ireland some important questions. Today, as the first generation of children born in the Second Irish Republic come of school-going age, I will repeat the Prophet's glorious words,' said John James, scrunching up his face and putting that wild eye on us again.

'How can an idea be anything but an idea? What is a nation but a collective thought? Therefore let our thoughts be thoughts of beauty,' roared John James, shaking the podium like a battle sabre and bearing his tea-stained teeth.

'Today the first children born into the glorious age of the Second Irish Republic begin their education. The first minds uncorrupted by the logical fallacies and aesthetic paucities of our past take the first steps on the path to enlightenment. Guided by the scholarly hands of these High Priests of Jessie, your children will elevate themselves into the realm of the superconsciousness,' said John James, motioning to the teachers sitting in a row behind him.

The Da shifted in his chair. A few coughs could be heard at the back of the hall, but all in all there was silence. Everyone waited for more.

'And what, you may ask, will they learn in the realm of the superconsciousness? And I answer: They will learn the eternal language of the gods. They will wash their ears of mortal filth and learn the language of eternal beauty. Their words will pour forth in verse. Their lungs will fill the air with melody. Their hands will carve exquisite forms, and their thoughts will be brimful of beauty.

When every child of the Second Republic turns their thoughts to beauty, how can our nation fail to be beautiful? How can an idea be anything but an idea?' said John James, closing his eyes and taking a deep moment of reflection.

The gobshites in the hall closed their eyes too.

'Children!' roared John James, scaring the bejesus out of the Da, who had started falling asleep, 'Today I tell you you are finally free: free from the tyrannies of sophistry; free from the machinations of industry and free from the quagmires of banality. Here in the first Jessholic school you are finally free to dream, so dream, dream, dream...'

Needless to say I hadn't got a smell what this looper was shouting about. The others got mad into it though. They all jumped onto their feet, started punching the air and chanting along like a bunch of loolahs. As if that wasn't bad enough, the Priests of Jessie pulled out guitars and fiddles and flutes and started playing a song.

Now if there is one thing I hate more than people writing down a load of bleedin waffle, it's people singing a load of bleedin waffle. At least you can ignore a book. You slam the thing closed, fuck it in a corner and leave it there to rot. Try doing that with some head singing at the top of his lungs. Doesn't matter how far away from him you go, you'll still hear the bastard. Like the Da and his poxy sitar for example. It didn't matter how many hats I pulled over me head; it didn't matter how much tissue I stuffed in me ears; no matter what I did I'd still heard the shagging music. And as if that wasn't bad enough, after the Da had finished playing, the tune would be stuck in me head. I'd slam me head off walls. I'd scream till I was blue in the face. I'd try and poke it out with a pencil, but no matter what I did I couldn't get the music out of me head.

So yeah, John James and the teachers and all the mas and das were singing.

'He searched for her each and every day,
But found nothing but strands of her hair turned grey...'

They were all linking arms now and swaying back and forth and sobbing and all. I could feel the sneaky fucker wriggling into my ear and decided to take action.

I jumped under the chair and put me hands over me ears.

'In a darkened cell Benjamin Murphy
Still kisses the strands of her hair turned grey...'

The bastards were roaring it now. The fiddles and flutes and accordions were egging them on from the stage. The tune was getting into me head. The thought of having the thing stuck in me head all day made me so fucking angry that I thought about getting up and kicking the shins off each and every one of them. It was only me promise to Helen that stopped me. I stayed under the chair, pulled my sack over me ears and began repeating facts in me head. I didn't list the thirty-two counties or do sums or recite FA Cup winners or anything stupid like that. I just repeated stuff I had learned; stuff I wanted to remember; important stuff that could fill me brain up and keep this rubbish from squeezing in through me ears. Stuff like:

1) If something is worth doing it's hard to do.
2) The distance between first and third is bigger than the distance between third and last.
3) Competition will reveal all weaknesses.
4) You're only as strong as your weakest muscle.
5) Power is nothing without flexibility.

How long did they sing the anthem of the Second Irish Republic? How long were they pumping their fists through the air, linking arms and bawling crying? Ah you're just dying to hear if the rumours are true aren't ya? You're dying for me to tell you about doctors letting grannies die cause they were lost in a three-hour saxophone solo or bridges collapsing because architects decided their rights to expression should not be limited by Newton or Boyle or anybody bleedin else. You want the juicy bits. The bits that Blondie over there and me agent will splash all over the cover. Well sorry to tell ya, but you've been ripped. I'm not gonna harp on about that shite. I'm here to tell my story and my story alone. I'm not here to fucking waffle on and on about the politics of the Second Irish Republic. God knows there's enough people doing that already. So if you want to know how long they sang for, then repeat my five facts; the facts I listed above; repeat them about two thousand times. I'll wait for ya....

    Well there ya go. That's how long they sang for. I hope that got you all warm in your knickers.
    Anyway they eventually stopped singing. They'd probably been stopped a long time before I realised, cause when the dwarf pulled me out from under the chair all the mammies and daddies had gone.

    I don't remember much after that. I know we did the rounds of the school. We were shown the gym, meditation chambers, music room, sensory deprivation tanks and canteen. We were introduced to the teachers, caretakers, secretaries and dinner ladies. I'm sure they waffled on about what we'd be learning and all, but I guess I blocked it all out. I was probably just repeating facts in me head and waiting for home time; cause I knew one thing for certain: after home time I was never coming back.
    The Da could get me dressed in the morning, but he was gonna take one hell of a kicking to legs. I'd battle him all the way down the stairs. I'd attack him with me breakfast. I'd lash into him as he tried to get me on the bike. I'd then give the bike a good beating. We'd set off for school all right, but the Da's legs would be in such a state he'd be dying on the climb up the Captain's Hill. He'd slow down to a crawl and then I'd jump off the bike and sprint back down into the village. The Da would catch me all right, but he'd never make it up that hill twice. No chance. We'd cycle back home. And

once the Da was beaten he was beaten. He was a good-for-nothing stoner, but at least he knew when to quit.

So yeah, I spent me first day in school waiting for it to end.

I remember sitting cross-legged on the floor. We had weird orange and purple cushions with shiny bits of mirror on them under our arses. There were four of us around this low wooden table that had fellas with elephant heads and snakes and mad-looking knives carved onto the sides of it. Mr. Chivers had been waffling on for hours. He'd been talking to flowers and chairs and drawing pictures and doing weird stretches, but now he just stared out the window.

'Let us go then, you and I,

'When the evening is spread out against the sky,

'Like a patient etherised upon a table,' said Chivers, turning away from the setting sun and pushing his half-moon yellow glasses up his nose before motioning for us to stand up.

No one moved cause no one had a clue what this looper was on about.

Chivers gripped his temples between thumb and forefinger. He exhaled sharply through his nose and then pushed the palm of his hand back over his forehead and down the length of his skull. He clawed his long girly hair and the tension made his face all taught and weird. His eyes bulged behind the yellow glasses. When finished stroking his hair, he exhaled slowly through his nose before giving a loud sniff. The meaning of that sniff was something I came to know all to well, but at the time I just thought we had a pooper in our ranks.

'When all we need to say is said

Dreams call us to our beds,' said Chivers placing his palms on his knees and flashing his weird green eyes from side to side behind his yellow glasses.

Still no one had a smell what this fella was on about, but I was fairly sure I had heard the word *bed*. I didn't know about the rest of these snot-nosed whiners, but I knew where my bed was— it was at home. Now, I had no intention of sleeping in it. I had no intention of even lying on it. God knows today's carry on had cost me enough training time, but if pretending to go to bed got me out of this madhouse then that was fine with me.

I started stretching and yawning and blinking slowly and all. It probably wasn't the best performance in the world, but having never been tired meself, having only ever seen other people yawning and all, it was the best I could do.

Anyway, Chivers bought it.

'And the journey into the superconsciousness begins,' laughed Chivers, clapping his hands together and spinning 360 on his toes.

'Very good, hmmmm, Peter. Very good, Peter,' said Chivers reading me name tag, 'And seeing as it's hunter-gatherer month let me give you this little map, young man.'

Chivers gave me a piece of paper and a slap on the back. Seeing the praise I got, me classmates started an elaborate display of yawning and stretching and groaning. One fella down the back even took to the floor and started snoring like a bear.

'Excellent, class. Excellent. The journey begins.... When all we need to say is said dreams call us to our beds,' said Chivers opening the classroom door and leading us all out into the hall.

Finally, I thought, we're off home. We went down long corridors with pointy roofs on top and pointy statues at the sides and pointy tiles underneath. Mr. Chivers walked at the front of our line and kept waffling on about dreams and words and journeys and all. The other kids hoping for some praise before they went home kept up the yawning and stretching, but even in this game (a game I had no interest in playing) I was better at than them.

All the pointy crap suddenly ended. The windows became square. The doors became rectangular. Even the smell got less pointy. There was no smoky rotting pong anymore. There was just flat cold air. As we walked along, I realised we had entered the modern rectangular yoke that stood beside the ancient pointy yoke. They must have found those loopers in the woods, I thought. We're slipping out the back door.

We arrived at a big brown door at the end of the corridor. Chivers got us all lined up straight and started handing out weird see-through books.

'Let our dreams be dreams of beauty. Let our dreams be dreams of Jessie,' said Chivers, holding his palms over our heads with his eyes closed. 'Lord, hear us. Lord, graciously hear us.'

Chivers held his book against his forehead and my classmates followed suit. While they moaned and groaned and rocked back and forth, I thought about throwing the book in the corner, but decided it would probably just hold up the show.

Eventually the groaning and all finished and Chivers opened the door. It was pitch black outside. There were no lights anywhere. Even the moon and stars were turned off.

So yeah as we walked through the yard it took me a couple of minutes to realise me waster Da hadn't arrived yet. The fucker was probably stoned in the sitting room right now. Helen will get home from work and find him pissing around on the sitar. She'll have to scream and roar to get him off his fat stoner ass.

None of that was surprising. What was surprising was that none of the other parents had arrived either. I'd always believed me waster Da to be a special case. I believed other parents worked and exercised and cleaned the house and washed their armpits. Maybe I'd been wrong. Maybe all adults, except for Helen, were bleedin' wasters. God knows me uncles and aunts were.

Seeing as no one was there to pick us up, Chivers led us into one of the massive box things to wait. With the loopers hidden in the woods nearby I was more than happy to wait inside the box.

We all squashed into a narrow hallway, and Chivers punched some numbers into a keypad. Something started hissing and a door rolled open. Cause the hall was so packed, the second the door opened we all kind of just spilled into the room.

Why didn't I do a runner there and then? Had I no cop on at all? Well I've asked meself that question more than anyone, and the only explanation I can come up with is that I had gotten so used to the idea that I was heading home that I couldn't put two and two together. And at four years old you don't think your Da, even if he is a waster good-for-nothing stoner, would abandon you to a load of head cases.

So yeah, I saw the room full of bunk beds. I saw the white sheets all neatly made up. I noticed the lockers. I even had a quick nosey in the jacks and admired the size of the shower room. I saw it all, but I didn't think for a second it had anything to do with me. No doubt whoever lived here enjoyed scrubbing up in that shower room and more power to them, but I was heading home.

'Ahern, Boyle, Doherty, Egan...' said Chivers, lining us up against the lockers in alphabetical order.

'Now as vulgar as it maybe, in the interests of practicality and convenience, and owing to the, as of yet, untrained nature of your ears, I will proceed in prose,' said Chivers, all sad and all.

'If you will look behind you, you will find a locker,' said Chivers. And sure enough, behind me was a locker with Peter J. Smash written on it.

'And if you will now open the aforementioned article you will find your sleeping attire. And exquisite sleeping attire it is too – donated by the connoisseurs of such articles, i.e., the Pyjama Wearers' Liberation Army.'

I opened me locker, and just like Chivers said, there was a pair of silky pyjamas with swirly-wirly patterns all over them.

'Now, if you will kindly shed your uniforms, which, might I add, are a credit to your religious devotion and a joy to the heart of Jessie, and dress for bed.'

And that's when all hell broke loose around me. There was me, oblivious to the facts, watching the other kids screaming and roaring and bawling and crying.

'Can we please dress for bed without the hysterics?' said Chivers, picking kids up from the floor and pulling others out from under the beds.

Dress for bed? He said we're dressing for bed. I'm gonna be locked up in here all night with these snot-nosed whingers. They're trying to keep me here. They're gonna try and make me sit in the classroom all day listening to Chivers talk rubbish. They're gonna try and steal me training time and force me to read and write a load of waffle.

The penny had dropped. It had dropped like a fucking ten-tonne nuclear bomb. While Chivers grappled with kids climbing up the bunks, hanging off doors and hiding in toilet bowls, I looked on with a dumbfounded expression. I didn't stand still cause I had accepted me faith or nothing. I stood still cause as the events of the last couple of months came into focus, I was totally stunned. I realised the Da had been planning this for ages. I realised Helen had been in on it. I realised the brilliant kicking sack was my school uniform. I realised the eye protectors were part of the uniform too. The book in me bed; the silent breakfast; Helen giving me a present; it was all part of the plan. The Da wanted Helen all to himself. The good for nothing waster had been plotting for months, and I'd let him pull the wool over me eyes.

This final realisation made me so fucking angry that I lost it all together. I started kicking. I could see the terror in the other kids eyes', but the fact that they had realised what was going on before I did made me even angrier. I unleashed shin-cracker axe kicks on anyone who crossed me path.

Why did I kick them? They were in the same boat as me. Why did I break their legs? Well, if you're asking me that question you must be a woman. All men know it gets to a certain point and then any target will do. We can't get at god. We're not allowed to hit wives or children or mothers or fathers or the disabled or the elderly or our boss or any of the people destroying our lives. So every day you're soaking it up, but it gets to a point where someone has to pay. You can't let it go anymore. You can't let this fucking shit go unchecked, so what do you do? Well, you kick the daylights out of whatever happens to be around. And does it make you feel better? You're bloody *right* it does.

The frightened cries were all becoming screams of pain as I worked me way around the room. By the time Chivers realised what I was up, to half the kids were rolling around on the floor gripping their shins.

'Desist!' shouted Chivers, catching me mid-kick.

He slowly set down the kids he had under each arm and pushed his yellow glasses up his nose. Everyone moved aside and we faced each other down.

I threw a couple of exhibition kicks to show I meant businesses. Chivers ran his hand through his hair and sniffed the air.

'Raising angry fists to your father,

Only makes your lessons harder,' said Chivers, dropping into the falling boulder stance of Northern Fist Kung Fu.

It was my first fair fight. I say fair cause me waster Da couldn't fight his way out of wet paper bag. Me uncles and cousins were pussies too. But this head, this Chivers fella, he had some training. He'd studied Shotokan, Kung Fu and Burmese Boxing. He could block flurries of punches. He could sweep a kicker off their standing leg. He could unleash a multitude of strangles and locks from close quarters. This was something I came to learn over the years, but in that first fight I knew nothing about his skills and he knew nothing about mine. If he had known anything about me he'd never have taken up a stance that exposed his shin so badly. I launched me jumping 720-spinning shin-cracker axe kick and heard the sweet snap of bone when it connected.

As Chivers joined the others screaming on the floor I tried to figure a way out of the room. Me kicks had no effect on the solid steel door. The windows were covered with a metal grill. The drains in the shower room were bolted shut and the toilets were too narrow for me to escape through the sewerage system. I was reduced to banging on the metal door with me hands, hoping someone outside would open it.

When the lights in the room went out and a siren started screaming, I knew I probably wasn't getting out of there alive. A red light on the ceiling started spinning around. The twisted faces rolling around on the floor, changed from red to black and black to red. It hid screaming mouths for a second and then revealed them again, teeth flashing red in front of screaming black holes. They were like a pack of wolves creeping forward, surrounding me in the woods, crazed eyes flashing violence when I swept a flaming torch from left to right, waiting for the first attack.

When the door did open I was too dizzy and nauseous to react. Three tall men in long white coats and white facemasks entered. I tried to steady meself for an attack, but when the fuckers saw me taking up a fighting stance they pulled out a piece. Holy shit they're gonna shoot me dead, I thought. I hadn't researched my opponents before accepting the fight. I hadn't prepared for the weapons they would bring to bear on me, and I was gonna die.

There was a loud pop and a sting in me left leg. I looked down and there was a bleedin' dart stuck in me leg. As the poison began crawling up me legs, I added a sixth rule to me list.

6) Know your enemy.

A valuable lesson, but scant conciliation seeing as I was about to be browners. As me whole body went numb I crumbled to the floor. The fuckers in the white coats were able to prod me and put their ears to me chest and look into me eyeballs and all. They didn't get as much as a kick in the balls for it. They picked me up and slung me into a bag. What with the poison and lack of oxygen, I passed out.

Chapter 3

Now as we all know some people love waffling on about their dreams. They're almost proud of the rubbish their minds make up while they're lying around wasting time. Oh, I dreamed a clock was melting on a table. Oh, I dreamed a fox was doing the butterfly stroke in a birdbath.... That's the kind of shite you'll hear them say. They expect a pat on the back for it, but the only sane reaction to that rubbish is: Congratulations! You're even more retarded in your sleep than you are when you're awake.... I didn't think it was possible—well done!

Even worse than the people who love to waffle about their retarded dreams are the people who love to listen to other people waffling about their retarded dreams. They'll hear all about foxes and owls and melting clocks and then they'll go – Oh, that means you want to fuck your Ma and kill your Da. Gobshites.

I've always wanted to murder me Da. That's hardly breaking news. And as you know, me Ma died while giving birth. I left her privates looking like the entrance to Dante's Inferno – something me Da loves to repeat when claiming I'm the spawn of Satan, which is one of the many reasons why I want to murder the bastard.

Anyway, I thought I'd just get that all out there before I told you about this dream. Just so you know I'm not boasting about it. And so it's clear that I always wanted to murder me Da and that me Ma is dead.

In this dream I was training in the living room. I was on me last set of burpees and me thighs were burning like holy hell. I knew the Da was out cause there was no sitar twagging in the house. He was probably out buying hash or something.

Anyway, me lungs were bursting and me heart was beating out of me chest when I heard some grunting coming from the kitchen. Me legs were all shaky after the workout so I pottered along slowly.

I opened the kitchen door and found an enormous hairy man standing with his back to me. I could see the power in his latissimus dorsi, triceps and glutes. Even the fucker's neck was ripped.

'You lost, buddy?' I asked.

He didn't turn. He didn't even twitch, but I noticed a big double-peaked mole on his arse just like me Da's. But this wasn't me

Da. Me Da was a stoner waster with the body of a twelve-year-old girl. He couldn't be standing naked in the kitchen cause he was out buying hash somewhere.

'You deaf?' I called.

Again there was no response, but then Helen's head appeared, at crotch level, from behind the man's bulk.

'Peter go back into the sitting room,' she said before disappearing.

The man started grunting again and the mole on his arse throbbed in time.

'The fuck I will! Hear you! Turn the fuck around!' I shouted, kicking the man up the hole.

There was a weird strangling sound followed by a thud. The man started turning around slowly and as he did I saw Helen sprawled on the floor, her face all blue and her eyes pointing different directions.

'You bastard! I'm gonna kill you!' I screamed, kicking the man up and down.

His face was covered behind a mop of hair and a thick beard, but one thing I could see was his cock. The sight of it standing up like that made me feel sick. I wanted to fight, but felt too disgusted.

'Put on some trousers, you sicko. Pull up your pants and then I'll kick the shite out of you,' I said backing away from the cock.

'I'm not gonna fight you little man,' said the hairy bastard stepping forwards with his big purple-headed cock bouncing up and down like a mad dog on a leash.

'For Christ's sake, put on some pants,' I said, backing away.

'I won't fight you little man. There is no need to fight,' repeated the man with a smile.

'You bastard!' I screamed, wanting to fight, wanting to see blood and hear bones breaking, but not while his cock was swinging around in the air, not while he was smiling at me and holding his arms out and all.

So I turned and ran, but cause of my gruelling training session I couldn't run fast. I gave it everything I had, but I kept moving slower. I felt like I was under water. I couldn't get away.

'Don't worry. We don't need to fight,' I heard him say as he clapped a hand on me shoulder.

I swear to God, Blondie, if you giggle once more, I'm gonna rip off your arm and beat you to death with it!

You think I'm confessing some big secret here, do ya?

You really think I'm dat[sic] bleedin[sic] tick[sic], do ya[sic]?

You reckon I'd keep a secret for twenty-nine years and then let it slip by telling you about a dream like that?

You think you get into the 151st Ranger Unit if you don't know how to guard intelligence? You think you get promoted to chief assassin if you don't know how to perform counter-interrogation techniques. I've been tortured for months and not let as much as me name slip. Nah, Jonathan, I know you perverts like to think all men secretly want to do you up the arse, but we don't. A true-blooded male like meself wouldn't spit on a degenerate like you if you were on fire.

That's right, Jonathan, if I had me way you'd all have your bits chopped off. In fact if you don't wipe that smug look off your face, I'll knock you out and go get a shears from the garden shed.

Right. As I was saying. I'm only telling yous about this dream cause this book is called *The Truth*, and the truth is that when I woke up in a pitch-black cell (some hours or days or weeks after I'd been shot) I was scared fucking shitless. I thought the big hairy bastard in my kitchen had me locked up somewhere.

As me senses returned, I realised I was sitting on a hard, wooden chair. I stretched me hands out around me and found a hard, wooden table. Me head was pounding and when I put me hands onto me head I realised I was soaked from head to toe. Had I been sweating like mad, and if so why was I now freezing cold? Nah someone had doused me. I did a quick inventory of me body, I had a few bruises here and there, but everything seemed to be in decent working order.

Me eyes were starting to adjust to the darkness and just as I began to suspect I was not alone in the cell a blinding white light snapped on.

'So you like kicking, Mr. Smash,' grumbled a voice on the other side of the table.

I hid me eyes behind me fingers and remained silent.

'I have to admit I'm fond of a well-executed kick myself," the voice continued. 'I studied Taekwondo for several years, and I have the utmost respect for the sport. Its practitioners are some of the most dedicated martial artists I've ever encountered. My teacher, Grand Master Kim, was a great man. You have probably heard of his legendary school on the foothills of Seoraksan and the fine athletes it has produced, but as you progress in your training, Peter, as your palette of martial arts is widened, you will, in all probability, spurn the acrobatic superfluousness of Taekwondo in favour of the simplistic beauty of, say, Burmese Boxing,' said the voice behind the white light.

He was in range for a head butt. That could be followed by an overhand right, but remembering Rule Six, I decided to wait a while and figure out who exactly this fella was.

'You see, Peter, martial arts are a lot like poetry. That is to say, all actions performed in the realm of the superconsciousness, in other words all actions performed under the guiding hand of God, all those actions have in them an innate poetic nature. So, like poetry is not an exercise in picking the most polysyllabic words or technically difficult pentameter, martial arts is not about executing the most spectacular kicks or impressive combinations. A true master of martial arts will not only spurn the most spectacular move, but he may also, at times, spurn the most effective. You see, he's not concerned with winning or losing. He has entered the realm of the superconscious and seen the truth: victory and loss are but illusions. He knows that the only reality is the reality presented to him by God in the eternal language of beauty. As a result, a true master will always find the middle path between exhibitionism and competitiveness. He will walk the path of beauty.'

I hadn't lived with Rule Six for very long. I hadn't repeated it thousands of times to keep other crap from creeping into my head. I suppose this meant the rule was more like a guideline at that time. Whatever the reason, Rule Six went out the window, and I tried to stitch your man a loaf.

Me head butt missed and my overarm right was deflected into an excruciating arm lock. The fucker levered me arm, and me face slammed into the table. I felt me shoulder was gonna pop out of its socket any second.

'I'll put some smacht on you yet, ya young pup,' growled the man, moving his face into the light.

I instantly recognised the crazed left eye squinting at me. It was that mad aul fella from the assembly earlier.

I tried to squirm free, but a jolting pain froze me in me tracks.

'Lie still while I tell you something or I'll rip this appendage clean off your scrawny little frame,' said John James, the smell of tar-black tea and bacon fat following his words. 'We're going to make a poet out of you whether you like it or not. You'll be speaking and writing and painting and sculpting works of art before too long.'

'Never!' I shouted.

'Oh really?' laughed John James, wrenching me arm and bringing his hot breath down against my ear. 'We found that photo in your sack Mr. Smash. We know who it is. We know where to find her. Do you know what the penalty for photography is in the Second Irish Republic?'

I said nothing. Helen had betrayed me. Helen had helped me stoner Da land me in this mad house. What did I care what they did to the bitch?

'The Historians' Alliance will string her up stark dressed at the crossroads and the PWLA will stone her to death. Once she's bloodied and battered out of all recognition, they'll cut her down and feed her body to the dogs,' said John James.

Good – that's what she deserves, I tried to tell meself. I wanted to hate her, but I kept remembering the time she picked me up and held me against her chest and she smelled all nice and was all warm and all. I remembered falling asleep and not feeling vulnerable or nothing. I remembered her jade-blue eyes and felt scared something would happen to her.

'What do you want?' I said through gritted teeth.

'I want you tell me what those chairs have to say about life,' said John James, releasing me from the arm lock.

'You what?' I said falling down.

'I'll leave you three alone to talk. There will be no distractions in here and no excuses for failing to reach the superconsciousness,' he said, each syllable of waffle adding to an already overwhelming case for kicking the living bejasus out of this gobshite at the nearest possible opportunity.

'Elevate yourself, Mr. Smash. Transmute the inanimate into the realms of the divine. Find the path between exhibition and competition. Find the path of beauty.'

There was a cold laugh.
I tightened my fists.
The door slammed.
I flexed my quads.
In the darkness it was only me and the chair.

    I suppose locking me up with no one to talk to was meant to be a terrible punishment. But as you know, I hated talking to people. I wasn't bothered with waffling on to wasters like me classmates. Nah, what I loved was training. Training for dishing out ass-whoopins. So yeah this set-up was nearly fucking ideal. I did no talking and lots of training.
    I put me legs up on the chairs and did jumping press-ups till me pecs gave out. Then I dropped down and did normal push-ups till I maxed out on that too. Finally I got down onto me knees and did ladies' press-ups till I reached total muscle exhaustion. Chest done, I started me arms. I gripped the edge of the chair, stretched me legs out in front and did a couple of hundred dips. Triceps done, I scouted round the room for a ledge or a handle on the wall. While standing on top of the stacked chairs I was able to reach a small ventilation hole in the wall. I gripped it with one arm, did pull-ups till my dorisis and biceps were gone, switched to the other arm and finished with two-arm pull-ups. Chest, arms and back done, I worked through me usual routine of cycle crunches, Russian twists, one-arm planks, lunges, squats and leg-lifts.
    I eventually collapsed face first onto the floor and lay there smiling a smile only champions know. A smile that comes lying half-conscious on the mat knowing that every muscle has given every single ounce of energy it had to give. It's lying there half-dead, and knowing you can rest. You can rest cause you have no *choice* but to rest.
    Now, by my calculations, I had been locked in the cell for five hours. And what a five hours they'd been. I picked meself up off the floor and without any fear of the Da or me cousins or me aunties interrupting me, I began me stretching. I worked me way through an entire Hatha Yoga routine and finished off by putting a foot up on either chair and doing the splits

I judged that to be seven hours of uninterrupted work. Christ, I hope they leave me in here for a couple of weeks, I thought. I'll be a fucking animal by the time I get out.

Having done the best training session of me life I drifted into a little doze on the floor.

'Food,' said the dwarf, sliding open a hatch and pushing a metal tray into the cell.

I picked the metal tray off the floor, pulled a chair up to the table and started shovelling the grub into me gob with me fingers. From the first mouthful I knew I was in trouble. It was lukewarm crap that tasted like cardboard boiled in muck. All there was to mop it up with were flat bits of stale bread. No meat, no eggs, no milk, no butter: no fucking calories. The energy required to chew and digest this crap was greater than the energy I was getting out of it.

Fuck it, I thought, the Da was feeding me similar crap for a long time before I passed out. They'll open up before it gets that far.

So every day or night or afternoon or evening (was hard to tell in total darkness) I did a complete conditioning and stretching session, and every morning or night or evening or afternoon I got the same sloppy crap for breakfast or lunch or dinner. The training was making me stronger, but the food was making me skinnier. Before long I was all out of body fat and me muscles started to waste.

The beautiful feeling of muscles pulsing with blood after a good session was gone. I no longer felt them growing under me skin. Instead I felt them knotting and cramping and telling me they weren't gonna do it again. They weren't gonna keep following orders if I wasn't gonna hold up my end of the bargain and feed them the protein they needed.

It was around that time, maybe three weeks, maybe longer, that John James paid me a visit.

I was in the middle of a set of bicycle crunches when the door burst open. John James stooped under the doorframe, swung his spazzy, retarded bad leg in front of him and slammed the door behind him.

I was in the best shape of me life. I couldn't check the curves and contours in the mirror, but I didn't need to. Everything was toned up and hard. Even John James, with that wonky left eye, could notice the development.

'I know that smell,' he said, sniffing the air. 'That's the smell of a man in training.'

I said nothing and looked back at the big ugly fucker with a blank expression.

'So you're a man in training are ya, Smash? Very good. Very good...but tell me this and tell me no more - what makes you train?' said John James.

'Appears to me tis nothing but your own will; nothing but your own ego. Your acts are performed outside the realms of the superconsciousness. They are not guided by God. They are but the gross egotistical presumptions of a gobshite. Who are you to train if God has not willed you to train? You're an arrogant young pup in need of a clip round the ear, that's what you are,' roared John James.

I flexed me pecks and kept me mouth shut.

'Oh you've grown muscles all right, but why? Your muscles have grown without purpose, and they will waste without purpose. You will drop. You'll fall to the floor, but that chair there will continue to stand. It will stand because we built it to do so! It doesn't presume to do anything else. It knows its purpose. What were you built to do? You haven't even asked that question. You don't have a fecking clue what your purpose is. That dumb chair knows more than you and will, in the end, outlast you,' said John James, opening the cell door and leaving me alone in my dark cell.

Three or four days later, when the cramps and diarrhoea started, I realised they weren't gonna bring me any more food.

The dwarf came all right, but now all he delivered was a cup of water. I tried to shout at the little fucker. I tried to plead with him. I tried to reason with him, but I never got a word out before the shutter closed again. I even skipped training to wait by the hatch, but every time I was either half-asleep or busy picking me toenails when the fucker arrived. I never got as much as a word in edgewise.

It wasn't long till the training had to be abandoned. The stretching even got too much. I lay there doubled up with cramps, groaning and moaning, but the whole time the chairs just stood there. The fuckers were silent, but they were too silent. You knew by their half-folded postures that they were laughing inside. They had heard John James telling me I was gonna drop and they were gonna keep standing. The cocky fuckers thought they were gonna outlast me.

227

A couple of days before, I could've kicked the legs off them. I could've bashed them off the wall. But I hadn't, and now I was too weak. No, if I was gonna beat the giggling cunts, I was gonna have to play them at their own game.

I straightened meself up, crossed me legs and focused on steadying my breathing. I needed to use as little energy as possible if I was gonna beat these fuckers. I relaxed me toes. I relaxed me calves. I relaxed me thighs and abdominals and pectorals and shoulders and even began to relax me mind. They weren't laughing now. Now they were worried, but I didn't pay them any attention. I kept focused on being relaxed and thinking about nothing.

I'd always thought that thinking about nothing would be the easiest thing in the world. Turns out it wasn't. All kinds of crap tried to distract me. I heard insects in the wall. I heard strange scratching under the floor. I felt cold. I felt sick. I felt weak, but one by one, I beat those things away. Next, something strange starting happening. I started picturing me Da playing sitar with the copper banging away on a tabla. I started imagining Helen being stoned to death by a bunch of crazy bitches in pyjamas. I started seeing the wolf-wild faces of me classmates flashing in and out of the shadows of the woods.

They were surrounding me and I was twisting and turning and swooshing my torch through the air trying to watch for Chivers. They all wanted to sink their teeth into me, but I knew it would be him first. They'd only attack after he'd made them brave.

I backed into a tree, and the wolves closed in tight. I felt the solid wooden trunk behind me and smelt the hungry breath of the pack closing in on my flesh.

I jumped up and grabbed a branch. I could hear mouths snapping at my heels as I pulled myself up. I started climbing like a mad man. I didn't have time to pick a route. I scrambled from branch to branch, fleeing the chasing pack.

All of a sudden I ran out of tree. Me head peaked out the top of the leaves and I had nowhere left to go. I couldn't climb higher, but I'd be damned if those bastards were gonna drag me back down between their teeth. Nah, I'd rather jump. I'd rather make the decision to fall to ground. I'd be the one who acted even if that act meant I cracked my skull open.

So yeah I jumped, but I didn't start falling. Me jump kept momentum. Nothing was pulling me back down. I just kept going up and up and up and up. The wolves were lost in the dark. The tree was a speck below. I hung up there with the stars and looked down on the entire world.

Then I spotted meself sitting cross-legged in my cell. From up there it seemed like the stupidest thing I'd ever seen.

'What the hell are you doing, ya gobshite?' I said to meself below.

'These cocky fuckers think they can outlast me, and maybe they can, maybe they can, but I'll be damned if I'm going out without a fight,' I answered from my cell.

'That's the stupidest thing I've ever heard,' I said.

'Not as stupid as giving up,' I shouted in reply.

'But they can't possibly beat ya, you ejiot. If you're not there to call them chairs then they're not chairs.'

It was then that I realised I'd lost me mind. Not only was I talking to meself, but I was talking nonsense about chairs. I'd been in total isolation for god knows how long. I'd been abandoned by me waster Da. I'd been threatened with the death of the one person who could make me sleep. I'd been starved of protein and then just plain-old starved. I'd challenge a full grown adult to endure that, let alone a four-and-half-year-old boy. So yeah, I had me first mental breakdown at age four. It took me a long time to recover from it, and even longer to realise what exactly had happened, but once I did I swore the fuckers were gonna pay.

Now the revenge I wanted wasn't gonna be a small-scale thing. This couldn't be squared away with a kick or a punch or a head-butt. This required a full-scale apocalyptic retribution of Homeresque magnitude.

That's right, Blondie. I said, 'apocalyptic retribution of Homeresque magnitude.'

Surprised I have the vocab?

Well, you shouldn't be. If you'd grown up in the dark days of the Second Irish Republic, you'd have a head full of useless shite too. You'd promise yourself you'd never use words like diaphanous, obstreperous, defenestration or confabulation. You'd swear bits of Shakespeare and Chaucer and Dante would never cross your lips. You'd try your best every minute of every day to talk plain, but then you'd get angry or upset or excited and some useless shite, some shite you were sure you'd forgotten, would come blurting out and remind you that no matter how old you got, those bastards had scarred your mind for life.

Anyway. I wanted revenge. I wanted the school reduced to rubble. I wanted the teachers' heads on spikes. I wanted all the chairs in all of Ireland stacked up to the sky and for astronauts on the international space station to shake with fear at the sight of the approaching flames.

I was so fucking angry that I was able to bend my every impulse towards one goal, i.e., revenge. I reacted to nothing. Poetry classes, nineteenth-century novels, tin whistle, chess club, endless waffling on about Jessie and Ballyfarnon and Dr. Benjamin Murphy: I soaked that all up and didn't say boo to a goose. I kept it all locked up in a box in me head. Every day the box got tighter and hotter to handle, but I kept it closed by repeating Rule Six.

Know your enemy, I said when composing verses of Gregorian poetry. Know your enemy, I said when painting cubist portraits of fat aul ones in pyjamas. Know your enemy, I said when caught up in a ten-hour Chinese chess battle.

I suppose you want a day-by-day account of all that shite. You want to hear every little juicy detail, don't ya? Well, tough. This book is called *The Truth*, and the truth is that I only have a dim picture of all that. I can remember certain things clearly, but mostly I just have a general feeling bout it. Just an overall vibe and then a clear picture of the big events. I'm sure other sports stars have given you a detailed description of the first girl they fancied and the ribbons she wore in her hair and the way she walked and the exact words she said and all. Well I hate to break this to ya, but they're lying through their rotten teeth. They're just adding in all that crap to fluff out the story. There will be none of that out of me. I'll give you what I remember and nothing more.

After me spell in solitary I was laid up in Nurse Mona's office getting fed the proper grub. I got me strength back fairly quickly, but it was a while before I got me head straight again. There were days where I raged, foaming at the mouth, trying to attack any chair I could see. There were nights were I cried like a baby, hiding under me covers, claiming wolves were trying to eat me. But as I built meself back up, the attacks got less and less frequent, and eventually Nurse Mona marched me back to class.

We walked into the classroom and everyone stopped drawing. At the front of class sat a fat aul one, tits perched on rolls of belly fat. She gazed out the window trying to look thoughtful and all, but she just looked like one of those America hicks that turn up naked in fields claiming to have been raped by aliens.

Realising no one one was drawing anymore, she turned to see what the distraction was. Chivers, who had been smoking by the window and admiring the model's arse, threw his joint into the schoolyard, grabbed his crutches and came towards us.

'One young man ready to be filled up with facts and figures,' said Nurse Mona, pushing me forwards.

'Education is not the filling of a pail, but the lighting of a fire,' replied Chivers.

The nurse grunted.

'What do we do class?' continued Chivers, swinging a crutch over the kids' heads.

'We elevate ourselves into the realms of the superconsciousness, sir,' answered the class before launching themselves back into their drawing.

The classroom filled with the noise of sharp lead scratching across paper and thick fingers smudging lines.

I'd been away for a stretch, that was for sure. A stretch long enough for Chivers to have these gobshites singing from the same hymn sheet. As I looked around, I noticed that some of the class still had casts on their legs. It takes ten to twenty-four weeks to heal a broken leg. I'd been in the hole somewhere in the region of three to six months.

'You know best, Mr. Chivers,' grunted Nurse Mona, slipping out the door.

'Table six, Smash,' said Chivers, pointing down the back with his crutch.

I walked down the back and nearly started laughing at the sight of the goons I was gonna be sitting with.

I suppose I should take a second to describe them for ya. Set the scene like...well, here goes:

Jim McGrath: Brown eyes, snot nose, skinny body, goofy feet, torn uniform, lop-sided glasses, messy hair.
Maraid Keane: Stoat eyes, bird beak, boxer's chin, 'mad woman who lives in a house full of cats' hair.
Gary Nolan: Block head, flat nose, pointy teeth, cauliflower ears, delicate mouth, sausage fingers.
Bobby Fence: Sperm whale forehead, centre parting, soft nose, soft eyes, soft chin, gappy smile, wheezy (but gigantic) set of lungs.
Ciara Fenlon: enormous chin.

I grunted a quick hello and stayed standing. Jim looked like he was gonna cry. Maraid looked like she was chewing on a lemon. Nolan stabbed his pencil into his picture and slashed viscous lines left and right. Ciara Fenlon's chin started wagging, but the sight of that massive thing moving was so shocking I didn't hear anything she said. Bobby Fence smiled, filled his lungs with air and started to blow.

'Smash, isn't it? Yeah I heard all about you, the leg breaker, the shin cracker, the ninja turtle, the power ranger— not that I know what any of those things are of course. Me big brother's friend's uncle told me about it, and now he's dead so there's no one to tell on even if you did want to tell on someone for watching T.V. Anyway, I missed the kicking cause I was in hospital meself. Guess why? Go on, guess why? Oh, you'll never get it. No idea huh? I had a broken leg! Crazy or what? I fell off the garden shed. Don't ask what I was doing up there. No really, don't ask. I couldn't tell ya even if I wanted to. Oh all right, I'll tell you. I was hunting insects. Don't ask me why! No really, this time I'm not telling. Seriously, I couldn't even if I wanted to. So yeah when you were breaking legs I was already in hospital with a broken leg eating jelly and ice cream and sleeping all day long. You know what? If you feel like breaking another leg just give me a call. That hospital life beats the hell out of this school crap...'

'Mr. Smash, sit down and start drawing,' shouted Chivers from the front of the classroom.

'Quick,' said Bobby pulling up a chair for me, 'Sit down before 'Gives me the shivers' Chivers takes points off our table. Do you like that? Shivers-Chivers! Made it up meself.'

'You never made that up, you dirty liar,' hissed Maraid, arching her back.

'Liar!' shouted Nolan, breaking the nib off his pencil with a viscous stab.

'Jim came up with that and you bleedin well know it,' said Maraid, knuckles on the table.

'Bleedin well know it,' repeated Nolan.

'Well in fairness, like, I didn't like come up with the whole thing, like,' said Jim, pulling his fringe down across his eyes.

'You called him Shivers didn't you?' shrieked Maraid, turning her glare on Jim.

'You did. You did,' growled Nolan, tearing his picture to shreds.

Jim's lips started to quiver, his breathing fell into irregular gasps and eventually his whole body started to shake.

'We did it together like. I said Shivers like and Bobby put it together with Chivers. It was a team effort like,' whimpered Jim.

'No, Maraid you're right. Absolutely correct. I shouldn't be taking credit for other people's work. Got a bit carried away there. I'm very sorry about that, Jim,' said Bobby, offering Jim a handshake.

Jim looked from Bobby's smile to Maraid's scowl and collapsed face-first onto the desk, crying.

'We did it together,' sobbed Jim over and over.

Maraid dropped her arched back and shifted uncomfortably in her chair.

'Oh come on Jim don't leave me hanging here. Accept a man's apology,' said Bobby, still waiting for his handshake.

'Why would he accept an apology if he thinks you did nothing wrong, you gobshite,' screamed Maraid.

'Gobshite,' repeated Nolan.

'Table Six is at it again, I see. Talking out of turn and failing to complete work as instructed. Minus two points,' said Chivers, walking over to a score board and removing two of our stars.

Jim cried harder. Maraid started pulling hair out of her head. Nolan snapped all our pencils and rulers in two. Ciara's chin

233

wobbled up and down, and Bobby tried to pull me down onto a chair.

I kicked the chair away and squatted down on all fours instead. After the experience I'd had with chairs, I wasn't gonna be putting me arse on one ever again.

I suppose I should get this out of the way now. Well here goes: The press made a big deal out of the fact that I stood for the duration of the Sports Personality Awards. 'A mark of arrogance,' they said. 'Another sign of the egomania of Smash,' they wrote. Some even thought that standing cause I knew they'd call me name was enough reason for the award to be revoked. I didn't answer any of those accusations at the time, but now you know the reason: I don't like chairs. It's not a phobia or nothing. I'm not scared of them or anything. I'd fight any chair. I'd kick the legs off the sturdiest of the fuckers. It's just that I'm not gonna be all hypocritical and sit on them and pretend they are relaxing or nothing. They are responsible for me first mental break down, and I hate the fucking things. End of story.

Anyway I didn't sit down with Jim and Maraid and Gary and Ciara and Bobby. Eventually Chivers spotted me squatting and deducted another star.

Table six went into complete meltdown, but I just squatted there wondering why they cared so much about a bunch of stars bandied about by 'Gives me the shivers' Chivers.

I got me answer at dinner time.

'...so me brother Andy picks him up by the neck and squeezes and Colin Fallon's eyes look like they're gonna pop out of his face and who comes round the corner? Go on guess? You'll never guess. No idea huh? Jimbo Knob Nose James. Gave him one month solitary! One month in the hole – can you believe it?' said Bobby, as we queued in the cafeteria with our metal trays.

'I did somewhere between three and six,' I said watching the dinner ladies scan student cards before dishing out the dinner.

'Three to six weeks for a first classer! Holy shit,' said Bobby almost dancing with excitement.

'No three to six months,' I answered stopping Jim and Bobby in their tracks.

'Liar,' said Maraid, spinning around to glare at me.

'Fucking liar,' added Nolan, heat-butting his dinner tray.

Ciara darted between us and started talking. Everyone stood transfixed, watching her enormous jaw move, but the sight was so incredible we missed everything she said.

'Then why is Chivers' leg still in a cast?' I said, breaking Ciara's spell.

'Cause he has a broken leg, you thick,' said Maraid, squinting her eyes and hissing.

'Thick,' roared Nolan, slamming his tray down on the top of his head.

'And who broke his leg?' I answered, cool as a cucumber.

'Dunno,' said Maraid, turning back around.

'Now in fairness, like, we know Peter done it, Maraid. I mean I'm not saying nothing we don't already know like. We saw him do it with our own eyes, sure,' said Jim, hiding from Maraid's glare behind Bobby's back.

'I saw nothing! And how would it prove he was in the hole for three months even if I did see it?' screamed Maraid, spinning back around and pushing Bobby aside to glare at Jim.

'No like. I'm not taking sides, like. I'm just saying in fairness, like,' said Jim, lips starting to quiver.

'Well it does prove he was in there for a least three months actually, cause that's how long a broken leg takes to heal,' said Bobby with a massive grin.

'And how the fuck would you know?' said Maraid.

'Cause I broke me own leg a while back,' said Bobby pulling up his sack to reveal a jagged scare on his shin.

'If yous lot want any dinner, yous had better hand over them student cards fairly sharpish,' said the dinner lady.

Maraid glared at Bobby once more before handing over her student card.

The dinner lady scanned the card, looked at the computer screen and shook her head. She wiped the card on her apron and scanned it again, but whatever she'd seen the first time she was seeing the second cause she gave it one last go.

'For Jessie's sake what have you lot been up to?' she said with more sympathy than anger. 'Yous would want to cotton on to yourselves fairly quick smart now or you'll be skin and bones again the week is out.'

Lecture given, she took Maraid's tray to a vat at the back of the kitchen. While we stared at juicy bacon, roast potatoes, fat peas, fried chicken, grilled sausages, shepherd's pie, lamb chops and cauliflower drizzled with cheese, we were spooned out a grey lukewarm slop. The moment I laid eyes on the slop me mouth filled with the taste of mucky cardboard, and I began to wretch.

We sat silent at the table, pushing grey slop around our trays, while all around us kids laughed and joked and shovelled the proper grub into their gobs.

'Fuck,' I muttered to meself.

'Ah it's not that bad once you put some salt on it,' said Bobby wolfing it down while reaching across the table to empty an entire salt shaker onto my tray.

'Not that bad? Not that bad! If you'd only kept your bleedin mouth shut we wouldn't have come last. Table two were miles behind us,' said Maraid pulling at her hair.

'Miles behind,' added Gary, slamming a fist into his slop and sending it flying in all directions.

'Think you'll find you were the one who started the argument, Maraid,' said Bobby, casually wiping Gary's slop from his face while adding yet more salt to his own.

'You were trying to steal Jim's joke, you liar,' said Maraid, tightening up for attack.

'Liar,' said Gary sending another fountain of slop into the air.

'I think we agreed it was a team effort didn't we Jim?' said Bobby, starting to help himself to Jim's untouched pile of slop.

'I think we are all on the same team here,' said Jim, trying to sneak a spoon into his food between Bobby's attacks.

'Stop eating his food, you thief,' screamed Maraid.

'Thief!' boomed Nolan, slamming his tray on the floor and bringing us to the attention of Chivers up on the teachers' table.

If this kept up it meant more points dropped. And more points dropped meant less food. Up until now I had been happy to let this pack of gobshites fight it out. I don't go in for teamwork. I don't like some other ejiot fucking it all up for me. I don't like some other

236

fucker getting all the credit for my work, either. In team games both those things happen with regular fucking occurrence, but they never happen in individual sports. No, in individual sports you win when you win and you lose when you lose. If you're crap, you've nowhere to hide, and if you're a champion, no one can deny your genius.

But here I was in a team whether I liked it or not, and we had a classic imbalance of power. Maraid had Gary on her side, but he was, as far as I could tell, as thick as a plank. This meant Maraid could win the battle of brawn but not necessarily the battle of brains. She needed another member on her side for a clear 3-2 majority. Bobby wasn't falling in line, so Maraid needed Jim, but Jim was a big softy and preferred Bobby's talking to Gary's grunting. That meant there was a two v. two scenario, with me as the key vote. Well if I was gonna be in a poxy team then there was only one way it was gonna work – I'd be the leader.

'Well we can fight about who said what, lose more points and be back eating this crap tomorrow, or we can figure out a way to never come last and be eating bacon and sausages and cauliflower with cheese every day,' I said, silencing the bickering.

'And how are you gonna do that?' sneered Maraid.
'Not sure. But I'll tell you one thing, Maraid.'
'What?'
'It won't take ME three months to figure it out.'

So for a couple of weeks I kept me eyes and ears open and calculated my next step. If I was gonna get revenge I was gonna have to get strong. If I was gonna get strong I was gonna have to get fed. If I was gonna get fed I was gonna have to figure a way around this scoring system. God knows we didn't have the talent to be notching up scores in the poetry and painting and singing and all.

Until I could figure out a plan I just went through the motions. Every morning we woke at dawn and dragged our arses out into the woods, where we meditated in little beehive huts made out of stone. The birds would start singing, the sun would dance on the dewy leaves and me skin would shiver in the vanishing night air. I'd find meself thinking about Helen. I'd start thinking about scaling the wall and making me way back home. I imagined the big hug I'd get off Helen and the smell of her clothes and the soft rising of her chest. I could almost feel meself falling asleep, but then I'd remember me

Da and Chivers and John James and the chairs, and me teeth would start to grind. I couldn't go back till I got even.

After meditation we'd go in and do some light stretching that Mrs. Vicky tried to pass off as yoga. Not once did we try to touch our toes off the backs of our heads. Not once did we perform headstands with our legs wrapped around our necks. Pouring saltwater down your nose or vomiting bile out your belly were not even mentioned. Yoga, me arse.

After stretching we had a spot of breaky and then it was time for class. Chivers went through the usual shite. All the time waffling on about the superconsciousness and Jessie and the prophet Benjamin Murphy and the future of the Second Irish Republic and all that shite. It was during these long blabbering speeches that me plans for revenge started to form. But like I said, if I was gonna get revenge, I was gonna have to be strong, and if I was gonna be strong, I was gonna have to get fed. So I'll tell you how I got round the scoring system first.

Under their system only the last team in each age group got the slop. With six classes of six teams that gave a total of thirty-six competitors. Presumably the school administration had reckoned that with so many teams, last place would constantly be changing hands. The slop would act as a little prick in the arse for a team that had stopped pulling their weight.

According to Bobby and Maraid, it had started out like that all right, every team occasionally coming last, but things quickly turned sour. The weaker members of each team found themselves being ratted out and squealed on for every little thing till they all got taken out of their teams and put in one team together. Apparently the same thing had happened in the other classes too. This resulted in each class having one shit team. Now instead of last place rotating around thirty-six teams, it was only moving between the six worst. Things were also complicated by the fact that it was impossible to study, compose verse, draw portraits, sing hymns and run your ass off in P.E. when you were crippled with pangs of hunger. The fuckers couldn't get themselves out of the situation, and soon found they were eating slop over fifty percent of the time.

My solution was simple. Every day we would volunteer one of the teams to come last. We'd make it known what score they were going to get that day. All the rest of us had to do was to get a few points more than that team. Not only would each team only be eating slop once every thirty six days but the other thirty five days could be spent safe in the knowledge that if they didn't feel like composing a Portuguese love sonnet, then they really didn't have to. No matter how little work they did, they still wouldn't be coming last.

After a little gentle persuasion from Gary and Maraid, most teams saw it our way. One team, consisting of the smartest kids in all the school, who referred to themselves as The Dream Team, were not proving to be good sports. So after communicating with them through Bobby and Maraid, and even sending Ciara to mesmerise them with her chin, I was forced to intervene personally.

The schoolyard was full. Children were sprinting left and right and screaming and shouting and creating general havoc. Mrs. Vicky was on yard duty. We'd made sure it would be her and not Jimbo Knob Nose James, who made more use of one good eye than most people would of ten. We'd even sent Bobby over to discuss karmic philosophy with Mrs. Vicky, ensuring our operation would go unnoticed.

'Were are they now?' I asked Maraid.

'Jim is luring them over to the dorms just left of the woods,' she answered, biting into a big red apple.

'Gary in place?'

'He's ready,' she answered, taking another bite.

'Lets do it,' I said dropping me head and walking quickly across the yard.

'Well, Bobby, that's a very interesting point. I had no idea that you were so interested in the teachings of Krishna,' said Mrs. Vicky as we passed her and Bobby under the basketball nets.

'They're in place,' hissed Maraid as we established a visual on the targets.

Children parted to our left and right as we charged towards the dorms at the back of the yard. Everyone knew what was coming. Everyone except Linda, Andrew and the rest of The Dream Team.

A circle of girls playing jump rope scurried out of our way and it was only then, when we were already on top of them, that they spotted us.

'Oh, um. HI, um,' said Andrew, little rat eyes skipping left and right hoping to find a burrow to scurry down.

'So that's why you've been talking to us you little traitor?' said Linda, red cheeks puffing out at Jim.

'We just want to have a little a chat, like,' said Jim, moving behind my back and away from their accusing stares.

'Well, we don't want to chat to ejiots like yous,' said Linda, crossing her arms confidently.

I gave Andrew a stun upper jab to the nose and Maraid smashed her apple into Linda's face before Gary hopped out of the woods and bashed the others. The fight lasted five, maybe six, seconds. Before they even knew what was happening we bundled them into the woods and out of view.

'I'm going to tell on you and you're going to be in so much trouble,' cried Linda.

Maraid replied with a kick to the chin.

'Everybody finished?' I asked calmly.

I could see the fear in their eyes. They knew Mrs. Vicky couldn't see them here. They knew their cries would only melt into the screams of the other children. They knew I could fucking bury them right there and then.

'Well it's sad that it has to come to this, it really is. I'd hoped you'd see reason. After all, all I want is for everyone to work together for an easier, fairer and more enjoyable life.'

'You want us to do nothing so you can get away with doing nothing too,' said Linda.

Maraid lunged forwards to deliver another blow, but I held her back and turned to answer Linda.

'No, no, Linda. You've got it all wrong. We don't want to do nothing. We want to do loads of kicking and punching and running and jumping and spitting and cursing. See we're really good at all those things. If they handed out points for that stuff we'd be first every day. Fact is they don't. They hand out points for waffling on about poetry and novels and all that shite. Now yous lot are great at writing poems about butterflies and singing songs about roses. We on the other hand are not so great. To make matters worse, they've put us all on one team. And worse again they're feeding us so little food that we can't even compete. You see the game's not fair, so we've decided to change the rules. We've decided to invent a new game. Now you're angry cause you might not be the winner in this game each and every bleedin day. But why should you be angry?

Unlike yous we're not gonna make you eat crap everyday. We're not gonna starve you half to death. In our game everyone will only have to eat slop once every thirty-six days. In your game we ate slop every other fucking day. Your game nearly bleedin killed us, but we're not looking for revenge. We're just looking a bit of fair play. So what have you got to be angry about? If anything, we're the ones who should be pissed off and ranting and raving, but are we? No, we're not. Look at my friend Gary here,' I said motioning towards Nolan's snarling face.

'There's nothing but love and compassion in that face,' I said, offering Linda and Andrew a hand up off the floor.

'Love and compassion!' shouted Nolan, slamming his fist into the palm of his hand.

'Tomorrow you guys need to get a score of ten and everybody will be happy. At the end of the day, it's the only fair thing to do,' I said, looking without pity at the bruised and bloodied members of The Dream Team.

'Fair for who?' snorted Andrew.

'Fair for everyone,' cried Jim, springing forwards to intercept the angry fists of Nolan flying towards Andrew's face.

Jim took two square digs to the face and collapsed on the floor.

Everyone was stunned. The Dream Team were shocked because Jim was known all over school as a wimp who wouldn't lift a finger to a fly let alone throw himself in front of two full-force digs from Gary Nolan. Don't get me wrong— we were shocked by that too— but what completely flabbergasted us was what the action meant. It meant Jim actually believed all that fairness and equality shite we'd been selling. He believed in it so strongly that he was willing to get smashed in the face to prove a point.

In truth – if I had been in The Dream Team I'd be doing exactly what they were doing, viz, I'd have been winning. I wouldn't give a fuck about some bottom feeders starving half to death on cardboard-flavoured muck. I wouldn't eat shit once every thirty-six days to save a single one of them. Jessie, I wouldn't eat it once every ten years to save a million of them. Fact was, I wasn't on The Dream Team and I couldn't compete with them on level terms, but like all true champions I was determined to find a way to win. This fairness jive was just a load of bolllix we needed to sell the others so we could start winning. I knew it. Bobby knew it. Maraid knew it. Christ even Nolan knew it, but much to our surprise Jim fucking believed in it.

Yeah so Jim's leap of faith gave our whole operation a kind of stamp of authenticity. We looked like the real fucking deal; genuine martyrs to the cause.

'Ten points is a little low isn't it?' said Andrew helping Jim up off the floor and dusting off his uniform.

'I usually get ten points for a single poem,' laughed Linda.

'Well consider it a challenge then. I'm sure The Dream Team won't shy away from a challenge,' I said, offering a hand to seal the deal.

'We'll try our worst,' laughed Andrew shaking my hand.

'All the worst then,' I said joining the laughter as I shook hands with all the remaining members of The Dream Team.

The day arrived and everything started smoothly. The Dream Team submitted stick man drawings for the life drawing class and after a brief lecture about the dangers of Dadaism, Chivers awarded them zero points. In the class debate, Andrew was attacked by fits of giggles, Linda mumbled around in circles, John went on a wild tangent about the public misconception of earwigs, Michele littered her speech with curses and Graham openly farted.

P.E. was far easier to throw seeing as there wasn't a developed muscle between them. Linda even managed to get some points deducted by scoffing every time the miracle of Jessie was mentioned in history class.

Coming towards the end of the day, The Dream Team were living up to their rep as overachievers. With a grand total of one point it looked like they were going to get the worst score in the history of the school.

'And team one I suppose we must allow you the opportunity to redeem yourselves, although on today's form I find it highly unlikely that you have composed anything worth gracing the ears of humanity,' said Chivers, flapping his hands around as if annoyed by a pack of shit-eating flies.

'Well let's hear it,' said Chivers, sniffing the air with disgust.

Linda stood up, cleared her throat and shuffled the papers in her hand.

'A smash hit,' announced Linda, getting sly giggles from all quarters.

'A chair cannot be a chair
If I am not there
To call it a chair
Even the table's positions unstable
If I am unable
To say it's a table
One cannot presuppose
The pen up me nose
Continues to write
When all becomes night.'

Linda sat down and struggled not to laugh as all around her people howled and whistled and jeered.

As you've probably guessed I was not laughing. I was not jeering. I was not whistling. I was deadly still, wondering how the fuck she'd found out about me breakdown. How had she written down my thoughts? Had she told Chivers of our plans for cheating the system? Had John James given her all the juicy details of my madness?

I was ready to scream, cry, laugh, run, jump, hate and love all at the same time. How dare she make me feel something with a fucking poem. A million feelings rushed around me head, but as Chivers began dissecting the poem one feeling came to the fore: I felt naked. I felt naked and then I felt vulnerable. I felt vulnerable and then I felt very fucking angry.

'...without any consideration for metre, the poem is most certainly better spoken aloud than read in silent contemplation. Some would argue that this factor alone renders it unworthy of serious consideration, but I personally believe spoken word to be the fountainhead of all verse and so will turn away from such discriminations. The childish clumsiness of the rhyming scheme, if indeed you could call it a scheme, and the general lack of form add to the satirical nature of the piece. Indeed this tyro-like bundling serves as a metaphor for the lack of sophistication in the modes of thought, which the words themselves have set out to ridicule. It is a brave attempt at breaking the rules to create effect. The lack of craft in the verse communicates the lack of craft in the philosophy it's presenting. Therefore, the lack of craft becomes a craft in itself. That said, I believe poets should master the rules before wilfully breaking them and in this way fully understand the full effect their rebellions will have on the reader. I do, however, commend the bravery displayed in this instance, and in the interest of encouraging such free-spirited creativity in the rest of you, I will award them ten points,' said Chivers, adding the points to leader board and causing general pandemonium in the class.

Students began frantically composing songs and poems and plays and short stories in a last-ditch attempt at avoiding the slop. My team did nothing; nothing but control the urge to rip Linda's head off.

Linda had fucked up our system. Not only that, but she'd openly slagged me off by composing a poem about me breakdown. This was a critical moment. If I let Linda's actions slide, I'd lose all authority and our team would be back eating slop every day. I was gonna have to make an example of Linda. I was gonna have to make her name synonymous with torture and pain and horror.

Class finished and we started walking down the halls towards the cafeteria. The Dream Team, thinking we were gonna break their legs at the nearest opportunity, hurried after us to smooth things over.

'Peter! Peter! Wait a second, Peter! I have to explain,' shouted Linda as she bounced up behind me in the hall.

'Should we brain her now?' hissed Maraid in my ear.

'Not here,' I ordered before spinning around to smile at Linda, Andrew, Michelle and Graham.

'Oh, Peter, Peter,' panted Linda, cheeks pulsing red, 'I'm so sorry about our little mishap there. I mean all day we managed to get bad marks; terrible marks; probably the worst marks in the history of the school. We were sure the poem would land us another fat zero too, but...'

'But it landed you a perfect ten,' I said clapping my hands together and roaring a harsh cold laugh.

Linda dipped her head and started twisting her foot on the tip of her shoe. Andrew's eyes darted from left to right, and seeing no support coming from his teammates, decided to take over.

'In fairness. In all fairness now, it was the worst poem Linda had ever written. I mean everything about it was bad. The rhyming scheme was bad. The metre was crap. Even the idea itself was a crock of shit. It was the most childish bunch of waffle I'd ever heard,' said Andrew, keeping his eyes glued for an attack from Maraid or Nolan.

'The most childish bunch of waffle you'd ever heard eh?' I said staring hard into Andrew's eyes, imagining meself gnawing his nose off with me teeth.

'Yeah chairs and tables and pens up noses and whatnot. It was a pile of shite,' said Andrew, summoning some nervous laughs from his team.

I waited for them to stop, and then started roaring laughing meself. I laughed and laughed and laughed until I could feel a silence, tight as a drum, all around me.

Andrew and Linda exchanged looks, and the poet picked up the pace again.

'I'm glad you see the funny side of it, Peter. I mean we could never have known that Chivers would have thought we were writing crap poetry on purpose as some kind of crappy metaphor,' said Linda, biting her lip and looking at me from under her eyelashes.

'Oh I know that, Linda. You could never have known it was so bad it was good! Only Chivers could come out with that kind of crap,' I said lifting Linda's bruised chin gently with my fingers so I could look down into her eyes.

'I'll get Andy to write the poem next time. I'm just no good at being bad,' said Linda, gazing up at me.

'Oh you're bad, alright. Just not everyone realises it,' I said releasing her chin and letting her stumble forwards.

'Well, you've got thirty-six days to practise writing shit poetry, Andy,' I said, turning away from Linda.

'But shouldn't we do it tomorrow seeing as...'

'It would raise too much suspicion.'

'He's right, Andy. We can't be too obvious,' said Linda, linking an arm through Andy's.

'Sorry again, Peter,' said Andy.

'These things happen.'

'Well we better get moving or the food will be gone before we get there,' said Linda pulling Andy away.

And off they trotted; giggling; trading smiles; thinking they had pulled one over on Peter Smash; believing their brains could out manoeuvre any trap I put in their way. Their food was gonna taste good tonight, but soon, very fucking soon, when the consequences of messing with Peter W. Smash were felt, they'd be willing to trade every piece of tasty grub they ever ate for the one bowl of slop they hadn't.

Over the coming days, we discussed our plan for revenge. We hatched kidnappings, half-drownings, three-quarter hangings, fourth-degree burns and all sorts of lovely stuff. Everyone got involved. Even Ciara, through a series of sketches and hand signals, managed to lay out a plan that involved ripping Linda's limbs off using an ingenious series of pulleys and ropes.

The only member failing to get involved was Jim. He still believed in all that fairness bollix. He even tried to convince us that the other teams, given enough time, would logically come around to our way of thinking because it was the right thing to do, and people, if given enough time to think, always do the right thing. I said that was bollix. Maraid said it was bollix. Bobby said it was bollix. Ciara even wrote a little note that read 'bollix.'

Yeah, so we thought Jim's idea was a load of bollix, but we humoured him for a bit just to avoid the waterworks and all. But as the days passed and the teams one by one took up Linda's tactic – team three submitting a painting with lines splatted all over it, swearing it was shite, but getting ten points – the girls on team two screeching like Japanese rape victims, swearing to Jessie they thought it was the worst crap they'd ever heard, but again getting ten points – as all this crap came to a head, I couldn't take Jim's shite any longer.

'So you're telling me those two giant red squares they've painted on that black background are an honest attempt at losing?' I said to Jim as team five, today's assigned losers, submitted their painting.

'In fairness, like, I'm sure they elevated themselves into the realms of the superconsciousness and that was the crap that flowed out of them,' answered Jim, hiding behind his fringe.

'Well what the fuck are they elevating themselves for? Can't they just lash a couple of stick men down or draw the Mona Lisa with a moustache? We all know Chiver's hates that shit,' I argued.

'They probably don't want to be too obvious. They're probably just worried about getting us all caught, like. And at the end of the day, Peter, old habits die hard. Every little thing they've done in the last year has been in the realms of the superconsciousness. It's hard to just stop that, but if we give them some time they'll logically come around...'

'Logically me hole!' hissed Maraid.

'Me hole!' added Nolan, punching the table.

'Now, now, let's take it easy,' said Bobby. 'I mean, Jim has his beliefs. I admire him for it. I mean, I love fair play as much as any man, but Jim, you have to admit that if the fuckers are elevating themselves into the realms of the superconsciousness then any attempts at shitness can only be beautiful statements about shitness and therefore not shit. I mean we all know that, Jim. So really if they're elevating themselves, then they know full well their shit isn't going to be shit.'

'I don't think they are, like, purposefully—'

'You don't have to believe it, Jim! Just like you don't have to believe one plus one equals two, or the sun spins around the moon, but it's still a fucking fact,' I said, getting hisses and punches and chin waggles of approval.

'Well, I'm not saying they're playing fair, like,' said Jim.

'Not playing fair? Not playing fair! They're fucking robbing us blind and laughing at us gobshites who wanted a fairer and more enjoyable life for everyone. They're making a joke of us right now. Look!' I said, pointing towards team five who had just 'unexpectedly' received ten points for their painting of two large red squares on a black background.

Jim stared hard across the room, and as he watched team five laughing and joking and cheering, something rearranged itself behind his eyes. His fists started to clench. He began to heave in heavy breaths, and tears bubbled up in his eyes.

'A few bad eggs are spoiling it for everyone,' said Jim, voice gurgling up from the pit of his stomach.

'That's right, Jim. A few bad eggs are wrecking it for everybody, so we've got to let them know we're not gonna stand for it,' said Bobby, throwing an arm around Jim's rigid body.

'The bad eggs have to go,' said Jim, paying no heed to Bobby and drilling holes in the heads of team five with his eyes.

'Smash the bad eggs,' hissed Maraid.

'Smash em,' roared Nolan.

'Oh we'll smash em, alright, but first we take out the chicken that's laying them,' I said, pointing to Linda.

So yeah, Jim got on board with our plans for revenge, but his motivations were still off kilter with the rest of us. You see, the difference between Jim and us, even at that early stage, was that Jim loved the game. He believed totally and utterly in the rules we'd set out for a fairer world. He was convinced it was the only game people should play. Not only that, but he believed it was the only game they should *want* to play. Meself, Bobby, Maraid, Ciara and Nolan didn't see it that way. We knew there were as many games and sets of rules as there were people to play them. Cause if you ask every person in this world how things should be run they'll all give you a different answer. The only thing you'll find in common is that the game each person suggests is the one they stand the most chance of winning. That's why you never meet a communist monarch or a laissez-faire coal miner. And that's only right. Why should people not want the best they can get? You see that was Jim's problem – he was unnatural. For example, if I was poor I would be a egalitarian socialist, but when I got rich I'd naturally become a free-market capitalist. That's just common fucking sense. But Jim wouldn't change. No, Jim would continue supporting an idea or a cause or a moral even if the thing was diddling him out of food; even if the thing was losing him money; even if the thing was gonna get him killed. So like I said, Jim's motivations were unnatural, but he did come up with our master plan for revenge. It was a bleedin ingenious plan. One guaranteed to scare the bejesus out of the other kids and get us away scot-free. As long as Jim was coming up with plans like that, who the fuck cared what his motivations were?

The night of the big showdown arrived. We lay in our bunks, pulses racing, toes twitching, hands fidgeting and ears pricked for the signal. It seemed like we'd been lying there for hours. Nolan even started snoring like a grizzly bear. I began worrying that Bobby's little incendiary device had been a dud. But just as I was giving up all hope, the fire alarm ripped across the schoolyard and the emergency lights began blinking in the dorms.

The bolts on the dormitory doors opened automatically and meself, Bobby, Jim and Nolan charged out the door.

The teachers were fast on the scene. They called for calm and started arranging the children into orderly lines. That all went out the window as secondary devices, planted at the end of each dormitory, went off.

Children ran screaming in all directions, their wild eyes flickering in and out of the shadows as the flames started to engulf the dormitories. Even Nurse Mona and Mrs. Vicky began to panic, charging around in circles, screaming for calm.

It had been raining all day and the yard was slippery. Naturally enough, with all this screaming and running and all, people started going arse over tit. The sight of kids rolling around on the deck, writhing in agony from imaginary shrapnel wounds added to the panic.

In the middle of this madness Ciara and Maraid cornered Linda, winded her with a few uppercuts to the solar plexuses and dragged her off towards the woods.

Meself and the lads arrived at the meditation cell furthest from the school and found Linda stripped naked and tied to four posts on the floor.

It was the first time I'd seen a naked girl in the flesh. I'd seen dirty pictures that Nolan had drawn. I'd even seen a photo that Bobby's big brother's friend's uncle's dead nephew had given him. The first thing that popped in me head when I saw Linda starkers was that she looked better with her clothes on. I wasn't the only man in the Second Irish Republic who thought women were better fully dressed. When extreme sects of the PWLA went marching through the streets of Dublin in their birthday suits, the rate of traffic accidents quadrupled. Manys a driver, turning onto Dame St. to see rolls of belly fat and swinging tits, threw their eyes to heaven only to slam into a double-decker bus. Hundreds of pedestrians, struggling to hold down their lunches, clamped their hands over their eyes and found themselves under the wheels of a truck.

Now Linda wasn't disgusting or nothing. She wouldn't make you lose your lunch. She was just flat as a pancake.

The beehive cell was lit by a single candle, and our shadows loomed large on the curved walls as Linda squirmed on the hard stone floor.

'Oh, Peter. Peter. What are you doing? Why are you letting them do this to me?' she cried, trying to appeal to me like a friend.

It's a tactic losers will try every time. When they're sure they've no hope of winning, they'll try and make you feel guilty.

'Shut the fuck up, you stupid cunt,' I shouted.

'Oh god! Oh god!' whimpered Linda, looking desperately around the room for a sympathetic face, but finding none.

'We tried to be reasonable with you, Linda. All we asked for was a bit of fairness, but instead you cheated us and then tried to play us for fools...'

'I didn't try to cheat you. I didn't mean to...'

'Don't lie to us, Linda. It will only make it worse,' I said, giving Nolan the nod.

Gary drew the stick back, grinned and then whipped it down onto the soles of Linda's feet.

Her scream made the candle flame shiver and every shadow inside the cell vibrated with her pain. We all tensed, watching as the line across the soles of her feet turned red.

Linda sobbed, hiding her face in the nape of her arm, before deciding she had to convince us of something. She had to convince us of anything that would get her out of here alive.

'Peter, listen to me. Please, just listen to me for a second,' she pleaded.

'All the talking in the world is gonna do you no good,' I answered.

'But, just listen. Just listen. That poem. That poem I got ten for. I swear. I swear on my mother and father's life that I thought it was shit. I remember writing it. I remember steadying my breath. I remember elevating myself into the superconsciousness and I remember writing the shittiest thing my mind could muster. I swear the shit just poured out of me. I was absolutely convinced it would get me a big fat zero. You have to believe me. You have to believe me, Peter, I didn't try to cheat you,' said Linda, her flat chest rising and falling rapidly.

'So you admit that you elevated yourself?' said Bobby, kneeling down beside Linda and looking down into her frightened eyes.

'What do you mean? Of course I elevated myself,' said Linda, her old confidence flashing forwards.

'Well you knew your shit wasn't going to be shit then didn't you?' said Bobby, hovering a couple of inches above Linda's mouth.

'What?' cried Linda, turning away from Bobby's lips. 'Peter, what is he talking about? Oh God, Jim, are you going to let them do this to me? Oh God, will nobody help me?' cried Linda, desperate for an ally.

'If you're elevating yourself into the superconsciousness then your shit can only be a beautiful expression of shitness and therefore good,' said Jim from the doorway.

'Oh God, you're all crazy. You're all insane,' said Linda.

'No, you're insane,' replied Jim, 'You're the one who's mad cause you can't see that our way is the right way to act. If you could see that it was right then you'd logically do it. You cannot – therefore you are sick.'

'Help! Help!' screamed Linda.

Those screams quickly lost all language as Gary let loose on her with the stick. He worked her over for a good five minutes, and when he stopped the soles of her feet were a bloody mess of fat and tissue.

'Oh god. Oh god. Please let me go. I didn't do anything wrong. I didn't do anything wrong,' whimpered Linda, sweat pouring off her brow, hair spread in a tangled mess behind her head.

'That's not what we want to hear,' I said motioning for Gary to give her some more.

'Nooooo! I'm sorry, Peter,' said Linda.

I caught Gary's arm and waited for what we all knew Linda would eventually say.

'I'm sorry, Peter. I shouldn't have written a poem like that. I shouldn't have elevated myself. I'm sorry I didn't play fair. It will never happen again. Please forgive me. I'm begging you to forgive me,' said Linda, finding composure from god knows where.

'Maraid, undo the ropes,' I said.

'She's lying,' said Jim stepping in from the doorway.

'What?' I asked.

'She doesn't understand what she did was wrong. Her mind cannot logically see that it should choose actions that are fair and right. She is sick and she will make others sick. We must stop her before it's too late,' said Jim, voice gurgling up from his stomach.

'Ah don't worry, Jim, she's learned her lesson alright. She won't be cheating us again anytime soon,' said Bobby, walking over to throw an arm around Jim's shoulder.

'She will cheat us again at the nearest opportunity because she thinks it is right to do so. She's sick. She must die,' said Jim, springing forwards, landing two knees on Linda's chest and starting to throttle her.

All five of us tried to pull him off, but his fingers were locked like vices around Linda's neck.

'You're gonna kill her,' we shouted, but Jim didn't even blink.

Linda's lips were turning blue, but Jim just looked dead ahead. There was no expression on his face. No anger. No passion. No strain. He could've been brushing his teeth or washing the dishes or taking a piss. This was an action that simply needed to be performed. It was not an action that required thought.

As Linda's eyes started rolling back in her head, I began peeling Jim's fingers away one by one. I eventually broke his grip and we bundled him into the corner. Even with five of us holding him down, Jim wouldn't give up. He started biting our arms and legs till I was forced to get him in a triangle lock and knock him out.

'Fuck, what time is it?' I asked.

'Eleven fifteen,' answered Bobby.

This was not good. We'd already been away for fifteen minutes. At this point we should have been climbing into the girls' dorm through the bathroom window. We should have been wrapping ourselves in water-soaked bed sheets. We should have been crawling under the smoke in the dorm and carrying Linda to safety. We should have been hailed as heroes.

Instead we had two unconscious bodies to carry all the way back through the woods and no plan for hauling them up through the dorm window. In short, our plan was fucked.

By the time we got back to the edge of the woods we could see all the classes had been arranged in lines. We could see the fires had all been put out. Worst of all, we could see the teachers searching the dormitories for us.

We brainstormed ideas, but no one could come up with a plausible explanation for why we were carrying two unconscious bodies, one of which was naked and bleeding from the souls of her feet. In the end we decided on a pact of silence. It was a stupid bleeding tactic, but I'd challenge anybody to come with something better under the circumstances.

We stumbled out of the woods and surrendered.

Nurse Mona and Mrs. Vicky carried Jim and Linda to the nurse's office, while Chivers started demanding answers.

'What in Jessie's name happened here?' said Chivers, yellow-tinted glasses all fogged with sweat. 'Why are that young girl's feet dripping blood? You answer me, Smash!'

'They don't seem to be in the humour for a chat, Mr. Chivers. I think we need to give them a little time to arrange their thoughts,' said John James, fixing me with his good eye.

I knew where we were going. I knew what would happen there. I also knew that kicking and punching and screaming would only mean I'd be in there for longer.

'Put them in the hole,' ordered John James.

So yeah, I started me second stint in solitary. Was it easier the second time? Had me first trip to hell prepared me for the second? No, of course not. A stint in the hole isn't like running a marathon or something. You don't hit a wall at thirteen miles and console yourself with there only being another thirteen miles to go. You don't see the last hill and smile through the pain cause you know it's the last hill. In the hole there are no markers or signs to tell you how far you've gone. Every hill could be the last, but it could also be the start of a fucking mountain range. And that's the agony of it. You know you're going to get out at some point, but you can't allow yourself to believe that point is anywhere in the near future or the disappointments will drive you mad. In the hole, you have to run without any hope of the running ending if you are to have any hope of running to the end.

After a couple of weeks, or a month, or a month and a half, me cell door burst open and in hobbled John James.

'No longer a man in training Mr. Smash?' he said, looking at me slumped in the corner.

I said nothing and had no muscles to twitch.

'Well that's a pity now, isn't it? All that hard work gone to waste. All those hours down the drain. All your labours laid to waste for want of a purpose. Did I not tell you it would happen that way? Did I not tell you the chairs knew more than yourself?' said John

James, pulling up a chair that made a cackling noise as he dragged it across the floor.

The fucker stared hard into me face before hocking up a mouth full of phlegm and spitting it against the wall.

'As you've probably guessed, your teammates have long since cracked. They've spilt the beans on your little plot. We know who masterminded it and we know what your goals were,' said John James, the smell of black tea wafting off his breath.

I suppose I was meant to be shocked by this. I suppose I was meant to feel hurt and betrayed and alone. Truth is, I always felt alone. Truth is, I expected nothing less from my so-called teammates. You see, when a team wins, the praise is shared, even though it's the leader who berates and beats the bastards to victory. But when a team loses, leaders find themselves short of volunteers to shoulder to blame. You get all the shit and not nearly enough of the spoils. John James was telling me nothing I didn't expect to hear.

'So?' I answered.

'So...I come here in the spirit of contrite humility, Smash. We misconstrued your laconic behaviour for guilt. The information garnered from your peers has, however, thrown everything into a new light. Your terseness is nothing but a symptom of misplaced loyalty. This loyalty is a characteristic, when put to work in the correct fashion, that can bring glory to the Church of Jessie. After all, not everyone finds their muse in the ancient halls of the scribes. Some men, arguably even more noble men, find their muse on the battlefields of the warriors,' said John James.

'What?'

'Jim confessed to planning Linda's abduction. The details were corroborated by your teammates. We know everything, Smash. In fact we were expecting a paradigm shift far earlier in the school year. It's a source of deep disappointment in the faculty that it took our students almost a year to plot a coup like this. Our programme of deprogramming has yielded results more slowly then we had anticipated,' said John James with a sigh.

'What the...'

'To your immature minds there may not appear to be a design in our methods, but believe me the greatest thinking in Educational Science is being brought to bear on your schooling. Of course, all experimentation will yield positive as well as negative results. It took far longer for you to revolt than we had hoped, but we have located an idealist amongst you. That rarest of gems will be taken, polished up and set in the crown of Jessie to shine forth in all its glory,' said John James, standing up and addressing some invisible crowd.

'So am I getting out of here or what?' I said, abandoning any attempt at understanding this waffle.

'Of course you are, young man. You're getting out here this very moment and I think you'll find the next phase of your education a little more in tune with your Spartan sensibilities,' said John James, helping me up off the floor and out of the cell.

'What's going to happen to Jim?' I said as we walked up the hall.

'He will be shown the glory of the flesh become word,' said John James proudly.

I asked no more questions; I didn't need to ask any more questions: Jim was fucked.

Did I feel any urge to fess up to me own part in the plan? Did I think about taking some of the blame to help Jim? Did I feel sorry for me old teammate at all? No. No, I didn't. The stupid bastard had tried to strangle Linda. Now don't get me wrong, there was nothing necessarily wrong with wringing the bitch's neck. There was, however, something seriously fucking wrong with messing up our plan. He'd landed us all in the hole, not only that, but he'd revealed our plan to cheat the school scoring system. After a long stretch in solitary we were coming back into a situation we had no handle on. After all our hard work we were back to square one. I was no closer to getting Chivers' head on a spike, John James' balls in a jar or Dr. Benjamin Murphy's beating heart in my fist. In fact, revenge was further away than ever. Jim deserved everything he had coming to him.

We walked along the long rectangular corridor, into the big pointy building and arrived at my classroom door.

'Peter Smash reporting back to class,' shouted John James, throwing open the door and pushing me into the classroom.

Strange music with whale noises and drunken voices and tribal drums was playing over the sound system. Chivers, sitting cross-legged beside an open window, exhaled a massive plume of smoke into the lazy rain and cast a casual glance towards the door.

Suddenly realising the principle had arrived, Chivers threw the joint into the school yard and hopped up onto his feet.

'Ah, Principal James, good to see you,' said Chivers, scurrying over to offer a handshake.

'I've warned you about these epicurean tendencies before, Chivers,' said John James, ignoring the outstretched hand and swinging his bad leg past the teacher.

'Well I...'

'Using the tools God has gifted us, to open new doors to the superconsciousness is all well and good if your intention is to create something meaningful from the experience, Chivers. But what you appear to be engaging in is a stimulation of the senses in pursuit of base pleasures,' said John James, scrutinizing the piles of books on Chivers' desk.

'Not at all, sir. I assure you that I am not enjoying myself in the slightest,' said Chivers, saving items from the floor as John James roughly tossed them back onto the desk.

'Don't lie to me, Chivers. I saw you with my own good eye reclining there in a drug-induced stupor. You have about as much intention of composing a poem now as my shoe...'

'No really, sir...'

'What kind of example are you setting for these young minds? Is it any wonder it took them almost a whole year to achieve a paradigm shift?' said John James, suddenly halting his tour of Chivers' table and turning to inspect the teacher himself.

'Well I would never contradict you, sir. I can only say that you may have misinterpreted what you have seen,' said Chivers, shrinking under John James' glare.

'Misinterpreted?' roared John James, spittle splashing against Chivers' yellow glasses.

'Well you see, sir. The thing is, sir. In truth, sir, I have been exposing myself sir to prolonged periods of drug-induced hallucinations to gather material for a poem on the folly of perusing such a path in life,' said Chivers, wiping his glasses on his shirt.

'What in the name of Jessie are you blathering about, Chivers?'

'Well, sir, you see, sir, much like a doctor, sir, who exposed himself to the plague in order to find a cure or Thomas De Quincey exposed himself to opium, sir. I am suffering so that others may read of the suffering such a life causes and not fall into that trap,' said Chivers with a nervous smile.

'De Quincey, eh?'

'Yes, sir. I'm working on a poetic rendering of drug-induced hallucinations using the argot of our age. I wish it to be a modern reworking of De Quincey's *Confessions of an English Opium Eater*,' said Chivers, smile growing more confident.

'You, Chivers, could never hope to achieve the heights of a man like De Quincey. You don't have a word of Greek, for one thing, and your learning is typical of the pathetic warehousing of facts and figures peddled by the universities of the First Irish Republic as an education,' said John James, wiping the smile off Chivers' face.

'I do, however, admire the ambition,' he continued, turning to face the class, 'and that's what I want to see from all of you this year. I want to see ambition. You fell way short of the expectations we had for you last year. Don't disappoint us again.'

John James glared from left to right as the sound of pan pipes, tigers rustling in long grass and a screeching tsunami siren played in the background.

'Well you heard Principle James,' said Chivers, ordering children back to their painting.

As Chivers apologized and bowed and kissed arse I wandered towards the only empty desk in the class. It was behind Maraid, in front of Bobby, to the left of Nolan and to the right of Ciara. It was a perfect bleedin location. The lads were all gaunt, but they gave me a smile when they saw me coming.

'They got Jim,' whispered Bobby as I sat down.

'No, Bobby— Jim got Jim,' I said over me shoulder.

'Yeah, he fucked himself,' hissed Maraid.

'Fucked himself,' shouted Nolan, causing John James to pause at the classroom door.

Everyone launched themselves back into their painting and with a few more bows and apologies from Chivers the big man left.

Chivers walked back to his desk and collapsed in exhaustion. As he cursed under his breath and slapped the table, we continued to paint.

I took a good look around at the canvases. There were pictures of drowning skyscrapers, suicide jumpers sinking from the

88th floor. There were oil blue canvases with quicklime skulls suspended in the rib bones of whales. There were pock-marked islands heaped high with mounds of tangled limbs, a finger at the summit reaching towards a pure white sun. There wasn't a stick man or moustached Mona Lisa in sight. Everyone was elevating themselves.

I looked over at Linda in the far corner. The marks of Jim's fingers could still be seen on her neck. Her feet were still bandaged and wrapped. Didn't they realise we'd do it again? Weren't they afraid?

'Okay, finish up now, please,' said Chivers as the music stopped.

Finishing touches were frantically applied to the paintings. Kids started carving in texture with pallet knives. Kids jumped up on the their desks to fling ropes of paint across the canvas. There was even the momentary appearance of a penis before Chivers brought everything to a close and collected the canvases.

Chivers lined the easels up in front of the interactive whiteboard and numbered them.

'Now class, if you'll take out your tablets, please,' said Chivers.

The second I heard the word tablet I feared the worst. They've started drugging us, I thought. They are going to pump us full of chemicals so we're too fucked to think for ourselves.

When everyone started pulling out slim computer screens, instead of pills, I was even more confused.

'Ah, yes...Smash. I nearly forgot about you,' said Chivers, starting to search through his desk drawer for a spare screen.

'What the fuck?' I whispered over my shoulder to Bobby.

'The teams have been disbanded. We're all one nation under Chivers now,' answered Bobby.

'Here you are, Smash,' said Chivers, sliding the screen onto my desk. 'You list your preferences one through to five. You don't have to use all five preferences, but obviously the more preferences you give the more effect your opinion will have upon the final outcome.'

'What the fuck?' I whispered to Maraid.

'Pick your favourite five pictures and list them one to five,' she replied without lifting her eyes from her own screen.

'Okay class, if you could please get ready to vote. Remember we are particularly interested in colour and contrast this week, so you may wish to weight your choices accordingly. Okay here we go. Submit your choices in 5, 4, 3, 2, 1...'

All eyes rose from their individual computers to the interactive white board at the front of the class.

'Right, let's see the results of the first round,' said Chivers, tapping some buttons.

A bar chart popped up on the white board and there was a collective 'Ohhhh' from the class.

'Oh, it's close run race today. Andrew's cubist piece is first past the post— good choice considering its brave use of green and blue. Will his excess votes transfer to the impressionistic tendencies of pictures two and eleven or will there be a drive towards the modernism of nine and eighteen. Let's see,' said Chivers punching some more buttons.

'And that's two more past the post now. As expected, Sarah's impressionistic piece benefited from the transfers, but we have an unlikely surge bringing Graham's classical Renaissance stylings across the line. Perhaps some tactical voting is going on there. Are the class willing to vote in a less skilfully rendered portrait piece in order to keep the modernists out of the running? There's only one way to find out.'

The computer churned figures for a few minutes before spitting out the final result. All kinds of cheering and booing and cursing broke out across the class.

'Well there you have it. It just goes to show you can never predict the vacillations of this class. As expected, painting eleven stumbles home after two sets of transfers but then out of no where Nolan's piece, black swirl on white, leap-frogs all the others and will go before the adjudication panel this evening.'

And that's how the rest of the day went. The entire class composed poems, sang songs, performed plays, executed Zen calligraphy, wrote proofs for mathematical theorems and expressed problems using Boolean logic. All the pieces went before the class and through a process of democratic election were whittled down to the best five creations. At the end of the day our selections would go before a panel of teachers, priests, mathematicians and natural philosophers for grading. The class was awarded points as a whole and these points were then used to buy food. There was of course a catch.

The catch was that the best five students in each class were assigned the job of sharing out the food relative to each team member's contribution. If you wrote crappy poems they gave you crappy food. If you wrote a gorgeous song they gave you a gorgeous steak. There are no prizes for guessing who the top five in our class were every day. It looked like The Dream Team were gonna be dishing us out cardboard-flavoured muck all year. But things took another twist at P.E.

The entire year was in the sports hall. Nobody but nobody, regardless of physical impairment or injury or illness, was absent. Not even Linda, with her bandaged feet, was aloud to sit down. But apart from the large numbers, it started out like any other P.E. class. Mrs. Vicky led us through a light stretching routine that she tried to pass off as yoga and then Mr. Flatly took over. We performed a full routine of plymetric jumps, one-arm push-ups, bicycle crunches, suicide sprints and belt-assisted back flips. After the explosive work was finished we did farmer's walks, fireman's' lifts and other core-strength exercises with the kettle drums and medicine balls. It was a murderous session, but then again it was a new year. We were hardly gonna be confining ourselves to five sets of thirty all the way through school. We were here to develop.

Mr. Flatly gave us a moment's breather and we were all ready to begin our cooldown stretches when in walks Principle John James.

'Line up!' roared John James, sending children scampering in all directions.

'Yoyi stance,' he ordered.

Everyone snapped to attention, fists clenched at waist height, feet shoulder-width apart and eyes dead ahead.

'Left fighting stance! Itch!' shouted John James.

Just like that everyone popped their left leg forwards and put their guard up – left hand slung low around chest level and right hand up against their cheek.

'Ready,' said John James, setting everyone bouncing on their toes.

I felt meself getting giddy with excitement. We could only be about to learn one thing. After all the waffling and reading and painting we were finally going to learn something of fucking use. We were gonna learn how to smash someone's head in.

'Nolan, get out here,' said John James, pulling Nolan up in front of the entire year, 'One step roundhouse kick to the head, roundhouse kick to the body, back knuckle, reverse punch, jump back side kick. Itch.'

Nolan snapped the roundhouse kick a good foot over his own head height and without dropping his leg followed with another kick to the gut. Having remained perfectly upright while throwing the kicks he was able to execute the punches the moment his foot hit the floor. After finishing his punches he stopped on a dime, reversed momentum completely and launched himself backwards through the air to throw the side kick. The move had everything: balance, power, technique and aggression.

I'd definitely been in the hole for more than a month. I had some catching up to do.

'That's how I want to see it done. Ready. Itch...Ni....San...,' said John James.

And off we went, kicking and punching our way up and down the hall. I gave it everything I had. I was so excited, so overwhelmed with joy, that even when me legs were full of battery acid and John James was calling out twelve-hit combinations I still threw everything at maximum speed, maximum extension and maximum power.

This new system might have The Dream Team telling me how much food I deserve and acting like they were better than me and all, but if I got to train like this every day it wasn't all bad. I'd find a way to get the food I needed. I'd get strong from this training and when the time was right I'd get my revenge.

'Yamai,' said John James, giving us a breather and walking off towards the interactive whiteboard at the top of the gymnasium.

'Teachers, if you'll please hand out the voting apparatus now,' said the big man.

The teachers started passing out the tablet computers and a large cage was rolled into the hall.

'All right now, children, if you'll please select the five fighters you wish to see represent your class in the cage. Place your votes in 5, 4, 3...'

The votes were cast and there are no prizes for guessing who got elected. We weren't contributing beautifully worked proofs of trigonometry theorems or elegant Boolean expressions for breaking ASCII passwords, but the Lindas and Andrews and Grahams of this world were gonna make damn sure we contributed blood and teeth and bones instead.

The cage door slammed behind meself, Bobby, Maraid, Nolan and Ciara. We stood with our backs against the cage looking out at the opposition. I suppose I should take a minute to describe the bastards. I suppose you'd like to know who their parents were and what state jobs they held in the Second Irish Republic and whether their places in society meant their children were given preferential treatment in Jessholic School. You'd probably love a sub-plot thrown in with a love interest and conflicting feelings and all that shite. Well, I'm sorry but I can't help ya. Truth is, I only knew their names. They were in a different class, you see. And when you're seven, a person in a different class may as well be from a different fucking universe. Anyway I'll give you what I have:

Fighting Bill Tracy, Jr.: Tall, wide, huge neck, no chin, hairy hands, big feet.
Hammer Harrison: Female, two plates jutting from back of head, flattened nose, impressive biceps.
Mickey Knuckles: Pretty face, slimy hands, constant bulge around groin.
QuQu Kim: Slanty-eyed Chinese chick from Korea.
Ginger Ciaran: Enormous ginger eyebrows.

'Well it's not much of a welcome back for you, Peter,' said Bobby, shadow boxing in front of me, 'but I have to say I'm pretty happy to have the shin-cracker, the power ranger, the teenage ninja mutant turtle here in the cage with us today ready to unleash that world-famous, universally feared bone-cracking shin kick!'

'Let's kill these fuckers,' hissed Maraid.
'Fuckers!' roared Nolan, banging his fists on his chest.

'Class One versus Class Two. You know the rules. Protect yourself at all times. No gauging. No biting. No striking to the groin. The fight is over when all your opponents have been tapped out or knocked out. Ready? ' said John James, over the excited shouts of the students surrounding the cage.

'FIGHT,' said the big man.

Before I even knew what was happening, Ginger Ciaran and Mickey Knuckles had wrapped themselves around me legs and I was anchored to the spot. I started raining punches down on their heads, but could only land blows to the tops of their skulls, which was doing more damage to my fists than their heads. I stopped my flurry of digs and caught sight of Fighting Bill Tracy, Jr. lumbering across the cage and starting to cock his world-famous right hook. It was a punch so exaggerated in swing that I had time to knock Ginger and Mickey's heads together, give them a few well-aimed digs to the nose and completely sidestep Bill's right hook.

I watched Bill's fist swing through the air, changed stance, loaded me left leg and delivered an unmerciful kick to his right shin.

The sight of the big man keeling over like an old tree took the wind out of his comrades.

Maraid caught Hammer by the pigtails and executed a beautiful hip throw, ripping the hair clean out of Hammer's head in the process.

QuQu Kim peppered Nolan's face with technically exquisite, but completely ineffective kicks. After attempting blocks, parries and other high-brow manoeuvres, Nolan decided enough was enough. As Kim threw another kick, Gary boxed her in the shin. As she hobbled on one foot, Gary stood on her toe and, having rooted her to the spot, stitched her a good, hard loaf.

With all our opponents grounded, we moved around at our leisure choking them out with arm bars. The crowd went nuts, cheering and shouting and hanging off the edge of the cage. It was the first time I looked into the eyes of so many people and saw reflected there a truth that I had known all along. A truth that the whole world would come to know: Peter Smash is a champion.

'Back in your lines, please. Back in your lines,' ordered John James, pulling children off the cage and sending them back to line up.

'Fall in line,' said John James, opening the cage door and giving each of us a little wipe across the brow with the magic sponge.

Class Two's fighter had to be helped out of the cage, but despite suspected broken bones and serious concussions were made to line up with the others.

'Well, there was a clear victory there for Class One,' said John James, setting off a bout of cheers from our classmates.

'Quiet!' roared the big man. 'A clear victory in terms of knockouts and strangles, but a paltry effort in terms of form. Are shin kicks and heat butts the hallmarks of a mind in tune with the superconsciousness? Is ripping the hair out of a girl's head the sign of divine inspiration? Where is the beauty in these techniques?' asked John James.

'The beauty is in the winning,' I answered, getting cheers of approval from my classmates.

'Ah yes, Smash. The man in training. The big, all-conquering champion. Did I not tell you once before that a true master of martial arts does not care about winning. A true master has entered the realms of the superconscious and seen the truth: victory and loss are but illusions. He knows that the only reality is the reality presented to him by God in the eternal language of beauty. As a result, a true master will always find the middle path between exhibitionism and competitiveness. He will walk the path of beauty,' said John James, getting nods of approval from all the teachers.

'Well, I'd rather be an ugly winner than a beautiful loser,' I said, but my classmates were no longer cheering. They were, as you'd expect from a pack of fucking cowards, backing down at the first sign of trouble.

'We'll see about that, Smash. We'll see about that,' said John James, fixing me with his good eye.

'The points will be shared – five points to Class One for the knockouts and five points to Class Two for the form,' said John James, glaring from left to right, daring the students to howl or whistle.

No one said a thing. No one said a thing cause no one really cared. They weren't the ones getting thrown in there to beat the holy hell out of each other. All they had to do was keep voting us mugs into the ring and watch us bleed.

As the weeks wore on, I began to realise John James was right. Not right about winning in general, just right about winning in this particular circumstance. Meself, Bobby, Maraid, Nolan and Ciara could bash anyone, and I mean anyone, to pieces. The problem was that we did it ugly. That invariably meant we got less points than we deserved, but when we tried to do fancy spinning kicks and foot sweeps, we ended up with thick lips and black eyes. But that's not where the shit ended. Not at all. You see, The Dream Team, invariably the five highest scorers, were responsible for dishing out the points relative to what they reckoned we had contributed to the classwork. When we won ugly we got less points, so The Dream Team reckoned we deserved less food. When we fought beautiful we got more food alright, but we also got our faces rearranged. We were winning the battles inside the cage, but we were losing the war outside it. We needed a plan. We needed to find a way to *win*.

After one of our attempts at winning beautiful we sat down to ham, cabbage and potatoes that not one of us could eat due to missing teeth, fat lips or bruised jaws.

'Fuck. It's too sore to eat,' I said, pushing my tray away.

'It's torture. The first time in weeks we get some decent grub and we can't even eat it! Do you reckon we could persuade someone to swap us for slop and then give us their good food when our faces are better?' said Bobby, scouting around for potential traders.

'Anyone who's eating slop today is eating slop every day,' hissed Maraid.

'You're not wrong, you know. You're not wrong. It's the same people stuck with the shit every bleedin day and the thing is it doesn't even make any sense. I mean, The Dream Team are producing maybe ten or eleven pieces that would get maximum marks from the adjudication panel every day, but instead of those pieces getting points for everyone they're just let go to waste, and half of us end up eating slop,' said Bobby, abandoning his attempts to chew some meat.

'It's a fucking waste, that is,' said Maraid.

'It's a fucking!' cried Nolan.

'Imagine if we could sell off their extras to the other teams in return for food credits. Everyone would get higher scores. Everyone would get more food and our class would be sitting pretty,' said Bobby.

'Good look getting that shower of shites to part with their precious works of art,' said Maraid.

'Shites to part!' shouted Nolan, stabbing a potato.

'They would if it saved them from the cage,' I said, and that stopped everyone in their tracks.

So yeah, that's how the seed for our plan came about. The growth of the fully formed plot was something that took months. It required the cooperation of not only our classmates, but students in other classes too. This resulted in so many drafts, clauses, sub-clauses, footnotes and technical small print that if I was to lay it all down here, my autobiography would be trebled in length. Anyway, it's not important what you say you're going to do, it's only important what actually gets done. So, here's what happened:

First: We whipped up bad feeling between The Dream Team and the rest of our class. We used the usual horseshit about everybody being equal and individual success being impossible without the support of a team. We convinced gobshites who didn't know their sonnets from their pantoums, ejiots who couldn't tell a Monet from a van Gogh, and thick mullahs who didn't know their Pythagoras from their Fermat that they were entitled to the same amount of grub as the swats on top. Naturally, enough our classmates were only too willing to believe us. Only a madman rejects an idea he stands to profit from.

Second: I got Bobby, the chief architect of our little plan, to open up diplomatic channels between us and our sworn enemies, i.e., the fighters in the other classes. It wasn't an easy thing to do. We couldn't be seen talking in the yard or rumours would start, and having a little chat in the cage before we beat the fuck out of each other wasn't really a possibility, either. The only other time we were all together was at Jessholic mass. Having a chin wag down the back was out of the question, so we had Bobby volunteer to be altar boy. He sang like a canary, swished around the incense, cleaned the chalice, rang the bells, locked the tabernacle, poured the wine and, most importantly, he handed out the Eucharist. While standing at the front of the altar, right under John James and Baba O'Brien's nose, Bobby passed notes to our fellow fighters.

Now the odd time, scrappers like Fighting Bill Tracy, Jr. or Ginger Ciaran might knock out a member of our crew, but nine times out of ten, we pasted them. It got us fuck-all points cause we pasted them the ugly way, but we pasted them all the same and they were...well let's not say 'scared' cause that would be disrespectful. They were, after all, warriors each and everyone, so let's just say they had a healthy respect for us. Anyway when we offered less batterings in return for them forcing their artists to buy pieces from us instead of making their own, they quickly saw the logic.

Third: We presented our plan to The Dream Team. Bobby pointed out that it was grossly unfair that only five of their pieces could be considered by the panel at any one time. He demonstrated with the use of Venn diagrams and bar charts how the sale of pieces to other classes, to be submitted for consideration, would raise the standard of living across the entire school. Mr. Fence finished by highlighting that as the producers of the works, our class stood to be the most prosperous, well-fed class in the history of Jessholic school.

Fourth: After The Dream Team told us to take a hike, we told the rest of the class about their decision. The fury at their selfishness was intense. People were baying for blood, and it just so happened that we had a way of giving it to them. We convinced everyone to vote The Dream Team into the cage for the next P.E. lesson.

We stood in the gym, sweat pouring off us, as the teachers handed out the computer screens to vote in today's fighters. Everyone was smiling and joking and all. There wasn't a hint of what was coming.

'Okay there now, teams,' said John James. 'If you'd please prepare yourselves to vote in the fighters you wish to see representing you in the cage today. Right, here we go in 5, 4, 3, 2...'

The results came up on the whiteboard, but seeing as they'd been the same for months now, John James didn't bother to check them.

'Team One and Team Two, yous are first up,' said John James, opening the cage door.

Meself, Bobby, Maraid, Nolan and Ciara remained in yogi stance, eyes fixed dead ahead.

'Well come on then, Smash, we haven't got all bleedin day,' shouted the big man, fixing me with his good eye.

'Not today sir,' I answered with a blank expression.

'What in the name of Jessie do you young pups think you're playing at? Is it another trip down into the hole yous have your hearts set on?' said John James, trundling forwards and loading up the back of his hand.

'We are not the democratically elected representatives of Class One today, sir,' said Bobby, halting John James' hand two inches from my ear.

Chivers started coughing up a lung. Mrs. Vicky began punching buttons on the computer. Ripples of applause and cheering broke out along the lines of students. Nurse Mona waddled over to slap Chivers on the back. Mr. Flatly grabbed our computer screens to check for faults.

As all hell broke loose, John James continued to look me straight in the face. For a split second I thought the fucker was about to smile, but he turned away, squinted at the whiteboard and then moved forwards for a full inspection of the facts and figures.

'Linda, Andrew, Graham, Sarah, Victor... looks like you're finally getting an opportunity to put all that hard training into practise,' said the big man, walking back towards the cage.

To say the little weeds were scared would be the understatement of the century. They were shitting bricks. They were pissing their pants. They were so fucking scared that they started to smile like morons. They looked into the faces of their classmates expecting them to start laughing; expecting them to tell them it was all a big joke.

'Well there has been some mistake. We need to have a rerun of the votes. There was some confusion over the labelling of candidates. I'm sure it's just a mistake,' said Linda, stumbling around like a twelve-year-old girl who's one Bacardi Breezer away from surprise sex.

'Yous are joking. Yous are having us on. Oh, yous are such jokers. Such big jokers, aren't ya?' said Andrew, turning this way and that, hoping to catch a laughing face.

This state of disbelief lasted all the way into the cage. They were still wearing dumb smiles as Class Two lined up in front of them.

It was only when the cage door slammed behind them that the flight instinct kicked in. Now, I know scientists and biologist and all those wankers will tell you that everyone is born with both a fight *and* a flight instinct. But you only have to see the crap your average person takes off bosses, spouses, landlords, parents, policemen, taxmen, priests, dentists, car salesmen, mechanics, electricians, real estate agents, old-age pensioners and computer technicians to see that most people, even given perfect provocation, will never throw a good dig. No, they'd run for the hills before they'd punch some lippy granddad demanding a seat on the bus. So yeah, like I was saying, ninty-nine point nine-nine percent of people are pussies. They might have trained in Brazilian Jujitsu for ten years. They might be fifteen-degree black belts in Taekwondo. But if they don't have the fight instinct, they're gonna get bashed by the fella that does.

    The Dream Team did not have the fight instinct. Linda started crying and begging for help. Andrew started climbed high up the cage walls and clung to the roof for dear life. Graham lay down on the floor and curled himself into a tight ball. Sarah screamed high C above G, and Victor in a flash of genius decided to pass out.

    'Fight!' shouted John James, dispensing with formalities; hoping Team Two would silence the screams that were threatening to deafen us all.

    Fighting Bill Tracy, Jr. and company delivered. Sarah found herself anchored to the floor by Hammer Harrison and Ginger Ciaran hanging off her legs. Over lumbered Bill, throwing his massive right hook. Sarah didn't duck, but instead closed her eyes and brought her scream up to a B# over G. After a few minutes, the screaming stopped and Sarah was out cold.

    After dealing with the imminent threat of Sarah's screams, Team Two reined in the pace. This was all about making a point. This was about bringing The Dream Team around to our way of thinking with some good old-fashioned pain and suffering. So they thickened their lips, bruised their eyes, winded their stomachs, stamped on their toes, cauliflowered their ears, twisted their fingers and pulled their hair for a good half hour. It was methodical and it was ruthless. Only when John James threatened to even up the fight himself did Team Two bring it to an end with some quick strangles.

    We'd beaten the holy hell out of The Dream Team. Not only that, but we'd done it all above board. They couldn't rat us out to Jimbo James or Chivers or anybody. They'd been democratically elected into the cage, and that was that. When Bobby went to talk to them for the second time, he didn't bother with a sales pitch. The shit was already sold. What he did talk about was the new asking price. As organisers, facilitators and enforcers of the new system, we'd be taking an administrative fee of twenty-five percent. Everybody agreed that was fair.

Having seen the pummelling The Dream Team had taken, the other classes quickly fell into line, and any remaining pockets of resistance were quickly cleaned up with a trip inside the cage.

A new era of peace and prosperity began. The Dream Team did what they did best and were banging out top-drawer merchandise. Bobby collected works every day, sourced buyers, sold pieces to the highest bidders and then collected debts when the points had been awarded. Scores soared across the school. The teachers kept waffling on about the First Renaissance of the Second Irish Republic. There was talk of twenty new Jessholic schools opening next year. Everybody was better off – the teachers, the students, the swats, the gobshites – everyone. Meself, Bobby, Maraid, Nolan and Ciara especially. We were the most well-off members of the most well-off class. We were winning.

Now that I no longer had to worry about making art all day, I was able to turn me noggin towards revenge. Now the way I saw it, all this cheating the system shite was just a stop-gap measure. I mean, we could keep coming up with ways to cheat the system, but they'd also keep coming up with new systems. They were the ones setting the pace. They were the ones in control. If we wanted to win, we needed to kill the fuckers in charge and set up our own system. And who was in charge of the Second Irish Republic? Dr. Benjamin Murphy, that's who.

Now whacking Murphy was gonna be no easy task. First of all, none of us had ever seen him. We had no idea where he lived and owing to the blanket ban on photography, nobody had any real idea what he looked like. Sure, we had portraits and sculptures of the great man, but could he really have a purple triangular nose, eyes under his chin and red hair shooting from his ears? Was it possible that he was twenty feet tall and had arms thicker than an elephants legs? No, of course it wasn't. That was just more impressionistic bullshit produced by gobshites elevating themselves into the superconsciousness.

One thing we had been promised, however, was that the top five students, democratically elected at the end of the year, would be presented with medals by the great man himself. Now I obviously wasn't gonna get elected on merit, but luckily enough, this was a democracy, and we were rolling in the cash. I decided to pitch it to Bobby, Maraid, Nolan and Ciara as just rewards for our hard work. I'd convince them that it was the stamp of approval that our operation needed. I'd talk about the power of symbols and myth and legend and all that shite. We'd get up on that stage and when Murphy lent over to hang my medal around my neck I'd cut him.

The event itself was a ways away, but you can never begin your preparations too early. So, one evening I walked over to Bobby's dorm room to get me plans under way. I found one corner of the room cleared of beds and Bobby sitting in a big black leather chair behind a solid wooden desk. He was tapping figures into a laptop with one hand, texting with the other and shouting instructions down the handset of an office phone.

'What the hell?' I said.

Bobby glanced up for a second and motioned for me to take a seat opposite him.

'No, listen Gary, he's had three weeks already. Tell him he pays now or we take the pencil case he put up as collateral,' said Bobby down the phone.

As you know, I don't sit on chairs as a rule, but this one was so deep and luxurious and all. I decided to make an exception. I planted me arse down and felt something groping at me back.

'What the fuck?' I said jumping back onto my feet and giving the chair a good kick.

'Uh huh. Uh huh,' said Bobby, catching my surprise and putting the phone down against his chest, 'Massage chairs. Just got them in this morning. Guaranteed by the United Republican Masseurs Association to put five years on your life.'

I didn't care what they guaranteed to do, I wasn't having any fucking chair touching me up. I squatted down on me honkers and waited for Bobby to finish on the phone.

'Okay, okay, he's clearly not understanding the words coming out of your mouth, Gary, so put him on the phone to me there,' said Bobby, tossing his mobile onto the desk and slamming his laptop shut.

271

'Sorry about this, Peter. I'll only be a moment,' he said, taking a deep breath.

'No problem,' I said looking around at the piles of merchandise surrounding Bobby's desk.

There were things essential to our day-to-day business – notebooks of poems, sheaves of lyrics, paintings, relief carvings in wood, sound installations and plaster moulds. But there were also things that seemed a little less than essential. There were piles of pillows, shoes, pencil cases, sacks of oats, hundreds of jars of pickles, engine oil, motherboards, microchips, mobile phones and even a small greenhouse full of plants.

'Sean, listen to me and listen to me good. You're going to give Gary what you owe me...No listen, Sean. LISTEN. You give it to Mr. Nolan now or you take a trip inside the cage tomorrow. Do you understand what I'm telling you? Good. I've given you your choices. This conversation is over,' said Bobby, ignoring the pleas from Sean and slamming down the phone.

'Sean Doyle?' I asked.

'Who else?' laughed Bobby, leaning back in his chair and putting his feet up on the desk.

'Nice little set-up you've got going on here, Mr. Fence,' I said tapping the hardwood desk.

'Why thank you, Mr. Smash, and might I just say that none of this would be possible without Peter W. Smash's legendary shin-cracker axe kick around to put the fear of compound fractures into the electorate.'

'It's going well then?'

'Our enterprise is growing every day, Peter. Every day we're bigger, and not only bigger but more profitable too. Our second-quarter results were off the charts. But I'm sure you read all about it in the quarterly report I emailed you?'

'You emailed me?'

'Yes we've had to have a computer system installed. The accounting and tracking was getting too complicated what with the opening up of international markets and whatnot,' said Bobby, cracking his fingers and putting his hands behind his head.

'Are you not worried about what Chivers is gonna say about all this?' I said pointing to all the stuff strewn everywhere.

'Chivers knows which side his bread is buttered on,' said Bobby.

'What?'

'My guy is getting him weed that's double the quality and half the price of that shite he was smoking before. He's not going to start fucking with us.'

'What guy?'

'An associate of our head of I.T. support'

'We have a head of I.T. support?'

'A close colleague of our sales rep in Dublin.'

'We have a sales rep—'

'Listen Smash, I'd love to sit around and chat, but I have to check Class Four have finished tweening Linda's animation movie, then I have to check on the patch stitching that Class Five are doing for Andrew's wall hanging, and finally I have a meeting with Nurse Mona about creating a more customer-driven health service here in the school because, quite frankly, the thought of one of our top talents missing a day's work because the nurse is busy tending to the needs of someone like Sean Doyle makes me sick to my stomach,' said Bobby, standing up to shake my hand.

'Why are Class Two doing in-betweens for Linda?' I said, shaking Bobby's hand.

'Outsourcing,' said Bobby, sitting back down, opening his laptop, texting on his phone and answering another call on his office phone.

'No, we only except payment in Chinese RMB. Because the punt is worthless on international markets, that's why. Administrative charges? Listen to me now, Finton, if you start trying to pull this shit on me, you'll find yourself out of the loop faster than a thirty-year-old divorcee drops her knickers! You're damn right you'll have it for me this afternoon...'

Needless to say I had more questions for Bobby. Why did we have a sales rep in Dublin? What the hell was outsourcing? Why were we receiving payments in Chinese RMB? But one glance at Bobby screaming down the phone told me I wasn't gonna be getting any answers today. I also had the sneaking suspicion that when I did get answers they were gonna make no sense whatsoever. And if you ask someone a question and their answer makes you even more confused, it can mean only one thing: they are trying to pull a fast one. Allow me to explain:

Everybody knows I'm an athlete not an intellectual, but that's not to say I'm thick. You see, being an intellectual has very little to do with being smart. All intellectuals really do is study and memorise stuff that smart people have come up with. Being an intellectual has about as much to do with being smart as being a sports commentator has to do with being an athlete. In other words, it has sweet fuck-all to do with it. Now, the way these intellectuals get by in life is through intimidation. You see, your average person thinks big words mean big brains. They presume the intellectual wafflers can understand shit they can't and so they're too intimidated to demand an explanation in plain English. I never fall for that trick. The second someone starts banging on in techno-jargon and using words longer than a St. Stevens' Day shite that's when I know they have no real understanding of what they're talking about. All they're doing is repeating something they were told by someone else who was probably repeating something they were told by someone else who was trying to pull a fast one. Bobby was up to something, but if he could keep it up long enough and buy us those medals, I didn't care.

As the weeks passed, I kept a close eye on Bobby's operations. Every time I swung by the office there was some new addition. One week there were eight clocks installed to tell the times in Tokyo, Beijing, Delhi, Moscow, Berlin, London, New York and Los Angeles. Next week there was a partition wall put up and you had to get permission from Ciara (now working as Bobby's secretary) before you'd be let in to see Mr. Fence. So yeah shit was changing fast, but one thing stayed the same – each and every time you came in, Bobby was talking at break-neck speed on the phone and gulping back black coffee.

Outside the office, things were changing too. We'd started off with just the swats producing works of art, but as Bobby found more and more buyers on the international markets, more and more outsourcing was necessary. It got to the point where the whole school was working harder than it had ever done before. People started grumbling. 'Why are we breaking our balls?' they asked. 'Why not just produce what we need?' they complained. Bobby called them filthy communist bastards and had them elected into the cage. After he'd won the battle of brawn he also tried to win the battle of brains. He called a general meeting in his office and stood up on his desk to deliver a rallying speech.

'There's been a lot of questions floating around recently and a lot of uncertainty among you all, and I have to accept that as leader of this company it is my responsibility to make our mission very clear and keep us all pulling in the same direction. Some of you have been asking why we're working so hard and producing so much work? Well I would point to your mobile phones, laptops and well-fed waistlines. Much like Class One became the dominant class in the school through ingenuity and hard work, I'm attempting to make us the most dominant school in all of Ireland, if not Europe, and so enjoy an even higher standard of living. Once we've established ourselves as the dominant force, we can focus our efforts on innovation and outsource much of the menial labour to poorer schools. We work hard now to secure a happier, healthier and wealthier future,' said Bobby, jumping down off his desk.

'Now let's get back to work and make it happen,' ordered Bobby, picking up his phone and starting to chatter away in Chinese or Japanese or some shit.

People slowly filed out of the office and into the yard. Nobody talked about what they had just heard. They didn't talk about it because they had no idea what the hell it meant, but they weren't gonna go asking questions in case everyone else understood.

The only problem with people not understanding an idea is that it's hard to get them to suffer for that idea. The students' hearts weren't in the endless sketching and stitching and moulding and sanding and varnishing jobs. The quality of work was slowly deteriorating. Bobby tried to do as many quality-control checks as possible, but he couldn't catch everything, not when running a business operating in eight different time zones. When Bobby did find some shoddy workmanship, he tried to get the culprit elected into the cage, but found no support from the other workers. The donkey didn't like the look of the carrot and Mr. Fence had lost his stick. I saw an opportunity to push me own plans forwards and went to visit Bobby in his office.

'Yes, sir. No, sir. Well you see, sir, a lot of companies face these sort of managerial problems when moving from a small business model to a multinational structure. The corporate culture, communication channels and operational protocols have not been fully engrained at the work-a-day level. Our employees will, with time, become far more efficient in their new roles,' said Bobby down the phone, massaging his temples with thumb and index finger.

'Absolutely, sir. My first loyalty has always been, and will always be, to the shareholders. You have entrusted me with your money and quite rightly expect to see dividends,' said Bobby, listening to a tirade of shouts.

'Well no, this quarter's results are not what we would have hoped for, but the previous three...no, sir. Absolutely not, sir. The future is all that interests us here at Fence Global,' said Bobby, going pale.

'I assure you that won't be necessary, sir. We are up to the challenge. Yes, sir. Absolutely, sir, and I'd just like to...'

I heard the phone go dead. Bobby slowly lowered it from his ear and dropped it into the cradle. He kept his hand hovering over the phone, away from his body, like someone who has touched something diseased.

'Trouble?' I asked, jolting Bobby out of his twenty-yard stare.

'Smash,' said Bobby, shifting uncomfortably in his chair and scratching the back of his head.

'Jessie you don't look too well, Bobby. You know I'm not the world's biggest fan of lying around all unconscious and vulnerable and all, but you look like you could really do with some sleep,' I said, crouching down on my hunkers in front of him.

'Sleep is the last thing I need to be doing. Christ, if the papers found out I'd gone below when the ship was heading for the rocks, the markets would have our shirts by the morning. Then we'd hear the shareholders really go off. Fucking bastards are already calling for my head. I've given those assholes returns they could never have dreamed of, and now we hit one little glitch and they're calling for my resignation!' said Bobby, slamming a fist onto the table.

'Profits are down?' I said, feigning surprise.

'Of course they're fucking down. You've seen what has been going on out there. They're cutting corners left, right and centre. I don't have time to check it all. Half the time I only hear about it when the markets nail us. Those lazy little freeloaders out there are gonna bring down the whole shoot and shebang,' shouted Bobby, getting out of his chair and pointing an accusing finger towards the schoolyard. 'When they're back eating slop every day of the week, I won't be held responsible.'

'Are you sure the markets aren't getting it wrong? I'm mean the stuff doesn't look that bad to me,' I said, drawing the fool in.

'The markets are never wrong. If everybody decides something is worth shit it's worth shit. End of fucking story. Fence Global is going down and those cunts out there don't give a shit.'

'Sounds like you need something to put the fear of God into them,' I said so very helpfully.

'That's exactly what I need, Smash. That's precisely what I fucking need. Fancy breaking a couple of shins?' said Bobby, teeth clenched and eyes wide.

'Could break a couple, but then I'll be in the hole for a month, and you'll still have the same problem,' I said, mournfully.

'Then break all their bastarding shins!' roared Bobby.

'Then you'll have no workforce for a fortnight. No, no, I have a more subtle plan, but I'm gonna need some guarantees from you first,' I said feeling the fish on the hook

'Name them.'

'I want to get elected for student of the year.'

'Christ is that all?' laughed Bobby.

'Yep.'

'Hang on... why the fuck do you want that? Is there some cash prize I don't know about?' said Bobby, eyeing me suspiciously.

'Nah, just a medal,' I said, playing the dignified competitor.

'Ah look at you, Smash. Always chasing the medals and the glory. Two more like you in this school and we'd be going places...the medal is yours. What's the plan?'

There in Bobby's office, I sketched out Operation Fear of God. Bobby loved it. He loved it so much he wanted to get me all five medals for student of the year. The stupid prick actually thought he'd found a fellow entrepreneur. He thought he'd found himself a good little helper in the world of commerce, but there's only one person Peter Smash helps, and that's Peter J. Smash.

Operation Fear of God started at mass. The chapel was at the very back of the big pointy part of the school. It had big pointy coloured windows all along the pointy walls with pictures of boys turning into books, men walking from burning buildings, women beating soldiers with wooden spoons and thousands of people singing with arms wrapped around each others' necks and all. The pews were hard wooden yokes with little bronze plaques on them saying shit like – Mossy Smith, Zen Calligrapher, R.I.P 1964 – 2011. On the back of every pew was a little cushioned ledge for kneeling. You were only meant to kneel at the really holy bits, but owing to me phobia of chairs I knelt the whole while. Not only did I get away with me kneeling, but John James chalked it up as some sort of pious devotion.

We all stood at our benches, translucent volumes of the book of Jessie in our hands, listening to Graham riff away on the organ. Then the bells rang. The organ stopped and in walked Bobby swinging the incense and ringing the little bells and looking all holy in his thick milk-bottle glasses. Babba O'Reilly followed Bobby up the centre isle and John James took up the rear.

They lined up at the front of the altar and bowed low to the statue of Dr. Murphy. We all followed suit, pressing our heads off the book of Jessie and muttering the commandments.

'How can an idea be anything but an idea. How can...'

Bobby and John James peeled off to the left and right of the stage respectively as Baba O'Brien took his place behind the granite altar.

Now I know this isn't my usual style. I don't normally go in for describing how people looked or talked or smelt or nothing. I don't do it cause this book is called: The Truth. And the truth is I don't normally remember all the little details, but I remember everything about Baba O'Reilly. Why do I remember everything about him? I remember because he was a foreigner.

What the fuck are you giggling about, Blondie?
You think it's funny that I'd never seen a foreigner before?
Do ya[sic]? Do ya[sic]? No, I won't stop slapping ya [sic], bitch.
Do you still think it's funny?
That's right, have a little cry.
Fag.

So anyway, like I was saying, this fella was foreign. At the time that's all I could say for certain. We had stories and songs and poems describing foreigners alright, but they were all written in the superconciousness, which meant that they didn't worry about little things like truth or accuracy. Baba O'Reilly could have just as easily been from Iceland as from Japan, in my eyes. Of course when I escaped from the Second Irish Republic, I got to learn all about where yellow and brown people were from. Today, if I had to guess, I'd say Baba O'Reilly was from Brooklyn.

He had wiry black hair that shot out in three spikes from his head. He had a black beard that came down in a spike too. He looked like he'd been impaled vertically and horizontally with black wooden stakes. That night of the living dead look was reinforced by his eyes, which were a bright gold surrounded by huge orbs of bloody red. His teeth were bright yellow and so gappy that it looked like he'd stolen them from a dead baby and pushed them into his gums himself. He wore a bright yellow scarf and a big purple sack. The sack was made of a very light material, and when Baba O'Reilly stepped into the light it became almost see-through. Jessie save ya if you happened to be looking around crotch height when he came near a window.

'Ohm Jessie Jessie Jessie Ohmmmmm,' said Baba O'Reilly, leading our first chant of the morning.

'Let us pray. Jessie, Son of Mary, flesh become word, grant us the wisdom/ to see dem/ gifts of beauty/ and shake our booty/ to raise our voice/ to rejoice/ in the glory/ of the flesh become story/ and forgive them who cuss us/ Jessie, hear us,' rapped the Baba.

'Jessie, graciously here us,' we replied.

'Jessie, Son of Mary, flesh become word, when it's money o'clock/ and down on the block/ my bitch is in shock/ guide my glock/ to the right spot/ so they know O'Reilly got/ more than a lot of swinging balls/ and never falls/ away from a fight in the Brooklyn night/ Jessie, hear us.'

'Jessie, graciously hear us.'

'Jessie, Son of Mary, flesh become word, when cops/ come to snatch my crops/ give em nothin/ leave em tuttin/ let em see me/ suckin tits from a bikini/ let her swallow without fuss/ Jessie, hear us.'

'Jessie, graciously hear us.'

'Sit your ass down,' said Baba O'Reilly, moving from the altar to the pulpit.

The Baba's feet had never been seen. His robes trailed behind him for six or more feet. When the Baba moved, it wasn't with the bouncing, swinging step of a two-legged animal. He kind of floated forwards. There was no upper body movement whatsoever. This led to two different theories about what exactly was under those robes. One camp was convinced that Baba O'Reilly had not two, but somewhere in the region of two hundred legs. This, they claimed, explained his caterpillar-like movements. The other camp scoffed at this theory, pointing out that two hundred legs would mean two hundred feet and one thousand toes, all of which couldn't possibly fit under Baba O'Reilly's robes. Instead, they believed he was a slug-like being who slid along on a slimy fleshy mass. He didn't look like he was walking because he wasn't walking. Both camps had fanatical supporters. I could've believed either. What the fuck did I know about foreigners?

'The time is comin/ when all the fussin/ and all the runnin/ will be at an end/ and you'll have to contend/ with an all-seeing eye/ you won't be able to buy/ his gentle favour/ or make his judgement waver/ no mercy will be given/ cause from the beginnin/ you were told/ whether you are young or whether you are old/ you must change your entire outlook/ to that of the divine book/ the flesh became word/ you all heard/ you can't mess/ with the righteous Jess,' said Baba O'Reilly, clapping his hands over his head and closing his golden eyes.

Everyone traded worried looks. The time was coming? What time was the time coming? They were all stressing, but inside I was all smiles. Baba O'Reilly was playing a blinder for Operation Fear of God.

'Repent!' screamed the Baba, snapping open his eyes and leaning far across the pulpit to glare at the startled students.

'Repent/ before your days are spent/ in fiery agony/ from which no plea/ will ever set you free/ before you're dragged to hells gate/ for the love of Jessie elevate/ your mind/ and you'll find/ salvation... Ohmmmmmm Jessie Jessie Jessie Ohmmmmmm.'

The rest of the mass was the usual craic. We had a guided meditation focusing on the illusion of sensory reality. Baba O'Reilly banged away on his weird wooden block and led us through our mantras. John James did a reading from the Book of Jessie, and then it was time for communion. The post-it notes were transmuted into the pages of Jessie and we all lined up to receive the Eucharist.

Bobby stood in the centre aisle handing out the post-it notes. Right under John James' nose, Bobby was handing out messages about tonight's emergency meeting. You could see everyone whispering and wondering what the big news was.

The timing couldn't have been better. Not only had Baba O'Reilly blasted them with threats of eternal agonies and all, but our meeting now seemed linked to it. Everyone knew about finding salvation by elevating themselves, but they also knew that sometimes they elevated themselves and still got a D. Had they elevated themselves into the wrong place? Had it been the devil that inspired them to make something ugly? All that crap was buzzing around their heads before we even started Operation Fear of God.

Everyone turned up for the emergency meeting. Bobby had to move some of the crates and boxes out to make extra room. Even with most of the heavy freight moved, latecomers still had to stand in the hall.

'Quiet, please. Please, ladies and gentlemen, if you would please settle down, we can begin the meeting,' said Bobby, standing up on his desk and waiting for the prattle to die down.

'First of all, thank you all for coming. I realise it's very short notice, but I think when you hear what I have to say, you'll agree a meeting was absolutely necessary,' said Bobby, pausing to let the tension simmer.

'Well, what's this all about then Bobby?' said Linda, unable to take the suspense.

There was a bought of shouting and pushing and jeering, which only added to the tension when order was eventually restored.

'Well, there is no easy way to tell you all this, so I'm just going to come out with it,' said Bobby, sucking his teeth, casting his eyes to heaven and holding out the palms of his hands.

'This morning, before Sunday mass, I got to the sacristy a little earlier than usual and was busy preparing the paper and chalice and whatnot when I heard John James and Baba O'Reilly come in. I was hidden from view by the rail of robes so they didn't realise I was listening,' said Bobby, crouching slightly and dropping his voice to a whisper.

'Well, what did they say?' snapped Andrew.

There was another bought of shouting and shoving, and a tussle broke out in the hall. It was a good five minutes before order was restored and when silence eventually fell it was wrapped up in the smell of violence.

'So, I was hidden behind the robes and Baba O'Reilly and John James were talking. It was hard to make out what they were saying at first so I got down on all fours and crawled between the robes to get closer,' said Bobby re-enacting his stealthy moves.

'And then?'

'Then I heard John James ask – So how many students do you think will pass the test? And then Baba O'Reilly said – at least three quarters heading for the slaughter, only the best will pass the test,' said Bobby, re-enacting himself stifling yelps of terror behind the robes.

There was absolute silence. There were just so many questions to ask nobody knew were to begin.

'What test?' I screamed to get the show on the road.

'I suppose it has something to do what Baba O'Reilly was talking about today in mass,' said Bobby.

'A test of elevation!' shrieked Linda.

'Oh God! What day is it on? What time is it at?' cried Andrew.

'It could be any time, any day,' said Bobby, looking around the room for an examiner.

'It could be tomorrow,' I added.

'It can't be tomorrow. I need time to study, ' cried a voice.

'Oh Jessie! What if it's tomorrow?' shrieked another.

'What the fuck should we study?'

'Where's my accordion?'

'Don't touch my etchings, you thieving fuck!'

'We're all going to fail!'

The panic spread like wildfire. How to prepare for a test-taking place at an unknown location, on an unknown date, at an unknown time, on an unknown subject? All you could do was trust in the superconciousness. All you could do was practise elevating yourself and hope that when the test arrived you were able to reach Jessie for help. At least that's the horseshit we fed them.

Art production went through the bleedin roof. You could go nowhere without encountering some fucking mosaic mural depicting the flesh become word, or a bunch of shagging shrubs clipped into the shape of Jessie. Some gobshites abandoned language altogether and communicated by singing improvisations around jazz scales. Others turned everything from washing their hands to blowing their nose into an interpretive dance routine. One day after taking a shite, I reached for the toilet roll and found that every last inch of the bog roll had been covered with poetic streams of consciousness. There was no escaping the endless stream of bullshit the fuckers were spilling forth. As more and more of this shite appeared, the legend of the test grew more and more ridiculous . The image of a bearded examiner with white robes and stone clipboard became universally recognised. A black hooded man with an F-shaped blade became synonymous with failure. Entire histories were written. Everything from how the world was created to how it would be destroyed was blathered on about. Graham, the fucking ejiot, even parsed the language of the Devil. Apparently, His Evilness had been appearing in Graham's dreams night after night to mock his attempts at studying for a test of unknown subject, unknown date and unknown location. Everyone was working like their lives depended on it; because, well, the goons actually believed their lives did depend on it.

   Me?

   I just grinned. As ever the only sane one in the fucking madhouse.

   Even Bobby, the ever resourceful entrepreneur,was breaking his bollix over the whole thing. You see, all this extra material needed logging, evaluating, shipping and auctioning. He tried to take on more staff, but people, stressed up to the eyeballs about the coming apocalypse, told'em to go and shite.

   There was one unexpected advantage to all this test shite however. Everybody wanted into the cage. After all, as the madcat theory went, the test could just as likely involve fighting as dancing. The fuckers elected themselves for punishment. Not only that, but they fought tooth and nail once they got in. I never got beaten or nothing, but I could feel them pushing me. I had to stay focused. This did wonders for me training. Doing me last set of squat jumps, I could see their crazed eyes. Doing biceps curls, I could smell their panting breath. Doing me final set of hill sprints in the woods, legs hanging off me, I pictured them picturing me and did one more set.

All of which was good, cause I was gonna have to be sharp. With the money rolling in, Bobby was gonna be able to pay off the teachers and students and get me that medal without even putting a dent in his funds. Then as Benjamin Murphy lowered a medal around my neck I'd put a knife in his.

But that assassination, one that would bring down the whole shoot and shebang, required some specialised training. Problem was that me day was already pretty full. I had to go to assembly. I had to be there for PE. I was voted into the cage each and every day. Me meals were regulated by the powers that be and were anyways essential for providing me with the protein necessary to grow the muscle I was building each and every evening in the gym. Me personal preference would have been to mitch off the classes. But if Chivers caught me bunking off tabla or slam poetry or metaphysics I'd be in the hole quicker than you can say, 'Go fuck your ma with a pair of scissors.'

It got to the point where I was seriously considering suspending me evening weights sessions or at least cutting them down from three hours to an hour and a half, but again this could've led to unwanted questions. Is that Peter Smash leaving before he's squatted 150 kg? Is that Peter Smash sneaking out before he's benched double his body weight? No, what was needed was a spot for the specialised training within my existing routine. You see there's one thing you don't want to do if you're planning a covert operation, and that's deviate from your existing routine. You don't want to spook your prey with some sudden change in behaviour. You want to be doing the shopping and picking up the kids and watering the flowers, but on entering the shed, just to put back the watering can, be slyly sharpening the shears you'll slit your neighbour's neck with.

Me morning run was the only thing that could provide me with such cover. Problem was that I was already pretty fast.... No, no— let me rephrase that: I ran like an Ethiopian after a bread van. So, improving on my PB was no simple matter. Not when you're running five miles in 26 minutes. Not when a fair whack of that run is uphill. Not when you need to lob 60 seconds off that bad boy to give you enough time for your secret ops training in the woods.

Losers think training is most difficult at the start. They think it all gets easier with time. They think once you've built yourself up it becomes effortless. Nothing could be further from the truth. The hardest training you will ever do is at the top. The effort it takes to improve your time when your time is shit is nothing. The effort it takes to improve your time when your time is already world-fucking-class is immense. But Peter Smash is a man for the immense.

    I'd have gotten me time down a lot fucking faster if it wasn't for the fact that I also had to master the technique of running with a bleedin razor blade gripped between me toes. Now, it wasn't necessarily the running with a blade that was the problem— I'd trained me toes up to a good gripping strength already—it was the removing the blade from between my toes at assassination speed that was tricky. You see I needed to arrive at me spot in the forest where I'd hung a paper-mache head from the tree. I had to slow me breath down. I had to reduce me heart rate. I then had to execute, at assassination speed, the following manoeuvre:

1. From a standing position drop into a crouch with left foot forwards and right foot back.
2. Spread toes of left foot apart without allowing blade to slip onto floor.
3. Grip blade with thumb and forefinger of left hand.
4. Jump upwards and forwards utilizing left leg in initial movement and adding power of the right as the angle of attack engages gluts.
5. At full extension of jump, execute slashing motion, bringing blade into contact with carotid artery of target's neck.

    Obviously, when I began trying this lark I'd only reduced me 5 mile PB by 15-20 seconds. Now let's just be clear, that's the kind of progress you cunts out there running with your fucking dog on a Sunday morning can only dream about. But nonetheless it wasn't giving me lots of room to play with in the neck-slitting department. Even with my powers of recovery, which even at that age where world-fucking-class, me heart was thumping and me lungs were heaving. I wasn't 100 percent composed. I wasn't 100 percent focused and if you're not totally in the zone that's when small mistakes creep in. At the top level it's small margins that decide winners and losers. Many's a time I'd rush the crouch and slip. Other times I'd pull out the blade too soon and cut the bejessie out of me toes. Even with these errors eliminated from me technique, there were times I missed the carotid artery and maim rather than kill the target. But after each and every one of those disappointments there was no time for feeling sorry for myself. There was no time for having a little cry like a fucking loser. Not unless I wanted to raise suspicion by arriving back late from me morning run. Is it only 26 minutes Smash is doing it in now? D'ya here the Smash fella is slowing down? Past his best they say? On the way out, sure! If that shit started then the entire operation would be in danger. No, what I had to do after each and every disappointment was man up and run 5 miles in world-class time.

    It was on my way back from exactly such a run that I found Maraid and Ciara sitting on the steps of the dormitory playing Chinese Chess.

    'Good morning,' I said quickly recovering my breath and making sure there was no blood left on my toes.

    'Fuck sake, I almost had it,' screamed Maraid.

    'Had what?' I said wiping foam from the left corner of me mouth.

    'I almost had the inspired move in me head, but you had to go and open your big fucking mouth,' said Maraid, pulling clumps of hair out of her head.

    Confident that they'd twigged nothing unusual in Peter Smash's post training appearance, I crouched down and took a quick glance across the board. The game was still in its early stages – an hour had passed, maybe less. No piece had crossed the river. They were still amassing forces and fighting for the centre of the board.

    'What do you need inspiration for? Just slide that cannon in behind your advisor there. It's textbook shit,' I said, looking at Ciara for support.

    Ciara whipped out a pen and notebook.

    'Said that two hours ago,' she wrote.

    'You've been thinking about this move for two bleedin hours?' I said.

    'No, that's exactly what I've been trying not to do. I'm trying to elevate myself. I'm trying to get ready for this test. It could be tomorrow. It could be fucking today. Oh Jessie, if I fail, me da is gonna kill me,' said Maraid, hiding her head in her lap.

It was hard to believe Maraid was actually crying. It was harder to believe she was crying cause her dad was gonna give out to her about her test results. I mean, she just didn't look like the kind of person who had parents. You couldn't imagine someone hugging her or putting saliva on her face or nothing. You definitely couldn't imagine anyone having the balls to give out to her.

'Ah take it easy, will ya? Don't be getting yourself all in a tizzy over a fucking test,' I said.

'Don't worry?! I'm gonna be dragged down to the gates of hell and tortured for all eternity, and when me da finds out he's gonna go ballistic,' cried Maraid, dashing the Chinese Chess board into the yard.

'That's a forfeit,' wrote Ciara on her notepad.

'Oh Jessie. I'm fucked. I'm totally fucked,' sobbed Maraid, following the chessboard onto the deck like a dying swan.

'How long has she been carrying on like this?' I asked Ciara.

'Too long,' scribbled Ciara.

'Where's Nolan?'

'Joined one of those interpretive dancing sects,' wrote Ciara.

'I see.'

Ciara drew a broken heart and shrugged her shoulders.

'Get up off the bleedin ground and cop yourself on,' I said, giving Maraid a kick in the ribs.

'Oh, I'm copped on already, Smash,' hissed Maraid, rearing up into my face, 'I'm copped on enough to know I'm fucked.'

She charged past me, grabbed her rucksack and emptied the contents onto the ground.

I looked down at the worst collection of drawings, etchings, carvings, mathematical proofs and logical inferences I'd ever seen. Maraid was cracking.

'Christ, you're bad,' I said.

'See, even Smash thinks they're shit,' cried Maraid, storming off into the dorms.

After that scene with Maraid, I began to notice a lot more people in the same boat. You could see the fear in their eyes, but more than that - you could see it in their art. Their paintings were full of fiery demons and screaming children. Their music was played in minor cords and accompanied by growling voices. All the dancing became this monkey-like flailing of arms and legs. Shit was getting dark.

Bobby, the ever-watchful entrepreneur, didn't like this new dark period, and neither did the markets. Mr. Fence tried spreading more cheery rumours about the test. He started scrawling some of the more optimistic pieces of the Book of Jessie on the walls of the school. He even tried drugging students' food with some chemicals he imported from Colombia. Nothing worked. The legend of the test had become a living, breathing monster. Nobody could bring it under control now. All we could do was wait to see what happened. And if everyone is waiting for something to happen, then it always does.

We were sitting in the classroom listening to Chivers explain how this one-thousand-line piece of object-orientated programming could be condensed into one elegant line of rational programming when there was a knock on the door.

'Ingress,' called Chivers from the whiteboard.

There were two more knocks on the door. Chivers pushed his yellow glasses up his nose and sniffed the air. Another flurry of knocks began.

'Yes, yes, come in. Ingress, for Jessie's sake! Ingress!' said Chivers.

The door opened, and in stumbled a baldy-headed boy with milk-bottle glasses and a slightly translucent complexion. The class froze. You could almost hear the cunts. Was this it? Was this the day of judgement? They waited for a man with a white beard and a stone clipboard to follow, but instead we got Nurse Mona.

'Another student looking to get their fire lit by Mr. Chivers,' announced Nurse Mona, waddling forwards with hands on hips.

'You've been reading the Yeats I gave you?' mumbled Chivers pulling a reddener.

'I'd take in anything you gave me Mr. Chivers,' said Nurse Mona, moving forwards with a hungry look in her eye.

'Well it's very good to have you back, young man,' said Chivers, positioning himself behind the baldy boy.

Nurse Mona didn't stop her advance, and soon the boy was trapped in a cage of flesh. Chivers' stomach was in front, Nurse Mona's stomach was behind and her heaving breasts were above. The two adults began trading whispers and meaningful looks, but everyone else focused their attention on the boy.

He'd grown about four inches. He'd put on at least five kilos. His mop of hair had been completely shaved, but when he managed to free his face from Nurse Mona's navel, we saw those big brown puppy dog eyes and knew it was Jim McGrath.

What was that noise?
That fucking buzzing noise. What was it?
Stand the fuck up and spread em.
What's this?
I know it's a fucking mobile phone. What the fuck is it doing here?
Who have you been texting?
Who have you told my location?
What the fuck is that noise in the hall?
No, I won't calm down!
It's a knife, Jonathan.
Well if the shit goes down I want to be sure I slit your throat before I get shot.

Chapter 4

  Well that was a bit of a laugh wasn't it?
  Ah come on, Blondie, don't take everything so seriously.
  Well yeah fair enough, but you have to admit this place is a lot more swanky.
  You're telling me you prefer piss-stained alleys to rolling hills?
  Well good, you fucking keep them on the screen.
  I'll tell you what you're not getting paid for?
  Taking two-hour lunches and texting your fucking boyfriend.
  Glad to hear it.

  So anyway, Jim was back. He didn't want to talk about where he'd been. He didn't want to talk about what he'd seen. He didn't want to talk about what they'd done to him. In fact he didn't talk at all. He just kind of floated around the school with a dumb fucking smile on his face. Thing was, with the whole Armageddon-damnation thing flying around, that smile was mighty appealing. People just started hanging around with Jim to feel calmer. That was all well and good, but then the fucker suddenly decided to speak.
  Maraid had just lost another game of Chinese Chess, and was hyperventilating on the hard, wet schoolyard when Jim walked over.
  'What is wrong, my child?' said Jim, out of the blue.
  'I'm not your fucking child,' hissed Maraid.
  'My child, please, it hurts me to see you in such distress. Tell me what vexes you, and I will do everything in my power to relieve your suffering,' said Jim, offering Maraid a hand up off the floor.
  The hand was rejected.
  'Is it in your power to cancel the test?' hissed Maraid.
  'We all must sit the test,' conceded Jim.
  'Well then you can't fucking help me then can you, Jim? I'm gonna fail the test and that's that isn't it Jim?' said Maraid, springing to her feet.
  'All things have been created by Jessie and...'
  'Yeah all things including a test I can't pass,' cried Maraid
  'Yes, the test was created by Jessie just as you were created by Jessie. Why would Jessie, who loves you, create a test he knew

you couldn't pass? What would be the point of your existence? Why create you to fail?' said Jim, causing murmurs of excitement in the surrounding crowd of gawkers.

Maraid was stunned. Ciara was stunned. I was bored fucking stiff..

'So...so...I won't fail?' said Maraid hopefully.

'Those who believe in Jessie cannot fail,' answered Jim with a loving smile.

'So I don't need to finish this ten-foot tapestry?' asked Andrew.

'Those who believe in Jessie cannot fail.'

'Can anyone think of a word that rhythms with antediluvian?' said Linda, bursting through the crowd in a panic.

'Fuck the poem. All we have to do is believe!' shouted Maraid.

'Says who?' asked Linda with wild-eyed excitement.

'Says Jim.'

'Those who believe in Jessie cannot fail,' repeated Jim.

'It's over. Oh thank Jessie, it's over!' shouted Maraid.

'Jessie, it's over!' added Nolan, abandoning his dance troupe and returning to Maraid's side.

There was an outpouring of relief from all quarters. Epic poems over ten thousand lines long were torn to smithereens. Sand sculptures over ten feet high were trampled to the ground. Never averse to a bit of smashing, I even got involved meself. Everyone linked arms and started singing the anthem of the Second Republic with tears of joy streaming down their faces.

I hardly need to tell you that Jim's new take on the whole test thing was bad for Bobby's little business. Some art was still getting made. In fact it was a lot sunnier than the doomsday gear being produced before. The problem was that it was getting made in much smaller volumes. Why bust your balls creating hundreds of pieces of art if all you had to do was believe in Jessie to pass? Bobby tried calling meetings where he revealed progressively more horrific details of the test, but people were all out of fear. They'd had the bejessie scared out of them for too long and they decided that they liked Jim's optimistic view of things a lot better. Me only worry was that the fuckers might realise money was just as pointless as art.

Paying the pricks off so I could get me medal might in that case prove problematic. In addition, all this happiness meant Bobby was looking at disastrous quarterly results, and the shareholders in Fence Global were baying for blood— which wouldn't have bothered me in the slightest if I hadn't been exploiting Bobby's bankroll for me own ends.

Concerned that I may miss out on my medal, and resulting neck-slitting opportunity, I popped around to Bobby's office and found a cage, intercom and retinal scanner had been installed. I pushed the buzzer.

'Who is it?' crackled Bobby's voice.

'Smash.'

'Look into the scanner please.'

The cunt was getting a little too fond of dishing out orders for my liking, but I did as instructed. Two red beams of light started scanning me eyes.

'Okay, Mr. Smash. Please push the gate when you hear the buzzer.'

The buzzer went off and I was admitted inside the iron cage. I looked around for a button to get through the next gate, but found none.

'Desist from tampering with the gate or it will be electrified,' shouted Bobby down the intercom.

The fucker was now actually raising his voice to me. Oh, the time would come. It would come with the sound of snapping shin bones.

'To your right you will see two fingerprint readers. Please place your thumbs onto the pads for scanning.'

I did as instructed, imagining my thumbs gauging out the upstart's eyes, and after a few minutes another buzzer went off and I was out of the cage. All this bleedin messing and I was still only at the office door. The door slowly rolled open to reveal a perspex box. Ciara, now busier than ever as Bobby's secretary, glanced up from her paperwork, Just beyond the doorway was a metal detector. I was made to throw away me pens, paper clips, pencil sharpener and razor blade (which I was training my toes to hold for hours on end) before the box opened.

The whole security area had been lit with bright white light. But here inside, the office was lit with weird purple UV lamps.

Anything white glowed. You could see every fleck of dust and fibre on the carpet. Ciara's red hair looked blue, as did her lips, and the whites of her eyes glowed a toxic kind of purple. The secretary of Bobby Fence Global was blathering away on the phone. I know this cause I could see that enormous chin wobbling around at lightening speed. It was a sight so disturbing that you couldn't make heads nor tales of what the ugly bitch was saying. Given the speed of the yapping, and the volume of the replies blaring out the other end of the phone, it seemed fair to presume this was not another happy customer calling up to pass his compliments to Bobby Fence.

Ciara slammed the phone back into its cradle and it immediately started ringing again. Her enormous chin started to quiver. She ran a hand through her flaming blue hair and gave me the big aul puppy dog eyes like she expected me to sympathise with her fucking problems or something. I mean, if you're bleedin stupid enough to be anybody's lackey, then what do expect from life? Of course your boss is gonna shit on you. Why will they shit on you? Firstly, because you're the kind of idiot that lets themselves be shat on. Secondly, cause you're the kind of fucker that gives people who don't let themselves be shat the big old puppy dog eyes and expects them to feel sorry for you instead of doing something about it yourself. But if you are the type of idiot who lets themselves be shat on, you deserve no sympathy. You deserve contempt. So that's what I gave to Ciara. A big old dose of contempt.

'Can't trust you to do the security anymore, no?'

Ciara's chin wobbled about.

'Too much of a fucking thick to keep out unwanted visitors are ya?'

Ciara stood up from her desk and wobbled her chin around faster.

'Listen I've got shit to do so just buzz me in or knock on the door or do whatever fucking menial task it is that you need to do to let the important people talk to each other.'

Ciara was out from behind her desk, and judging by the length of time she held that big old chin down around her chest I'd have to say that she was screaming at me.

I spat on the floor and waited for compliance.

Ciara grabbed her notepad off the desk.

'Oh, for Jessie's sake, open the fucking door will ya?!'

But no, she had to have her little scribble. She had to have her little say.

'I have training to be doing, you know,' I said truthfully, and time in relation to that training was of the essence cause I'd just handed over me razor blade and was gonna have to source another one before morning if the required progress was to be made.

So yeah I read the little note just to placate the bitch and get shit moving.

'You think I have no voice of my own,' it read.

That clearly was not a question and if it was a question then it was a rhetorical question and Peter J. Smash does not, under any circumstances, answer rhetorical questions.

I spat on the floor and crossed me arms. But would she open the door? No fucking chance. Out came the notepad once more and as she scribbled I began to feel like a good 360 Degree Jump Spinning Shin Cracker Axe Kick might be in order.

'Just because I'm ugly you think I have no right to be heard,' read the next note.

'Oh here we fucking go,' I said tossing the note in the air. 'Surprise sur-fucking-prise. Another ugly feminist who wants to be heard.'

Not that I have anything against feminists. They're just a bunch of chicks who realised that the rules of the game were written by men for men. Men made the game and men win the game. Feminists are trying to make a new game that they can win. Fairly standard shit. If I was a bitch I'd be at the same thing meself. Fact is, however, that I am in possession of a healthy slab of penis. Rules as they are suit me fine. I'm winning. Now what a feminist has to do is knock me off me perch. And the ones who try to do that by brute force I have time for. I'll kick the bollix out of those bitches all day, but I'll shake their hand at the end of it. But if you're too weak to go down the violent feminist route, and let's face it most bitches are far too weak to step up to Peter Smash, then you're best off going down the sexy bitch route.

What the sexy bitches realised is that 99 percent of men are ruled by their micky. They may be animals in the boardroom. They may take names and numbers on the squash court. They may be bloody-minded stubborn gits who'll buy and sell their mothers to get ahead, but put a sexy bitch in high heels and a tight ass and a big pair of tits in front of them and they'll go to pieces. The fuckers will chase pussy across the seven seas. They'll risk life and limb for a smell of it. They'll humiliate themselves for a whiff. They'll enslave themselves for a taste. And that's how sexy bitches go about getting themselves some power. But chicks like Ciara are neither violent nor sexy. They are weak and ugly. So instead of accepting the fact that she was a fucking loser and staying the fuck out of the way, she tried to make winners feel sympathy for her. She tried to make them feel guilty. She tried to whine and moan and complain her way into power. It was enough to make ya sick.

'You're only interested in what women have to say if they are beautiful,' read the next note.

God I was sick of this. Not only was Ciara an ugly cunt, but she actually thought that I gave a fuck about what any woman had to say. I didn't, don't, and never will, give a bollix about what anyone has to say. Now I know that's not literally what the big-chinned bitch was trying to express with her little note. She was trying to say that I would pretend to listen to some bitch if she was hot just so I could fuck her later. But you see I wasn't one of those losers either. I wasn't gonna chase after some slag who might or might not let me stick my dick in her if I jumped through the right hoops. I wasn't gonna go waffling on with a load of romantic shite to try and persuade some chick to let me give her the ride of her life. Nah what I would do is become an undisputed champion. I'd become a winner amongst winners. Then it was just a matter of genetics that I'd be fucking the hottest chicks. Cause they all want to sleep with the top monkey. They can't help swaying their asses in his direction. But I wasn't explaining all that to Ciara. She was a loser and could stay a fucking loser for all I cared.

'Ciara you've got exactly 10 seconds to open that door before I break both your shins,' I said, beginning my count down.

She knew I meant it. She knew I'd snap those bones. But she was a redhead and she had a redhead's temper.

'Someday I'll speak and all you pricks are gonna listen,' read the final note that she jabbed into my chest before punching the button that let the important people talk to each other.

As I entered the office Bobby stood behind his desk, knuckles pressing into the wood, looking all Night of the Living Dead under the UV lamps: lips a zombie blue, eyes a toxic purple.

'I think you're gonna need a new secretary, my friend,' I said, slamming the door behind me and brushing some illuminous flecks of dust off my shoulder.

Bobby's whale-like forehead scrunched up like an accordion. 'Why? What's happened? Is she injured? Is she killed?' he said, purple eyes flashing around in a panic.

'Worse.'

'Oh my God...Oh my God help us...' said Bobby reaching for what looked very much like a medieval crossbow.

'Yeah I'm sorry to break this to you Bobby, but your secretary is a raging lesbo.'

'What the fuck are you saying? How many are there? Are they armed?' he said, taking aim at the door.

'I'm saying she's an ugly fucking feminist; a raging lesbo and she's out there armed with a load of clap trap, a notepad and a pencil.'

Bobby looked through me rather than at me. But slowly, noticing I was cool as a cucumber, returned to his senses.

'She's out there by herself?' he said, keeping the crossbow trained on the door.

'She was when I left her.'

'And she is alive and uninjured and under no immediate threat of either loss of life or injury?' said Bobby.

'Well if she keeps up the feminist clap trap she is in very serious danger of me breaking her fucking shins for her, I'll tell ya that for nothing,' I said taking a seat, crossing my legs and putting both feet up on Bobby's desk.

'And why would you do that to her, Smash?' said Bobby, turning the crossbow on me.

Now as you might guess Peter Smash does not take well to threats. He especially does not take well to people pointing medieval crossbows at him from what is effectively point-blank range. I was also aware that I needed a certain bankroll to secure my medal. What I did not need was a dead CEO of an international corporation on my hands. That I adjudged to be a fairly fucking major deviation from my daily routine, and, as I already mentioned, a successful assassination relies on the maintenance of exactly such a routine. So I didn't spring across the desk and gouge out Fence's eyes and bludgeon him to death with his own paperweight statue of Benjamin

Murphy. I did not stick the crossbow up his arse and fire the arrow. I did not mutilate his body with the letter opener and feed his fingers into the shredder. I remained calm and let good old Bobby know how I felt about this sudden development.

'This is not the kind of customer service I've come to expect from Fence Global,' I said, raising my hands behind my head and stretching out further in my chair.

Bobby shook himself like a man attempting to exercise his demons before slowly lowering the weapon.

'Little tense today, Bobby, aren't we?'

'Sorry, I just thought that somebody had hurt my...I mean everything is all right isn't it? Ciara my...my secretary is fine. That is to say nobody was hurt, were they, Smash, eh?'

I snorted and spat the phlegm on the floor.

Fence shook himself once more, silenced the remaining voices in his noggin, and went to sit down, but suddenly stopped and got down to check for suspect devices under his chair.

'Are you messing or what?' I said.

'Precautions,' answered Bobby, finally taking his seat.

'Precautions against what? World War Three?' I said, noticing a gas mask and multiple sticks of dynamite on the desk.

'Close.'

'Ah come on, Bobby, the shareholders have to expect losses sometimes. It's the name of the game,' I said ever so sympathetically, knowing full well if Bobby tried to pull out of delivering my dividends— i.e. the medal that lead to the knife – then it would be Bobby's throat that I'd be slitting.

'There's been some new developments,' said Bobby, throwing a file down on the table and burying his face in his hands.

I came to the table and opened the file. The first shock was that there were photographs inside. I mean I'd seen the odd few photos that Bobby's sisters ex-boyfriend's dead cat's vet had given him, but nothing of this size. You couldn't hide these bad boys down your sack. They were about the size of a hardback book.

The second shock was that the people in these photos were gagged, tied and stripped naked. I looked up expecting to see a big grin on Bobby's face. There was no grin.

'No wonder you've got so much security. If Chivers caught you with these you'd be in the hole for a year,' I said, closing the file.

'It's my family,' said Bobby quietly.
'Your family?'
'My family.'
'I see,' I said, clogs beginning to spin in me noggin

'The IRLA sent them to me. They're gonna kill them if I don't do what they say,' said Bobby, starting to cry.

I nearly did a dance there and then. You didn't need a PhD in international relations to guess what the sworn enemies of the Second Irish Republic wanted out of us. It sure as fuck wasn't paintings and sculptures of Jessie created in a state of elevation. They'd be wanting hearts on platters. They'd be wanting heads on pikes. Oh Bobby Fence was gonna be needing the services of Peter Smash now all right.

'That Saudi buy-out was a front. Our real owners are stationed in Donegal. Our real owners are the Illusionist Republican Liberation Army, ' said Bobby, sliding down in his chair so that only his eyes were visible over the desk.

'Well fuck, we'll have to tell Chivers,' I said, playing the innocent little lamb.

'If we tell Chivers, they die.'

'Well, we'll have to pay them off. We'll tell the others. They'll gladly create pieces to save your family,' I said, surprised at the very convincing nature of me performance.

'It's too late for that. These people can't be negotiated with. They don't care about money. They've just been drawing me in to get at someone else,' he said, slowly rising up in his chair.

'To get at who?' I enquired with a look of complete naive wonder.

Bobby checked the security cameras. He put banging dub-step on the stereo. He turned the stereo up to eleven. He beckoned for me to come closer and cupped two hands over my ear.

'They want us to kill Dr. Benjamin Murphy,' whispered Bobby.

'I see,' I said, knowing this was not merely luck: this was the kind of opportunity that always presents itself to those who know how to seize it.

'What should I do?' said Bobby, wringing his hands.

298

'You should kill Murphy,' I said a little too quickly, a little too casually, a little too like I didn't give a flyin fuck about Bobby's family, a little too much like I didn't give a shit about his global operations, a little too much like I knew money was just some shit that somebody else decided the value of, a little too like I wanted to be the one who decided what shit was worth.

'But what about the greater good?' cried Bobby, collapsing onto the desk and, like the loser he was, failing to note the little slip in my disguise

'Oh yeah, well it's a very difficult choice. An impossible choice, but this is your family,' I said, reopening the file for effect.

Bobby's bottom lip began to quiver looking down at the photos.

'They want me to kill the greatest mind of a generation. They want me to kill a pioneering librarian, prophet and imaginary revolutionary. I know it's wrong. I know I'll go to hell for it, Smash, but I can't let my family die. I just can't do it,' said Bobby, looking to me for forgiveness.

'Nobody should have to make choices like these Bobby. Nobody,' I said, standing up to put a consoling arm around Fence's shoulder as he broke down once more.

Needless to say I didn't share Bobby's moral dilemma. But I still had to listen to the fucker go through the whole soul-searching, philosophising, excuse-making bullshit. The prick was actually beating himself up over what he called 'the greater good'. He banged on about society and social responsibility and civic pride and all kinds of horse shit. Even when it was clear that we were gonna have to whack Murphy, Bobby still had to put on his little performance. He had to seem like he was doing it all against his will. He had to piss and moan about the injustice of it all. Then finally after a couple of hours of this shit he did what any sane man does and put his own interests first.

You could see the switch flip. You could see the adrenaline kicking in. You could see him seriously considering killing the father of the nation. But mostly you could see that the little man was very, very scared. He was no killer. It was then, in his hour of need, that I offered myself so selflessly.

'Don't worry Bobby,' I said, patting him on the back. 'I'll kill the fucker for ya.'

Bobby rose from his seat with hope in his eyes, and I knew by the way he looked at me— like I was a saviour sent by Jessie, like I was his bestest buddy in the whole world— that we were a go.

'I knew you wouldn't let me down, Peter,' he cried with relief, 'I knew you wouldn't let me down.'

He was relieved cause the thought of his ma and da being chopped up into little pieces and spread all across Ireland terrified him. And even though me ma was already dead and me da dying in excruciating pain would have given me the greatest pleasure in the world, I could understand why you might be terrified by someone threatening to hack up your family. I could understand it, but I sure as fuck wasn't gonna sympathise with it. Nah, what I was gonna do was exploit it for me own ends.

You see, training had been going well. It had been going very well. I was doing 5 miles in just over 25 minutes. If you took off the 60 seconds it took me to do the aul throat slitting routine then that time would earn me an Olympic medal (if the Second Irish Republic hadn't been banned from all international competitions apart from the Arirang Games in North Korea). Not only that, but the springing motion I'd perfected was generating such height and length that with a few slight alterations I was sure I'd put in a very respectable performance in the long and high jumps. But as cool as it was to know that me physical prowess would see me rise to the top of whatever event I chose to train for, me focus was still on kicking ass. I didn't want to be the champion of jumping over bars. I didn't want to be the champion of soaring over sand. I wanted to be the champion of kicking fucking ass. Cause it's all well and good being the world champion of table tennis, but it's not much use when some piss poor judo practitioner, who didn't even finish in the medals, can beat the fuck out of you in the dressing room and steal your gold. Nah, what you want to be is the champion of champions. A fucking warrior.

Anyway, me point is that me training had been going well and I was as prepared as any warrior could be. There did, however, remain the small problem of me escape. Springing forward at lightning speed is all very well, slitting the throat of a pioneering librarian is all well and good, but with the PWLA running the security detail, how the fuck was I gonna make good me escape? With teachers and parents and students all over the kip, how was I gonna get away? With the school located in the middle of the Second Irish Republic, how was I gonna make it to a boat or an aeroplane or a helicopter? Was I planning on swimming across the Irish Sea or what?

I'm not thick. Those were questions that I'd asked meself. But they were not ones I had answers for.

Now I know what you losers will be thinking. You'll be thinking, 'So you just ignored this fairly large gap in your plan? You just trained yourself up for an event that was sure to get you killed? Why bother training at all?'

Exactly the kind of bullshit questions losers always ask. Exactly the kind of play-it-safe wank you hear out of your average pleb. Yez want to know the answers to all the questions before you'll begin. Yez want to be sure of the outcome before you'll put in the effort. What a pack of fucking cunts! It's never safe at the top. There's always unanswerable questions. The outcome is never certain. A winner knows that, and instead of trying to control things that can never be controlled they control the one thing that they can – your own body and mind. They train to the limits of human endurance and then they train some more. They pour their fear into preparation. They sharpen their reactions to such a point that they have the best possible chance of seizing the chances presented to them. The kidnap of Bobby's family was just such an opportunity. I was sharp enough to seize it and use it to overcome the little problem of my escape.

'I'll slit Murphy's throat for ya. Don't worry,' I said, returning Bobby's big old smile before delivering my demands. 'But you've got to get us a ticket out of here.'

'Of course. Of course. We'll escape. We'll get a plane. We'll get a chopper. We'll organise something… with our bankroll…with our contacts… something will be possible. Yes! I'll get us a ticket out of here. But first things first. You'll slit his throat, you say. But shouldn't we... I think maybe...'

After agreeing on our goals, the arguments about how best to achieve them began. Show me a full-blooded revolution that doesn't descend into civil war. Show me an overthrow of a system that doesn't lead to bitching and backstabbing. It's something that happens whenever there's an aul rupture in the head space. You see I'd been planning to cut Murphy's carotid artery for months, but for

Bobby the assassination of the father of the Second Irish Republic, the pioneering librarian, the world's first imaginary revolutionary, was a bit of a headfuck. So a period of arguing about how to change the entire world as he knew it was bloody annoying, but inevitable.

First Bobby wanted to use his position as an altar boy to place a replica book of Jessie in the tabernacle, which would explode at the exact moment Benjamin Murphy was scheduled to give his reading to our assembly in the Church. This was a plan that relied on the timing of several external parties. A cycle jam on the roads could delay the cavalcade and fuck things up. Murphy arriving earlier owing to other pressing engagements could scupper the whole plan. Then of course you were relying on the bomb actually going off. Or worse still, blowing us to kingdom fucking come as we tried to wire the bleedin thing. It was a plan with too many variables and as Bobby banged on and on and on about it, I replied:

'I'll just slit his fucking throat. No messing. I'll just slit his fucking throat.'

There was no denying the simplicity of my plan. It had no external variables. It relied on only one person and that person happened to be the best-trained ass-kicker for a thousand miles. So Bobby was forced to drop the book bomb bullshit, but he couldn't accept the neck slitting just yet. You see, he was destroying his whole worldview. He was plotting to undo the very system that had produced him. The thought that I could do all that by simply putting a knife in Murphy's throat freaked him out. He wanted an ingenious plan. He wanted something sophisticated and clever. He wanted a plan worthy of the results it would bring about.

So yeah, this shite went on for a while. I'd come around to the office. I'd go through security. I'd trade insults with the ugly feminist, and then I'd be forced to listen to yet another one of Bobby's brilliant plans. There was the poisoned chalice plan. There was the sleeping gas in the ventilation system plan. There was the trapdoor plan. There were bombs of endless fucking number: bike bombs, sandal bombs, bombs in seats, bombs in the pulpit, bombs in microphones and bombs in door handles. Bobby was seriously starting to piss me off. We had an assassination plan that would work. What we needed was a plan for escaping afterwards. But I was also aware that I had to lead the fucker along the merry path. I had to give his poor little noggin time to come to terms with the aul paradigm shift. So I just kept repeating:

'I'll just slit his fucking throat. No messing. I'll just slit his fucking throat.'

My complete and utter confidence in this plan, my complete and utter resistance to engaging in any other plan and Bobby's complete and utter inability to come up with a better plan all started to bring Fence around.

'...and after the acid has burnt through the rope and the trapdoor is released, a pair of falcons will drop a flare onto the altar, thus igniting the gunpowder that will explode with a flash that not only kills Murphy but also blinds everyone present— except of course for us two who will have inserted specially made contact lenses onto our eyeballs that will filter the exact wavelength of light emitted by the explosion before running to the window, gripping the zip wire, and flying across the schoolyard to a pair of quad bikes that we'll drive off a ramp that will be erected to help us clear the perimeter fence before driving down through the village to the river where a speed boat will bring us to a set of underground tunnels emerging at a helicopter pad invisible from the air where a chopper with the ability to scramble radar and avoid surface-to-air missiles will fly us to a secret location.'

'I'll just slit his fucking throat, Bobby. No messing. I'll just slit his fucking throat.'

'Oh for Christ sake! How will you slit his throat? Show me how you'll slit his fucking throat!' cried Bobby in exasperation.

Now why didn't I just show the fucker how it was done there and then in his office? Couldn't we have set up a little target on the table or something?

Of course we could. But what Bobby wanted to see was not something that simply worked, but something that worked because of the effort and planning and ingenuity that went into it. He wanted something that justified its ability to kill off his entire concept of the world. He wasn't gonna see that in the office. All that'd be seen by the untrained eye— and Bobby's eye was highly fucking untrained— was the effortless result of months of training. It would just look like a freakish natural talent for doing a simple task. He wasn't a champion. He wasn't a world-beater. He'd didn't understand (or like all losers, he didn't want to understand) that it's training yourself to do the boring everyday simple things very, very well that makes you a champion. And he sure as fuck wasn't gonna have it recreating the world for him.

'You know what time I do my morning run?' I said, standing up before I had to listen to another bullshit plan.

'7.00 a.m.?'

'5.30 a.m.'

'Uh, okay, that's nice, but shouldn't we look at another...' said Bobby, reaching for another set of blueprints and maps that he had strewn all over his desk.

'You're coming running with me at 5.30 tomorrow,' I said opening the office door.

'What? No, wait! Why am I coming running with you at 5.30 tomorrow?' said Fence, abandoning the maps and coming out from behind his desk.

'I'm gonna show you how it's done, Fence. I'm gonna fucking show you,' I said, ignoring Ciara who by the movement of her chin must have been saying something to me.

'Just open the fucking door, will ya, you ugly feminist cunt,' I said, crossing me arms.

Ciara wobbled her chin around some more.

I snorted and spat on the floor.

'Please don't talk to my...my ehh...my staff like that Smash,' said Fence, scurrying out after me.

'Then hire better fucking staff,' I said heading for the door

'Well, we can discuss these plans in the morning then,' he called behind me.

'Just be there at 5.30,' I replied, making good me exit.

Pink Flamingo Soup

Chapter 7

The creation of Europe's first modern theocracy was always going to ruffle some feathers. Our point-blank refusal to honour any debts run up by the First Irish Republic caused the collapse of the Eurozone and, needless to say, the Germans got a bit grumpy about the whole thing. We reminded our Arian friends that at their greatest moment of political upheaval, viz. the death of Adolf Hitler, it was our president alone, Mr. Eamon DeVelera, who sent a letter of condolence to the Third Reich. Not one other country, on the entire globe, sent as much as a mass card. Could they not now reciprocate those sentiments in our hour of need?

  The French took the emotive approach of pointing out all the benefits we'd received from European funding. Were we not grateful for the motorways, tunnels, ports, community centres and libraries that had been built with European funding? We tactfully pointed out that the French nation had also benefited from Ireland. We had allowed one of our most beloved sons, Mr. Samuel Beckett, a writer far exceeding the calibre of any Frenchmen, to compose several pieces of literature in their native tongue. Yes, they'd given us things of concrete and steel that would, with the passage of time, crumble into nothingness. But we had given them the greatest literature ever written in their pompous language. A son of Eire had gifted them works of eternal beauty. We were more than even.

  The American's didn't know what in the hell to do with us. Their whole Irish eyes are shining, leprechauns, rebel ballads, pints of Guinness view of Ireland was completely at odds with the emergence of a theocracy based on aesthetic ideals. The revolution did, however, have the undeniable support of the Irish people and so the Yanks could not very well, even with their high threshold for rank hypocrisy, object to the uprising on democratic grounds. It was only when we tore down the central points of financial failure, i.e. the banks, that the Americans got their knickers in a twist. They started peddling the usual shite about laissez-faire markets being essential to democracy. We pointed out that by distributing banking to each and every member of our society we were actually the purist realisation of Dr. Freedman's Chicago School of Economics ever witnessed in the short, grim history of capitalism. If a citizen of the Second Irish Republic wanted a loan of, say, two hundred thousand punts, he uploaded a loan torrent onto the Internet, and if two hundred thousand of his fellow citizens thought he was worth a one-punt bet then he was away. The Americans responded by placing us on the Axis of Evil. We promptly sent ambassadors to all the members of this illustrious club: Iraq, Iran, Cuba, North Korea, Libya, Syria, Belarus, Zimbabwe and Myanmar. These nations, not used to acts of good faith from the international community, were delighted by our hand of friendship and became our sworn allies. Within six months, Ireland found itself the subject of more than a dozen UN resolutions. Endless teams of nuclear inspectors scoured our countryside for evidence of WMDs, but could find nothing. Our friends in Iran proved invaluable here, and we successfully evaded detection until the detonation of our first bomb. With our position in the club of nuclear nations secured, Ireland began hosting the annual International Congress of the Axis of Evil. All sorts of lucrative trade deals were done. The Second Republic became a distribution hub for everything from handguns to heroin.

It was at the end of another successful International Congress of the Axis of Evil that I found myself seated in the VIP box of the Galway races surrounded by the colonels and chairmen and rahbars that ran those fine nations. Dr. Benjamin Murphy entertained Marino Murillo with tales of Castro in his youth. McFee laughed and joked with President Mugabe. Inspector Biggington chatted causally with members of the Belarus secret police, and I attempted to resurrect my Korean, which had fallen into disrepair, by conversing about today's runners with Kim Jong-un.

'The next race will be the 4:15 steeplechase,' came the announcement.

The sound of the crackling speaker was made worse by the metallic echo from the roof of the stand.

'Respectfully, Little Brother, what would be your educated choice if a genuine seeker of knowledge was to beg your opinion?' said Kim Jong-un, communism having done nothing to dampen his impeccable Korean manners.

'Respectfully, Big Brother, a genuine seeker of knowledge would flatter me with such a request. Of course what little I know I would gladly share. If Big Brother would kindly turn his eye to runner number eight, I think his sagacity would not fail to recognise the potential of that runner,' I answered, smiling as my old fluency in Hangungma began to return.

'The wisest sage is the one who acts on wise counsel, Little Brother. Number eight is a lucky number. Let us see if the facts match the omens,' said Kim Jong-un, pulling out the form guide and beginning to study the horse's statistics and breeding.

'Thoroughness is the course to correctness,' I said, giving a half bow to the North Korean leader.

Below the grandstand where our box was located, bookies shouted odds and punters waved fists full of cash in the air. Today, women were granted a one-day reprieve from the dogma of the PWLA and dressed up to the nines. Hats of outrageous plumage, skirts of scandalous length and heels of dizzying altitude were all on display. Half-cut young fellas who had never witnessed the transforming powers of things like makeup, fake eyelashes, bottle tan and Wonderbras walked around with their tongues hanging out of their heads.

'Yes, Little Brother, the calibre of this athlete cannot be denied. She was studded by Roy Keane. She is the daughter of Michelle Smith. She was trained in the stable of Glaxo-Smith-Klein. That is all very good, but what of the conditions, Little Brother? Do these soft conditions suit her?' said Kim Jong-un, his impressive jowls lifting as he smiled.

'Truly, Big Brother, you leave no detail unattended to. I had not considered the turf. Is there nothing in the form guide as to her ability on soft ground?' I said, knowing full well Saipan Incident (our steed) had romped home in the soft on several occasions, but allowing my senior the opportunity to correct his own mistake.

On the track the athletes were being herded into the gates with cattle prods and long wooden poles. The growls and curses of the steroid-ridden steeds was audible even from our position at the finishing post. Once the raw power of the athletes was boxed into the gates, the jockeys dropped in on their backs. Another bout of kicking, growling, punching and hissing began. The jockeys were pitched about from left to right and desperately tried to calm these sub-human monstrosities.

'Little Brother. I do not think these conditions will be a problem,' announced Kim Jong-un, closing his form guide resolutely.

'I never doubt your word, Big Brother,' I said, pretending to be pleased at this new information.

Shouting and roaring broke out at the gates. One of the runners, Tokyo Panty Vendor, had bucked his jockey and was flapping him around by the legs like a rag doll. The trainers distracted the raging beast with prods from their poles, and the jockey was pulled out of the box and stretchered off to an ambulance. A replacement midget hurried out in his purple silky gear and tried his luck with the beast.

'Little Brother, what should be our wager?' asked Kim Jong-un, eyes narrowing at the mention of money.

'Big Brother, if we risk too little we gain too little, but if we are reckless our losses are heavy. We should seek the middle path,' I said, foolishly forgetting the anti-religious leanings of Kim's communist dynasty: my allusions to the teachings of Buddha were not well received.

'I will bet one hundred thousand of your punts,' said Kim Jung-un tersely.

'Fighting!' I exclaimed, attempting to lighten the tone with some playful Korean slang.

The bets were placed and we waited for the race to start. The shouts of the bookies faded. The punters all hassled and harried for viewing points. The bobbing of feathered hats stopped. All eyes turned to the gates where the jockeys could be seen clinging on for dear life to the backs of their muscle-bound steeds.

'And they're off,' crackled the speaker as the gates snapped open. 'They're all away cleanly. Tokyo Panty Vendor taking an early lead with Shadowfax in second. Then it's Dr. Hopzinger Hand Job, Varanasi Canoe Club, Fred West Gardening Ltd., Saipan Incident, Charlie's Aunt and, in last place, Oroonoko.'

Down the side of the track, running on a motorised rail, shot a small tea table laden with pills and powders and hypodermic needles. The sight of their beloved pharmaceuticals shooting off down the track set the steeds sprinting on all fours in pursuit.

As they approached the first jump, Saipan Incident found herself hemmed in beside Fred West Gardening Ltd. and Charlie's

Aunt. I felt Kim Jong-un growing more tense and agitated by the second. Matters were only made worse as Mugabe and Murillo yelped with joy at Tokyo Panty Vendor's early lead.

I began to wonder if I had seriously blundered when, as it always does, good breeding came to the fore. Saipan Incident, a true descendant of Roy Keane, grew tired of the hassling and harrying of Fred West and gave him the studs in the ankle. Fred crashed head-first through the first jump. The runner was uninjured owing to his colossal strength and lifelong diet of pain-numbing drugs, but the jockey was killed instantly.

Freed from the trap, Saipan Incident began eating up the distance to the leaders.

'Fighting!' screamed Kim Jung-un, springing to his feet.

Mugabe and Murillo's yelps of joy dipped in volume. Had their runner got the legs to hold the lead to the finish? Had Tokyo Panty Vendor gone out too quick?

Fred West Gardening Ltd., now free of a rider, abandoned the race altogether and made a beeline for the spectators. A few young fellas got the hiding of their lives, and a number of young ladies were treated to a spot of sexual assault before the snipers, stationed on the top of the stands, were able to get a clean shot. The first shot hit the poor animal in the base of the neck as it mounted a particularly buxom young filly. Blood shot in a pulsing jet across the spectators, but the beast continued to thrust itself deep into the rear end of the unfortunate woman. Several more jets were opened up by the snipers, creating a fountain of gore, which only ebbed once the beast had spilt its seed.

As the racers came around the corner it was Tokyo Panty Vendor followed by Varanasi Canoe Club and Saipan Incident. The jockey was giving Tokyo Panty Vendor a good taste of the whip and shouting her on, but you could tell by the tossing of the athlete's head that she didn't have the stamina.

As Varanasi Canoe Club and Saipan Incident went around the outside, Mugabe and Murillo retook their seats in disgust. Dr. Benjamin Murphy offered his sincerest condolences, and I had no doubt that Tokyo Panty Vendor's jockey would be dead within the hour.

Kim Jong-un sensed victory was within his grasp and grew hysterical. Owing to his high-pitched tone and use of esoteric

Pyongyang slang, I am unable to provide you, dear reader, with a translation of exactly what was said, but suffice it to say it was not the type of material you'd be using around the dinner table.

As they came around the final corner it was Varanasi Canoe Club by a nose. The entire stand was on its feet. Punters were waving betting slips and form guides in the air. Women's' hats were knocked to the grown. Pints were being spilled over dresses. Wayward hands seized the opportunity to squeeze some flesh. Screams of encouragement, beseechment, unexpected pleasure and horrified violation filled the air. Bookies, having given 10:1 on Saipan Incident, wrung their paddy caps in their hands. Would this freak victory wipe out the weekend's profits?

As they came into the final straight, the jockey started whipping Saipan Incident for an all-out sprint. The world and its mother could see it was too early, but the jockey was absolutely convinced this was the best course of action.

Saipan Incident began trading heated words with her jockey. The jockey responded with more of the whip. The jockey and steed now started openly cursing each other and issuing threats. I didn't need a form guide to know what would happen next. Saipan Incident bucked her rider, sat in the middle of the course and refused to play the game with such a pack of amateurs.

Kim Jong-un looked at me in total disbelief. The Korean Peninsula did not, unlike the Emerald Isle, have a tradition of conscientious objectors in the arena of sports.

'Little Brother, I do not understand,' said Kim Jong-un as Varanasi Canoe Club romped home.

I desperately tried to construct a coherent explanation for this display of fanatical individualism, but could find none that would make sense to a man raised on the philosophies of Confucius and Marx.

'Excuse me, sir. I have a message for you sir,' interrupted a young man dressed in the uniform of the Second Republic's Army.

'Thank you, young man,' I said, taking the envelope and, with much relief, excusing myself from Kim Jong-un's presence.

The feelings of relief where, however, somewhat short-lived when I read the note, written in the impeccable hand of Captain O'Reilly, summoning me to a clandestine meeting on a matter of 'life and death' regarding 'you know who' and the insurgency from 'you know where from'.

From Ballyfermot to Pluto: A portrait of a magician

Chapter 10

It was August. The wind beat clouds across a pale blue sky that seemed so high you believed the oppressive half-lit days of winter could never descend. As golden lakes of light chased each other across the fields and hills, exact negatives of the clouds above, you wondered how such rolling and rollicking motion could cease. How could the myriad shapes and contours of these charging nimbuses be replaced with a flat hegemony of November grey? Those short, tea-warmed days spent avoiding views out windows seemed impossible. For now, the mountains and valleys of Donegal were alive with shifting shade and fluttering shadow.

The mountains crossed like penitent fingers, and in the narrow valleys small cottages knelt with bowed heads. In the back of one of these valleys, where the spray of waves mixed with the smell of sheep dung and ditchwater, stood Mrs. Harris.

Behind her was a cottage whose door was open and whose metal roof had turned a deep orange-brown. Mrs. Harris looked up the narrow lane, past the blackberry bushes, over a broken stone wall and then up the mountainside.

What the mountain lacked in height it made up for in gradient. The clouds of the coming months, after a weary trudge across the Atlantic, would gladly lash this mass of land with rain. Elsewhere, a jungle of vegetation would have sprouted – colossal trees, orange and indigo flowers, sweet fruits and twisting vines. But here there was only grass; dark, bitter grass and sudden outbursts of rock whose jagged edges served as a violent reminder of who held power here.

The wind picked up. The sound of waves collapsing onto the cliffs was carried over the hills and reached Mrs. Harris as a faint, but deep, vibration. The wind whipped salt across the fields, robbing the valley of that warm, rotting smell of fecundity. Mrs. Harris crossed her arms against the chill and watched a lake of golden light dash up the mountain. Three quarters of the way up, she spotted Hughey Harris, his ten-gallon jugs glinting under the golden light.

The magician held a pole across the back of his neck and shoulders. At either end of the pole hung the jugs. Hughey did not look up from the bruised green grass. He simply watched the slow footfall of his sodden boots. Hair fell about his face. Sweat hung from the tip of his nose. He did not shake his head. He did not wipe his face. The magician just climbed, and heard the great war of the waves reduced to a faint vibration, and felt the salt weave itself into his hair and sting his sweating pores.

Hughey picked his way through the jagged rocks, pitching dangerously from side to side under the weight of the jugs. Here, at the first of many false summits, there appeared a stream. It ran under the sky for less than twenty meters before disappearing underground once more.

Hughey lifted the pole off the back of his neck and slid the jugs onto the grass. Now he dipped the lips of the jugs into the sprinting silver and felt his fingers go numb. This stream was never warmed by the sun. Hughey's legs throbbed with blood as he knelt with the jugs. The gurgle of the captured water grew higher and higher in pitch until it drowned out the giddy babbling of the stream. Hughey lifted the jugs out onto the grass and shook off the cramps that threatened to cripple his descent.

The magician positioned himself under the pole, took the strain across his shoulders and stood up. Hughey gazed down the mountain, not to spot Mrs. Harris at the cottage below, not to watch the lakes of sunlight running across Donegal, and not to see their negative image in the clouds above. Instead, the magician looked out at the horizon and fixed his eyes on infinity. Now he lowered them to his sodden boots and watched heavy footfall follow heavy footfall.

Mrs. Harris saw Hughey's descent and turned back into the cottage. When she came across the threshold into the kitchen she felt uneasy. Emptiness seemed to shrink the room. The same pictures of uncles and cousins and pilgrims and popes hung on the walls. The shelves still held the china and the silver and the holy water and the carriage clock. The house was not empty of objects. It was empty of the dramas of youth. When Mrs. Harris grew up in this house, the hurl never lay in the corner collecting cobwebs. Instead it clattered shins and sliothars in the laneway. The carriage clock did not silently mark the passing time. Instead it screamed forth the hour of dances and markets and exams and illicit meetings in hidden alleys.

Mrs. Harris was overcome with a claustrophobic absence and rushed to open the window. She noted Hughey's progress and then turned to prepare dinner.

She stood at the sink and turned on the tap. She watched the water run down the drain. All it took was the twist of her wrist. She could let it run all day and there'd be no public outcry. Water was easily got. So why did he climb that mountain every day? Why did he only drink and wash in water he'd taken from the stream? Mrs. Harris had watched it every day – the climb, the descent, the drink and then the wash. He'd use ten litres at most, but instead of saving the rest, instead of sparing himself another climb, he walked to the ditch and emptied the remaining water into the muck.

Mrs. Harris pictured the blank expression on Hughey's face and shuddered. She grabbed a plug stop and rammed it into place. She began washing the potatoes and carrots. The water in the sink gradually turned a thick brown, but Mrs. Harris could not bring herself to pull the plug. Instead she worked the vegetables over, one by one, with a brush.

The light in the cottage changed.

The sounds of the salt-whipped lane grew muffled.

Mrs. Harris dropped the potatoes and turned around. The bright daylight rendered the personage a black silhouette in the frame of the door. The silhouette was, however, inimitable.

'He's up on the mountain,' said Mrs. Harris returning to her vegetables. 'You can sit down like a civilised human being or you can stand out in the cold. I don't care either way.'

Marley rode into the cottage and swayed gently back and forth on the unicycle. The low roof meant the clown was forced to put his chin on his chest, and even at that his hair swept the cobwebs from the rafters.

Hearing the rhythmic squeak of the unicycle wheel, Mrs. Harris issued a final warning.

'I swear to God, Kempe, it'll be the last thing you do!' shouted Mrs. Harris.

Marley, jolted by the sudden outburst, lost control of the unicycle. He smashed the back of his head off a rafter, which righted him on the saddle, but also knocked him unconscious.

Despite being out cold the clown maintained a perfect posture aloft the unicycle. It seemed he would never fall, until Hughey Harris walked in slamming the cottage door behind him. This slight vibration broke Marley's equilibrium. The clown hit the wall and slid down onto a kitchen chair.

'And we wonder why the legs are falling off our chairs,' said Mrs. Harris, looking to Hughey for action.

The magician was still hunched over from carrying his load down the mountain, but his vacant look of determination had been replaced with a smile.

'Have you news?' said Hughey, ignoring his wife's anger and addressing the clown.

Marley snapped his eyes open and feigned total confusion as to his location. He pointed at his unicycle and then at the rafter and then at the wall. He then executed a thorough search of his person and, not finding what he sought, arranged his features into an elaborate frown.

Hughey linked his fingers behind the small of his back and stretched. Several loud cracks shot from his spine.

Mrs. Harris exhaled sharply out her nose, spun back around and pulled the plug from the sink. She turned the tap on full and attacked the vegetables with renewed violence.

Marley eyed the married couple cautiously and then without warning began violently coughing, retching and convulsing. He gripped the table with two hands and slowly a cylindrical object began emerging from his mouth. When a good six inches was protruding from his gob the clown stood bolt upright, gripped the object with two hands and pulled it out. Marley burped, sat down and opened the blueprint.

Hughey pulled up a chair opposite and eyed the helicopter spec suspiciously.

'Will it get us there?' said Hughey, casually removing dirt from under his nails.

The scraping and scratching stopped at the kitchen sink.

Marley Kempe contorted his face into an expression of tortured sorrow and nodded.

'Well that's all we need it to do is it not?' said Hughey, pushing the blueprint back to the clown and opening the newspaper. 'Get it ready.'

Marley opened his mouth and then slowly closed it. Mrs. Harris dropped the scorn potato into the water.

'Is everything else in place?' said Hughey from behind the newspaper.

The clown mournfully honked his nose to indicate a reply in the affirmative.

'Then we go as soon as the chopper is ready,' said Hughey, studiously ignoring the tension in the small cottage and flipping to the tide report in the paper. 'Big swell for tomorrow, my friend.'

Marley tapped his wrist with a quizzical expression. Mrs. Harris began slowly peeling the potatoes once more.

'Dawn is twenty past five. Be here at five,' said Hughey.

To these orders Marley gave a salute of such exuberance that it launched him backwards off his chair onto the floor. As the clown scrambled to his feet, Mrs. Harris advanced with the potato peeler.

'I told you what I'd do, didn't I? I told you,' said Mrs. Harris, throwing the peeler across the room as tears of displaced anger began bubbling up under her eyes.

Marley didn't need a paper to know which way the tide was turning here. He snatched his unicycle and fled for the hills.

Pink Flamingo Soup

Chapter 8

'How can an idea be anything but an idea? How can you create more energy than you are given? God charged your body with divine energy, but who charged the thick black oil hidden deep underground? I tell you that the devil is in that fuel.'

This is the word of Jessie.

There is of course no doubting the rectitude and profundity of the comments. They are something of an inconvenience, however, when a man of my elder years is forced to ride a bicycle from Galway to Donegal on highly sensitive state business. You cannot help feeling, after the first hundred miles or so, that a car, under the circumstances, might be the lesser of two evils. Then again the path of the truly devout, in order to impart humility, and to encourage the holy mortification of the flesh, is often beset with obstacles requiring self-sacrifice and suffering, and thus becomes the path of the penitent. Had Dr. Benjamin Murphy, the prophet, the father of the nation, the visionary librarian, not himself chosen to take the form of an enfeebled and frequently catatonic man of flesh and blood? Had Jessie, blessed be his name, not chosen to come down amongst us as an innocent child of severe ocular impairment and sacrifice himself to the word that was then read amongst us?

It was with thoughts such as these that I sustained myself in the protracted and agonizing cycle from Galway, where I had been entertaining the esteemed members of the Axis of Evil, to Donegal, where Captain O'Reilly was commanding the nation's tenth consecutive summer offensive against Hughey Harris and the IRB. O'Reilly had come into the possession of information which was for the entire nation, and this according to a man disinclined to exaggeration of any sort, a matter of 'life or death'. Discretion was paramount in this instance and as such precluded my commandeering a tandem-drawn state carriage and a pair of well-seasoned cyclists. The procurement of a horse, especially given my starting point at the Galway races, would not have been beyond the realms of possibility. The sight of my person riding across the landscape would have been conspicuous in the extreme, however, and as such did not meet the requirements of secrecy as laid out in

Captain O'Reilly's communique. Too much was at stake to risk discovery. So despite the very severe objections of my bad leg, I gritted my teeth, got forward in the saddle, made my substantial frame as aerodynamic as possible and attacked the various long and snaking hills characteristic of that coastline with a pilgrim's faith in the purifying properties of the trials and tribulations of travel.

Dawn was just breaking when, wind-lashed and soaked to the bone by stinging torrents of rain, I summited the final gradient and began my free-wheeling descent towards the badlands. Needless to say that a senior member of the Second Republic's Revolutionary Council offered a prime target to insurgents operating in the badlands. With this in mind I had armed myself appropriately. In the style of Fionn mac Cumhaill, I carried a heavy-gauge hurl and a dozen sliothari in a satchel slung across my shoulder. For closer combat, I carried the Ssaysudo two-handed sabre, which I wielded in the ancient Korean style of Han Kyo. Then of course I could fall back on to my vast knowledge of Burmese boxing and Taekwondo if a situation requiring hand-to-hand combat was to arise. Heavily armed as I undoubtedly was, there did remain significant risks to my person as I shot down the hill and into the valley. The running dogs of the First Republic, degenerate infidels that they were, were known to utilize mechanised transportation running on oil and other debased fuels. A machine gun mounted on a pick-up truck would prove problematic against my hurl and sliothari. A tank with heavy gauge cannon would go some way to nullifying the threat posed by my two-handed sabre. A lone sniper, hiding somewhere along this roadside, could perhaps shoot out my tyres, launch me into the air, and taking advantage of my dazed state, shoot me dead. It was for reasons such as these that I rode with absolutely no lights whatsoever. I also employed evasive manoeuvres, shunning the straight path and employing instead an erratic zig-zagging motion that made use of the entire width of the road. The condition of the byway, given years of retreat and advance and shelling and outright sabotage, was not what one would expect from a nation of such advanced ideas as the Second Republic. On more than one occasion I narrowly dodged a pothole the size of Carlingford Lough, which given the speed I was traveling at, may well have done me in.

Despite the agonies being endured in my bad leg, I was forced to rise from the saddle and shift my body weight into the ever more rapid turns I executed during my decent. The windchill seemed to strip my bones of flesh. The rain, laced with more than a little Atlantic salt, stung my good eye and closed my bad eye completely. At the acme of this suffering, I even mistook my own rattling breath for the sound of an approaching helicopter and narrowly avoided falling from the bicycle in fright. But as the prophet has often counselled during our brave nation's many struggles – If Jessie brings you to it, then Jessie will bring you through it.

I held my faith and nerve and was in due course rewarded with the sight of one of Captain O'Reilly's vanguard checkpoints. Such was the elation that I felt on sighting members of the Second Republic's armed forces pointing guns in my general direction that I failed to view my zig-zagging, wind-lashed, hurl and sabre wielding advance from their perspective. Their order for me to 'halt or be shot' came as a complete shock, especially as it seemed fairly obvious to even the most tyro of cyclists that an immediate stop was, at this pace, nigh on suicidal. The high-powered spotlight they attempted to trail on me only disorientated me further and seemed at the time, given the high probability of snipers in the area, to be an outright betrayal. My screams for them to 'turn the fecking light off before the snipers find range' would, in retrospect, have only exacerbated paranoia regarding my insurgent status. This is probably why all verbal warnings were abandoned and my line of advance was cut off by a hail of machine gun fire.

I brought the bike to a halt just behind the line chalked in lead across the road and on placing my feet on solid ground, that is to say on grounding myself in the landscape rather than flying across it on my steed, the impression my advance must have made began to dawn on me: I looked like a candidate for the suicide bomb if there ever was one.

'Delta Delta YoYo,' I said, shouting out the codewords before I was blown to kingdom come.

'Echo Mayo Mayo,' came the hesitant reply.

'Foxtrot Foxtrot Tango Mango,' I replied and heard the distinct sound of rifles being lowered and long-stored breaths being exhaled.

'Well, why the fucking hell didn't you bloody well say so earlier, you fucking moron? We were seconds from blowing your fucking head off,' screamed the sentry emerging from behind a pile of sandbags to reprimand me.

I pulled my scarf up across my mouth and lowered my hat to obscure a view of my brow.

'You got a fucking death wish or what cycling around in the badlands at this time of the bleeding night,' continued the guard.

The young pup was no older than seventeen, fresh out of Jessaholic school, and if he knew he was talking to in such a filthy and disrespectful manner, he'd probably shit himself, before turning his rifle on himself, to avoid the types of punishments we reserved for young men who demonstrated such insolence to their superiors. On this occasion. However, there were bigger fish to fry.

'Here are my papers,' I said, handing the upstart the handwritten orders from Captain O'Reilly himself.

The sight of O'Reilly's florid signature was of course accompanied by a complete change in attitude from the little fucker.

'Very good sir...We weren't aware sir...I mean to say we didn't realise...' babbled the sycophantic little shite, removing his helmet, lowering his weapon and picking up my bicycle from the ground.

I ignored his flapping, hocked up a worryingly dense wad of phlegm and spat it on the ground between us before beginning to drag my bad leg towards the check point barrier.

'You have been injured sir...if you'll just...I can get...,' waffled the little fucker hurrying after me, trying desperately to undo the offense he had done to an unknown, but undoubtedly important, guest of Captain O'Reilly's. 'Deco, get your arse up and help this man!...Sir, if you'll just wait for Private Long to come...we can assist you....DECO FRONT AND CENTRE YOU LAZY PRICK!'

There are those who enjoy the worry-inducing influence their presence has over others. They gain great satisfaction on seeing people hopping to attention, running in fright and offering the most obsequious of welcomes at the mere mention of their rank and title. For a man of Jessie, however, such goings-on can lead to despair for they indicate one thing and one thing only: these men have not truly let Jessie into their hearts. For if an individual has truly understood the beauty of the flesh become word then he does not need to run and bow and apologize and perform when a superior arrives unexpectedly. He does not need to do this for he has absolutely nothing to hide. He has Jessie in his heart and he is submitting himself to his will. That these pair of gobshites were drinking bootleg whiskey and playing cards and talking about floozies dressed to the nines in utterly unrevealing clothes was evidenced by their drastic efforts to appear to be bastions of Jessoholic morality. They peppered their speech with misquotations from the Holy Book, they muddled their aphorisms and in attempting to ingratiate themselves to me only damned themselves further. For there is no surer sign of an alcoholic with bad brains for drink than the man who makes a big show of refusing a pint. No clearer sign of the young whore than the woman who in her later life turns to the nunnery. If I had been free of the shackles of secrecy I would have taken the young men in hand myself. As it was, I simply ordered them to take me to Captain O'Reilly without further delay.

'Yes, sir. Right away, sir. We will deliver you, Jessie willing, praised be his most holy and blessed name, safe and sound, for if Jessie brings you round it he'll land you in it, as the prophet Murphy once said,' babbled the young pup as he helped me into a tandem carriage, whose deep blankets provided me with the first hint of warmth my body had encountered in 36 hours.

We passed over a dozen checkpoints en route, and at each one the handwritten orders signed by O'Reilly himself accelerated the necessary checks and security measures designed to detect improvised explosive devices or hidden electronic equipment.

Being as I was well acquainted with Captain O'Reilly's views regarding the corrupting effects of home comforts on soldiers out in the field, it came as little surprise to find that the command centre of the nation's war efforts had been set up in a drafty old barn, which had half its roof cut away— not, as might be imagined, to allow access to new-fangled telecommunications devices (devices the captain had little faith in), but rather to allow the hardening elements of rain, sleet and snow to have full play on the men at all times. This hardening effect of the elements, in contrast to satellite imagery and telecommunications systems, was something the captain had complete and utter confidence in, having built an entire career out of hardening the battle wills of men by first hardening their weather-beaten skin.

Around the barn, which contained no chairs or restful apparatus whatsoever, there were dotted tents of standard army-issue green. Not a one, this being the late hour of 45 minutes past dawn, was occupied. Indeed the embers of fires, used to cook Spartan breakfasts of beans and hot water (caffeine of all sorts being classified as a home comfort by O'Reilly), had long ago died under the relentless drizzle of rain. I did not need to hear the voices of a hundred-strong choir breaking forth in five-part harmony to know where O'Reilly's men were and to what activity they were devoting themselves. I had undergone the same exercises each and every morning I served under Captain O'Reilly in the 151st Ranger Unit.

    I ordered my two escorts to remain with the carriage and began walking through the mucky field to the men's position at the rear of the barn. As luck would have it, I arrived at the tail end of the exercises and only had to wait for the men to perform Santiano's 'Frei Wie Der Wind' whilst executing star jumps and a medley of Friedrich Silcher whilst pumping out push-ups and a stirring version of 'A Londonderry Air' whilst doing pull-ups before Captain O'Reilly noticed my presence on the fringes and indicated to his subordinates that they should lead the warm-down routine in his absence.

    I expected O'Reilly to return to the relative privacy of the barn where the men's singing would mask our conversation from any prying ears. When he instead began striding off across the field towards a bloody big hill, I thought the man had lost the run of himself entirely.

    There's precaution and there's precaution. This was plain old paranoia. As battle-hardened as O'Reilly undoubtedly was, these past five years out on the frontline, directing advance after advance while under constant threat of being blown to kingdom come, had obviously taken its toll. I was not, however, going to start roaring shouting across the field at the captain when I had so carefully maintained a low profile for the last 36 hours. There was nothing for it but to follow. My bad leg began to groan before I even started to climb, but I gave it a good old thump, gritted my teeth and got on with it.

    Despite my physical impairments I had always been a good climber and I maintained a steady pace, which was aided in no small measure by the rousing version of John Tavener's 'The Lamb' being belted out by the men below. Despite this, O'Reilly was pulling away from me at a rate that indicated that ostentatious fucker was jogging if not outright running up the fecking hill towards a square concrete building on the summit. As I climbed through the fog I began to pick out the silhouette of a metal radar dish on top of the building's roof.

Even as I mounted the summit, the strains of the men singing were still audible and it was on these sounds, rather than my arrival, that the captain concentrated his attention.

'Was it absolutely necessary to-', I began.

The Captain raised a finger to indicate that silence was, for the moment, an absolute necessity. But alas what O'Reilly heard below was not in slightest pleasing to him. Even my ear, as out of practise as it was, could detect a flat in the tenors, a number of sharps in the bass and some God awful examples of sliding up and down to notes in all three sections of the choir.

'You're sharp Private Scullion. You're bloody well sharp you tone-deaf bastard,' screamed Captain O'Reilly, his moustache bristling with anger as his eyes bulged out of his head.

'And he's not alone,' I added in sympathy.

'Fools! Musically inept buffoons! I'll flay them to shreds when I get down there,' roared O'Reilly, slashing the air with his military baton.

'And they'd be getting a lenient punishment at that, Captain.'

'You take your eyes off the blaggards for a moment, just one moment, Corporal James, and they're missing notes and skipping a push-up and pulling out of that high C. But they'll learn to meet my standards yet. By Jessie they'll learn or they'll have their thick skulls bashed in with the hard end of my stick,' declared O'Reilly, bludgeoning a sod of grass with the metal ball on the end of his baton.

The singing finally ceased and O'Reilly snorted, smoothed down the worried ends of his moustache and looked me over in the manner of a seasoned breeder of horses.

'You were not identified in the course of your travels?' said O'Reilly, narrowing his eyes.

'I was not,' I confirmed.

'Very good, Corporal,' said O'Reilly, whipping his baton up under his armpit.

Captain O'Reilly seemed in little hurry to proceed any further in the conversation and stared out across the badlands as if lost in thought.

'With all due respect, Captain, I presume you didn't bring me here for the view,' I said.

O'Reilly shook his head as if clearing it of a concussion and spun away from me on his heels.

'Do you know what that is, Corporal?' said O'Reilly, pointing his baton towards the square concrete building that accompanied us on the summit.

'A radar system of some description?' I ventured.

'Very good, Corporal. I see civilian life has not completely undone the training I instilled in you. This is indeed an anti-aircraft radar system,' continued O'Reilly. 'But tell me, o you know what this is?'

Before I had an opportunity to identify the object, it was airborne and sailing towards me over the captain's shoulder. If I'd any inkling as to the nature of the object I'd have let roar at O'Reilly to quit the fucking messing. If I'd the slightest idea of what I was catching I would have employed more than one hand and quadrupled the dosage of care I employed in its retrieval. It was only when the fecking thing was already in my hands that I realised the nature of the threat.

'O'Reilly, you fucker! Tell me you did not just throw me a bomb! ' I shouted, a cold sweat breaking out on my brow.

'I will tell you no such thing, Corporal. It is indeed a bomb of a fairly respectable size. But as you can see from the shoddy wiring and messy shaping of the charges, it is without doubt the work of untrained amateurs, with no appreciation for the fine art of bomb making. It's the kind of shite I am forced to put up with day in, day out around here Corporal. Every young gobshite with an internet connection thinks he is a world-class terrorist. There's no pride in the craft. There's no dedication to the acquirement of the skills so necessary for good and meaningful warfare,' said O'Reilly.

'It's certainly not up to your standards, Captain,' I said, feeling not a jot less threatened by the substandard craftsmanship and beginning to fear that it could at any moment prematurely detonate and blow me to smithereens.

'Do you know how many of these have insulted me with their presence in the last 24 hours?' said O'Reilly shaking his head slowly like a man losing faith in the very fabric of the world he once knew.

'One?' I said hopefully.

'54.'

My feet took a step back under their own volition in anticipation of more examples being launched through the air towards my hands.

'Are you aware of how many anti-aircraft radar stations guard our borders with the badlands, Corporal?'

'54?' I said with a growing sense of foreboding.

'Exactly. And at all 54 locations a bomb, such as the one you are currently holding, was found primed and ready to explode at 12 noon tomorrow,' said O'Reilly, spinning around and pulling the bomb from my grasp and replacing it with a folio of documents, which I foolish believed could pose no such threat to my health.

'As you can see from the intelligence report we have reason to believe that Harris and his operatives have gotten hold of a helicopter,' said Captain O'Reilly.

I opened the file and began scanning photographs of Harris and Kempe, and blueprints of aircraft, and intercepted communications, and lists of bank account transactions.

'The trail of money leads somewhere very worrying, Corporal. Somewhere very worrying indeed,' said O'Reilly.

Our list of enemies was not a short one. It was, however, dominated by those who'd had the arse fall out of their bank accounts when we refused to honour the debts of corrupt, immoral and traitorous swine who dominated the political life of The First Irish Republic. Of the 37 known assassination attempts against Dr. Benjamin Murphy, 21 had their origins in that imperialist whore that is America; unsurprisingly 12 plots had been hatched by our old enemy across the sea, and the remainder came from internal terrorist organisations such as Harris' IRLA, usually with the financial backing of the Brits or the Yanks.

'Don't tell me North Korea have gone and turned tail on us now?' I said fully ready to cycle back to the Galway races and give the young Kim a swift clip round the ear for his troubles.

'If only, Corporal. If only. This I am afraid is a situation far more worrying. Have a close look at the final page of the documentation,' said O'Reilly, narrowing his eyes as the tips of his moustache began to tremble.

The money trail began innocuously enough with a transfer to our close partners in Pyongyang before moving on to our allies in Zimbabwe, northwestern Pakistan, Tehran and Chechnya. Here the trail took an abrupt and highly unusual turn into Switzerland where it bounced around several deposit boxes and unnamed accounts before emerging once more in Iceland. From Reykjavik the money made a quick dash to the Cayman Islands before doing a tour of Jersey's Financial institutions and finally landed, to my shock and horror, in the account of one Fence Global registered at the address of our flagship Jessholic schools.

'The little bollix!' I roared, making ready, there and then, to descend the hill, mount my bike, cycle across the country, grab Bobby Fence by the collar and beat the living bejessie out of him.

'You turn your back on them for one second, Corporal,' said O'Reilly in sympathy.

'I'll flay the fuckers alive,' I shouted.

'And it would be a punishment too lenient for them,' added the captain.

'No doubt the little bollix has got others in his employ,' I said.

Captain O'Reilly heaved a heavy sigh and nodded gravely. 'Smash?'

'I'm afraid so,' said O'Reilly with an uncharacteristically feminine air of sorrow.

'Our own weapon! Our own warrior! Used against us! Used against his very creators! Is there no sense of moral decency with these animals at all!' I said in complete and utter disgust.

'It does indeed come as a great blow. Especially as Smash was showing such…such pure…such untainted military promise,' said O'Reilly, now nearly on the point of tears.

'I'll fucking kill them!' I roared.

O'Reilly hunched over his baton like an old man on his walking stick and emitted a pair of pathetic sobs that would not have been out of place in the despicably sentimental novels of Jane Austen or Emily Bronte. This alarming collapse was then completely reversed as the captain straightened bolt upright, made two slashes through the air with his stick and set his jaw, moustache and eyebrows into one hard cold line.

'Yes, you will,' said O'Reilly with an eerily detached viciousness. 'You will submit them to pains they never imagined possible, Corporal. But not until they've submitted to our will. Not until they are our weapons once more. We let them make their assignation attempt. We let them try and kill the father of the nation. We let Harris come within striking distance and then we snuff them out for once and for all with one killer blow.'

This statement confirmed a suspicion that had slowly and steadily been impressing itself upon me in regards to Captain O'Reilly's mental state. The man had, following the years out on the ground, the endless assaults of wind and rain, the Spartan meals, the complete abstinence from alcohol and caffeine and home comforts of any kind, and the constant barrage of insurgent attacks and mortar fire and IEDs, gone stark raving mad.

'Have you lost the run of yourself all together, Captain?' I said in exasperation.

'On the contrary, Corporal, what I propose is not only a logical choice, but from a military perspective the only viable option if we are to finally secure a victory against those who would threaten the sovereignty of our fine nation,' said O'Reilly with the alarming calm of the maniac.

'It's logical from a military perspective to allow the attempted assassination of the father of the nation in my own bloody school by my own bloody students?' I said, almost laughing at the ridiculousness of the proposal.

'You are dealing in personal emotions that have nothing to do with national security, Corporal. For ten years we've been trying to locate and kill Hughey Harris, and now we know where he will be and what time he will be there. We can capture and kill him. But only if we allow him to think his bombs have exploded. Only if we allow the helicopter to fly across the border. Only if we use as bait the greatest mind our country has ever produced,' said O'Reilly, moustache curling upwards.

'This is madness. The life of the prophet, the pioneering librarian, the leader of the world's first immaterialist revolution, must not, under any circumstances be put under threat,' I stated.

'Ah but it is already under threat, Corporal. It is already under threat from all sides. Students in your own school are plotting to kill him. Your core supporters are starting to rebel. The general population is beginning to doubt the leadership of the revolutionary council.'

'And do you doubt it, Captain?' I cried in outrage.

'As the commander of the armed forces and sworn protector of the constitution that represents the will of the Irish people I could not, without rendering my role in public life a base hypocrisy, ever doubt the leadership of the revolutionary council,' said Captain O'Reilly in consternation.

'And yet you dare suggest that we may fail to realise our goals of the world's first nation under Jessie with its people fully elevated into the super-consciousness?'

'Ah yes, the golden utopia forever glittering on the horizon, but will we get there, Corporal. Will you or I live to see this heaven? I do of course believe the ideals of our nation are achievable in the generations to come. But as military men we have a responsibility to take the practical steps necessary to bring them into being. We must create the conditions under which they may flourish. There is discontent in the general population. There is an ever-present threat from insurgents. The Pyjama Wearers' Liberation Army are operating like a law unto themselves. Our authority must be exercised. An example must be made. What better example than Harris? What more effective boost to public confidence than the capture, torture, prosecution and public execution of the most notorious enemy of The Second Irish Republic?'

I am of course not the first to note the correlation between men possessing true military genius and the mental attributes of the psychopath. Indeed, much academic research has been performed in this area by the NSA and CIA who have devoted large amounts of public money to locating psychopathic members of the American public and enlisting them in the service of the national security agencies. Often, these men and women are put on express promotion tracks and quickly find themselves in positions that require the ordering of tens of thousands of deaths a year. The cool logic required for such work calls for a character completely devoid of the bothersome impediments of empathy and sympathy and pity. That Captain O'Reilly was just such a man of genius was clear to me now. For as repugnant as risking the life of my mentor was, even with the extensive precautionary measures that no doubt would be made, there could be no doubting the logic of O'Reilly's plan from a military point of view. Our immaterialist revolution had not yet been coupled with the kind of cultural revolution so necessary for the full realisation of our vision. The propaganda of Harris and Kempe and the IRLA corrupted the consciousness of the people and stopped the nation reaching a collective state of super-consciousness that would usher in our promised utopia. But first, the mind of the nation needed to be wiped clean of past stains. Captain O'Reilly's plan, exposed the Father of the nation, at whose side I would remain at all times, to minimal risk, and offered us maximum results. It offered us the tabula rasa. A chance at rebirth. A chance at salvation.

'How do you know Harris will be the one flying the helicopter?' I asked after some time.

'He's the only one amongst those bunch of amateurs with any training whatsoever in aircraft of that description,' said O'Reilly with disgust.

'But can you guarantee Dr. Murphy's safety?'

'I will personally see to it that the Father of the Nation comes to no harm, Corporal. You yourself will be involved in double checking every aspect of his security arrangements. Then our targets will be lured in, captured and neutralized.'

'What our chances of success?'

'Total.'

From Ballyfermot to Pluto: A portrait of a magician

Chapter 11

Faint clouds hung on the horizon like fingers running through smoke, and the first hints of orange crept into the navy pre-dawn sky. The cliffs stood guard, sheer walls of black holding back the incessant advances of the waves. On the other side of the world, palm trees had been uprooted, roofs had been torn off houses and sea walls had been breached. From all those thousands of miles away, these waves had travelled, and you could see it in their foaming beards and scarred faces.

Through the dark green fields, over crumbling stone walls and rusted barbed wire fences there wound a trail. It was not a path. No tarmac or concrete marked the way. Nothing maintained the trail apart from the feet that trampled it. Beyond the last outpost of sheep and goats, where the trail began its treacherous descent, two men stood. They wore black boots, black gloves and black hoods on black wetsuits. They tucked their white surfboards under their arms and began picking their way slowly down to the sea. Birds in nests squawked warnings as they past. Others hovered on the wind, watching the imposters with unblinking yellow eyes. Hughey Harris and Marley Kempe followed the zigzagging trail. Their feet fell into the rhythm of the booming waves whose noise rattled their eardrums and drowned out the nervous hammering of their hearts.

There was a small beach at the foot of the cliffs, which disappeared and reappeared with every attack and ebb of the waves. Further to the left the cliffs fell away and the beach widened, but paddling in from there would require half an hour's work. Instead, the surfers followed a jut of rocks that curved away to the right and brought them just beyond the break.

The fact that these rocks had survived millennia of punishment meant they were hard and sharp. But an ability to maintain balance in extreme circumstances was one of the many benefits of Harris and Kempe's profession. They held their surfboards on top of their heads and picked their way through the razor-sharp rocks without as much as a stumble.

Once at the tip of the rocks, Hughey began to watch the swell. There was no time to appreciate the rugged beauty of this place, the very end of the old world. They could not enjoy the ever-changing shades of cloud. They watched the swell and tried to make their entry before yet more monstrous waves arrived to sweep them from their perch.

Hughey went first. He dove off the rocks, flat onto his board, and paddled with all his might. He made no progress at first. This was simply a struggle for position, and as the swell ebbed Hughey shot down into a valley of hissing foam on slate-black water. He paddled under an endless sky and towering cliffs and monstrous waves. His two hands pulled against the will of an entire ocean. The magician rose up the face of a wave that got steeper, and steeper still, until it seemed gravity must take over. Hughey would surely slip from the board and go down into the foaming mass. But the surfboard poked over the crest of the wave. The board tipped like a see-saw and Hughey disappeared into another valley.

Marley quickly followed suit, paddling hard and fast. There was no room for slapstick here. If the waves swept you onto the rocks, there would be no escape. Not even a clown wants to make a joke of his own death.

Having made it to relative safety, the pair straddled their boards and bobbed on the swell. They were twenty-five meters apart and traded neither look nor comment.

The apex of the sun breached the horizon and shot a line of sparkling light across the crests of a million undulating waves. The cliffs awoke and moved under their blankets, sending birds swooping out over the heads of Harris and Kempe.

The magician and the clown steadied their breathing and listened to their beating hearts. Not until they had fully recovered would they paddle for a wave. Anything short of absolute commitment would mean death.

The waves broke left to right as you looked in at the beach. If you were dumped off the wave at the very start, you would be heading for the rocks. If you fell midway, you were in for a long battle against the breakers. If you rode far enough to the right, you could paddle back in around the break in a long arch and catch another wave.

Hughey turned his board to face the shore. He lay down flat and watched the waves over his shoulder. The magician let two waves pass before committing to the third. He paddled with head down and toes pointed. He felt the wave take the board, raised his head, gave three final pulls and popped up onto his feet. He hung up on the crest of the wave for a split second before shooting down the sheer face. As Hughey reached the base of the wave he adjusted his weight to the balls of his feet and cut back up the wave. Once more he reached the foaming crest and dug in his heels to turn back down. The magician crouched low now and built up incredible speed. With the wave rising up behind him, Hughey took several short breaths and one final lungful.

He now did what he had come to do. He ditched into the water and put himself at the mercy of the wave. The water crashed over him and Pluto Von Paradise went into the rinse. Legs went over and under and over his head. He tumbled and flipped and twisted, limp and helpless against such raw power. All direction was lost. He could not swim up because there was no up.

Suspended in the raging water, Pluto Von Paradise wore the same passive expression seen on his mountain climbs. Panic was the enemy here. Panic meant an increased heart rate. An increased heart rate meant greater demands for oxygen, and oxygen was something he did not have to offer.

There was a slight moment of calm as Pluto, still submerged deep underwater, slipped out the back of the wave. The magician felt the buoyancy of his wetsuit guiding him to the surface when another wave arrived and he went into the rinse once more.

Again, Pluto was lost in the tumultuous water. His lungs began to scream. The urge to inhale the slate-black water rose up his throat and quivered on his lips. Pluto swallowed the urge back down and ground his teeth. He barely noticed the flipping and twisting of his body as he battled with the seductive urge to inhale. Just one lung full of water and all the pain would stop. He started to feel his mind go and that realisation, the realisation that he was on the verge of death, gave him a burst of adrenaline, which demanded information from the senses one last time. And then Pluto felt it. He felt himself lifting. The wetsuit was pointing the way to the surface. The magician kicked and paddled. He could see the border between water and air. He burst through it and gasped in a lungful of oxygen. The magician floated flat on his back. His vision was obscured by black spots of oxygen deprivation. His arms and legs were incapable of movement.

Marley Kempe soon arrived at his side. He slid Pluto onto his board and paddled them to the beach.

Pluto collapsed onto to the sand and smiled up at the morning sky.

'How long?' he asked, watching birds circle above.

Marley showed him the time he'd spent underwater on his digital watch.

'Fourteen minutes twenty two...We're getting closer,' said Pluto.

Marley sat down beside his old friend. The sea had washed the makeup from his face. His hair hung limp and lifeless on his shoulders. The clown frowned, but there was no white makeup to animate the worried lines of his brow. There was no bright red lipstick to sweeten the sour turn of his mouth. Marley put a hand on Hughey's shoulder and sighed. How much closer could they afford to get?

'Well I suppose another run would be inadvisable under the circumstances. We had better call it a day,' said Hughey, struggling to his feet.

Kempe was not relieved. The clown did not break into an enormous smile. Instead he looked at the magician with horror. Had Hughey actually been considering a second attempt?

Peter Smash: The Truth

Chapter 5

Dya wanna see what I showed him that morning, Blondie?
Ah, you do. I know you do.
Well it wasn't really a fucking question so get your arse up against the wall there.
Yes, bring the laptop, by all means.
What's it look like I'm doing? I'm taking off my shoes and socks.
Cause it's a little difficult to pull a razor blade from between my toes when I've still got me fucking shoes on, that's why.
Ready?
Yeah well I'd give over the typing now for a minute if I was you.
...
Ah, go on out of that you big girl's blouse, ya.
Sure ya'd do worse shaving, ya would.
Go on. Take out your little handbag. I'm sure ya've [sic] sum plasters and shite in there along with your bleedin [sic] makeup and tampons.
Faggot.
I knew ya had em [sic]. Right, ya finished havin [sic] a little cry?
Good.

So as you saw for yourself, the technique was devastating. Not only that, but the run required to get to the forest on time would've killed Bobby if I hadn't given him a ten-minute head start. The sight of the prick sweating like a pedo in a playground made me sick. Plus he'd stretched me patience to the absolute limit with all the planning and soul-searching and shite. The CEO of Fence Global, the money-grabbing entrepreneur, the hirer of ugly feminist secretaries, the family-loving queer, had annoyed me just about as far as I was willing to be annoyed. So when it came to the aul neck-slitting technique, I couldn't help asking Bobby to step up for a ringside view. This of course had the advantage of letting me practise on a living target. It also allowed Bobby to witness firsthand, up close and personal, the impossibility of escape.

'Peter, are you sure this is a good idea?' said Bobby, standing in the woods, kicking at some dead leaves and sweating like a pig.

'I wouldn't move or talk now if I was you,' I said, bringing myself into a state of absolute concentration.

I lowered me heart rate. I controlled me breathing. I reached complete focus. I dropped into a crouch. I spread the toes of my left foot. I gripped the razor blade between the thumb and forefinger of my left hand. I pushed forwards with my left leg. As my gluts engaged, I added the power of my right leg. At full extension I executed a slashing motion towards the target's carotid artery. I landed in left fighting stance and looked up at Bobby's face white with fear. There was, just like the little tickle I gave you, Blondie, a trickle of blood on his neck.

'I'm cut,' he whimpered, holding his fingers away from his face like he'd just put them in dog shit.

'You're grand,' I said, giving him a friendly slap in the face and dragging him along for the rest of the five-mile run.

By the time we reached office security Bobby was too incoherent to argue against my throat-slitting method. If a little demo had put him at death's door, then the real thing was sure to succeed. Ciara did all kinds of chin wobbling and finger pointing and note writing as I carried Fence into the office. But all the prick needed was a sit-down and a glass of water. I told the ugly feminist as much and left to get on with my day.

After that demo, the planning entered a new phase. There was no more James Bond bullshit. We'd just slit his fucking throat. No messing. We'd just slit his fucking throat. The simplicity of that plan also seemed to rub off on Bobby's thinking for the second phase. There was no more quad bike jumps or jet-ski rides or sky dives bullshit. No, what we were working towards now was a simple suicide-vest threat to keep the fuckers at bay till we made it up the back stairs onto the roof of the church, followed by an Illusionist Republican Liberation Army chopper ride across the border into Donegal. Simple.

Now I hadn't trained for my assassination attempt with that weight of dynamite strapped to me chest and I sure as fuck wouldn't have been able to run 5 miles in under 25 minutes with the extra load, so that job was gonna have to go to Bobby. The only question was if Bobby could pull off a convincing Jihadist lunatic hungry for his 27 virgins. Could he do the crazy towel-head-willing-to-blow-himself-and-everyone-else-to-kingdom-come look? Could he get that fanatical look in his eye that would convince the PWLA and John James and the teachers and the parents that he meant business?

At the top there are always unanswerables. At the top the outcome is never certain. We controlled what we could – our bodies and our minds. I trained the fucker till you could've sworn he was a goat-shaggin Musi straight off the Afghan hills.

'I've just slit Murphy's throat and John James is sprinting across the altar. What do you do?'

'FREEZE MOTHER FUCKER OR I BLOW YOU PRICKS TO KINGDOM COME, INSHA'ALLAH,' screamed Bobby, springing up from behind his desk and baring his chest strapped with rows of dynamite.

'A member of the PWLA is reaching for her rolling pin. What do you do?'

'IF YOU FILTHY INFADEL WHORES SO MUCH AS MOVE THEY'LL BE FINDING PIECES OF YOUR TAINTED FLESH FROM MIZEN TO MALIN HEAD, INSHA'ALLAH,' roared Bobby, bulging his eyes like I'd taught him and gathering a healthy dose of foam around the corners of his mouth.

'That's not bad, Fence, not bad. Now don't forget the good-terrorist, bad-terrorist routine. Just like I taught you, now,' I said.

'TELL THEM NOT TO MOVE SMASH. TELL THE INFADELS NOT TO MOVE CAUSE I'M FEELING TENSE HERE. I'M GONNA DO IT. INSHA'ALLAH, I'M GONNA DO IT,' he said, waving the detonator around just the way I'd shown him.

'Nobody's gonna move, Bobby. Everyone's just gonna stay nice and calm and we'll all live through this. CHIVERS MAKES A LUNGE FROM BEHIND! WHAT DO YOU DO?'

Bobby sprung to the left, pulled a hunting knife out of his pants and delivered a shot that would definitely maim if not kill.

'ANYBODY ELSE WANNA PLAY THE FUCKING HERO? ONE MORE MOVE LIKE THAT AND I'LL BLOW THIS PLACE SKY HIGH, INSHA'ALLAH.'

'Not bad, Bobby. Not bad,' I said, motioning for him to relax.

So yeah, he was about as well trained as he was gonna get. Whether he had the balls for the real thing remained to be seen. But there was only one way to find out.

Fence made all the necessary donations to students and teachers and judges and other interested parties and secured me a student of the year medal. To be honest, I deserved the fucking medal anyway. I was by far and away the main man. Some pricks might have been better at the aul surrealist poetry or abstract painting or freeform jazz, but nobody dominated their area of expertise like I did. That I had to bribe my way into the medals said all you needed to know about The Second Irish Republic's so-called education system. When a true champion, a winner amongst winners, cannot make the medals cause the rules are fixed for verse-spouting faggots and piano-twinkling pussies, you know a country is fucking sick. The rules needed changing and that meant changing the fucker who made the rules. I'd slit that prick's throat, and then we'd see who was winning and who was losing.

The day of the medal-giving ceremony arrived. Everyone was gathered in the church. It was a clear sunny day and light was streaming down through the stained-glass windows with their pictures of boys turning into books and women attacking soldiers with spoons and historians hanging from the gallows. The students were decked out in their finest sacks and specs and sandals. To a man they were muttering prayers. They were all rapidly rotating their rosary beads. There was not a single one of them who wasn't trying to look all elevated and holy and shite as they knelt in their pews stiff as rapist's erections under the watchful eyes of Chivers and Nurse Mona and the largest collection of ugly looking how'a'yas you'd ever seen.

The PWLA were everywhere. Dressed in their standard-issue pyjamas, dressing gowns and slippers. But there was nothing standard about their ugliness. They weren't simply avoiding makeup and shampoo and all that shite. By the looks of their skin, they must have been rubbing grease into their pores. By the state of their hair they must have been dipping the shit in oil. Jessie only knows what kind of black gunk they were using to stain their teeth. They were, each and every one, armed to the gills with rolling pins and wooden spoons and spatulas. They stood a maximum of two feet apart all the way along the aisles of the church. There was even a load of the cunts upstairs with Graham on the organ. They didn't look left and they didn't look right. They were fully focused. Above and around us, the cream of the year's artwork was on display. It hung from the rafters. It was stuck to the walls. It was laid out on the floor. It covered every conceivable surface. This swirling-whirling explosion of colours and forms made the kneeling students and the rigid pyjamas wearers look even more tense.

So, was I feeling nervous? Was I having second thoughts? Was I thinking of calling the whole thing off? Was I, shite!

The bells rang. Graham stopped playing the organ. The PWLA stiffened their grips on their weapons. Chivers pushed his yellow glasses up his nose. Nurse Mona adjusted her ceremonial dressing gown. Everybody took a good deep breath.

In walked Bobby, swinging the incense and ringing the bells. Baba O'Reilly followed. The stakes of hair that impaled his head had been sharpened at all four points for the occasion.

Then we saw him; the pioneering librarian; the prophet of the Church of Jessie; the father of our nation; the soon-to-be browners: Dr. Benjamin Murphy. He had hair coming out his ears. He had hair coming out his nose. His eyes were locked shut with layers of yellow pus. There was a pool of drool in his lap. *This* was the great man? I almost laughed. Why had no one killed this fucking loser before now?

'She was the queen of the St. Steven's green mall. He had a job in a department store,' sang Baba O'Reilly.

The entire congregation burst forth from the silence, singing at the top of their lungs. As Dr. Murphy moved up the centre aisle, the students bowed low and touched their heads off their Books of Jessie. There were tears in the gobshites' eyes. You'd swear they were meeting Roy Keane or Steven Roche or something.

Bobby and co. reached the front of the altar, got down on their knees and prostrated themselves to the prophet. They eventually rolled the retarded old fart up onto the stage, and the mass began.

'Ohmmmmm Jessie Jessie Jessie Ohmmmmmmmmmmmmmmmmm....,' chanted Baba O'Reilly, raising his game for the occasion by dragging the final ohm out for a good three minutes.

I watched Bobby out of the corner of me eye, and even with that blurry image I could tell the fucker was shitting himself. He kept fidgeting with his robes. He kept wiping his glasses. He kept retying the rope around his waist. He kept looking at the members of the PWLA to see if they were looking at him. If he kept up this craic, the whole jig would be up.

I turned me head, as if rapt by the grand occasion, and gave Bobby a huge big smile. Bobby looked into my eyes. He saw the complete self-control and confidence of a champion and steadied himself.

'Jessie, Son of Mary, flesh become word/ you honour us today/ in a most righteous way/ with presence of a prophet/ motherfuckers know he got it/ shepherd of the sheep/ keeper of his peeps/ bitch-ass niggers can't get near us/ Jessie, hear us,' rapped Baba O'Reilly.

'Jessie, graciously hear us,' came the booming reply.

'Jessie, Son of Mary, flesh become word/ cops try to make fuss/ gangs try to mess us/ realise we're the bestest/ pump them full of something more deadly than asbestos/ believvvvvvvve/ we'll make your momma grieve/ Jessie, hear us.'

'Jessie, graciously hear us.'

'We will now have a reading from THE Book of Jessie,' announced the Baba, nodding to the altar boy to supply the prophet with THE book of Jessie locked up in the tabernacle.

Now, I was not worried about them discovering the suicide vest under Bobby's robes. We'd strapped that dynamite on good and tight. It wasn't gonna slip. I was also unconcerned about them noticing any strange bulges under the robes cause those bad boys were nice and loose and you could've worn a sumo suit under them and nobody would've been any the wiser. What I *was* worried about was that Bobby, given the job of putting THE Book of Jessie into the lap of the so-called father of the nation, was gonna have an attack of all that 'greater good' bollix. During our training sessions I'd tried to give him all kinds of tasty details about the agonies his family would face if hacked to death. I'd told him they'd remain conscience till the end. I told him they could spend days in writhing agony. But what could I do now as he took the flesh become word out of the tabernacle? What could I say as he knelt before Benjamin Murphy with THE Book of Jessie raised over his head? What could be done as he laid that load of translucent rubbish into the retard's lap?

Nothing.

Bobby was shaking like a leaf. I began to worry that he'd spaz out so much it'd set the detonator off and blow us all to kingdom come. But to everyone else it was just a young man doing what any of them would have done when laying the book in the great man's lap. Of course he was bricking it. With the principal and the teachers and the parents and the PWLA all watching, who out of all these fucking pussies wouldn't be bricking it?

Bobby stepped back from the catatonic prophet and everyone drew breath. They all waited to see the thing they'd been told about their entire lives.

Dr. Murphy gripped the book. His eyes darted around under his eyelids. His arms shot up over his head and his entire body began to shake violently.

'Ugly urban duckling pecking condoms all along the banks of the royal canal – crack fox conspirators coughing golf balls down hepatitis holes- mojo finger headache – pawn scum facial – Tel Aviv foreskins weaving diaphanous tapestries under screaming minarets – the flesh became word – THE FLESH BECAME WORD!' said Dr. Murphy, eyes snapping open and sending yellow shrapnel flying across the congregation.

Everyone was silent. Everyone was rapt. Everyone acted like they knew exactly what this bullshitting spazzer was on about.

Murphy struggled to his feet. He shuffled over to the pulpit. He raised the book before us. He looked into the eyes of his idiotic followers. He began to tell them what they'd come to hear.

'How can an idea be anything but an idea? How can your education be the accumulation of other peoples' thoughts? Jessie gave us all wings with which to soar in the superconciousness. Who is it that chains you to the ideas of the past? I tell you those chains were forged in the furnaces of hell,' said the waffling fucker.

'Amen,' replied the congregation.

'How can an idea be anything but an idea? Jessie blessed your minds with gifts so that they may flourish in the soil of his children and feed the imaginations of all men. Who is it that twists your talents to selfish ends? I tell you, it is the devil who twists those hands.'

'Amen,' they bleated, and I kept a close eye on our resident twister to selfish ends, but me tales of terrible torture were holding Bobby's will steady.

'How can an idea be anything but an idea? Jessie filled your bodies with his power and strength so that you may carry his word and toil in the fields of his kingdom so that all will proclaim the glory of his name. Who is it that channels your powers into stagnant pools for the drowning of your fellow man? I tell you, it is the devil who digs those channels.'

'Amen,' I said, visualising my razor going through this prick's carotid artery and leaving him on the floor to spray the last of his heart beats across the shocked looks of the front row.

Murphy finished his speech. He placed the book of Jessie on the pulpit. His face lightened. He became meeker. He became kinder. He gave them the big old benevolent prophet shite and they lapped it up.

'Be seated, my children' said the spaz— and how grateful the pricks were. How happily they all sat down. You'd swear the fucker had told then to take a year off to sunbathe, drink beer and sleep with supermodels and afterwards send the bill his way.

'My children, I have been given the pleasure of coming before you today to award medals for students of excellence,' he said bringing himself one step closer to death.

'The work that this Jessholic school does is the crowning achievement of our nation under Jessie. The poets, musicians, painters, artists, idealists, entrepreneurs and warriors necessary for the development of the Second Irish Republic are nourished here, in the fertile soil of the superconsciousness so that they may flourish and eventually feed the imaginations of their fellow man.'

I might stab the prick twice, I thought.

'It is no coincidence that this immense responsibility of running these schools has been placed upon my most entrusted and dearest comrade – a brilliant librarian, an erudite scholar, a man of deep faith and poetry, a true elevator of the collective consciousness – Principal John James,' said the spaz, giving a nod to old knobbly nose and nearly making the poor fucker cry with happiness.

Everybody clapped. The PWLA banged their wooden spoons and rolling pins together. Graham played a little flourish on the organ. Baba O'Reilly pumped his fist in the air. The decorations on the floor and ceilings and walls swirled and pulsed with colour. After all the tension, the pricks were just dying to let off some steam. But not me, and not Bobby. We made eye contact. We traded nods.

Murphy raised a hand, and the crowd grew silent.

'But now to award the medals for students of excellence…'

It was showtime. It was extreme focus time. It was a time for putting all thoughts of winning out of my mind. Cause if you're thinking about winning, then you're thinking about losing. What I had to do, what I did, what I still do today that makes me the champion I am, is focus on the process.

1. Await the call for medal.

'For consistent demonstration of excellence in this academic year… Peter Smash,' he called.

2. Walk up aisle to the altar.

The stupid pricks all wanted to shake my hand. They wanted to slap me on the back. They'd each and everyone accepted a bribe, but they still wanted to bask in my undeniable brilliance. I just shoved me way past, walked up the aisle and stood smirking at this old fart who thought he was good enough to be awarding me anything.

3. Receive medal around neck.

The spazzer prophet of bullshit was all gooey-eyed and gentle as he lowered the medal around me neck. The prick actually had the gall to playfully toss me hair. I might have to stab him three times.

4. Drop into a crouch and spread the toes of…

Ah, you know what comes next don't ya, Blondie?
You've seen the ruthlessness of that technique.
You've still got the scars to prove it, what.
So you understand how close the prick was to death.
But yeah, there was a deviation from the plan. A fairly fucking major deviation from the plan. It's a hard thing to describe this. It's hard to tell it so that you feel the kind of shock that was necessary to break my level of absolute

concentration. A state of focus where everything and everyone apart from the process and the target disappear. How to describe it in a way plebs like you can understand? Okay I've got it, Blondie.
Ready?
Right, imagine you're watching your favourite TV show.
Yeah, *Sex and the City* or some faggy bollix like that.
Right well it's the end of the series and you're snuggled up on the couch with your fucking cat or your hamster or some shite. You've got the lights turned down low. You're shovelling handfuls of popcorn into your fat gob. Now the ugly bitch with the curly hair.
Yeah, that bitch.
She's about to marry whatever Prince Fucking Charming that they've been setting her up to marry for the last fucking 10 seasons.
Yeah it's the fucking climax. They're about to put saliva on each other's faces and do the happily-ever-after bit. But now instead of reaching that climax, instead of you making real what you've always visualised, there appears, from Jessie knows where, a creature who stands between you and the screen, howling.
Of what height?
Of approximately 4ft, 3inches.
Of what width?
Of about the same width as a human.
Of what appearance? Weird. Very fucking weird.
Mask – wooden.
Ears – jutting straight out like hands crushed in an industrial accident.
Nose – aggressively rectangular with nostrils big enough for fists.
Eyes – long slits like gaps between slats in a pier.
Mouth – vicious and smashed and totally still.
Head – matted with fried electric wire.
General impression – weirdly two-dimensional.
General conclusion – not fucking good.

342

And as if shit could not get any weirder the fucking thing started to talk.

'How can an idea be anything but an idea? Jessie blessed our minds with gifts so that they may flourish in the soil of his children and feed the imaginations of all women. Who is it that twists your talents to selfish ends? I tell you, Bobby Fence twists your hands in that direction,' boomed the creature, without moving its mouth, but with an odd wobbling about its entire face.

Murphy had taken a step out of range. The PWLA were moving in to nullify the threat. Bobby Fence was shitting himself on the stage. The cogs in my noggin were spinning double time.

'How can an idea be anything but an idea? Ladies of the PWLA, Jessie sculpted our forms with his own hands so that he may happily gaze upon their glory. Who is it that builds aesthetic systems that convince us that our fat and our hair and our chins are something to be ashamed of? I tell you the devil of man is in those aesthetics,' cried the creature, waving a notebook above its head and giving the PWLA pause for thought.

The creature was speaking their language. Their women are as strong as men— bullshit language. They were on the toes of their slippers, but they held off the attack for the time being.

Bobby was near passing out and had propped himself up against the wall. Not the wisest move given the prick was wearing 20 sticks of dynamite on his back—dynamite we had to properly arm to ensure a convincing performance from the pussy. The congregation of students were gawking and gasping and ready to stampede the fuck out of there at the smallest chance.

'My child, what is it that troubles you so?' said Murphy, apparently unafraid of this freakish fucking thing.

'For too long the fascism of beauty has denied me a voice. For too long my words have been ignored because of the shape of my face. Yet if you would only listen, if you would only hear the truth found in my words, you would never lay a medal around the neck of a man like Peter Smash,' it said, opening its notebook as if to read.

The plan, my vision, the climax of my training, was fucked. Murphy was out of range for my neck slitting. If they caught us they'd kill us slowly. But we still had the vest. We could still escape. Bobby was weeping like a heartbroken lover, but luckily the creature was drawing all the attention. There was still time for him to get his shit together.

'Yes, Peter Smash, a man who is planning to undo the great work of The Second Republic by…'

As the creature talked it seemed as if I'd heard its voice somewhere before, and as I looked up at Bobby who was all lovelorn and shit it occurred to me who was behind the mask. Who it was dropping me in the shit. Who it was speaking and being heard.

What are you crying about, Blondie?
Oh you know what happens next do you?
Think it's mad tragic, do ya?
You ate up all that Anne Frank horseshit Fence had put around afterwards did ya?
Have a hardback copy of her notebook on your shelf, don't ya?
Bought all that beauty finding a way in a time of evil bullshit that Bobby waffled on about on CNN?
Think ugly feminists like herself and faggots like yourself deserve to be heard, don't ya?
Well ya don't, you prick.
Cause you're fucking irrelevant, that's why.
Nah, even when you're allowed to speak you're never given a voice.
No, no, no, no, you stupid fucker, you're only ever given a vent.
You can talk about beauty and love and truth and friendship and all that bollix. Oh yeah, they're more than happy to let you do that cause it's fucking irrelevant. But just try changing the game, Blondie. Just try becoming a winner. You won't be let speak then. No, no, no, they'll do what I did then. They'll slit your fucking throat.

I caught her flush in the carotid artery. The amount of blood was horrendous. I was fucking ankle deep in the shit before I saw Bobby with the vest open and the detonator shaking in his fist.

'YOU MOTHERFUCKING PIECE OF SHIT,' he screamed with a level of intensity far outstripping anything I'd gotten out of him in training.

344

The shocks just kept coming and the entire congregation were now scared out of their fucking wits. Even the PWLA seemed like they didn't want a piece of Bobby. Okay, we hadn't killed Murphy, but at least we'd whacked the ugly feminist and with Bobby's performance looking fairly convincing we might get out of this shit show yet. Murphy and John James started edging slowly towards the back door with Baba O'Reilly.

'NOBODY FUCKING MOVE OR I'LL BLOW YOU ALL TO KINGDOM COME!' roared Bobby, bulging in the eyeballs and gathering an impressive amount of foam around the corners of his mouth.

'Bobby, what is the meaning of all this?' said Chivers, taking a step forwards as Ciara's corpse started spazzing out on the floor.

'FREEZE, YOU INFIDEL GOAT FUCKER, OR THEY'LL BE FINDING PIECES OF YOUR BODY FROM MIZEN TO MALIN HEAD, INSHA'ALLAH,' screamed Fence with the kind of emotional commitment I'd never dreamed him capable of.

'Okay, Bobby, take it easy. Nobody's gonna do anything silly. We're all just gonna stay nice and calm and we're gonna get out of here in one piece,' I said moving things onto the good terrorist, bad terrorist routine.

'FUCK YOU, SMASH! FUCKING FUCK YOU! YOU KILLED HER! YOU WERE MEANT TO KILL MURPHY NOT MY CIARA! YOU'VE KILLED MY FUCKING CIARA, SMASH!'

Needless to say that revelation didn't go down too well with the congregation. And I was fairly upset meself. Bobby and Ciara? Bobby and fucking Ciara? I should've guessed the prick with the whale-like forehead would end up with the bitch with the whale-like chin. Was there no end to the depravity these fucking losers would sink to? And after me dragging the cunt, kicking and screaming to the point of victory, he was gonna sell me down the river for a dead ugly feminist bitch. No, no, no, this prick could not be allowed to beat Peter J. Smash.

'Take it easy, buddy,' I said, inching towards a distance at which I could lob off his thumb and get hold of that detonator. 'We can discuss this on the chopper yeah? Just take it easy.'

I was a little outside range, but I was starting from a standing position. I calculated that I'd gain a half foot extra in my spring. The only worry was the underfoot conditions. Ciara's throat and blood and shite had made things a little slippy. If I missed or even slipped, Bobby looked crazy enough to push the button, and that would be losing. That would be very much losing.

'DON'T FUCKING MOVE, SMASH! I'LL DO IT INSHA'ALLAH. I'LL FUCKING DO IT!'

'Relax, pal. I realise you're upset. But I did what had to be done. We'll discuss it on the chopper, yeah?' I said visualising the process.

Bobby bent down to pick up Ciara's notebook and I got myself that extra inch.

Now there are those who claim that what happened next was Peter Smash backing down. They bring it up like some fucking proof. Oh Smash is human after all. Oh even the champion of champions gets scared. But what those losers don't understand is that winners aren't governed by fear. They are governed by the rules of winning and losing. And when your target, fully aware of your neck-slitting ability, takes a step towards you rather than away, looks you in the eye, presses his thumb against the button, and dares you to do it, you know you're gonna lose. You're gonna permanently lose. You're gonna be blown to little pieces with no chance of making good your victory at a later date. I had then, like I have now, no fucking interest whatsoever in self-sacrifice. I wasn't one of those cunts who'd die losing in the hopes it would be called a moral victory by a bunch of misty-eyed poets who liked to dress up defeat as tragedy or some other bollix that makes them feel better about being losers themselves. As low as me chances were of escaping this school alive once Bobby had done a legger, they were better than me chances of winning once Bobby had blown us all to smithereens.

'YOU STAY, SMASH. YOU STAY AND YOU FUCKING DIE,' said Bobby, moving away from Ciara's dead body, and away from the PWLA and away from Murphy and John James and Baba O'Reilly and ascending the stairs as the sound of the helicopter filled the church.

Now I'm not gonna lie to you. I was scared. I was fucking scared. I had a whole battalion of the PWLA coming at me. Me classmates, turncoat pricks that they were, came close behind. Then of course there were the teachers and staff and dinner ladies who were all just queuing up to have a sly kick at Peter J. Smash once the first 30 fuckers has softened him up. But I wasn't going down without a fight. If they wanted their kick at me they'd have to fucking earn it. I had me blade. I had me shin-cracker axe kick. I was in peak fucking condition.

'Bring it the fuck on,' I shouted as they closed in. But you didn't need to be a rocket scientist to see that a lone defender against 200 attackers coming at him from all directions at once was not gonna work out well. What I needed to do was control the flow. What I needed was to narrow the battleground. What I needed to do was get them in a bottleneck so they could only come at me two or three at a time. What I did was cut a swath through three members of the PWLA and four of me ratbag fellow students before turning to take me stand in the stairwell Bobby had fled up.

As predicted, the hallway regulated the flow of fuckers looking for an ass whooping, but they were still throwing themselves at me with real passion. It was if the stupid bastards were taking my attempt to off Murphy all personal like. They fought for all the world like they were seriously fucking affronted by me neck-slitting plans. They launched themselves into the stairwell with teeth and nails and limbs flailing all over the shop. They'd no technique and they were easily taken down, but they sheer energy of the attacks was forcing me onto the back foot. The bodies were getting stacked so high that I had to retreat up the stairs to avoid a mountain of bruised flesh collapsing on me. And so it went: break nose, fracture arm, dislocate shoulder, crack ribs, take a step back to avoid the bodies piled up on the floor.

And off we go again: smash cheek bone, gauge eyes, take a step back to avoid bodies...

So yeah it wasn't long till I was at the top of stairwell and realised, in a rare reprieve from the PWLAs onslaught, that the sound of the chopper was still filling the school. Had Bobby had a change of heart? Had he realised I'd done him a favour slitting that bitch's throat? Was he waiting for me? I glanced behind me out onto the roof top and what I saw gave me such a shock that I momentarily lowered my guard.

Around the entire periphery of the rooftop there were soldiers with big fucking guns pointed at the helicopter. In front of the helicopter there was Bobby Fence lying face down with a dart sticking out of his neck and cable ties around his wrists and ankles.

Beside him, face up, but with an identical dart in the aul jugular, was a face as familiar as the devil's. We'd seen him in paintings of hell. We'd been threatened with his wrath from the moment we were born. Yet here he was hog tied and drooling down his own shirt. This fucking country can't even get its bad guys right, I laughed, before getting caught with a sly rolling pin that knocked me the fuck out.

Pink Flamingo Soup

Chapter 9

It was to be the trial of the century. An event that would attract crowds from the four corners of Ireland and beyond. Owing to the tourist revenues the event would generate, the location of the trial was the subject of intense lobbying from various local councils. Carrick-on-Shannon was an early favourite. The area had no lack of water, fine vantage points from the picturesque stone bridge and was in the general vicinity of Ballyfarnon. Unfortunately, the river flowed very quickly in Carrick and there were fears amongst the health and safety authorities that we may lose sight of the defendant before the trial had run its course.

A host of other venues now vied for the honour of hosting the trial. Everywhere, from the Cliffs of Moher to Blessington Lake, was given due consideration. It was a hard-fought race, but in the end it was decided that Glendalough would host the event. The ancient monastic site boasted a round tower, two lakes and breathtaking views of the Wicklow Mountains. It was also hoped that by choosing a mountain location we would keep the crowds expected to attend within a manageable number. The citizens of the Second Republic were of course hardened cyclists, but the climb to Glendalough would still challenge the best of them.

I oversaw the preparations for the trial personally. Two grandstands were constructed on the lush green banks of the lake. A small wooden pier was also built. It was located so that a man standing on the end of the pier would be placed exactly in the centre of the two mountain peaks that closed off the end of the glaciated valley. Several test runs were performed to insure the operational standards of the winch-and-pulley system. Vantage points complete with telescopes and easels were built on top of the grandstands so the army of painters, commissioned to commit the event to posterity, would deliver works of the very highest order. No detail was left to chance, and soon the day was upon us.

Dr. Benjamin Murphy sat in the VIP box of the grandstand surrounded by the Second Republic's political elite: Christoph

McFee, Inspector Biggington, Captain O'Reilly, Beyonce O'Neill and my very own theological prodigy, Jim McGrath. I stood at the end of the pier with the defendant, Hughey Harris, and his two co-conspirators Peter J. Smash and Robert Fence.

Paradise, despite the jeering crowd of onlookers, wore a reticent grin along with the straightjacket which was attached to the winch by a long sturdy rope.

Dr. Murphy rose from his seat, and the cheering and flag-waving ceased. Everyone awaited the words of the prophet.

'How can an idea be anything but an idea?' boomed Dr. Murphy, his sonorous voice echoing around the valley walls still wet with morning rain.

'How can human thoughts contradict the thoughts of their creator? Jessie stimulates your senses with beauty and compassion and love. Who is it that sullies your senses with banality and apathy and hate? I tell you, the devil breathes these thoughts.'

The great man gazed benevolently on his flock and allowed us all a moment of reflection.

'Hughey Harris,' roared Dr. Murphy, pointing a finger of judgment down upon the defendant, who continued to grin despite his coming end.

'You have been accused of heresy and witchcraft. You have been sentenced by the Execution Council of the Church of Jessie to stand trial by ordeal. Let the will of Jessie be done. If Jessie bids you float, then your knowledge of the dark arts will be revealed. If Jessie bids you drown, your name will be cleared and Jessie himself will welcome you into the Kingdom of God,' said Dr. Murphy, staring hard at Paradise, who began hyperventilating in fear.

'Let the trial commence,' shouted Dr. Murphy, motioning for me to push the defendant into the lake.

Harris panted in disbelief as I edged him off the pier. The lake was calm and crystal clear. A heron rose from the reeds on the far bank and began crossing the lake with the world-weary gait of a man who has attended too many funerals. The sun was unencumbered by cloud, and the woods released a sigh of mist as the morning rain returned to pale blue sky. As I pushed Harris off the pier, he took a final breath, and the same strange grin appeared on his face.

A roar went up as he hit the water. Flags flapped in a stiff breeze that suddenly sliced through the valley. Ripples began spreading across the lake. A front of clouds, banked high and bruising, appeared over the peaks of the mountains. A tense silence fell across the spectators. All eyes strained to see the magician sinking to the bottom of the lake. Was he twisting and contorting himself out of his restraints. Where would he surface? Would he try to escape with a desperate swim?

I stepped to the very edge of the pier and followed the line of the rope to the lake bed. The shadowy mass was not moving. It lay completely motionless and emitted not a single bubble of air.

'Some resistance leader! Fucker sucked in a lungful to spare himself the pain,' said Smash, with no apparent sympathy for his co-conspirator.

'Well don't you worry, Smash, you boys will get your chance to show us how it's done soon enough,' I said, leading to a whimper of fear from Bobby Fence, which quickly gave way to silence.

The sound of the woodlands rustling their autumn plumage died away, and the hum of insects began to rise in a pulsing rage. The bank of clouds pushed over the mountains and sealed the valley off from the sky. When the rain came, it came in cold sheets that blinded the eyes and turned the glassy lake into a mess of waves all crossing and double-crossing each others' paths. A worried murmur started to circulate through the spectators. What was happening below? Was he still lying motionless on the bottom?

I pulled on my goggles, dropped onto the flat of my stomach and dipped my head into the lake. Below the surface, away from confused echoes of a million individual drops, all was clear. I could see the magician lying on the flat of his back, green weeds swaying gently like ribbons around his head. As I looked into his vacant eyes, lost in the immeasurable depths of his final thoughts, my otherwise simple hatred of the man was complicated by a begrudging respect. He'd chosen to die rather than allow us to prove his guilt.

I raised my head and nodded to Dr. Murphy up in the stands.

'May Jessie have mercy on his soul,' said Dr. Murphy making the sign of the book before leading the congregation through their prayers for the faithfully departed.

As the throng muttered their mantras, I began cranking the wheel and drawing up the body with the winch. The pulleys screeched under the strain of the magician's dead weight and the noise fell in time with the cold pulsing of the insects that lay hidden in the reeds along the lakeshore.

The cadaver breached the surface; his open eyes rising up from the depths to stare hard at those offering up their prayers. His hair hung around his face and green weeds hung from his shoulders. The magician had been under for twenty minutes at most, but in that time he took on the look of an ancient wreck long banished from the kingdom of the sky.

The corpse was untied from the winch, removed from the straightjacket and laid out on the pier. Dr. Murphy and the other members of the IRB Supreme Council descended from their box to offer final prayers for the delivery of Paradise's soul.

'Let us pray,' intoned the prophet, kneeling beside the body and closing Paradise's eyes with a gentle stroke of his fingers.

It was at this point, with the clouds departing as quickly as they'd arrived and the insects ceasing their pulsing aural assault, that the unthinkable happened: the dead man drew breath.

Dr. Murphy sprung back to the pier's edge and clutched the Book of Jessie to his bosom. Beyonce O'Neil and the rest of the PWLA drew their wooden spoons. Captain O'Reilly drew his firearm. Jim McGrath's angelic face contorted under the weight of the coming philosophical crisis, and I in a state of shock raised my eyes up the mountain ridge, where the silhouettes of a thousand, ten thousand, twenty thousand men appeared.

Amongst them, in the centre of the mountain peaks, with the sun burning directly above his mass of hair, stood Kempe. I'd averted my eyes from what I didn't wish to see only to alight on something far more terrible. Unable to deal with the despair of the situation, my brain decided to stop relaying reality.

In a kind of detached daze my eyes returned to Paradise. We watched in horror as the cadaver's chest rose and fell. Then it began to laugh, a low, guttural, manic laugh. Feet shuffled in the stands. People began edging slowly towards their bicycles. Jessie had willed the man to drown but he'd lived. Did that mean he was innocent or guilty? What was God trying to tell us?

'Away, evil spirit. By the power of the Book of Jessie I command you to be gone,' shouted Dr. Murphy, attempting to regain control of the situation.

The corpse continued to laugh and rose to its feet like the hand of a clock sweeping towards our hour of judgement.

'There is no power in that book, just as there is no Jessie,' said the corpse, a gurgle of water distorting the already horrible voice.

'Heretic! Shoot him,' commanded Dr. Murphy, but Captain O'Reilly, hand shaking with fear, did not dare open fire.

'Beat him to death,' cried Murphy to the PWLA, but Beyonce O'Neill, sensing Murphy's despair, commanded her minions to stand at ease.

'You heard his words. As prophet of the Church of Jessie, I command you to kill him,' said Murphy, turning in all directions for help.

I should have sprung forwards. I should have taken out Paradise with a flurry of Burmese boxing, but instead I watched in disbelief as Kempe and the IRLA poured down from the mountain ridge into the valley. I didn't shout a warning or even move a muscle. The horror was delivered in too a potent a dose. I was unable to process the sheer gravity of the situation and, as a result, was incapable of acting to save us.

'How can an idea be anything but an idea? How can human thoughts contradict the thoughts of their creator? You set me to trial by ordeal and Jessie has found me innocent. Who are you to contradict the judgement of Jessie?' said Harris.

'How dare you lecture Doctor Murphy on theology! Shoot him!' I screamed, grabbing O'Reilly by the collar.

'Well, we did sentence him to trail by ordeal, Corporeal,' said O'Reilly sheepishly.

'And?'

'And as set out in Article 36 of the constitution, the outcome of that ordeal is representative of the will of Jessie. Now, as Jessie is the supreme leader of our country and I am sworn protector of the constitution, I cannot very well contravene his judgment,' said Captain O'Reilly, his bushy red eyebrows and bushier red moustache forming symmetrical apexes of stress.

'He denies the existence of Jessie, you fool. He is guilty of heresy,' I screamed in exasperation.

'Well, actually this trial by ordeal, representative of the will of Jessie himself, has proven him innocent of heresy,' countered

O'Reilly, setting off a chatter of philosophical debate amongst the onlookers.

'How can Jessie judge a man innocent if he denies his existence? How can Jessie will himself out of existence?' I cried.

There was a profound silence as the Supreme Council and throng of spectators considered this paradox. I gazed down the valley at the old round tower where the early Christians hid from the raping and pillaging pagans. Where was our succour? How had we found ourselves so exposed?

'God has killed himself,' declared Jim McGrath, and the sound seemed to set the entire valley into motion.

Wind traced darting shadows across the lake. Rocks crumbled from the mountaintops. The woods moaned and creaked. Kempe and the IRLA sent up an enormous battle cry. The throng, hitherto unaware of the attacking force sweeping down from the mountain ridge, began running and screaming in all directions. The entire world was uprooted and seemed to lurch perilously forwards.

'Silence!' I commanded, but my voice had lost all authority.

McGrath's conclusion was loose amongst the mob, and just when we needed total unity, just when we needed total faith to defeat our swarming enemies, a pandemic of atheism was beginning. Bottles and cans rained down from the stand, and the PWLA were absorbed in battling the riotous mob rather than preparing for Kempe's charge.

The splattering of blood and cracking of bones sounded strange under the gently swaying trees. The screams of blue murder were unreal before the reflection of sky and mountain on a lake that washed the ascetic hands of Ireland's first monks. We'd tried so hard to be beautiful, but it was all coming apart.

The gunshots of Kempe's charging men snapped me from my reverie. I saw Dr. Murphy standing on the edge of the pier as fighting proceeded all around him. The great man was huddled and scared. He clutched the Book of Jessie to his chest and looked around in confusion at his lost children.

Wooden spoons and rolling pins rained down on my school as I battled towards my mentor. I watched in horror as my former student, Peter Smash, crept forward and kicked the Book of Jessie out of the prophet's hands. Dr. Murphy fell to the ground in a state of catatonia. I surged forwards, laying about me with Burmese boxing techniques, and taking blows that would fell a ten-tonne elephant.

'I win, shithead,' laughed Smash before kicking the pioneering librarian, the prophet of the Church of Jessie, the impressionistic revolutionary and the guiding light of my life, into the lake.

Fuelled by an overriding desire for revenge I redoubled the blows with which I struck down my enemies, but as Smash took to the forest I realised I would be forced to make a choice; vengeance or salvation; Smash or Murphy. There was not time for both.

Bodies began to drop around me as Kempe and the IRLA came into range with their rifles. Captain O'Reilly and Beyonce O'Neill and Christoph McFee and Jim McGrath all added their bleeding bodies to those rolling around on the lakes of the shore. The grass became slick with blood. Mouths screamed up to me in pain. They wanted relief; they wanted help; they wanted consolation, but I could not give it to them. The mountains stood as they had always stood. The autumn leaves fell with disinterested ease. The lake accepted the blood of the fallen like it did the rain. The red swirled in the crystal waters; the myriad lives crossed and doubled-crossed each other until the patterns became a mess of living and dying that no human eye could penetrate.

I plunged down into those waters. I sought about me blind. From the very top to the very bottom I searched. I searched until my lungs screamed. I searched until my consciousness began to fade. In the mists of the dead and dying I thought I glimpsed him. He was just a little further. He was just beyond my grasp. I pitted my will against the demands of my body. I pitted my will against the demands of the mind. I touched the tips of his fingers. I felt a soaring elation in my soul. The mists cleared into a moment of perfect clarity, but then he was gone.

Peter Smash: The truth

Chapter 6

Right, now that we've got all the *Catcher in the Rye* shit over and done with, we can get into the good part of the story. I can tell you about how I got all the members of Girls Aloud, even the horrible ginger one, high as kites on coke and rode the holes off them backstage at the MTV music awards. I'll tell you about the time me and Christiano Ronaldo flew to Vegas on a private jet and blew a hundred grand in one spin of the roulette wheel only to win back double that in a single hand of poker. I'll dish the goss on Richard Branson's orgies down in his tropical mansion and tell you which members of the royal family take it up the arse and which ones spit or swallow. You'll get the complete lowdown on every pimp, pedo, alcho, smack head, bum boy and slag in the business. But best of all you'll hear about how I became the winner I am today. You'll hear about each and every one of my fifty-four knock-out victories in precise detail.

    What did you just say, Blondie?
    I said the publisher says we have enough.
    Did you just type that down you little cunt? I'm gonna fucking brain ya [sic].
    I don't think so.
    Wow hang on, what the fuck is this?
    It's a gun, Mr. Smash.
    Well you just put that little thing down now before someone loses an eye.
    Bobby Fence sends his regards.
    Wow, whoa now, Jonathan, whatever he's paying you....
    You lose, Smash.
    Fuck you. I never lose. You hear me, Blondie? I never fucking lose.
    BANG.

Printed in Great Britain
by Amazon